PRAISE FOR *AN ECHO IN TIME*

"In this beautifully written story of an old crime, a secret has shaped a family for generations until one woman goes in search of the truth that will allow her to reconcile the inherited traumas in her life. Celebrated author Boo Walker deftly explores the curious power of genetic memory in a modern American family . . . *An Echo in Time* vibrates at the sweetest frequency and pulls gently at just the right heartstrings."
—Kimberly Brock, bestselling author of *The Lost Book of Eleanor Dare*

"*An Echo in Time* is a beautifully written, emotionally powerful story of a young woman's journey to break the cycle of generational trauma . . . I found myself cheering for Charli at every turn and smiling at the deeply satisfying and nuanced ending."
    —Yvette Manessis Corporon, international bestselling author of *When the Cypress Whispers*

"*An Echo in Time* is a captivating novel about the generational legacy of secrets and shame and one woman's journey to love herself by righting the wrongs of the past. Walker has crafted a beautiful and moving tale of loss and healing that is part love story, part mystery, and all green lights."
        —Melissa Payne, bestselling author of *A Light in the Forest*

PRAISE FOR BOO WALKER

"Walker dazzles . . . the characters all earn the reader's emotional investment, and the pacing is perfect. Readers will fall in love."

—*Publishers Weekly* (starred review)

"Walker's attention-grabbing and surprising plot highlights the engaging characters in this tale of second chances. For fans of women's fiction such as Nicholas Sparks's and Kristin Hannah's work."

—*Library Journal*

"A heartwarming read."

—Historical Novel Society

"Boo Walker is a true talent, and his latest novel is a captivating tale of one man's journey to reconcile who he used to be with the person he's becoming. *The Stars Don't Lie* is a beautiful reminder that sometimes returning to the past is the best way to find your way forward."

—Camille Pagán, bestselling author of *Good for You*

"Boo Walker has written a book with a tender heart . . . a great story of redemption that carted me away."

—Barbara O'Neal, bestselling author of *When We Believed in Mermaids*

"The perfect mix of character-driven, heartstring-pulling drama and sharp-witted humor. Clearly, Boo Walker is an author whose time has come."

—Julianne MacLean, *USA Today* bestselling author

"I love books with breathing characters you can root for, a narrative of human life to which you can relate, a conclusion that can stop the heart, and an author who can bind them all together with passion and soul. Boo Walker proves he's that kind of writer."

—Leila Meacham, bestselling author of *Roses* and *Titans*

"If Nicholas Sparks and Maeve Binchy had a baby, he might sound a lot like Boo Walker."

—Jodi Daynard, bestselling author of *The Midwife's Revolt*

"I was swept away by Boo Walker's deft storytelling and incredibly complex characters. Soulful but also full of sharp dialogue and humor, [this] is exactly the sort of book you get lost in, then mourn when it is over."

—Suzanne Redfearn, #1 Amazon bestselling author of *In an Instant*

"Boo Walker is that rare writer who is both a master storyteller and a wordsmith all at once. This is a book to bring you to tears but leave you with a light in your heart."

—Eoin Dempsey, bestselling author of *White Rose, Black Forest*

"Bring tissues because there will be tears, but the good kind—the kind that let you know you are alive."

—Emily Bleeker, *Wall Street Journal* and Amazon Charts bestselling author

AN
ECHO
IN
TIME

ALSO BY BOO WALKER

The Stars Don't Lie

The Singing Trees

An Unfinished Story

Red Mountain

Red Mountain Rising

Red Mountain Burning

A Marriage Well Done

Writing as Benjamin Blackmore

Lowcountry Punch

Once a Soldier

Off You Go: A Mystery Novella

AN ECHO IN TIME

a novel

BOO WALKER

LAKE UNION
PUBLISHING

Text copyright © 2024 by Lemuel Harrall Walker III, writing as Boo Walker

Published by Lake Union Publishing, Seattle

www.apub.com

Amazon, the Amazon logo, and Lake Union Publishing are trademarks of Amazon.com, Inc., or its affiliates.

ISBN-13: 9781662516504 (hardcover)
ISBN-13: 9781662508790 (paperback)
ISBN-13: 9781662508806 (digital)

Cover design by Faceout Studio, Molly von Borstel
Cover image: © Andrea Pucci / Getty; © jakkapan, © Sablegear, © Buch and Bee, © argus, © ganjalex, © Faraz Hyder Jafrie, © Bykfa / Shutterstock

Printed in the United States of America

First edition

For my agent, Andrea Hurst, with whom I vibrate at
the same frequency

You chose
Fear over love,
Distance over touch.
You chose
Running and denial,
Burning words
And breaking hearts.
You chose
Ordinary over *extraordinary*,
Complacency over disruption,
Simplicity over greatness,
The *mundane* over magic.
You chose
Smallness over expansion,
Ease over beauty,
Solitude over *connection*,
Comfort over clarity.
You chose *over*,
And *over*,
And *over*.
And your choices
Challenged me
To choose,
Too.

I chose *myself*
Over you.

—Jenan McClain

Chapter 1

RED LIGHTS

Boston, USA
Present Day

After the day she had, Charli doesn't want to get out of bed, but her Great Dane is staring at her with his big dopey eyes, demanding attention. His tongue hangs from the side of his mouth like the slack of a belt that's far too long. She named him Tiny when he was small enough to fit into her tote bag, but now, when he stands on his hind legs, he's taller than she is.

If he only knew what she was going through, he'd let her spend another afternoon curled up in bed with a book in her hands, checked out from the world. He couldn't possibly comprehend the agony of being human, of working an uninspiring job, of constantly trying to live up to the overachievers surrounding you, of worrying and worrying and worrying about your parents, one of whom you don't even know why you care about in the first place.

It must be so nice being a dog, not having to make a living, not having to go outside unless you want to, not having a concern in the world other than always hoping to go to the dog park.

He's such a snarky canine that he'd probably reply, *You try eating the same thing every single day. And don't get me started on having my privates clipped off. Humans have it made.*

"You really are incorrigible," she says to him, setting her book down. "You know that, right?" *Wouldn't it be nice to just go away a little longer, fall back into a fictional world?*

Tiny pulls his tongue in and tilts his head sideways, as if he's trying to understand the language this two-legged creature speaks. He raises a paw as big as Charli's hand, holds it up like he's casting a vote. Then he presses it to her chest and whimpers, a strange sound coming from this dog that last weighed in at 161 pounds. But he knows how this action melts her heart and gets him what he wants, a guaranteed Pavlovian response every single time.

"I know, I know," she says. "We all know who wears the fur in this relationship. Give me a sec to collect myself, and then we can go to the dog park, okay?"

He hears *dog park* and pops up to a stand on the bed.

"Are you sure? We don't have to go to the . . . *dog park*."

The two words send him into a frenzy, and a smile rises on Charli's face. He's just about the only being who can do that to her, make her almost believe life is okay.

When she sits up, he leaps off the bed and scrambles clumsily down the steps of her loft to the living room. She hears his nails click on the hardwood floors as he races to the front door of her apartment. As if she could be ready in three seconds.

Charli throws on jeans and slips into an army-green sweater with shoulder ruffles, then follows him downstairs. She peels back the blinds of the large windows that look out over Washington Street in Boston's South End. A streetlight casts an orange glow over her living room. Snow falls for the second day in a row, the flakes dancing in the wind. It's already dark outside, and the hint of the day's warmth has surely dissipated. Still, Boston is alive with activity, drivers smashing their horns, pedestrians moving like cattle toward their evening affairs.

With Tiny shooting those adorable eyes at her, Charli zips up her puffer jacket, puts on her hat and gloves, and reaches into a basket for the Chuckit! launcher she uses to sling balls across the park. Right then the dread of having forgotten something hits her like she's left a candle burning somewhere.

The sinking feeling in her chest makes it hard not to be disgusted with herself. Her mother would thoroughly enjoy this moment and let her have it. *What a surprise, Charli. You forgot to do something. You dropped another ball, space cadet. Way to go. Really proud to be your mom.*

Was it a work engagement? Charli wonders, trying to ignore her mom. Did she forget to do something at work? Or was it . . . dog food?

The thing she's forgotten wraps its icy hand around her heart, and she wants to cry. Her fingers go limp, and the launcher falls to the floor.

Before it even settles, her mind goes to work conjuring up potential excuses. Bad traffic coming back from Arlington, a deadly wreck. Someone pickpocketed her. The Russians are attacking; she can see the paratroopers from the window. It doesn't matter, does it? Her relationship with Patrick is coming to its due end.

She glances at the Agatha Christie clock on the wall. Agatha's character Hercule Poirot stands in the middle, and his arms perform the task of the hour and minute hands. This clock is supposed to be hanging in her bookstore—the one that never got off the ground. Thank you for the steady reminder, Agatha. You're correct. I can't do anything right. You and Mom would have loved each other.

Charli finally looks at the time. It's three minutes till six o'clock. She was only reading for maybe thirty minutes, and now she has three minutes to get out the door and cross town, a comical notion with the traffic outside.

Patrick will be disappointed in his own sweet way. How many times did he tell her of tonight's importance? Dammit, how could she have forgotten? She'd set a reminder on her calendar but hadn't even glanced at it. Patrick's been working nonstop, so they haven't seen each other in days.

But you know what? What's the point? She should have ended it weeks ago. Things were already going south. She could feel his annoyance when she would steer away from any genuine conversations about their future. Couldn't he see that there was no future?

Charli does a quick inventory of her appearance in the large mirror hanging above the long glass table pushed up against the wall. Her battered jeans have holes. The casualness of her pilling sweater is just shy of wearing a pajama top. Her dark-chocolate hair is too thick for its own good today, and her face doesn't match what's going on inside.

Charli stares deep into her own brown eyes and searches for the glimmer of the fighter that she knows is in there. She's better than the part of her that wants to pull out of their plans. No, she can't do that to Patrick.

Tiny's pressing up against the door as if a mound of treats waits on the other side. "I can't, sweetie. Sorry, I have to go."

He doesn't get it and sits and wags his tail, waiting for her. With the leash still dangling on the coatrack, she runs back up the steps and riffles through her closet. Her mind races so quickly now that making any rational decisions feels like putting on makeup while riding a roller coaster. All she manages to do is change into some black jeans and a camel-colored cashmere sweater, both recent thrift store finds.

She races back down the stairs as she considers the best method of transportation. A catapult might be the best way. Then he'd feel sorry for her as she landed with a crimson splat on the sidewalk outside the restaurant. It doesn't seem like that bad a way to go. A taxi is another option, but it might be faster to drive. In the bathroom, she realizes she's a mess. Never in her life has she applied foundation so quickly. She'll do the rest en route.

Tiny is impatient now, whining as if she's taken away his food.

"I'm so sorry, buddy." Her heart goes out to him, but there's nothing she can do.

Looking for her keys in a frantic scramble, she pushes aside the mail cluttered on the table by the door. Charli can hear her mother's condemning voice: *So typical . . .*

Patrick is surely making excuses for her, how she has a high-maintenance dog, a new job . . .

"I can't believe I forgot!" Charli cries to herself, imagining the worst, seeing Patrick's eyes as she dashes into the restaurant looking like . . . like this. She pulls back pillows and opens drawers, trying to find the keys. As she runs out of options, she accepts that she'll have to call a cab.

On her way out the door, she gives one last apology to Tiny and offers him a Himalayan dog chew as a consolation prize. She steps into her L.L.Bean snow boots and rushes down the three sets of stairs, her feet smacking the steps in what sounds like a herd of buffalo racing across the plains. Maybe twenty minutes late won't be that bad. It's snowing and dark outside. People are late all the time.

She hears Patrick's voice from three days ago as she busts through the doors of her building out into the snow. "Charli, please. My mom is punctual and old-fashioned. Just be on your best behavior, okay? She comes into town once a year, and I try not to rock the boat. Besides, I'm excited to introduce you."

"I can't wait to meet her," Charli had replied, feeling a shovelful of trepidation. His mother is only in town from Rome for two nights—she's some kind of marketing exec there.

Charli should have said no the moment he brought up introducing her to his mother. They hadn't even been dating for six months. Come to think of it, why didn't Charli pull the plug on their relationship right then? She vaguely remembers deciding that she could stomach this meal with his mother so that she could put off the breakup for a few more weeks. That would give him time to get the message. Maybe he'd end things himself, which is always Charli's preferred option.

Her breath transforms to fog in the cold. She thrusts her hand into the air and calls "Taxi!" but a guy in a business suit beats her to it. She goes to the edge of the curb. Snow falls around her, flakes the size of fingertips. A juxtaposition of quiet and loud exists, as is always the way in the snow in Boston. Without a taxi in sight, she looks at the Uber app. A text from Patrick is waiting for her. Friendly reminder about tonight! She doesn't know how to respond.

After taking what feels like forever for the Uber app to load, she types in the restaurant's name, only to see that there is a surge fare, which means she's going to pay four times the regular price because of high demand. She's already going to be late, might as well not be fifty in the hole too. A cab will be just as fast.

She jaywalks to a location where she has better luck flagging down a taxi. Eight minutes later, she's in the back of one, creeping along Huntington Avenue toward Brookline. The driver is a chatty woman with gray hair pulled up in a bun. On the screen in front of Charli, Jimmy Fallon tells a joke that she's too distracted to follow.

"Why don't you try Tremont?" Charli suggests through the glass. "I have to be there five minutes ago."

"Five minutes ago is a tall order," the woman says.

"My whole life is a tall order. Please get me there as fast as you can." Charli scrolls to her messages and types out a quick note. The traffic is awful. We're catching every red light. I left twenty minutes ago.

Through her therapist, she's learned that she fibs to avoid conflict, an aftereffect of being raised by an abusive mother. She's tried to curb the habit, but it's difficult, especially in a case like this. Charli is no stranger to being a lot of things, including a bad girlfriend, but she hates to be a disappointment. It's why she bails when everything is still golden.

Charli hopes for a quick response, stares at the screen. Hopes for the three dots to show he's responding. Maybe he and his mother are also stuck in traffic.

But probably not. Fully aware of traffic patterns at this time of day in Boston, he'd plan accordingly. She can already feel his mother's eyes looking her up and down, judging whether Charli is a good fit. No, Patrick's Mom, I'm not a good fit at all. I play the game well, but then it falls apart. In fact, I'm wondering why he's still hanging around. I couldn't possibly be *that* good in bed.

Patrick doesn't write back. Charli grips the phone but diverts her gaze out the window. The traffic is a tortoise race. Horns beep. A biker smacks his palm onto the hood of a car that nearly slammed him into the back of a garbage truck. Pedestrians bob and weave around stopped cars on the crosswalk. More cars are stuck in the intersection.

Red lights.

A long line of red lights stretches like holiday decorations down Huntington Avenue, carving out a path toward her doom.

"We have to get off Huntington," Charli says. Barring a miracle, she'll be thirty minutes late.

The cabbie tries a few tricks, cuts down Parker and even tries an alley. But a garbage truck is blocking the way, so they have to reverse. They finally get going, and the cabbie presses the gas to beat a yellow light. They barely squeak by as they're assaulted by a barrage of angry honkers.

"Thanks for trying," Charli whispers inaudibly. "Sorry to storm in here in such a rush. I'm late to meet my boyfriend's mother for the first time."

"Oh, I remember that day well," she says. "I'll do the best I can."

"Thank you."

Charli looks at her phone again. Nothing. She feels sick inside, knowing how much she's letting him down. A memory barges in, as if it were waiting on the other side of the door for the opportune time to ambush her. She was ten or eleven—shortly after their housekeeper had quit because Charli's mother, Georgina, had screamed at her for not vacuuming under the couch. Charli had been forced to take up some of the slack, and she seemed to always have toilet duty. She remembers being on her knees, wearing giant yellow rubber gloves pulled past her elbows and breathing in bleach, as her mother stood over her, saying, "This is about all you're good for."

They hit more red lights. They haven't caught one green light since they left. She texts Patrick again, assuring him she'll be there.

Finally, he responds in short: K.

Ugh. He's pissed and has every right to be.

She squeezes the phone like she's strangling an intruder and watches as every red light slowly turns green, as the cars in front inch forward. Finally.

Finally, Colton Four comes into view. The restaurant doesn't have a sign and doesn't need one. The *Boston Globe* raves about them constantly, calling it the hippest place in town. After winning a competition on television, the chef is now taking over New England.

Charli reaches into her purse. Of course she doesn't have cash, and she's misplaced her debit card. She hands a credit card over as they slide to a stop outside the restaurant. Waiting for the damn machine to run and print a receipt is agonizing. But walking inside will be worse.

As she's climbing out of the car, the cabbie turns back to her and says through the glass, "Just be yourself."

Charli lets out a breath she's been holding entirely too long and whispers, "Thanks."

Three minutes later, she scrunches her hair to give her roots some height, but her physical appearance is the least of her worries. She has to win over Patrick's mom with all the humor and charm that Patrick has certainly promised. From the way he talks about his mom, she sounds like Cruella de Vil meets Miranda Priestly from *The Devil Wears Prada*.

Charli stops shy of the entrance. People push by her. Fear splashes down on her like a waterfall. She closes her eyes and attempts to steady her pulse.

"You got this," she says to herself.

Charli comes through the door with her best strut. The small restaurant is packed, people talking over one another, servers winding by with trays of delicate cuisine. Patrick and his mother are not at the bar. She walks through the restaurant, one table at a time.

No sign.

She goes back to the hostess stand. "Do you have a Patrick Hannigan here tonight? I'm supposed to meet him. I'm late. Party of three."

The hostess, wearing a dress and high boots, scans the book and shakes her head. "I don't see a Hannigan. Could it be under another . . . ?"

"I don't think so." Charli casts a look back toward the restaurant, as if she missed a table.

"You're sure it's this location? You know we opened the place downtown too? On Washington, near the Opera House."

The words of the hostess drive a stake into Charli's heart. She's at the wrong location. Patrick had told her a few times that he was switching it because his mom had opted for the Mandarin Oriental over "intruding" at her son's place.

"Do you want me to call them?" the hostess asks. "You're probably twenty minutes away."

Charli looks up as tears sprout under her eyes. She's twenty minutes and ten red lights away from everything in her life. "No . . . no, thanks."

Outside, the snow still falls. She looks up and down the street. Sure, she could catch another taxi, but what's the point? She texts him. I just got here. To the Brookline location, the wrong one. I'm so sorry, Patrick. She tucks her phone back into her purse. There's no use trying now. No use even catching a cab. Peering up the street toward her house, she decides to walk in the snow.

⌒

The bell of her apartment rings two hours later. Tiny's head perks up from his position on the floor. Charli took him to the park, and now she's reading a book on the couch. Charli gets up to answer, assuming it's Patrick, but she hasn't checked her phone since she last texted him. She feels like a younger version of herself, hiding in her room in her family's Beacon Hill row house, waiting for her mother to storm in and explode.

Patrick enters so much more gently than her mother would and says hello to Tiny and gives him a rub. Her boyfriend—for now—doesn't say

11

anything for what feels like five minutes. He holds his wool hat in his hands. A look at him now confirms the inevitable: they're over.

Charli likes him; she really does. He's kind and sweet to her. Opens doors, listens without judgment, brings her flowers. But he likes the best of her, and she's tired of pretending. That's the way it's always been with men. She's into it for a while, but eventually it fizzles. All that work of being your best self gets old.

Before Patrick, there was Adam. He was great at first but fell way too hard. She pulled the rip cord after three months. She was pretty sure he had a ring in his pocket when she said, "It's my fault; I'm not ready." Before him, it was Ben . . . Ben, Ben, Ben. He was a journalist, and they loved to read together. That was pretty nice, actually. They could lie on the couch together for hours disappearing into their own stories. But then he got naggy, telling her she was the greatest thing that ever happened to him. Settle down, Ben. Desperation will get you nowhere.

The last remnant of her current boyfriend finally gives a weak smile. "Can we sit?"

"Yeah." Charli nods to the couch in front of the television. Her apartment was once a cigar factory, and the brick walls and tall ceilings suddenly feel cold, despite all the rugs she uses to cover the chipped and overworked hardwoods. Hundreds of the leftover books from the Bookstore That Never Was line the shelves and stand in stacks along the wall; even they can't mute the cavernous feel of her place during an awkward conversation.

They sit on either side of the couch. He seems relaxed, throws his arm up over the back. She studies his face. He's clean-shaven and smells of menthol. God, he's delectable.

"So . . . ," he starts.

"So . . ." She doesn't apologize again. It would feel like an insult to do so. "How's your mother?"

He shakes his head with the glimmer of a smile. He's done putting up with her. It's written all over him.

"Just rip off the Band-Aid, Patrick." She loathes her childish behavior, but it's coming up from her core. There's something about her turning into an asshole that makes life hurt less.

"What do you want me to say, Charli?" he asks. "You knew tonight mattered to me."

Her hands fly out in front of her. "And I tried. I got the wrong place, okay?"

He's equally animated, as if this moment has been coming to a head for a long time. "But did you? I don't even know what to believe. It wouldn't be the first time you've bent the truth."

He's right.

Patrick sighs, letting it all out, all the frustration of dating such an impossible person. She was his first girlfriend in a while, as he'd been drowning in a surgical residency at Boston Medical Center. They'd met at the dog park. He was dog-sitting for a friend. Of course he was. He's pretty much an angel. Deserves to be with his female counterpart, an overachiever-with-wings-type figure. A heart surgeon who walks on water, arrives early to everything, and has a giant loving family.

Patrick speaks to her like he's sitting down to give a patient bad news. "I have tried. And tried. It doesn't seem like you want to be in this relationship." He raises a hand and lets it fall onto his lap. He has fine and steady hands, surgeon's hands that could undress her and touch her with tantalizing skill. Even more, she'll miss his arms around her.

Had he not brought his mother into the equation, they could have had a little more time together. Maybe if she were a different person, they could have had a lot of time together. She liked his spur-of-the-moment ideas, like riding up to Portsmouth for a play at the Music Hall and their Halloween visit to Salem last year, his way of making her feel better after she shut down her plan to open the store.

She fights off her silly romantic hopes. It's that he was dating someone other than the real Charli. Well, Patrick, the jig's up.

"What do you want me to say? I should have warned you." God, they always have to sink their teeth into you at some point, as if a man must conquer you and own you and put a leash around your neck. Why can't they be okay with having some fun and then moving along? Men are best rented and not owned.

He does what he does when he's frustrated with her, which is twist the ring his grandfather gave him. "You and I could be good together. But you're trapped in this . . . this . . ."

"This what?"

"I don't know what," he says. "This . . . darkness. This thing where you don't allow yourself to be happy. We could be great together, but you're not letting us. It breaks my heart to say it, but I think I'm done."

Charli presses an imaginary button in the air. "There it is. Exactly what I was waiting for."

He retracts the steady hands that will never touch her again. "You see. I bring up the end of us, and you suddenly look light as a feather. Let me remove the burden of *us*."

Her lips tighten into a thin line. "Once you get to know me, I'm not so pretty, am I?"

He looks flabbergasted. "Do you hear yourself talk? You have to stop. Yes, you're beautiful. You're smart too. Brilliant, even. I love our conversations. And you're fun to be around when you let yourself off the hook for a moment. You make me laugh more than anyone. God, I'd love for us to work out. But you're not ready. Tonight was another example of that."

Silence fills the room. In a way, she does feel freedom. He's right. The worst part is almost over. There's so much *trying*.

"I get it," she says. "And I'm sorry."

Patrick sits there for a moment, a befuddled look on his face. He slaps his hands on his thighs and stands to face her. "Do you mind gathering my things and leaving them with the concierge? I'll come by and drop off your stuff in a few days, make the exchange."

"Yep, sure." Why is an "exchange" the worst part for her?

Charli looks away as she feels herself disassociating from the moment. The sooner he's gone, the better. She backs up and avoids eye contact. He doesn't want her; he wants a better version of her.

Tiny slathers him with a last kiss. Charli watches, waiting for him to cross the threshold. Still avoiding his eyes, she says, "Have a good one."

Then he's gone.

She presses her ear against the door to make sure she can hear his footsteps. Once she knows he's gone, she slides down to the floor and folds forward.

Tiny wedges his way in.

She runs her hands through his hair. "It's back to you and me, lovey." She looks over at all the books on the opposite side of her apartment. "At least I'll get more reading done . . ."

Chapter 2

WHAT BEST FRIENDS ARE FOR

"You're kidding me," Vivian says, showing that radiant smile of hers.

"It's not funny," Charli whispers, paranoid of others eavesdropping. She and her best friend are at their favorite restaurant, but like everywhere else in Boston, real estate is valuable, so the restaurateurs squeeze their patrons in, leaving enough space between tables so that you won't elbow your neighbor. Charli has just recounted the sorry tale of how Patrick and her relationship had reached its conclusion.

Viv lets her smile fade and leans in. Her braids are long enough to graze the white tablecloth. "I know it's not funny. But still . . . you have to laugh a little. Losing your keys. Red lights. The wrong restaurant. There's some part of you that's doing this intentionally, because you and I both know you're not looking for anything serious."

"Yeah, well, we'd run our course."

Her eyes widen. "He was a good one, Charli."

"I know he was a good one." She pulls her wineglass toward her and twists the stem.

"Even if he's the best catch in New England," Vivian says, "you're going to find something wrong with him before too long. It's almost like you don't think you deserve a good man."

Charli whips a hand into the air. "Look at my competition, Viv. You should be the one dating him." Charli sighs as she takes in her friend. They're both twenty-nine, born a week apart. Viv has teeth that a dentist would put on marketing materials and lips that women would kill for. Her golden-brown skin belongs to a supermodel. She's great at being a friend, and so funny all the time, so happy. And talk about brilliant. She was the top of her class at Yale Law, and that was after four years at Harvard. She is unstoppable. When she eventually has children—after she's conquered the world—she'll make it look so easy.

Viv postures like she's addressing someone on the witness stand. "Tell me something. Why do you think I'm your friend?"

Charli is puzzled, as if Viv asked her what number she's holding behind her back. "Because we've been friends since we were kids. And because you like to surround yourself with inferiority?" She drinks to that and lets her lips bend into the slightest smile, because she is at least aware of her tendency to self-deprecate. It's soothing.

Viv stares Charli down. "I am besties with you because I see in you what you don't see in yourself. That part of you, I love being around. Don't get me wrong, I love all of you. But the really good stuff, your soul. Your heart. The way you've always been there for your father since the moment your mom broke his heart. The way you drop everything when I need you."

Her toes curl. "Would you please stop? Someone might overhear, and I have a reputation to uphold."

Viv lets the slightest smile grace her face. "And I shouldn't even tell you this, because you'll use it as an excuse, but your sarcasm is pretty darn entertaining."

Charli fidgets with her napkin. "You know I don't do compliments."

Viv sits back with a splash of attitude. "So sue me for giving you compliments. Maybe one day you'll actually hear them."

"Sue a lawyer, that'll go far." Charli slides her eyes left and right, sure that the wide-eyed youngsters dining next to them are listening in.

Or maybe the two women on the other side who are suspiciously silent. "I would prefer someone less than perfect."

Vivian shakes her head. "That's the silliest thing I've ever heard. What, you want a white-collar criminal who drinks too much? Doesn't give orgasms and leaves the seat up? Why would you want that?"

"Well, Viv, I realize now that it's best to undercompensate when it comes to men."

Viv retreats to her Manhattan, probably realizing she's pushing the limits. "You make no sense, girl."

"Try living in this skin." Now Charli's just venting and doesn't want to stop. "For whatever reason, I am not meant for love. And I don't think I'm meant for happiness either." She jumps in for more before Vivian can disagree. "But I'm happy in my unhappiness. No, that's not true. But I'm happier accepting what is, as opposed to spending my whole life chasing a carrot that I'll never catch."

Viv cracks a smile. "You're impossible. Do you hear what you're saying? I should record you and play it back. Give yourself a break."

"Easy for you to say when you're getting all the green lights." Charli sucks in a breath. She hates all this self-pitying victim stuff. "Look, you're meant for greater things."

Viv holds back what Charli is sure would have been a long lecture. She blows out a blast of air and picks up the menu.

"What I know, Charli, is that love and happiness are universal rights. As soon as you tell me you don't deserve them, I tune you out."

"Oh, thanks. What a great dinner pair we make." Charli slides her wineglass across the tablecloth. "What do you want me to do? I've tried all the things: therapy, yoga, meditation—both transcendental and whatever you call just regular, sitting there watching your thoughts, which are a whole thing, let me tell you. My apartment is drowning in self-help books."

"That's because of your leftover inventory from the bookstore. How many of the self-help ones have you actually read?"

Her friend's words are daggers to the heart. "Some of them."

Viv gives a chuckle that makes Charli consider tipping the Manhattan over on her. "Talk about metaphors," Viv says. "You're surrounded by the answers, but you're not listening. Those red lights? You're the one attracting them."

Charli's feathers are ruffled now. "How am I doing that, Viv?"

"You want me to be honest?"

"I would expect nothing less from you."

"By letting your mom win. By believing the crap she said to you." Viv sets her palms on the table and lifts her fingers. "I know you've done all this work to get better, but I'm not sure you're past it. You're funny. You're awesome when you let your light shine. You're beautiful, Charli. You're all the things. Guys are desperate to break through your barrier, but you're not letting them in."

Charli starts to argue, to make up an excuse, but what's the point? "What am I gonna do? I'm trying. My mom didn't hold me enough as a baby, and she smashed my dolls, and she told me she would throw me away if she could. Yada, yada, yada. I've already been down this road."

Viv frowns. "It breaks my heart that I didn't realize the extent of it."

Charli had hidden it longer from Viv than from her father, only sharing the details after they'd left high school. "What would you have done about it anyway?"

"I wish you had told someone."

An unwarranted tear is coming, and Charli bites it back. Would anyone have believed her?

Viv pushes. "You might have gone down this road, but you haven't come to peace with how she treated you. Georgina's still controlling the narrative."

Charli's teeth grind. "Please stop."

No one *really* knows how badly Georgina hurt Charli, not even her father. She was trying to protect him for some reason, holding back that her mother was the worst when he went away. So many of the things her mother said are branded into Charli's psyche—how she was a mistake, how . . . how Charli was put on this earth to torment her.

How she should be taken out with the trash. Georgina would always come back later with an apology and beg for Charli not to say anything to her father when he returned from his trips, a request Charli always abided by.

But it hurt. It still hurts. She made her—

Crack.

Charli looks down in time to see the bulb of her wineglass break from the stem. In slow motion, she watches the bulb crash down and wine splatter everywhere. The puddle spreads quickly over the heavily starched tablecloth to the edge of the table and lands on her lap before she can rise.

"Oh shit," she says, standing quickly. The whole restaurant turns to see why she cursed like a sailor's daughter.

Viv is on her feet, too, already disposing of the mess. That's the way she is. Never in shock, always moving forward, fixing the situation. She dries off Charli's phone and then notices Charli's hand.

"You're bleeding."

Charli lowers her eyes. Blood drips down her fingers and into her palm. All she can do is smile. "This is my life," she mutters. She looks down at the kids next to her, who are trying not to stare.

She holds her bloody hand out in front of her. "Just wait until you're my age."

⸺

Fifteen minutes later, the stain on Charli's dress is drying. She holds a freshly bandaged hand on her lap. She looks over at Vivian and feels all kinds of gratitude, as there's nothing better in the world than knowing you have a best friend who will never leave you, no matter how much you screw up. They've been friends since they were five, so it's not like Viv has much of a choice.

They met because their fathers were friends who'd been sailing together since their days at Harvard. Some of Charli's favorite memories were boating with both of their families. Her father was in his element, and her mother was always on her best behavior, showing the side of herself that Charli wished were the norm. Funny—or maybe not so funny—Charli and her mother had that in common, an ability to behave and be their best for a while.

Their parents had gotten along well, and Charli and Viv had latched on to each other, though Viv grew into an incredibly impressive woman, while Charli felt stuck on the sidelines. Sometimes she feels like Viv's charity case. Viv's best friend should be someone who attends royal weddings and visits the White House.

Charli has a fresh glass of wine and holds it gingerly. Viv has drunk her second Manhattan but seems completely sober and in control. She has a sharp mind that a little alcohol cannot dull. Nothing will stop her from swimming her laps at five in the morning.

As they wait for the salads they ordered, they chat about how Viv wants to find a new place to live, as her upstairs neighbor stomps on the floors. This topic segues into Viv's own troubles, and she vents for a while.

"Terry wants to get married. I'm not ready." Terry is disturbingly handsome and runs a LGBTQ nonprofit in downtown Boston. And he does triathlons. "Maybe after I make partner. But I'm not ready . . . to be locked down, have kids—'cause I know that's what he's thinking. He's going to reel me in and then knock me up. I want a few more normal years before I stop wearing makeup and my boobs turn into dairy udders and . . ."

Charli lets out a laugh. "Dairy udders?"

"Seriously. And forget about sleeping. Maternity leave for a lawyer in this town is about twelve minutes."

"Why twelve?" Charli asks.

"I don't know. Because thirteen is too long. It's hard enough staying ahead as a woman, let alone a Black woman. I can't imagine trying to work a baby into my schedule." Viv pulls her hair back. "Besides, I'm still working on me."

Charli's heard it all now. "You? What in the world do you have left to work on?"

Viv jolts her head. "You always do that. You act like I'm living the perfect life, but trust me, it's not easy for me either."

She's right, Charli realizes. She does always treat Viv like she's super-human, like she doesn't have her own share of difficulties. "I'm sorry," she says. "Seriously, though, you're kind of like a souped-up human. Like half-AI."

"You realize you're doing it again, right?"

Charli gives up on being funny. She looks down like she got in trouble for playing with matches. "Sorry."

"Forget about it." Viv leans in. "Did I tell you I'm seeing a spiritual guide?"

"Hold on, what?" Charli didn't see that one coming.

"Yeah, I've seen her twice now. Because my souped-up human life is not all that you think it is."

"Wait, you're seeing a spiritual guide, and you're just now telling me?"

Viv draws a circle in the air toward Charli's head. "We had to wade through your stuff first."

"That's fair. I'm sorry. Your turn now."

Her friend gets real, which is another wonderful trait of Viv. "I've just . . . I've felt a little superficial lately, you know. Do this, do that . . . but to what end? What's out there? A neighbor of mine has been working with a spiritual guide for a while, and I thought, 'What the heck?' Turns out, this guide is plugged in like no one I've ever met. She's changing my life—and that's only after two sessions."

"What is she, like a psychic?" Charli tries not to show that she feels left out.

"She's a soul reader, a kind of yogi or guru. I don't even know what happens in there. She sits across from me and pulls back the layers. I'm telling you . . . she can see inside me, see that I've always defined myself by my work, my grades, my accomplishments. She's helping me get to know myself better, you know?"

Charli leans forward on her elbows and listens intently. Not only because she wants to be a good friend, but also because she's intrigued. Why is the most perfect woman in America seeing a soul reader? Is she really dissatisfied with the life she's living? Because her incredibly hot and chivalrous boyfriend wants to take the next step?

"She has a retreat coming up in Costa Rica," Viv continues, "doing family constellation therapy. I'm dying to go, but there's no way I can get away from work right now. Which, I know, is counterintuitive to me trying not to work as much . . . but whatever. I still have to work."

"What is it?" Charli asks, noticing a server pass by with a delicious tray of food.

Viv starts talking with her hands. "It has to do with transgenerational patterns, memories, trauma. Being a Black woman, I can tell you without a doubt that trauma gets passed down. You've heard me talk about that. But it's more than genetics. With family constellations, a family exists within a cloud, a sort of energy field that includes dead family members. *All* my ancestors are connected to me. If something bad happened to them, *or* if they did something bad, I could be suffering from it too. Frances says the therapy allows the family to restore balance, taking away the suffering of not only you, but your family too. I know it sounds wack but . . ."

Charli hears a bell ring in her head. This could totally be what's going on in her own family. "No, no, it doesn't sound wack—not completely."

"You're looking at me funny."

"No," Charli says, "I'm thinking that it sounds like something I need more than you. And I'm thinking I'm the worst friend in the world for not being there for you, not knowing this stuff about you."

"Um, who was there for me when I caught my ex-fiancé—he who shall not be named—sleeping with his boss? I seem to recall you taking all your vacation from the bookstore in Rhode Island, driving up here to Boston, and hunkering down with me for two weeks while I complained about men."

Charli smiles at the memory. Maybe she isn't as bad of a friend as she thinks. "I gained five pounds in those two weeks, all that pizza and ice cream."

"You and me both." Viv lets out a smile. "You tried to get me to go skydiving. Remember that?"

Charli shrugs. "What better way to move on?"

Viv waves a hand in the air. "I could go run out into traffic, too, but I don't have a death wish."

They share another laugh before Charli gets serious. "Still, I'll try harder, okay? I know you have your stuff too."

"Trust me. It's not always easy for me, either, this life thing."

A quiet rises between them as they hold each other's gaze.

Charli is surprised at how raw the moment is. She doesn't have experience with such feelings.

"So, this therapy . . . ," Charli says.

"You should watch some videos. Mind you, I'm just learning about it, but the facilitator, Frances in this case, creates an environment where the dead family members can communicate to the people in the room."

Charli sits back and crosses her legs. It's like finding out Viv went on a girls' trip and didn't invite her. Not that she'd go, but that's beside the point. "Look at you."

"What?"

"I didn't know you were into woo-woo. Is this the new Viv?"

Viv looks offended, as if she's been pegged into a political party in which she does not belong. "I've always been into woo-woo."

"Oh, c'mon. You're a lawyer."

"And that means I can't have a little faith in the unexplained?"

"That's exactly what it means."

Viv bites her bottom lip and nods as if she's about to drop a condemning piece of evidence onto the judge's lap. "You want her number then?"

"Whose?" Charli asks, putting off the dare.

Viv wraps her cream-colored scarf around her neck. "What do you mean, *whose?*" she mocks. "My spiritual guide. Frances."

"*Frances,*" Charli says. "Shouldn't her name be something more . . . I don't know . . . guru-ish?"

Viv rewards her with the faintest smile ever smiled. "You might like her, Cha Cha." Charli hasn't been called Cha Cha in a long time, and it unspools a reel of childhood memories in Charli's mind, the good ones like the lemonade stand she and Viv used to host at the marina.

"What do I need a guru for?" Charli asks, as in: *What's the point?*

Viv turns into a mannequin, her face frozen in bewilderment. Though she knows Charli better than anyone, she probably can't tell whether Charli's joking or asking such a question earnestly. Charli would love to clarify, but she's not sure herself. Of course she needs a guru. She needs a guru and a better therapist, and probably a prescription of some sort. But the idea of it feels a lot like trying to shovel a sidewalk while it's still dumping snow.

The silence between them goes on for a long time, and hardheaded Viv seems to wait for a response.

Viv finally caves. She raises her hands and sets her index finger on the opposite hand's pinkie, ready to count. "Want me to list the ways?"

"You don't have enough fingers," Charli says.

Viv tilts forward. "You're going to call her then?"

"Give me her number. I'll call her."

Viv knows her too well and lets out a "Mm-hmm."

Chapter 3

BUMPER TO BUMPER

In the morning, Charli strips and stumbles into the shower. She managed to sleep without medicinal help, but it was her usual tossing and turning, grabbing her phone every couple of hours to take her mind off the endless hamster wheel of thoughts that gnaw at her.

Once Charli is dressed, she's racing. There's no time to eat, as she has to take Tiny for a walk. They step out into the madness of downtown Boston. Another dusting of snow came down around midnight, and people slip and slide over unsalted sidewalks.

Thirty minutes later, she drives to Arlington in bumper-to-bumper traffic. She used to take the Red Line and then switch to a bus but started driving when the T became unreliable. She taps her fingers on the wheel, hoping she's not late again. As usual, she listens to an audiobook—Barbara Kingsolver's latest, which deserves the Pulitzer—but her thoughts are elsewhere, so she keeps having to back up by thirty seconds. Eventually she waves the white flag and presses pause.

It's strange not to wake up to Patrick, or at least to a text from him. Of course, Tiny's probably happier this way. She's definitely not going to race into something new. It will be nice to be single for a while and allow herself to regenerate.

Eventually her mind drifts to Viv and her spiritual guide and the family constellation therapy. Charli has often wondered how she and her family have been dealt such a bad hand. Though her father was dragged into the mire, it was her mother's side that had all the problems. Georgina was a wreck who came from a long line of wrecks, people who'd done time, lost children, gone bankrupt, divorced often, died by suicide, and died young. Was it possible that there was a reason for their struggles? Something more than statistics or inherited genes?

Pulling into the parking lot always draws a sigh out of her, as if the mere sight of this nondescript building is enough to crush her spirit. But she's made her choices. It was Charli herself, shortly after last year's bookstore debacle, who said she wanted a job that paid well but required zero attention once she'd left for the day.

Charli tucks into her cubicle and resumes work on an advisory report for a local doughnut chain. She can barely get through a page without stopping to ponder what went wrong. Though it had all fallen apart, at least her father had done something with his life. He'd gone to Harvard, for God's sake. Charli had crawled her way through UMass on the five-year plan. He'd grown an importing business from his tiny garage apartment in Newton to a company that he could have sold for $30 million at its peak. He started out importing toys, but expanded quickly, including clothing, electronics, and other consumer goods. Now all that's left are a few articles in the *Globe* detailing its near demise before a competitor stepped in with an offer William had to accept.

Charli, on the other hand . . .

She'd finally found some chutzpah two years ago and started to do something great, but she collapsed under pressure. Having always been a book person, Charli was rarely without one in her hand. Her friends made fun of her because she'd sneak a page in any time she could, even in the elevator. It was only natural that she work at Barnes & Noble through college. Afterward, she joined an independent bookstore in Providence, Rhode Island, where she eventually conjured up the *brilliant* idea of opening up her own store in Cambridge.

For about five minutes, it was the greatest job on earth, all the social media excitement, the books pouring in from distributors, the coffee and pastry tastings in preparation to open her café. Then the location fell through, and she got cold feet. Yes, she could have found another spot, but all the momentum that had been building seemed to float away after that. If it wasn't the lease, it would be something else. Might as well have pulled the plug before she made herself an even bigger embarrassment.

She saved herself from further financial loss too. Though she had to return the Kickstarter funds, and she lost a chunk of savings to inventory, advertising, down payments, etc.—not to mention the time invested—it could have been far worse.

Marvin, her boss, creeps up and stands over her.

"So . . . did you make it on time today?"

She can't stand his voice. He slithers, all of him. His voice is a hiss, his skin scaly. But she needs the job, so she turns around and gives the fakest and merriest "good morning" she can muster.

"Right on time today," she says. "I'm so sorry about yesterday."

"Yeah, and the day before."

Charli shrugs. Truth be told, she was late again today, but thankfully she was able to sneak in discreetly. If he would be kinder, maybe she would arrive earlier.

"I really should fire you," he says in a half-joking tone. "You're late half the time and not very good at this job, anyway. I mean, the reports are fine, but Sam finishes his in half the time."

Charli bites her tongue. Anything she says right now will make it worse. Sam can go suck an egg with his big fat chompers. Collating these reports that advise fledgling companies on ways to avoid bankruptcy is the highlight of his life. He attacks the day as if he were born for this job.

Marvin sets a hand on the wall of her cubicle. He breathes as if he's plugged into a respirator. "But I probably won't. Because of my slacker of a son who has decided not to go to college, I have a soft spot for

29

people who can't get their acts together. Staff shortages what they are, my options are limited."

What an asshole, she thinks. "Then I want a raise."

"No."

"Then I'll quit." They both know she won't, as it pays better than anything else she can get. There may have been staff shortages, but she did not find it easy to land a job. Her résumé was all bookstores, and after having to abandon her own, she wanted nothing to do with them. Thankfully, her experience didn't ruin her love of books.

Marvin coughs out a laugh. "You're not going to quit."

Charli finds his eyes, really looks into them. She can play this game all day long. "As awful as you are," she says, "you remind me of my mother, so I understand you. And I'll continue showing up late, taking my time. But at least I'm showing up. Do we understand each other?"

He looks at her for a long time, a slight upward curl of his lips that indicates he likes the way she talks to him, which grosses her out.

When he walks away, she decides she will get Marvin back by taking a break from working. She pulls up the internet to search for "family constellations." A man named Alfred Adler coined the term, but it was German psychotherapist Bert Hellinger who ran with the idea and developed it into a therapy. Each piece she reads helps her wrap her head around the thought process. Viv had it right. Family members can feel and even suffer from trauma that existed in a previous branch of their family tree—even if they are unaware of the details.

Apparently it's more than genetics that provides a conduit for such pain to pass through. Believers claim that there is a morphic field, or energy cloud, as Viv had called it, in which family members, both alive and dead, reside. A traumatic experience can create an imbalance in the field, causing a collective suffering. The idea of the therapy is to rebalance the dynamic, which relieves the traumatic burden.

Charli finds the website of Viv's guru and reads the "About Me" section. Frances Graham is an American who was born into a family filled with violence. She fell hard into drugs and only resurfaced in her late twenties after discovering the power of family constellations.

Though Charli reads several articles debunking the concepts as pseudoscience, a tiny part of her wants to learn more. What if that's what's going on with her and her parents? Even before her mom started blaming her for everything, Charli had always felt guilty of something, as if she came out of her mother's womb consumed by it. She feels guilty now, searching the internet, instead of slogging out reports for the snake, guilty that Tiny is cooped up in her apartment, guilty for letting Patrick down and leaving his mother hanging. She'll never stop feeling guilty for failing to open the Bookstore That Never Was.

Thursdays, she goes to see her father, William, after work. Maybe it wasn't only her mother's side of the family that drew the short stick. William married into it, which made him the unluckiest of them all. He'd told Charli one time that his parents had warned him before the marriage that he was getting into something bad. William had loved Georgina, though, and nothing anyone said would make him feel differently. Wasn't love a real mensch, to tie you to someone that wasn't good for you? Poor guy never stood a chance.

When she looks past the sludge, Charli can remember Georgina being a good mother, like the times she volunteered at the school, helping with the field trips, and even the annual haunted house fundraiser. Georgina wasn't taking home any best-mother awards, but it seemed she was at least trying.

When Charli was nine, Georgina and William lost a baby—Charli's little brother, Jacob. He'd died after four days of complications with a heart defect. Afterward, everything changed.

Georgina spent weeks in her room, completely checking out of her maternal duties. And in that den of grief and rage, she snapped. She came out a different person, treating both William and Charli as if they were the ones who'd taken Jacob away.

William took time off from traveling to help keep his family together. He worked hard to be patient with Georgina, trying to bring her back to who she used to be. But she was gone. William eventually had to go back to work; he had a hundred employees counting on him. Each time he left, he would hug Charli and promise that he'd be back as soon as he could. Then he'd ask her to take care of her mom. No one ever asked if she was okay about losing her brother.

The days when he was gone were hell. Georgina would barely look Charli in the eyes. She'd drink or sleep all day, sometimes pop pills. Charli would tiptoe around, trying not to get in trouble, which she would often. The following four years were a nightmare.

Then Georgina asked for a divorce, which hit William unawares, like a fly ball striking a Red Sox fan mauling a hot dog up in the cheap seats at Fenway. There he was, being a devoted husband despite her deterioration, and she saw nothing but a monster in him. She was suddenly sure that he was cheating on her and lying to her.

She didn't fight for custody—not a shred—which had crushed thirteen-year-old Charli. Not that Charli had any interest in even weekly visits with her mother, but the idea of not being wanted by her mother stung.

Neither William nor Charli had known that she'd been running around with other men, a fact that had come out only after the ink had dried on the divorce papers and Georgina had walked away with two homes and half the money. The whole tragedy had left William scratching his head in the aftermath. He took the blame and started his own decline. He stopped traveling as much, stopped going into the office. Charli had tried to be there for him, to lift him up, go sailing with him, but even those days had lost much of their joy.

Tiny's wagging tail threatens to break a window as Charli drives them in her Honda across town to Beacon Hill. After her father opens the front door of his brownstone, Tiny barges in and throws his enormous paws up onto William's shoulders. He lets it happen, smiles even, which is rare for him these days.

Then it's Charli's turn. "Hey, Dad."

"Hi, sweetie." He leans in for a kiss, and she notices his skin is pale. He's dressed as gray and gloomy as the day outside. Sometimes she wants to shake him, to tell him to pull out of it.

As always, she's come bearing flowers and a book. It's her little way of trying to bring some light into his life.

"I don't think you've read *Pillars of the Earth*, have you?"

He takes the hefty tome. "No, but I've heard you mention it."

"Just trust me, okay?"

"Aye, aye, captain."

She remembers the first of the two times she'd read the story and how her apartment could have been on fire and she wouldn't have noticed, and she hopes *Pillars* might cart her father away from his troubles in the same manner.

They walk through the house, following Tiny, who has raced to the back door in a desperate frenzy to get into the yard. Having sold the house where Charli grew up, which is only two blocks down, William has been living here for ten years.

Rugs with a footpath worn into them stretch out over dusty floors. Paintings of sailboats cutting through the sea hang crooked on the walls. Pictures of Charli and her dad standing on the deck or hoisting up the mainsail or sharing the steering wheel can be found on almost every wall. There were some great photos of her mom on the boat with them, too—times that were truly delightful, but like the charming and happy side of Georgina, they're long gone now.

When Charli was a baby, as William started to make good money, he had caught the sailing bug and become obsessed. He'd bought a forty-five-foot Beneteau sailboat that he named *Just What I Needed* after the song by his favorite Boston band, the Cars. It's the only artifact left of those abundant days before his company had gone under.

Charli finds a vase and gives the flowers some water; then they go out into the backyard. Tiny leaps into the snow as if he's been penned up for years. William and Charli stand on the brick of the patio and watch the Great Dane come alive.

Her dad zips up his jacket and pulls on gloves, looks at her. "So . . . what's going on?" he finally says, his breath turning to fog.

"Oh, you know." She tries to inject some happiness into her tone, but it's so hard around him.

He pulls the furry hood of his jacket over his head. "How's work?"

"It's . . . it's . . . I don't know . . . a paycheck."

Their time together always starts out like this, like a car trying to warm up in the cold. She feels like she's being reeled into the sadness and fights back. "You know, it's fine. My boss is clueless, but what boss isn't? It's easy work, and I'm saving money. I'm glad to be doing something."

"You're a fighter, honey. Always have been."

She raises her fists. They both know that her failed bookstore cut her off at the knees, and it's taken a lot for her to come back to her normal self.

"Just like you," she says, slipping an arm around him. She wishes it were true.

As he kisses the top of her head, Charli considers her role in how his life played out. Could she have done something differently? Does he still hold on to the blame of what happened with Georgina, especially considering how Charli had once rubbed it in his face?

She'll never forget that day back in the summer of her junior year. As a teenager, she'd become difficult to raise for her single father. It was as if she'd listened to her mother berate her so much that she became the problem her mother always saw.

During a fight with her father over a Dave Matthews Band concert he wouldn't let her attend, all Charli's bottled-up frustration and rage had erupted at once. Without holding back, she'd admonished William for not sticking up for her more when her mother came down on her.

She'd even gone into details, sharing with him information that he'd never known, like the day Georgina had smashed her dolls.

He'd died a little inside that day, assuming a nearly impossible burden she wished she could take back. No matter how many times she apologized, no matter how hard she tried afterward to carry their household, she will always know that she had knocked the life out of her father. No matter how much it hurts that he wasn't there to protect her, she'll never bring it up again.

A year after that big fight, William sat her down and told her that his company had filed for bankruptcy, and that he'd lost most of his money. When she pressed him for a reason, he'd claimed that the industry had changed. She'd later discovered that he'd simply stopped caring, stopped paying the bills, stopped showing up. How could she not own some of the responsibility for that too?

Here he was now, almost ten years into working for the man who bailed him out of bankruptcy, and it must be nearly unbearable to walk through those doors every day. William barely travels at all now and spends most of his time on the phone and computer. Though he is definitely making more than Charli, she imagines he doesn't do much more than hide in that office and fixate on what could have been.

Charli takes a ball from her jacket pocket and plays fetch with Tiny while she and her dad chat about *Ted Lasso* and a few other shows that they both like.

Tiny won't stop. Ten minutes in and he's still retrieving the ball with gusto. A plane flies overhead, descending toward Logan Airport. They watch it quietly.

She hurls the ball all the way to the back wall. "Patrick and I are over." It's taken her this long to admit it, and her father knew better than to bring it up. If his hesitance to ever ask isn't a telltale sign of her love life, then nothing is.

Her father groans. "I'm sorry."

Charli hadn't even introduced them yet, almost as if she knew the end was inevitable. "Yeah, what do you do? And thank you for not saying that the right guy will come along when you least expect it."

"I wouldn't dare. Whoever he was, he wasn't good enough for you. I know that."

She slips her arm around him again, buries her head in his shoulder. "I love you, Daddy."

"Love you too." He abruptly changes direction. "Oh, I didn't tell you, but I think I'm gonna sell the boat."

Charli swivels her head to her father like a pinball flipper. "What? You love that boat."

"Yeah, she was good to me, but it's time. I'm getting older."

"Dad, you're fifty-five. There are people sailing out there in their nineties."

He makes a sound that illustrates his disagreement. "It's lost some of its luster as I get older."

Charli's concern widens as the impact of what he's saying registers. Aside from her, that boat has been his everything. No matter how hard he worked, or how badly Georgina was torturing him, he became a new man once he stepped aboard, as if even the sight of her charged his soul.

"First you stop going to the Harvard Club, now this. What's going on with you?"

"Everything's good," he says with his eyes on Tiny. He repeats himself in a whisper. "Everything's good."

She wants to fix him, but she's tried fruitlessly since her mother left them. She's done everything she can to bring him back to life, but he withers away, one day at a time. Come to think of it, she can't help but wonder if she's going in the same direction.

Her conversation with Viv pops up like a chipmunk from a hole in the driveway. Is there something larger at play? Why is it that all three of them—Charli, her mother, *and* father—are stuck in a tailspin?

William tosses the ball for Tiny and is apparently reading Charli's mind. "How's your mom, by the way?"

"What's there to say? She's asking for money again, thinks you're storing it all in your account in Switzerland."

"Yeah, she's texting me too."

Her mom took both the Cape house and the chalet in Stowe. Sold the chalet after she blew the millions she took in the divorce. And now she's down to the Cape house and a few pennies and a black heart made of ashes.

Charli sighs. "Let's *not* talk about Mom." She looks up; the stars are showing through a break in the clouds. "It's a beautiful night. Let's go open a good bottle of wine and cook together. And talk about how you're not selling the Beneteau."

"Honey, don't bother," he says firmly.

"I'm serious. Some of the best times I've had in my life were on that boat. Viv talks about sailing with you all the time. She'll be furious. Dad, you tell anyone who will listen that *Just What I Needed* is a symbol of all the hard work you put in."

"Yeah, I know . . ." William scratches his chin. "But she's a lot of hard work too. And they raised the slip fees again. You know the tough thing about being my age is you don't know when you're going to die. So you have to guess with your money. If you run out, you're in some trouble. I'd like to leave you something if I can. At least leave you the house."

"Don't worry about me. You love being out there, working on her, hanging out with the other sailors at the marina. You even like fixing the head, which is odd and disgusting."

She gets a smile out of him this time. "We'll see."

"No." She pokes him in the side. "Don't give me that 'we'll see.' You're not selling the boat. I'm not done sailing with you."

He's staring at Tiny.

"Dad?"

"Yeah, I hear you."

"I know I'm preaching to the choir, but have you thought about seeing somebody, a therapist? Maybe trying some medicine?"

"Some things you have to face head-on. I'll figure it out."

Will he? "I'm worried about you."

"I'm digging out of it."

She wishes she could believe him.

～

After dinner, she hugs her dad tightly. He tries to smile as she walks out the door, but all she sees is a man who is giving up. She wants to ask him if he's thought about hurting himself, but she can't bring herself to do it.

The drive back to her place leaves her puzzling over what to do. Sure, she's told Viv on occasions that she's okay living with her own bleak view of the world, but maybe she's not. She's definitely not okay with her father's decline.

What is she going to do about it, though?

The idea of calling Viv's person reappears, and she tries to push it away, but the notion is stubborn. Is she that desperate? Yeah, maybe. She certainly can't sit on the sidelines and let her father fall apart.

When she gets back to her apartment, she pulls out the phone. She's on the couch with Tiny. He rests his head on her lap. He's so big one of his legs is dangling all the way down to the floor.

Not allowing more time for debate, she dials the number Viv shared. A surge of adrenaline zaps Charli when the woman answers.

She stumbles over her words. "I'm calling . . . I might . . . a client of yours told me . . ." Charli takes a breath. "My name is Charli Thurman. I'm Vivian's friend."

"Hi there," Frances says warmly. "So glad I picked up. I was headed out the door. What can I do for you?"

Charli wonders where to begin. "My family is falling apart. Has been for almost as long as I can remember. My dad's in real trouble. And when Viv mentioned what you did, it made me wonder if there's some reason for it. I have to admit that I'm skeptical about everything,

but something keeps telling me to call you. I'm in desperate territory."
She pets Tiny's head. "Do you have any time to see me coming up?"

"Ugh, gosh, Charli. I am slammed right now and have a waiting list, which I'm happy to add you to. But I do have a spot for my family constellation workshop in Costa Rica during the first week of March if you're itching to get started."

That's a month away. "Viv mentioned that, but I don't think I can pull off a Costa Rica trip."

"It's only a few days. I've got a great group coming down, and it so happens that someone canceled, and a spot opened up."

A tiny flicker of hope sparks but dies quickly. "That's a long way to . . . how do I even know it would work?"

"I can't promise anything, but I suspect there's a reason you found me."

Charli laughs out loud. It's a hopeful laugh, a desperate laugh. And a doubtful one too. As if repairing her family's damage was so easy. "That is a big commitment."

"You're right, it is."

Excuses shoot off like fireworks in Charli's mind. It's a big trip to try out some holistic thingy that she'd never even heard about until last night. Second, everything. *Everything* is why. Tiny. Work. Money. Leaving her father.

She finally says, "My life is complicated right now. I have this big dog and a new job without any vacation . . ."

Frances lets Charli ramble.

Another thirty seconds into her excuses, Charli says, "Are you still there?"

"Yes, I'm here. I'm smiling."

"Why are you smiling?"

"Because something tells me you should join us."

"Why do you say that?" The other question: *Why does Charli feel hopeful?*

"I don't know," Frances says. "It's a feeling. How about you don't rule it out and tell me what's going on?"

Charli rarely opens up to people, especially strangers, but for the next five minutes, she spills out the troubles of her life, including how she's worried about her father and that she isn't too different.

"So now you know," she finishes. "I told you more than I've told anyone ever. You there?"

"Yes," Frances says. "I'm thinking. I know it's a big decision. But I might be able to help you if you can find a way down."

Charli thinks of Viv challenging her. She wants to be spiritually open-minded; she's certainly more so than Viv. But Costa Rica? She asks Frances a few questions, trying to understand more of what the therapy entails, including the cost and time commitment.

Charli isn't broke, as she squirreled away most of what she was going to use to open the bookstore, but she's trying to protect her savings so she has a cushion to fall back on if she ends up jobless again. At some point, she'd love to put more into her pitiful retirement account, but she's not ready to take the risk of letting it go just yet.

Frances gives her a two-minute rundown, concluding by telling her that she'll get a chance to participate in other people's constellations as well.

Charli says, "But I don't get it . . . what is the end goal?"

"Every experience is different, but most people leave here with less weight on their shoulders. Your father could experience a new breath of life. Same with you and everyone else in your family constellation."

Charli can't deny the optimism rising up her spine. "God, I would love that. But I don't even know if I should leave him right now."

"You'll know if you should come. Trust your intuition."

"Intuition?" Charli says. "It's my intuition that's screwed up half of my life."

"You have to make sure you're listening to the right voice."

Chapter 4

HERE'S MOMMY

Every time Charli makes the drive out to the Cape, she spends part of it pondering why she still stays in touch with her mother, let alone visits her. It's a duty, fed by this guilt that drives her mad, this guilt that makes her feel like her mother, in all her failures, is somehow Charli's responsibility.

Another reason propels her today, though. She wants to know more about her mother's side of the family. It's been two days since she spoke with Frances, and Charli can't shake the idea that she should consider the trip to Costa Rica. It's lunacy, really, but Charli's desperate. Seeing her father decline, hearing him talking about selling the Beneteau. Her own instability. Something must be done, and she's running out of time.

Her mother's place on the water is a masterpiece, four thousand square feet of perfection steps away from a private beach. In the summer, the gardens wrapping around the house evoke Versailles, but only because one of her exes pays for the landscaping—among other things.

Her mother, Georgina, greets her at the door, and Charli can tell she's already been drinking. It's not even lunchtime on Saturday. "I thought you were coming earlier," she says.

Charli swallows a snarky response. Here less than a minute, and her mother is already showing her claws. Georgina is dressed like she's still in her thirties, a tight turquoise sheath showing off her tiny waist, a constant reminder of her mother's abstemious efforts to avoid food at all costs. She has a tan that has no business on a woman in New England; it's from the tanning bed she bought a year ago on a credit card that still needs to be paid off. She wears a gaudy pearl necklace around her neck. Her puffy lips are enough to keep Charli away from getting work done for the rest of her life. Same with her mother's oversize implants and stretched face.

"Where's the dog?" Georgina asks. Charli often thinks of her mother as Georgina because she feels more like an evil stepmother than a mom.

"I left him at doggie day care," Charli says. "I didn't want him upsetting you again." Last time Charli visited, Tiny knocked over a lamp, and her mother threw a tantrum.

"Hopefully they're training him," Georgina quips.

Charli already regrets coming here. There is no lower blow in Charli's world than to insult Tiny.

"I brought you a book," Charli says, offering an advance reader copy of a Gabrielle Zevin novel that arrived as Charli was wrestling with the decision of whether to go forward with the bookstore. She never did get a chance to order actual copies of that one, as she'd let her dream go long before its publication date. What she should have done is bring her mother a self-help book, but such a gift would not go over well.

"This one was great, Mom. You'll devour it."

"I still haven't read the last one you brought me. Where do you get all this time to read?"

Charli shrugs. "I make the time."

They go into the living room, which feels cold with its modern decor. Charli remembers when her mother had replaced the furniture a few years ago, putting the new purchases on yet another credit card. Then she'd begged her second husband, Steven, to help bail her out of the payments. Charli looks through one of the floor-to-ceiling windows that face the sea. Waves are crashing hard over the beach. The water looks as frigid as her mother's blood.

"You want a glass of wine?" Georgina asks.

Charli sits in a chair with barely any give, noticing how clean the living room looks. Clearly someone is still paying for the weekly house-keeper too. "No. And haven't you had enough?"

Her mother ignores her as she goes into the kitchen and comes back with a generously poured glass of white, probably her standard pinot grigio. She sits across from Charli on the edge of a couch that looks like it was plucked out of MoMA.

"So . . . did you talk to your father?"

"About the money? No. He gets your messages, Georgina. He doesn't have any money."

She blows out a blast of air. "Asshole."

"Why don't you get a job? Or sell this place? You don't need all of it."

"This is my home, Charli. Why don't you give Tiny away?" Her mother makes no sense, makes the worst arguments.

Charli promises herself to resist a war between them. "I don't even know why I come out here. Can't you be nice for once?"

"Can't you be nice for once?" her mother mimics before knocking back a gulp of wine. She's lonely and sad like her dad. Behind all that makeup and plastic surgery lies a woman that hasn't matured past her fourteen-year-old self, the age she was when her father put a shotgun into his mouth and left the mess for his daughters to scrub from the floor.

Somehow Charli is able to muster enough sympathy to visit her mother because Georgina has no one else. After her third divorce, she's alone in a way that few people could truly know. Her hollowness is a monster that is days away from swallowing her whole.

After they chat for a while, mostly arguing about Charli's direction in life, her mom says, "Let's not forget I told you not to open the bookstore. You're not good in that way, Charli. Trust me. Some people aren't cut out to be entrepreneurs."

Charli wonders what it means exactly to have her mother's blood, to be dangling from this rotten family tree that's somehow still standing.

She ignores her mother's deep insult about the bookstore and asks, "Mom, do you ever wonder why your side of the family is so screwed up?"

Her mom looks up, as if to say, *How dare you.*

"Seriously," Charli says. "I'm really asking. Is there something that happened in the past? I mean, before your father killed himself. Do you remember your parents ever saying anything?"

"What in the fuck are you talking about, Charli?"

Charli rests her elbows on her thighs and exhales. "I'm talking about your family. What happened? I'm just trying to break the cycle, Mom."

"Break what cycle? God, you kids are so existential and think you have some mission in life. You all exhaust me." She says it like she's been forced to drink water instead of wine. And Charli is twenty-nine, a long way from a kid.

Aware that she is about to throw gasoline on a fire, Charli tells Georgina about the Costa Rica trip. She hacks her way through a vague description of the therapy as Georgina's wine disappears like sand in an hourglass. She's looking at Charli as if she has described last night's alien abduction.

"I know you think I'm a basket case," Charli says, "but I'm considering going. To figure out if something is lingering in our family history. I read about this experiment they did with mice. They trained them to fear the color red by showing them something red and then shocking them afterward. When the mice had babies, they showed the same fear of red. It's passed through their genetics—and quite possibly through other ways as well. I'm wondering if that could be the case with us." She stops before adding, *It might actually make me love you a little more.*

Georgina gives a wretched look that Charli is all too familiar with. She might as well scream, *How did you come out of me?*

"You're crazy, Charli. No, nothing happened in our family. We're as messed up as all the rest. Even if it did, what in the world are *you* going to do about it?"

"I know you think it's stupid. Shocker there. But please, humor me. Why did your dad kill himself? And my uncle, why was he so messed up? What about my great-grandparents? Do you remember them?"

"Of course I remember them." Georgina looks toward the still ceiling fan. "Henry and Susannah left Boston to help my mother with Kay and me after my father was gone. Moved about two minutes away."

"What were they like?"

"Our dad was dead. Their son was dead. We were all trying to get by."

"How about on your mom's side?"

"Sip and Eunice," Georgina says. "They were . . . normal."

Snickering inside at Georgina's surely skewed definition of *normal*, Charli does her best to get more information, but her mother is a dry well. All the hard years on her body and mind have impaired her memory.

Eventually Georgina sits up and addresses Charli in what seems like her best attempt to be a mom. "You're not going to find some reason that the world you're living in is terrible. Look around you. There are no answers to find. You live, you struggle, you screw up, you maybe have a good day or two, and then you die. Wash, rinse, repeat."

"I get it," Charli responds, reminded of the origins of her own bleak interpretation of life.

Georgina takes on a proud look, like she's done well just now, with her mothering. "These are the things we learn as we get older. At least it doesn't hurt as much once you know."

"Always there with the tough love," Charli says.

Georgina gives a plastic smile.

Charli shifts gears. "Did Dad tell you he's selling the boat?"

Georgina makes a face of disgust anytime Charli's father comes up. "No. Don't tell me he's still trying to pretend like he's broke."

45

"It worries me," Charli says, ignoring the money comment. "I think about your father taking his life, and I—"

"William is too much of a coward to kill himself."

Charli looks at the woman, incredulous that she came out of her womb.

Thirty minutes later, Charli races away from the Cape with a heaviness coming down all over her. She can feel the pain of her family in her blood. She can taste the disgust she feels for herself and the rest of her family. A part of her can see the appeal of swinging her steering wheel hard to the right and seeing what happens, finding some peace for once.

And yet she does want to break the cycle. She wants to find a way toward happiness. Maybe she hasn't done anything with her life. Maybe her mother is right, that life is awful anyway. But she wants to believe there is a way to escape the dark cloud that hovers over all of them.

She's known for a long time that the best thing she can do for this world is to make sure the family line stops with her. Never will she allow herself to get pregnant. There you go, she is doing something to contribute.

At a stoplight, she finds Frances's name in her phone and calls her. "I'd like to figure out going down to Costa Rica . . ."

"Guess what, Charli," Frances replies. "I was saving you that spot."

￼

February is a nightmare. Georgina won't stop harassing William about more money, claiming he's sitting on millions. He's listed the boat for sale. Every Thursday visit gets sadder and sadder. Charli encourages him to find a therapist, but he's not interested. And she gets it; her therapist hasn't done that much for her. Work is eating at Charli's soul. She's not much happier than her dad.

But she's finally mustered up the courage to ask her boss for a few days off so that she can go to Costa Rica. Just her luck, the two-day constellation session she's attending is during the week. A weekend thing would have been so much easier.

Marvin's office is a mess, coffee stains everywhere. Wadded-up tissues. "What kind of headache did you bring in today?" he asks, while he keeps his eyes fixed on his computer monitor.

Charli sits across from him. "I know I just started and don't have vacation time until next year, but I wanted to see if you'd make an exception. My mother's having surgery, and she has no one, and I was hoping I could go spend some time with her on the Cape. Take care of her."

"Flipping Friday," he says. "Everyone's got a reason to skip work, don't they? What if I said yes to all of you? We'd be out of business."

Charli places a hand on his desk, which causes him to look at her. She taps into her best acting chops. "She's having her ovaries taken out, and she's all alone."

"Your mom is not my problem," he says.

Her urge to quit is so incredibly strong, but she reminds herself of her salary and potential for quarterly bonuses. She raises her hands to her face and starts to sob. It's fake at first but turns real, a release she had no idea was coming. She cries for all the bad stirring around in her world, all the pain she feels, the loneliness. She has her shell of a father and her toxic mother, and that feels like having no one at all. Viv is distracted with a new case, and she hasn't even seen her since that night after Patrick ended things. All she has is Tiny.

Marvin sighs with his own flair for drama. "Oh my, you're good. Just when I thought I didn't have a heart, you're getting to me. Please, please stop the crying."

Charli opens her eyes and drops her hands. "It's four or five days," she says. "While she recovers."

He pinches his nose, clearly considering his options, and then decides he better get something out of it. *Please don't ask me for a date.* Instead, he says, "Give me fifty hours every week until you leave, and you can have your vacation. But I want you available if I need you."

Charli feels like she's won something for the first time in years. "No problem. Thank you."

Chapter 5

Costa Rica!

As she waits in the customs line at Liberia Airport in the northwest of Costa Rica, amid people wearing floral shirts and dresses, chatting it up about their vacation intentions—zip lines, massages, catamaran tours— Charli is thinking for the fiftieth time that she's been had. Seriously, she hasn't been on a big trip in forever—when was the last time?—and this one, a Hail Mary if there ever was one, is the first on her list?

Okay, there are worse places to be than Costa Rica, but still . . . How gullible could she be to take advice from a friend's spiritual guide and a few weeks later touch down in Costa Rica?

In the prearranged shuttle to Tamarindo, Charli sits next to a chatty couple from Indiana who talk her ear off about how she'll "just love it down here." They come every year and want to buy a place before the next big boom comes.

Charli's not up for much chitchat, but she's trying to remember she's partially on vacation, that she's escaped the snow and freezing temperatures. It does feel good outside, the sun spraying warmth into the humid air. March in Boston is so tough sometimes, the way the rest of the country is warming up while Beantown clings to winter like an insecure child would to her mother.

As reggae plays through the speakers, they drive the dusty and often bumpy roads past small villages where the inhabitants stare back from their porches. Chickens roam freely. A farmer crosses the street with a cow. There's an occasional fruit and smoothie stand. The farther she gets from the airport, the more relaxed she feels. Worst case, she gets a tan and reads a couple of books.

Her hotel is called La Linda, and it's on the bustling main strip, where bungalow-style restaurants press up against touristy trinket shops. The white stucco nearly glows against the jungle backdrop. As she climbs out of the shuttle, the salty ocean air hits her, and it's like a balm on her soul.

She checks into her room. Her balcony looks past the pool surrounded by sunbathers and then beyond the tall palm trees to the ocean, where she can see a lineup of surfers waiting for waves. A few jagged rocks poke through the surface of the water. Those wave riders better know what they're doing when they catch a ride. Closer to the horizon, a powerboat flies a red-and-white flag, signifying that they have divers in the water. Two Jet Skis dart about in sharp angles.

Back in her room, she unpacks, checks out the comfy bed, and flips through the hotel's booklet. Under the Wi-Fi password, she finds a request in bold that guests not flush toilet paper.

"Oh wow," Charli says out loud. "That's a first for me!"

Charli throws on her swimsuit and pullover; slides into her flip-flops; grabs her Kindle, some cash, and a towel; and heads out the door. Other than the Cape, which is poisoned by her mother's presence, she hasn't put her feet in the sand in a long time.

She walks by the pool. A few American children play Marco Polo. People drink fruity drinks with umbrellas poking out. At the gate, she kicks off her flip-flops and leaves them with the other sandals. It's a beautiful beach, jungle-esque with thick-trunked palm and banyan trees that lean over and cast spots of shade on the sand. Women massage tourists. Men try to rent her a surfboard. Peddlers offer their wares, but it's a less aggressive approach than her experiences in Mexico. Charli avoids eye contact with them; she hates being the target of street vendors. But a woman comes by with toasted coconut dusted with chocolate powder, and Charli takes a sample. Her mouth waters, and she buys a package with American dollars.

Finding a quiet spot on the sand, she sits and eats a few flakes of the coconut as she watches the tanned surfers. They ride the waves like they've been doing it all their lives; they probably have. She eventually stretches out on her towel and gets lost in her book.

That night, she slips into a midi dress she found on a discount rack in Anthropologie and steps into her Birkenstocks for the first time since last summer. She sits at the bar and has dinner: *gallo pinto y queso de freír*—black beans and rice and fried cheese. She drinks two rum drinks called *pura vidas* and then calls it a night.

~

After a surprisingly peaceful slumber, Charli takes an early dip in the water, then finds a cup of Costa Rican coffee that she takes back to her room. Turns out they know a thing or two about coffee in Costa Rica, and she enjoys every last sip of her macadamia-milk latte as she sits on her balcony, watching tropical birds fly by and the world come to life. At least she's trying, she decides, amid the splendor of the jungle morning.

The GPS leads her by foot down a gravel road that is busy with tourists poking their heads into trinket shops and surfers headed toward the ocean with their boards under their arms. She sees a modest wooden sign with an arrow that reads EL COLECTIVO. That's it, the place where Frances has rented to host her sessions. Charli cuts down a path that opens to several different artist studios. When she finds the right door, she hesitates. Please, please, please let there be some validity to all this.

Stepping inside, she finds polished hardwood floors and whitewashed brick walls. Clusters of potted plants fill the corners of the room. Twenty chairs create a circle in the center. Though she's no energy reader, she is certainly aware of the calmness that permeates the air along with the scent of flowers.

People are standing in different groups, chatting. She recognizes Frances from the photos on her website. She wears a fashionable silk blouse tucked into khaki pants, and her silver hair falls just past her shoulders. Breaking away from a group, Frances approaches with open arms and a smile that is slightly overwhelming to take in. Between the woo-woo nature of what's about to happen and the joy pouring from this woman, this is unfamiliar ground Charli's walking. For a moment she wants to be able to smile with such power. She wants to exude such positivity and strength. How can someone affect another so much in just a few seconds, with nothing more than a look and a hug?

After they embrace, Frances stands back and says, *"Bienvenida, amiga."* She looks into Charli's eyes, causing Charli to tense up.

"You're nervous," she says.

Charli looks away, embarrassed to admit it.

"Don't worry. Everyone is."

She puts her hands on Charli's upper arms, which causes Charli to feel slightly uncomfortable. She's not a big toucher. In fact, she's way out of her element in every regard.

Charli makes awkward conversation as they wait for the rest of the crowd. She meets people from Boston who have been working with Frances for a long time, but she also shakes hands with people from Italy, France, the Netherlands, and Brazil. Apparently Frances has built up a worldwide following with her blog and YouTube videos.

Though it's nice to be around people seeking similar answers, Charli's relieved when Frances finally asks everyone to take a seat. Charli sits next to Letícia, a woman from Brazil. On the other side of her sits a man from Venice, Florida.

Frances steps to the center of the circle with a basket in her hands. "First things first, would you mind turning off your phones and dropping them in here? I know it's a tall order, but you'll get them back in the afternoon." Her voice is as soft as goose down but full of life. The kind of person who can command attention with a whisper.

Frances takes the deposited phones through a door in the back that must be her office. Returning to the front, she says, "I'm so glad everyone is here. I know it's a bit intimidating, but know that each of you has found your way here at this exact moment for a reason, and we're going to do our best to figure out what that reason may be. My constellations can sometimes be uncomfortable, or even scary. Some of you will feel a tremendous number of emotions. Know that you're in a safe place."

She lets the promise resonate as everyone looks around the room, as if ensuring her statement is true, then looks at Charli. "Many of you are concerned that you don't have what it takes to sit in this room and jump into a constellation with me. Let me assure you . . . you have what it takes. Today is about faith. I know that's a hard word to wrap your head around. But let me tell you . . . lives have changed in this room, and if you open your heart and mind, the same will happen to you."

Frances takes a moment to smile. "You may be asked to be representatives in others' systems. Don't overthink things. Simply rely on your intuition. You may experience the emotions of others, of those who are no longer living. You may even have strong urges. It's okay to have these feelings, but I do ask that you avoid acting on any urges."

"What kind of urges?" someone asks. Charli was wondering the same thing.

"You'll soon see what I mean."

Everyone in the room becomes uneasy, muttering and shuffling their feet. Charli is *freaked* out. In fact, she's wondering about all this, wondering if she's in a room full of kooks. And yet something is telling her she's not. It could be the most real experience she's had in ages.

"Our past is alive inside of us," Frances says. "People connected to you, even those long gone from this earth, are still a part of you. And in more ways than one. Think of an oppressed people, any oppressed people. Their children feel that pain in their bones, even if they haven't been exposed to it at all. My expertise lies in focusing on what the

English biologist Rupert Sheldrake calls the morphic field. Has anyone ever seen a flock of birds, like starlings, dart around in the sky as if they're all connected? Or a school of fish that makes a turn in a second, far too fast to explain by writing it off as communication?

"These animals share a morphic field—as you do with your family. Think of siblings who can feel each other, know when something's wrong. It's bigger than that, though. It's not only your living members who are a part of your field either. This is your grander family. It doesn't have to be blood either. Adopted children are brought into the morphic field of a family as well. As are those who marry into a family."

Charli's father appears in her mind. Oh boy, did he marry into it.

"Right now," Frances continues, "you exist in a field with the rest of your family, almost a solar system, all of you spinning around one another. You are starlings in a flock."

Charli recognizes what Frances says from her own research—including Frances's videos, but it's nice to hear her explain it in person. "Sometimes, one of the starlings falls from the flock. One of the planets gets knocked out of orbit, which knocks the others out as well. In other words, one of the family members experiences exclusion from the group. When that happens, an imbalance occurs. It can affect everyone in the system."

Frances moves her gaze from person to person. "You might be suffering from this exclusion. You might be feeling a connection with this excluded person. For example, let's take a suicide. If one's grandfather killed himself, an imbalance is created. We might feel this missing piece in us. We might feel his pain. Think of him as lost in the void, his soul floating out there alone. What we need to do is bring him back into the field."

Images of her father's potential funeral pass by Charli with such verisimilitude that she feels her insides go dark like a city that's lost power. No, she has to do everything in her power to keep him alive, and to keep any imbalances from further fracturing her family.

"How do we do that?" an American asks. "My brother died by suicide." Charli almost chimes in about her grandfather but holds back.

"We're about to find out," Frances says.

Another asks, "But what if we're not out of balance in our constellation? How do you know?"

Frances nods. "You'll know."

Wandering around the room, Frances talks for a few more minutes, then stops and puts her hand on Charli's shoulder. "Would you like to go first?"

Every single head in the room swivels her way. Her heart thumps. She starts to shake her head. "I . . ."

But here comes that part of her again, the part that wants out of whatever she's in. It's pushing her along, like a skydiving instructor on a plane urging her to take that leap.

"Okay," she says quickly, before she can overthink it.

Frances waves her to the center of the circle, and Charli stands with false bravado. What has she gotten herself into?

Chapter 6

THE CONSTELLATION

Charli's the last person who would ever raise her hand to go first, the last person to ever volunteer if someone onstage asks, but she's doing all she can to act like she's fine.

Frances puts her hands on Charli, pats her down, almost like a frisk. But it's some kind of ritual, a ridding of negative energy. Charli exhales a giant breath to extinguish her anxiety. So much for pretending.

Frances asks everyone to close their eyes, and Charli obeys. A long tail of silence follows, which makes room for all kinds of noise in Charli's mind. Who is she to think she could exact any sort of change in her family? She can't even change herself.

Charli peeks to see Frances holding her hands out, palms up. When Frances looks at her, Charli quickly snaps her lids shut. She wonders if she could be ruining this experience for everyone.

"Charli," Frances whispers, "why don't you tell us a little bit about why you're here?"

Opening her eyes, Charli looks down at the floor and wonders where to begin, how open to be. She finally raises her head. Finding comfort and safety in Frances's eyes, she says, "I come from a long line of disasters, mostly on my mother's side." Charli elaborates, mentioning everyone she can think of who has suffered tragically, including her father, who might have suffered due to being absorbed by the awful that is the Hall family.

When she's done, Frances asks, "I'd like for you to take a moment and lean into how all this makes you feel. Even if it hurts, feel it and listen to it as intently and thoroughly as you'd listen to your favorite piece of music—with all of you."

Charli closes her eyes again and follows the instructions. She can feel a hole in her heart, the part of her she often ignores. To Frances's instructions, she puts all her focus on that sensation of . . . what is it . . . emptiness? A lack of backbone? A family tree that looks more like a Christmas tree still up in the living room in March.

After a while, Frances asks, "Can you tell me how you feel?"

"Like it's almost pointless, me trying to be different. Me, trying to fix whatever it is that's going on. I feel so helpless."

Frances moves closer. "Helpless in what sense?"

There doesn't seem to be much room for skeptics here. Charli casts away her doubt and tells herself to give this moment her all. "No matter what I do or try," she says, "I don't have and will never have a fairy-tale life." The hole in her chest grows like a tumor.

Her eyes swell with a rush of sadness. "Sometimes I don't see the point. My dad's given up. My mom's long gone. Why do I even think that I have a chance?"

Frances sets a comforting hand on her arm. "I promise you do."

Even in this bleakest of moments, Charli senses a glimmer of hope. "Point me in the direction. If that's true, I'll do anything."

Frances gives a look of pride that Charli turns to fuel. By God, if all this is real, she'll do whatever it takes.

"What does a fairy-tale life mean to you?" Frances asks.

Charli actually laughs, because she knows exactly what it means. "Oh, I can answer that one. Green lights. The opposite of my life, basically."

"What kind of green lights?"

Charli latches on to the hope she's feeling. "Green lights in everything: business, life. Love. I have friends who are getting married and having these big splashy weddings and talking about babies. And other friends who are becoming leaders in their field. I'm floating on top of the water like a dead fish."

Tears gather like dark clouds. "It's more than what my friends are doing there. I don't mean to sound that superficial. I mean, I am annoyed by all of them, but it's deeper than that." Charli feels into what's going on inside, putting all her focus on it like Frances instructed.

"It's not easy describing the essence of what I'm feeling . . ."

"No, it's not."

"But I . . . I don't think that I deserve any more than what I'm getting out of life. Sometimes I feel like . . . no. Most of the time I feel like I deserve to be punished, that I've done something wrong." Suddenly Charli is the size of an insect in her mind, and she's squirming on the floor, and a big foot is coming down on her, and then squash. "God or whoever else is out there wasted a body on me."

Charli's eyes are on her shoes, as it's too hard to look up. She's never been so honest in her life. The sunken feeling doesn't go away, but there is still that hope, like somehow this thing they're doing could make a difference. If not, then like she told them, what's the point anymore?

"You're very brave coming in here and opening up," Frances says. "Not everyone can do that." She pauses thoughtfully. "Do you know of anyone in your family history who had misfortunes, who experienced red lights in their life, particularly in terms of love, family, and work?"

Once again, Charli finds humor in Frances's questions. "I don't know anyone who *doesn't* have red lights in my family—at least on my mother's side. My mother and her several failed marriages. Her father dying by suicide. Her mother wasting away afterward. My brother dying when he was only four days old, which is a lot of what made my mother the way she is. My father, and how my mother destroyed the big ball of energy that he used to be."

Charli falls into a trance. Her lips are moving, she's giving answers, but she's not working to give them. Something in this room, something about Frances. She's cracking open the wounds and letting the poison ooze out.

She can't believe she hears herself add, "And as far as me, I grew up being emotionally and verbally abused by my mother. I hid it from everybody, my dad, my best friend . . ."

"That must have been a heavy burden," Frances says.

"Yeah." Charli feels as if she's going to be in trouble for ratting her mother out to these strangers. "She would threaten me, though. I didn't have a choice."

The heavy thud of the hammer crashing into one of Charli's dolls shakes her insides. She closes her eyes to hide from her mother's rage, but the memory comes at her like a rabid dog.

Her dad was somewhere in Asia. He was gone so much, Charli couldn't keep up. She was ten years old, about a year after her mother lost the baby. It was a morning before school. Her mom was running around talking to herself while subsequently shouting out the morning to-do list. "You need to make your snack, Charli. Surely you can do something other than play with your fucking dolls. You're ten years old, for God's sake. What girl plays with dolls when they're ten?"

The answer to her mother's question was Charli. *She* played with dolls when she was ten. Like books, dolls were an escape, a way for her to disappear into an imaginary world where her mother couldn't get her.

"Brush your teeth! Get your backpack by the door! And go change out of those awful sweatpants. Whose daughter are you?" Like now, Charli would close her eyes and wish away all that anger.

She was dressing one of her American Girl dolls in a ballerina costume when she saw her mother coming at her from the corner of her eye. Charli raised her arm to protect herself, but Georgina simply swiped the doll from her hands. As she collected the other three dolls on the table, her mother screamed, "What did I tell you? Stop playing with your damn dolls! I told you I'd throw them away."

"No, Mommy, don't throw them away."

"Forget throwing them away," Georgina hissed as she reached into the drawer where they kept a few tools. Drawing a hammer out, she waved it at Charli. "We won't have this problem again, will we?" She marched toward the door that led to the courtyard.

"Where are you going?" Charli ran from her chair to chase her. "Don't hurt my—"

"You made me do this!" Georgina holds one doll by its legs and brings down the hammer with such anger that she chips the concrete. The ballerina's head turns to dust as specks of plastic fly up into the air.

Charli finally pulls herself from the vivid memory and swallows. There were similar bad moments in her childhood, but it's that one that's buried the deepest, like a splinter that will never come out. That feeling of loneliness is as fresh today as it was back then.

When she's finally able, she looks up at Frances. "My dad knew she was awful—she was as bad to him, but he wouldn't leave her. So the two people who were supposed to be there for me weren't always there for me." A sigh rises out of her, and she skips over a few years. "I finally picked up the pieces and found the courage to open a bookstore, but I lost the lease and . . ." Charli looks away. "You get the picture."

"You're a brave woman, Charli," Frances says. Someone sitting down starts clapping, then another, then another.

Charli swallows back the vulnerability that's going to knock her to the floor if she's not careful. She offers a smile to everyone and whispers, "Thanks."

Once it's quiet again, Frances says, "You've had more than your fair share of challenges, Charli. Thank you for sharing."

Frances gestures toward the people sitting around them. "I'm going to ask you to choose someone who represents where the red lights in your family began. The occurrence that perpetuated the imbalance in your family's constellation. This could have happened long before you were born, thousands of years even."

"But I have no idea—"

"Choose based on your intuition. Think of each of the people you select as avatars that help your intuitive mind to re-create the imbalance that exists in your family."

Charli looks around, notices how respectful everyone is, how seriously they are taking this moment. It's a reminder to continue giving it her all.

"You can motion for them to come forward," Frances says, stepping away from the center of the circle. "Once they're up here, put your hands on their shoulders from behind, and guide them to where you'd like them to be."

Charli becomes slightly afraid, like she's going to mess up. "But I . . . how do I know where to put them?"

Frances answers like she's dealt with this situation a thousand times. "Go with instinct. There are no wrong decisions."

Charli closes her eyes and recalls Frances's request. *Someone who represents where the red lights began.* Once she has a grip on that feeling of pain in her family, she looks around the room. All eyes are on her.

She stops and looks at Frances. "I don't want to hurt anyone's feelings."

Frances takes a seat. "No one's feelings will be hurt, Charli. Don't overthink it."

Charli nods, then returns to her mission. She bounces her eyes from one person to the next until she lands on a man who appears to be in his early fifties, with a scruffy beard and thick-framed glasses. He wears a faded baby-blue polo shirt tucked into high-rising khaki pants. If she had to guess, he's a professor of history somewhere. Something within her says that he is the one. Hesitantly, she points her finger at him and waves him into the circle. He rises and joins her. It's a little awkward at first, probably both of their first times in a constellation.

Frances helps. "Herman, Charli is going to tell you where to go."

Charli walks behind him and puts her hands on him, feels his broad shoulders and collarbones. Doubt nips at her heels, but she pushes it away, and she guides Herman forward and then to the left. She has no idea what she's doing, but she trusts the process. She puts him directly in the center of the circle.

"Great, Charli. Now I'd like for you to choose someone to represent you. Put him or her where you think they should be in relation to this person who represents the red lights in your family."

Charli does so, more confident this time. She chooses a woman with short auburn hair cut in a forward angle who is probably a few years younger than her. A Chinese symbol is tattooed on her neck below her right ear. Frances calls her Millie.

Charli guides Millie without thinking and is surprised where she ends up. She's unintentionally set the two people facing each other, about three feet away from one another. She steps back and glances at Frances for feedback. She's gifted an assuring smile in return. Charli intuitively looks back at her choices. Her throat goes dry, and she's not sure why. A twinge of fear runs through her.

Frances's words come from behind her. "What does this feel like, to have him looking directly at you—or, in this case, looking at your representative?"

Charli swallows as she looks back and forth between Herman and Millie, absorbing their energy. "Awful, it feels like a military sergeant screaming in my ear." She's unsure how she's answering so quickly, and her words surprise her, because the depiction seems so accurate.

"Let's feel into that for a moment." They pause in the quiet. Someone coughs. Another person shifts in their seat. Herman and the young woman stare at each other. He's several inches taller and is surprisingly intimidating, far more than he was originally.

Frances must know this because she says, "Who is he?"

Charli shakes her head curiously. "I don't know."

"Is he a he?"

"Yes, most definitely," Charli answers. She doesn't know why she knows, but she knows with all of her. It's as if she actually knows him.

"You may get a sense of a time period," Frances says, "when he was alive. Or if he still is. Someone in your life now or from fifty years ago, one hundred years ago, three hundred . . . if you do get that sense, let me know."

It's asking a lot, to figure out who this man is, where he came from. However, she can't explain anything so far, so why not go with it? She looks at him again, his side profile. He doesn't seem like the man whom she'd called up, Herman. He's different, as if he is the avatar who has absorbed the person he represents. He's . . . he's older. Then it hits her. She has this strange sense that he's indeed dead, that he comes from a time long ago. She feels something else, too, something terrifying.

"I get this sense that I'm a part of him, like he's definitely my blood. My family. But from years ago, like . . ." She tries to tap more into this sudden well of information. "I don't know when," she finally says. "Long before me, that's for sure."

Charli awakens from this trance state she's in and wonders how in the world she just gave this answer. But it feels right to her.

"Good, Charli. Lean into it."

Charli continues to stare at Herman's side profile, but she's not seeing Herman. She's seeing someone in her family—feeling him, even. Though Herman is standing perfectly still with a stoic look on his face, Charli sees another image—almost like the ghost of him—berating Millie. There is no volume to his words, but he's screaming at the top of his lungs so harshly that spit is flying from his mouth. Charli feels like she's standing in Millie's place and is actually the victim of Herman's verbal assault.

"He's angry," Charli says. "Like completely full of rage."

Herman turns to her with a look of someone who is in way over his head. "Yeah, that's how I feel." He raises clenched fists. "Like I want to hit something."

"That's it," Frances whispers.

Millie looks uneasy as well, almost as if she's afraid of him. Though they might have been warned, no one in this room other than Frances could have known what they were getting into.

Frances doesn't say anything for a while, and Charli isn't sure what to do, so she watches both with a growing tightness in her shoulders, as if Herman might physically attack Millie at any moment.

Frances's voice breaks the silence. "Choose someone who is the original cause of his frustration, his anger . . . his whatever it is that you think he's feeling. The aggressiveness. That's how it appears. I saw you step away. Is he bothering you?"

Charli nods. "I'm sorry. I'm uncomfortable."

"Me too," Herman says.

A light round of warm giggles circles the room. Charli welcomes a bit of light, but she's fully planted into this scene. Whatever is happening is hard to doubt or understand. The energy in the room has changed. It feels like there are dead people standing among them. The hair on her arms rises at the thought.

Breathing through it, she follows the instructions and chooses an avatar for the source of this man's frustration. She picks a man in a sky-blue-and-white-striped soccer jersey. Frances calls him Fredrick. She's not a huge soccer fan, but she recognizes soccer legend Lionel Messi's name printed on the back as she places her hands on the man's shoulders and guides him to a spot ten feet behind Millie's left shoulder.

"It's like I'm protecting the man behind me," Charli offers. "Well, I mean, Millie is protecting the man behind her."

Frances is so calm, as if she's seen it all before. "That's great, Charli. Feel that. You might even get the sense of how they feel toward each other."

Charli stands back and takes in the scene—Fredrick looking over the shoulder of Millie to Herman. There's an energy there, this kind of animosity. "Yeah, it's almost like they're enemies, and I'm standing in between them. There's this really strong sense of responsibility that I have, this sense of wanting to protect him."

She hears herself talking, but it's like she's been hypnotized. If she wanted to, she could snap out of it, but she doesn't want to. There is something powerful at play, and her hope heightens.

Frances allows time to pass before speaking. "Okay, so remember Millie is your avatar. I'd like you to choose the avatar that belongs there facing Herman. It's not you and Millie."

Charli tries to put it together. "Do you mean that I have somehow been living my life facing red lights that weren't mine?"

"Quite possibly. I'm seeing a constellation come to life that existed long before you. Which means that there was someone else originally facing these red lights. At some point in your life, you stepped into that role."

A tingle races up Charli's legs. She and Viv dabbled with a Ouija board in high school. This is that on steroids.

"This is real, isn't it?" she whispers. "What we're doing."

Frances nods, as if there were never any doubt.

Charli resumes her work and scans to find the right representative. She lands on Letícia, who pops up when Charli nods to her. The newest of the chosen ones offers a kind smile, revealing a tiny gap between her front teeth. Lively curls dance over her tan shoulders. She wears a flowery sundress and leather sandals with gold buckles. Her pink-polished nails catch the light of the chandelier above.

Frances speaks to the woman with auburn hair who faces Herman. "Millie, you can step aside for a moment." Charli guides Letícia to take Millie's place. Letícia now faces Herman. The whole time, Charli is careful of him, as if he's about to pounce on her. She can't even bear to look at him.

Frances continues. "Now take Millie, who still represents you, and put her where you are in relation to these two people."

Trying not to second-guess herself, Charli puts Millie off to the side, looking directly at the side profiles of Letícia and Herman. She steps back to see her work, reminding herself who the avatars represent.

Though he has a slight hunch in his back, Herman stands a few inches taller. He's also wearing sandals, but his are way past their prime. He is the red lights in Charli's family, but it's more than that too. He's an angry man from long ago. She can still feel him screaming at her, his spit landing on her face.

Letícia is probably in her early thirties. Her legs are as tan as her shoulders. She's eyeing Herman with a fierce look. She represents the person in the family who first faced the red lights, somewhere way back in the past.

Fredrick, who represents the source of the angry man's frustration, stands well behind Letícia, as if she's protecting him. Millie, who represents Charli, is standing off to the side.

"Are you okay?" Frances asks Charli.

"Yeah, just thinking through things."

"Let's be with this moment awhile and see what comes of it," Frances says.

The room goes so silent that Charli can hear herself breathe. The feeling of other entities being in the room amplifies.

The temperature in the room drops. It happens in an instant, and Charli is suddenly shivering. Her teeth start to chatter. "I'm cold," she says.

"Me too," Letícia says.

She and Charli look at each other with open mouths. In the corner of her eye, she sees Herman, and Charli can't bring herself to look at him. She feels like he's staring at her, but maybe he's not. Either way, all this judgment and rage and fire radiate from him.

"He's so mad," Charli says, turning away from Herman as if he is a flame reaching out from a fire and trying to burn her. "It's like he wants to murder me . . ." She recalibrates. "But I feel like I want to look at him, like I have to."

"It's okay to look at him," Frances says. "What is that anger like?"

Charli finally directs her full attention at him. Herman's eyes are wide, and he's burning a stare at Letícia, who is looking off to the side in fear.

Any last doubts of what Charli's doing fall away as she sees and feels this exchange. If it gets any more intense, she's not sure she can take it.

"His rage is a full-on ten," Charli says. "Like no light whatsoever. Pure darkness."

"Yeah," Herman says, "I'm shaking inside. And I . . . my leg hurts so badly. I can barely stand on it."

Frances stands and takes a step toward the center of the circle. "Herman, stick with it if you can. Just a reminder that you should not act on any urges that you might have."

A sheen of sweat collects on his forehead as he nods.

Frances puts a hand on Charli's arm, and she jerks at the touch. "Sorry," Charli says.

"It's okay." Frances offers a smile that soothes Charli again, gives her the courage to keep going.

"Now that you're out of the dynamic," Frances says, "looking in on it, could you pick a figure to represent the green lights that you seek in the present?"

"What do you mean?"

"Think of all the things you want, all that goodness that awaits you, and choose a person who can represent it, almost like how a flag represents a country."

Charli takes her time and eventually gets a strange sense to pick a guy she's not noticed before. His head is shaved, and his biceps push at the sleeves of his tight shirt like he's just left boot camp. He's probably in his midtwenties but has a serious look to him, as if he's seen more than most at his age. If he's been to war, then that would explain it.

"Where does Parker go?" Frances asks.

Charli laughs as she reaches up high to put her hands on his shoulders. "He's almost outside of this building. Untouchable. Just like my green lights." She guides Parker against the brick wall directly behind

Herman, who stands between Charli's representative and her green lights.

Frances asks Charli, "Is there anyone else who wants to join the system?"

Charli considers the question. When no clear answers come to her, she shrugs.

Frances returns to her seat and says, "Herman, what does it feel like?"

"I . . . I . . ." He stumbles over his words. "I've never been so angry in my whole life. Like fucking . . . excuse me . . . I see red." He raises his fists out in front of him and says with a British accent, "Like I want to kill someone."

At that exact moment, Letícia drops to the floor.

Charli and the rest of the audience gasp. The room once again goes silent. Dead silent. Adrenaline pumps through Charli's body, causing her to feel dizzy.

On the floor, Letícia starts to cry as she pulls her knees to her chest. She calls out in desperation, "I'm so cold, so incredibly cold."

Frances grabs a blanket from the back of a chair and drapes it over her. "Everything is fine; hang in there a moment."

Charli can't move a muscle, can't even speak. The whole room must feel this way. What they're witnessing isn't possible, but it's happening.

Letícia is actually crying. Her face is wet, and she's wiping it. Her feet poke out of the blanket, showing the pink polish of her nails. Herman stands over her, still shaking with anger.

Frances steps to the center. "You've done an amazing job and set up a perfect representation of your red lights. Before we close, take some time and walk around, look at everyone, see what they're seeing. Breathe their air."

Charli does so, going from one avatar to the other. When she puts her eyes on Herman, Frances says, "It does seem like everything off balance in your world comes from here, doesn't it?"

Though the terror he's evoking is beyond any horror movie, Charli tightens her fists and stares him down. Whatever these red lights are, whatever it or he is, she wants it all gone from her life.

"You are tied to these people, Charli," Frances whispers. "Tied to him. And he is what is standing in the way of your life."

Charli looks down at Letícia, wrapped in the blanket and wiping tears.

"It seems like you have some sort of life debt to her," Frances says. "Something is certainly off balance here, and I don't know exactly what it is. Other than . . . I think it's clear that there was a death. Possibly a murder. He could have killed her years ago."

It seems obvious as Frances says it. The woman on the floor is the victim of a murder. Charli feels like she's both the murderer and victim at the same time.

"What . . . what do I do?" Charli asks. "Did someone in my family kill someone? Is that man in my family, for sure?"

Frances inches toward her. "I think it's possible, and it's important to find out what is going on. The only way to get to those green lights is by releasing the truth of what happened here. Who is he? Who is she? This is your debt." She touches Charli's arm. "I believe you've been chosen to break your family free from generations of pain."

Charli looks at her. "Why me?"

Frances smiles warmly. "I think you'll find out. And what an honor it is." After another beat, she says, "Let's close here. Thank you, everyone. You can get up now and return to your seats."

Once the dust settles, Charli asks, "Am I supposed to go play detective now and figure out what happened?" Everyone else listens for Frances's answer.

"I think what we've brought to light has already caused a shift in your family. I can feel it, and I suspect you will too. But I'd encourage you to find out more if you can. We've found the source of your imbalance. The more light you can bring into it, the more order you can restore. It's a cliché but a good one: the truth will set you free."

"What? All I have to do is figure out who these people were and what happened? And then I'm living the good life?"

Frances shrugs. "That's the simple version, but something tells me that if you can get to the bottom of what's going on, you might set free some positive changes that are due in your family's world."

Could she really help her father? Could she change her state? Forget the therapy and self-help books. This is the answer; it *has* to be. "So my dad giving up on life. And all the bad things happening in my life, the way I ruin everything. Is there a way out?"

"Not a simple one, but yes. There are strong forces in your subconscious that are creating patterns of bad luck and even tragedy in your life. The same might go for a lot of your family members. But until someone does something about it, those patterns will never stop. Let's take a break for now. As we explore others' constellations, you might find more clarity."

Charli has a million questions, a million concerns. She looks over at Herman, who somehow took on this evil energy that terrified her. He looks normal now, a sweet guy surely seeking answers to his own questions. Never in her life has she experienced something so out of this world.

Chapter 7

THE WYKEHAMIST

Winchester, England
September 4, 1880

Miles could not climb fast enough into the carriage. Whereas some boys might enjoy the days between summer and fall terms, he was eager to escape the hell that was his home. The only time there was ever peace at Elmhurst was when his father was away. Even then the man's energy lingered in every room, strangling the air and poisoning any joy that attempted to take root.

It was just under an hour's ride to Winchester, where Miles and his brother, Edward, attended Winchester College, a preparatory school for thirteen- to eighteen-year-old boys. Miles was seventeen and facing his last year before graduation. Typically the coachman would take the boys alone, but their father, a gentleman who carried a position in the House of Lords, had business to attend to in the city. Therefore, both the Honorable James Pemberton and his wife, Cora, had come along as well.

Like their father, the boys—or *men*, as they were addressed at the college—wore polished shoes, pressed shirts, and long waistcoats over trousers. James wanted nothing more than for his boys to be exact replicas of him, and it was this desire that fueled the feud between Miles and him. In fact, Miles was still seething from a fight with his father two days earlier. He could still feel the welts from the proper beating he'd endured.

Miles watched with a tight jaw as his father pulled himself up into the carriage and set down his cane. A horse had bucked him off when he was a boy, and he'd walked with a limp ever since. This particular cane had come home with him from London. The golden lion-head handle gleamed in the sunlight that shot through the windows. Lord Pemberton was a tall man, intimidatingly so, and his hat reached near the top of the carriage's roof. Rarely did Miles ever see him showing anything other than an agitated look on his mustached face.

"Let's go, Cora," James shouted to his wife, who scurried in as quickly as she could.

"I'm doing the best I can," she muttered softly, taking her place by her husband and adjusting her blue dress.

"Then we should have left an hour earlier," James replied coldly. "And we'll leave first thing tomorrow, no time for shopping."

"Yes, dear." Cora clasped her fingers together and rested them on her lap. She had her own bruises hidden under that velvet gown, and she surely had no interest in collecting another.

Cora came from a family in Southampton and had been pushed into marriage by her father, who owned a fleet of merchant ships and several sugar plantations in the West Indies. In a rare moment of both honesty and warmth, she'd once admitted to Miles that she'd never loved James but had been given little choice in the matter. A marriage contract had been struck between James and Cora's father.

Was it any wonder Miles grew angry when his father started telling him what to do? As the firstborn, Miles would one day inherit his father's position in the House of Lords. His entire life was already predetermined. Following a long line of Pemberton men, he studied at Winchester College and would attend New College at Oxford. Next, he'd return to his upper-class existence at Elmhurst, where he'd wave the

Whig flag and marry a woman of his father's choosing. What a miserable existence to have no say in how your own life played out.

Once they were underway, Miles kept his gaze out the window, brushing his brown unruly hair out of his eyes and watching the rolling hills of the Hampshire countryside pass by. Despite the beauty of the terrain and the sensational weather they'd been enjoying lately, he couldn't quite get away from the discomfort the four of them created in such a small space. The only consistent sounds were the clop of the horse's hooves and the movement of the carriage as it bounced up and down on the rather rutted road.

As they drew near to the city, James spoke to his youngest son. "Edward, you'll be joining the rifle corps this year, yes?"

Edward had been dozing off but stirred at the sound of his father's voice. "Yes, I will."

"Good, very good. If you keep it up, you might one day be able to outshoot me."

"It's certainly something to aspire to."

James nodded, seemingly satisfied with the interaction.

Miles wondered how many times his father had expressed his wish that Edward be the older son. He couldn't stand the way Edward snapped to his father's attention like a soldier to a general. The man hadn't earned such filial respect, no matter how much violence he used to attempt to command it.

As they came into Winchester, even the outskirts teemed with life. The new hospital had brought more people to a city already thriving as both the legal center of Hampshire County and a popular tourist destination due to its rich history. The ancient Norman cathedral, home of the bishop, loomed mightily in the distance as they crossed the gin-clear river Itchen and then rode along the grassy shore before cutting into town on College Street.

Founded by William of Wykeham in 1382, Winchester College was one of the finest institutions of England, a school that Pemberton men had attended since the late fifteen hundreds. As it was the arrival day, the street was overcrowded with carriages. The air was hazy from the dust kicked up by the horses' hooves and smelled of manure and cigar and pipe smoke and a thousand other elements. Miles looked at the men and their families pouring in through the porter's gate. Mothers asked for last hugs, and fathers issued final warnings as their sons hurried toward a new year. Miles did not feel the pride of following in the footsteps of his family, but he was excited to escape the prison of his homelife.

His father stuck his hand out of the carriage and waved and made small talk to the other gentlemen as they pushed through the crowd and turned left onto Kingsgate, where Miles would stay. The college had outgrown the boardinghouse, so only the scholars, who were the top of the class, slept within its walls now. Most of the men, including Miles, stayed in various boardinghouses down the street. Miles had been a part of Moberly House since his first year.

Miles peered down Cannon Street as they passed by. The opium dens and brothels would come alive at dark. "Lots of trouble that way," the housemaster told them every year. "And a caning if you ever choose to quench your curiosities." As stated in the rules, their boundaries as men of the college were explicit. They could not leave Kingsgate or College Street unless given permission.

Two short blocks down, they came to a stop at Moberly House, a two-story redbrick building that matched most of the others on the street. The grub house and housemaster's quarters were located downstairs. Upstairs was the bunkhouse, which provided room for about fifty men. Miles exchanged a wave with his good mate Quimby, who appeared in the upstairs window.

Miles climbed out and waited for the footman to take down his luggage. He didn't even acknowledge his brother, who remained in the carriage and was staying two streets down. James and Cora exited the carriage momentarily, if only to stretch their legs and mingle with a few other parents.

James soon approached. Miles could barely look at him.

"Come here, boy."

"Sir."

"Don't embarrass me, you understand?"

Miles gave a sharp nod. His father's words always landed like threats.

His mother was next and spoke to him like he was still a child. "Be a good boy." With that, she turned, and Miles watched his parents take their leave.

He felt an arm slip over his shoulder. "Good summer, mate?"

Miles turned to Quimby and laughed. "Simply marvelous."

The first month of school sped by. Miles fell into his routines, waking in the morning, bathing in the frigid water that came directly from the river, then dining in the grub hall before spending most of the day within the school's walls. They had mathematics first in the morning, followed by Greek and Latin before a lunch of boiled beef and potatoes. Afterward, they'd take a short break before continuing to French and German.

Though most of his studies were tedious and boring, he greatly enjoyed his time in the Shakespeare Society, a group that met three times a week to read the Bard's plays. If he had it his way, he'd trade his place at Oxford for a role in *Hamlet* in London without hesitation. Sometimes at night, when he couldn't sleep, he'd imagine what it might be like to take the stage with such greats as Henry Irving and Ellen Terry, absorbing the praise of an audience after giving his all to a character.

Of course, acting out the plays would have been too exciting for Winchester College, so their performances were simply readings at the end of each term. Still, Miles loved the way the Bard's words danced off the tongue, and the way he felt when stepping into another's skin.

Overall, though, he was torturously bored, and increasingly annoyed by the expectations put on him. He often found himself looking around at the other men his age who were eager to fall in line like his brother. Miles didn't understand it. Wasn't there more to life? Had he no choice as to his future? Now into his last year of secondary school and on the precipice of turning eighteen and becoming his own man, such questions demanded answers.

His frustration with the place where his desires clashed with others' expectations had led him toward rebellion lately. Sometimes it was by sneaking into the kitchen to find something actually decent to eat, like a leftover cut from the housemaster's lamb. He hated the rotten mutton typically forced down the students' throats. Other times, he might push the boundaries with a stroll up Cannon Street to witness the madness for himself, or take a quick walk through the city to see what he was missing.

One cool eve in October, about six weeks after his father dropped him off for the fall term, he decided to sneak out of Moberly House. He sat up from the bed amid a sea of sleeping men. Some snored, some stirred as he crept past. Even if they were awake, they'd assume he was going to relieve himself. He passed through the room and down the stairs, then found the window he'd left open during dinner. His heart pounded as he lifted himself up and went out headfirst. He came down into the street with a tumble, nearly knocking his head on a rock. But he'd made it, and he dusted himself off and stood to surveil his surroundings.

Miles was dressed in simple slacks and a shirt and wished he'd brought a jacket as he quickly walked toward the river in the brisk air. He guessed it was around midnight, and he was surprised to see so many people milling about. Hearing the river calmed him, and as he slowed to a stroll, he enjoyed the fresh free air and the star-filled sky and the river Itchen that held so many promises in its current, as if leaping in could simply take him away.

"Spare some change, sir," came a husky voice from the darkness. Miles jumped and turned to find a beggar wrapped in a cloak, huddled against the crumbling old wall that once protected the city. He was missing a tooth and shook a cup that jingled with coins. "Just a few pence for food."

Miles reached into his pocket, found a shilling, and dropped it into his cup.

"God bless," the man muttered back.

Miles felt on guard for a moment, his hackles up, as he continued along the shore. The darkness exposed a side of the city to which he was not accustomed. He soon saw light ahead of him—candles and gaslights—and he knew he was coming upon High Street.

A stone bridge crossed the river straight ahead, and he caught sight of a lone young woman driving a small carriage over it. She was about his age, maybe seventeen or eighteen. Her curly brown hair shimmered in the moonlight, and he was instantly spellbound. Perhaps it was the way she seemed so content, or the way she handled the horse, giving him a solid whip and whistling for him to carry on.

Miles picked up his pace. She barely looked at him as she passed by. He didn't care that she wore only a simple white frock with leather boots that begged to be polished. She was the most beautiful creature he'd ever seen, elegant in her movement, dazzling with her poise. Her eyes glowed in the night, not like a fox's, but like the stars themselves. She made no effort to lure him, but he followed her anyway, watching her gently bounce up High Street to the rhythm of the horse's gait. She looked utterly at ease amid the madness of the city, dodging drunk pedestrians paying her no mind.

She eventually came to a stop outside a pub. From inside came boisterous laughter and the clinking of glasses and a tipsy fellow attempting to carry a tune. She climbed off the cart and tied up her horse, took two jugs from the back, and walked into the pub. Miles seized the opportunity to get closer.

Through the window, he watched her set the jugs on the back bar. An older man said something to her before she started back toward the door. She made three more trips to the cart to unload more supplies before assuming her position behind the bar, pouring beers for the patrons. Another man, slightly older, possibly her brother, came and climbed on the cart and took it away.

Miles watched her for a moment. If anything, the light of the pub showed that she was even more beautiful than he'd first suspected. Brown hair the color of autumn fell across her shoulders. Her smile was enough on its own to light the inside of the pub.

A man left some coins and abandoned his seat at the bar. Miles couldn't take it a moment longer and stepped inside. People were so immersed in their own conversations that they barely acknowledged him. He sat at the bar and waited as she pulled pints for another customer.

She looked at him, or barely so. "What will you have?" She was so busy that she went about taking two glasses off the table while waiting on his answer.

When she finally gave him a second look, he smiled at her.

She chuckled to herself. "You gonna stare or have a drink?"

Miles smiled even wider. "A pint, please."

She nodded and went to pour him one.

"I saw you coming up the road earlier," he said.

"Oh, is that right? You followed me?"

Miles laughed to himself. "Maybe I did."

She slid the beer his way. "You hungry too?"

He shook his head.

"You're going to hurt yourself, staring like that."

"Would be a good way to go, I suppose." Miles sipped his beer. "What's your name?"

"Wouldn't you like to know."

He shook his head, feeling his dimples reveal themselves. She was feisty, this one—so very different from the dull and submissive girls with whom his father wanted to pair him. Miles had no interest in marrying a woman like his mother.

"Nothing to eat then?" she asked.

"A beer is quite fine. I'm called Miles."

She leaned toward him again. "Miles, you seem a little young to be out and about."

He answered quickly. "I'm in town on business."

"Hmm. I pegged you for a Wykehamist."

He felt like a burglar caught red-handed, and his face surely showed guilt. "What makes you say that?" Pupils of Winchester College were known as Wykehamists, deemed so after their founder, William of Wykeham.

The young lady who hadn't shared her name looked him up and down. "I spent my whole life here. You all stand out."

"If I were a Wykehamist, I'm sure I'd be tucked away in my boardinghouse by now." Being caught would come with grave consequences. He'd seen a boy caned toward the end of the previous year. The screams could surely have been heard in Scotland.

She nodded and walked off. Even as she cleaned glasses, she looked angelic.

When she came back around, she asked, "You really are going to watch me all night?"

"I can't think of anything I'd rather do. Other than know your name, of course."

She turned to him. "Name's Lillian."

"It's a pleasure to make your acquaintance."

They held a gaze that could have set the world on fire, and Miles felt as if he'd sprouted wings. "You work here?" he asked.

"A bright one, aren't you?"

Miles reddened in embarrassment.

"My family owns it," she said, saving him from further humiliation.

He wondered whether his father had ever passed through here.

"And what's your story, Miles, if you're not a Wykehamist?"

He took a long sip of his beer, seeking courage. "If only I could tell you in this short amount of time. Could we meet again?"

Lillian studied him, perhaps wondering if he would be worth her time. Miles held his ground.

Finally, she shrugged. "We'll have to see."

"What does that mean?" he asked, but she was already walking away.

He watched her climb a set of stairs in the back. Suddenly the man who'd moved the cart had taken position behind the bar. He looked at Miles and said, "Have another there?"

Miles shook his head. "No, I'll settle up now."

After paying, he glanced back at the stairs one more time before exiting the pub and walking—or floating, more like it—back down High Street. He figured that if he was to see her again, he'd best get back to where he belonged tonight.

Chapter 8

The Black Sheep

Present Day

Charli spends the next two days in a state of awe and wonder. As she's told Vivian and her father on the phone, this stuff can't happen, but it does . . . right in front of her, constellation after constellation. As if she needed any more confirmation, she witnesses seemingly impossible family dynamics come to life through the acting out of the sessions. People learn about kidnapped children, exiled uncles, and extramarital affairs that took place in the past.

For one constellation, Parker, the man who looked as if he'd been in boot camp, chose Charli to represent his dead grandfather. Apparently females could represent males and vice versa. She actually felt the grandfather's disappointment when his son stole his money. Toward the end of the constellation, as the person who represented the thieving father finally got his chance to apologize, Charli had burst into tears. Afterward, Parker reported feeling lighter than he ever had in his life. He had no idea that his father had stolen money from his grandfather.

In almost every other case, the other constellations apparently revealed what was needed for the healing of the main participant, and Frances suggested afterward that the imbalance had been corrected. A woman from Virginia who'd been having chest pains reported after her session that she felt better than she had in her entire life.

It's no surprise to Charli that her family has the one imbalance that a constellation can't restore. When Charli says to Frances that her family should win a prize for being the worst of the sessions, Frances gives a brief laugh and then replies, "Don't let doubt creep in. Don't forget what you've seen here. Trust the process. And no, your family is not even close to the most imbalanced that I've come across."

On the morning she is to return to Boston, Charli goes to say goodbye to Frances and asks, "Why me? Of all the people in the sessions, it seemed I was the only one who has to go play Sherlock Holmes."

"I think the better way to think of it is 'lucky me.' Lucky you, Charli. You have been given a great responsibility."

Frances takes a book from her bookshelf and opens to a dog-eared page. "Carl Jung writes, 'It often seems as if there were an impersonal karma within a family, which passes on from parents to children. It has always seemed to me that I had to . . . complete, or perhaps continue, things which previous ages had left unfinished.'"

Frances closes the book. "I think this is the case with you. I feel good about what happened during your family constellation. I feel good about you and your family, and I have hope for all of you. So much hope that it almost feels like a foregone conclusion, you finding your way. Finding your green lights." She puts her hand on Charli's shoulder. "Lucky you."

Charli wonders on the plane if she's been brainwashed. Those two days were magical, but what happened to her? What happened in that room? She wishes she'd recorded it or written it all down. She wishes she could recapture that feeling she had and bottle it and never let it go, because for a few moments there, she was a believer. She was sure that it was her calling to free her family of unhappiness and tragedy. Now, as the plane bounces in awful turbulence and the guy next to her crushes a burrito, she worries she might have been played. As much as she wants to be open to new possibilities, she's being pulled back to her old self, complete with her mother's voice in her head. No, there's no explanation for their misfortune. There's nothing Charli can do to bring a swath of light into her family's life.

Still, she can't shake the constellation from her mind as she takes the train from Logan and hops a cab to her house. It's twenty-seven degrees and windy outside—a far cry from Tamarindo. People run down the sidewalks to avoid the cold winter wind blasting through.

The dog sitter dropped Tiny off earlier, and he's waiting for her. He does what he always does, rushes to her for a kiss and then plops down on his back, begging for a scratch. She rubs his belly, and he groans with delight.

"I wish I could tell you what happened to me down there. But maybe it's best you don't know. I think I'm losing it."

She says these words but is still so intrigued that she stays up late researching her family on Ancestry.com and Family Origins. She's never spent a minute on these sites, never cared to look them up, but now she's curious for answers. And she can't deny that the part of her that loves to read mysteries is slightly enjoying the idea of falling into one herself.

That evening, she's lying in bed with her computer on her lap. An episode of *The Bachelor* plays on the television, but she's barely paying attention. She's busy accepting hints and suggestions on Ancestry. After a long while, she's successfully populated a lot of her family tree on both her mother's and father's sides going back several generations—all the way back to the seventeen hundreds in England and Ireland. Her father is who brings the Irish blood.

Staring at the names and reading obituaries and even discovering the occasional picture, she's taken aback by the idea that these people not only make up who she is but might exist in her constellation. Though they are dead, they are here. She shivers at the notion.

Tiny snores on the floor beside her. She drops her hand down to touch him, and he goes quiet. The drama on *The Bachelor* is amping up, two of the contestants yelling at each other. She can't help but watch for a little while, glad to not be caught up in such lunacy over a man, but then she's back to work.

The only piece that isn't falling into place is one particular branch of the tree on her mother's side. Whereas she can trace back centuries with most branches, one line stops with her great-great-great-grandfather, Samuel Hall. Ancestry.com doesn't offer any hints to further populate the tree. In all the other cases, the website had suggested a *Potential Mother* and *Potential Father*, allowing her to extend several more generations with nearly every other family member.

Not with Samuel. What could that mean? Another oddity that strikes her is that, unlike most of her other relatives, he doesn't even have a middle name.

She clicks on his profile. Born in London in 1863, married Margaret Taylor in 1900, and died in Boston in 1925. That was it, the sum of the man.

Clicking back out, she sees that Samuel and Margaret had two children, including Charli's second great-grandfather, Jeremiah Hall, who then had a son named Henry. Henry married Susannah Clemons and had Georgina's father, Barrett Hall. It's Barrett who shot himself.

If . . . *if* Frances isn't a kook and Charli is willing to keep her mind open, it doesn't take being Philip Marlowe for Charli to make an assumption here.

"Follow the pain," she says out loud. What caused Barrett to shoot himself? Was it *his* generation that committed a crime? A murder? Was he a murderer? Did he shoot himself out of guilt? Or was it further back? Why are there no records past Samuel?

Though her mother married a Thurman, Charli knows she's still a Hall through and through. These are her people, the people who have likely been suffering for a long time.

A thought occurs to her. She should go to Lowell to see her mother's sister, Kay. Though it's been a while since they've spoken, Kay always sends a piece of her pottery to Charli for her birthday, a gesture that reminds Charli how much she likes her aunt.

On Saturday morning, Charli braves a wintry mix and drives to Lowell to visit Aunt Kay, who said she'd be thrilled to see Charli after all these years. From the stories she remembers growing up, Aunt Kay was the black sheep for whatever reason, so Charli wasn't around her much and only knows that she's a pharmacist, never married, no kids. Seemed to avoid family get-togethers when she could. Looking at it with fresh eyes now, it seems apparent that Aunt Kay was quite possibly distancing herself from the wreckage that was the Hall family.

Charli parks and climbs out of her car in front of a turn-of-the-century Victorian that's due for a new coat of paint. An old yellow Mercedes is parked in the driveway. A colorful bottle tree stands in the lawn. An owl made of tin hangs from the portico roof.

Aunt Kay bursts out of the purple front door and runs down the steps in her clogs, a splash of sunlight. If there are two sides of the family, Charli wants to be on Team Kay.

As she gets close, her eyebrows arch tall with excitement. Her aquamarine eyes remind Charli of the sea glass she used to collect as a kid out on the Cape. "I'm so glad you called!"

"Me too." Though Charli certainly can't match the woman's enthusiasm, she's slightly pleased to see someone in the family not withering away from depression. Maybe there's hope yet.

Kay spreads her arms. As usual, Charli gets hugged without doing much hugging herself. She wishes she weren't that way, especially around her aunt, but she's doing the best she can.

Once she's set free, Charli says, "I'm sorry it took me this long."

Kay waves a hand loaded with costume jewels. "No, stop right there. I'm your aunt. I should have stayed in touch."

Charli waves her off. "You do. You share your art with me every year. I treasure them, really. You're so talented."

"Thank you," Kay says. "I do enjoy my little hobby."

"Do you have your own wheel?"

"Oh, yeah. In the basement. Which I would show you, but it's a mess. Come inside, though. Let's get out of this cold. I picked up Thai takeout, in case you're hungry."

"Oh, fun. You lived in Bangkok for a while, right?" Charli is reminded of how cool her aunt is. Georgina would often spin tales of Kay in a way where it sounded like her sister was always wasting her time trying to find herself, but Charli saw it differently, knowing that Kay was actually just taking life by the tail.

"Good memory, yes. Ages ago. Before I decided to come back home and get a real job."

Charli feels a longing for seizing life like Kay. She wishes she'd done something so brave before adulthood caught up with her. But maybe that's what she's doing now.

Aunt Kay invites Charli inside, where she is assaulted by two tabby cats who weave around her legs. "Meet Larry Bird and Tom Brady."

Having grown up watching sports with her father, Charli grins at their names and reaches down to pet them. "Hi, Larry and Tom."

They sit in the sunroom facing windows that look out over several garden boxes that will surely be bursting with life soon. For now, they carry patches of recent snow. Between the two women, a small table holds a pot of tea and two gorgeous mugs giving off steam. Larry Bird and Tom Brady post themselves on top of the back of Kay's chair.

"How's work going?" Charli asks. Kind of hard to jump right into . . . *so I went to Costa Rica and did a séance with a woman who fell on the ground, and I think that person is a victim of a homicide. That's why I think our whole family is completely screwed up . . .*

Kay sips her tea. "You know what. I adore it. We have a great team at the pharmacy; we're helping people. What else matters? How about you? Your mom told me about the bookstore. I'm so sorry."

Charli shrugs with embarrassment. "Yeah, that didn't work out too well."

"What are you doing now?"

Charli doesn't want to tell her. Though they don't stay in touch, she looks up to Kay, how her infectious positive attitude lightens every room. Why couldn't it be Kay who was her mother? "Just an easy job now while I figure out my next move."

They catch up for a few minutes, and then Charli seizes her chance. "I wanted to come see you, of course, but I have an ulterior motive."

Kay sets her mug down and sits up, intrigued.

Charli smooths her hands together. "I've been in crisis mode lately. Well, since the bookstore. Or maybe before. And I'm just trying to . . . I don't know . . . figure some things out. You're gonna think I'm not right in the head for what I'm about to tell you, but I'm willing to take the risk, as I think you might be the only one who can help."

"I'm on the edge of my seat, Charli. And I would never judge you. Try me. I've been on this earth a long time and have seen a lot. Nothing much shocks me anymore."

"This one might stand out," she says, her muscles relaxing. "About six weeks ago, I was hanging out with my best friend when . . ."

Charli talks for a while, stopping short of talking about the constellation specifics. "I'm looking into it, you know?"

Aunt Kay nods. She hasn't said much but doesn't look like she's judging.

"I do wonder why my mom's side of the family—your side—struggles so much," Charli says. "Well, everyone but you. You seem pretty great, actually. I've always admired you."

Aunt Kay smiles. "That's sweet of you, but trust me, I'm not without my problems."

Viv had said something similar, and Charli scolds herself for pretending she's the only one who struggles. "I guess we all have problems, but don't you ever wonder . . . like . . . why us? Why did your father kill himself? Why is my mom so broken inside? Why did she lose my brother? Why did she make me feel like such a piece of shit? Forgive my language but . . . not sure how else to say it. Why am I struggling to find my way? Why do I push away the men in my life? Not that it's about

89

me, but I guess what I'm saying . . . is . . . do you know any reason that there's so much negatively charged energy in our family? I feel like my dad absorbed all his crap by marrying my mom."

Kay sits back and studies the ceiling. "I knew," she finally says. "I knew how bad it was at your house. I'm sorry I didn't do anything."

Some discomfort catches in her throat. No one did, Charli thinks.

"I had a feeling that you were having a rough go at things," Kay says. "Your mom and I didn't talk much, especially after she lost Jacob, but I knew what living with her could be like. Honey, if I could have, and maybe I should have, I would have intervened."

Charli's eyes glaze over as the past tugs her back. She's ten years old again and playing with her American Girl dolls, her only friends who didn't live in books. Her father is out of town. Her mother won't let her play with the other kids in the neighborhood. She barely even let her go to Viv's house. That kind of lonely is not something you can even describe.

If Kay knew, then why didn't she get involved? Did Kay think that Charli was no better than the rest of the family, all people she needed to avoid? That line of thinking doesn't ring true with Kay, though. She'd always been kind to Charli.

Kay reaches over and puts her hand on Charli's knee. It's a loving touch, a sincere one, which quells some of Charli's frustration.

"I should have gotten involved," Kay admits. "But I was too weak, struggling with my own stuff. I get your point. Trust me. This family does feel damaged more than most. Losing Dad destroyed all of us, but your mom took it the worst. I tried to get through to her, but she was just . . ."

"What?"

"It was like she was possessed. We had some good times growing up, but now I can barely talk to her without feeling disgusted and sad. Losing Jacob made it so much worse, but she was already a mess."

Charli doesn't remember seeing the mess of her mom before she lost the baby, but then again, she was so young.

"I get it," Kay says, "and you know what . . . I love the idea that maybe something did kick-start this domino fall. Why not try to figure it out? I'll help any way I can, though I'm not sure how."

Excitement shakes Charli's fingers as she reaches into her purse, unfolding the family tree she printed out. "This is about all I have to go on." She wants to tell Kay about the constellation, that there could have been a murder, but she resists.

Kay takes the paper and looks at it for a few moments. Charli gives her a tour, talking about some of the family members. She points at the end of Samuel's line. "It's weird to me that Samuel's family tree stops here. Any idea why?"

Kay keeps her eyes on the tree. "It is a little weird, I guess. I don't know much more than you."

She must know something. "How about your dad? If you don't mind me asking, why did he kill himself?"

Kay pauses. "I've spent a long time wondering, and I truly don't know. His parents were good people, gave him a good upbringing. He seemed happy, and then one day he wasn't. Kind of like your mom, suddenly someone I didn't know."

Tom Brady jumps up on Kay's lap, as if he sensed her pain.

"I can't imagine," Charli murmurs, recalling how it had been both Kay and Georgina who'd found the body when they'd come home from school. "I'm sorry."

Kay sighs. "We're all dealt our blows. I wish I could help you more. I don't know of any particular event or situation that might have unfolded." Then a light bulb goes off in her eyes. "You know what, though," Kay says, suddenly standing. "I do have some pictures. You can have them if you like. Maybe something to show your kids one day. I don't know."

Charli doesn't mention that she's not going to have kids. Instead, she says, "Sure, I'd love to take a look."

Kay returns with a Tupperware container the size of two shoeboxes. "I haven't looked in here in forever." She sits and opens it up. A musty smell rises into the air, causing Charli's excitement to bloom. Her aunt pulls out a stack of photos tarnished by years of fingerprints and humidity. She shows them to Charli, pointing out the names of the subjects.

Underneath some loose photos, she pulls out a few frames. "Ah, yes, I thought I had one. This is my great-grandfather with his sister and his parents, Samuel and Margaret." She hands over the framed black-and-white photo, exposing some clay under her nails. "It's the only one I have of them. I suppose Samuel's your third great-grandfather."

"Is that how you say it?" Charli asks.

"I think so."

Charli carefully holds the faded photograph in her hands like she's holding a relic from a museum. The chipped wooden frame is nothing special. The family stands in front of a single-story house in staged poses. The children are not quite teenagers.

"Where was this taken?" Charli asks.

"I have no idea."

Charli examines the photo, thinking that the bad she's experienced ran through all these people as well. The four of them aren't exactly frowning, but not one looks happy.

She takes in Samuel and Margaret. They're probably in their late thirties. Margaret's not particularly attractive, looks like she doesn't even know what a smile is. And Samuel . . . he could be handsome, but he's not, as if his life has been one long trial.

Charli smiles to herself as she hears a photographer say, *Frown, everyone!*

"What year would this be?" She looks at the back of the taped frame but doesn't want to open it.

"Must have been over a hundred years ago," Kay guesses.

They look through a few more photos, and Kay shares what she can before Charli finally stands and says she's got to get back for Tiny.

"I'm so glad you came. We should spend more time together."

"Please." Charli really means it. She's reminded that maybe she's not all alone, fighting the battle of life. "Though I haven't seen you in a long time, I always considered you the bright light in our family. Someone I've always looked up to, as you don't seem bogged down by life like the rest of us."

Kay bats her eyelashes. "I appreciate that. And I've always felt the same way about you. I'm so proud to be your aunt."

"Thank you." Her words are comforting in a way that Kay could never know, and if Charli's not careful, she's going to start bawling.

Chapter 9

Miles to Nowhere

When Charli gets back to Boston, she walks Tiny and then spreads the photos out on her dining room table. There are twenty in total, five of them in frames. She takes her time with each of them, staring into the eyes of her young mother and aunt, of their mother, Priscilla. Then of their father, Barrett, who took his own life. In one photo, he's out working in the yard. Looks like a beautiful Pennsylvania day. He's in shorts and sandals, holding a shovel. Charli sees herself in him, the same annoyingly innocent brown eyes. It's an old photo, but they might share the same slightly dimpled chin as well.

"Why did you do it, Barrett? What hurt so badly?"

The answer waits for her in the next photo, the one that includes her third great-grandparents, Samuel and Margaret, standing out in front of the house. What was life like for them? What happened to Samuel or Margaret to pass it along to their children and then the next generation and so forth? They were so young to be troubled.

What year was this taken? She turns the frame over. The brittle tape is cracking. She breaks the seal and pulls back a piece of cardboard so she can see the other side.

A smaller photo slips out and falls to the table.

Charli's heart skips a beat as she reaches for it. Its condition suggests the photo is even older than the one behind which it was hiding. In it, a young couple, most likely teenagers, stand by a tree along the river. He has his arm around her. She is beautiful, exquisite even. Her thick bouncy hair is pinned down on one side by a flower-shaped hair brooch with a jewel in the middle that looks elaborate, despite the photograph's fading details.

The young woman's smile is bright enough to bring color to the black and white of the photograph. Her dress stops before some leather boots. He has dimples and wears a suit and tie and looks familiar . . .

"No," she says, squinting and leaning in. "Is that . . . ?"

She looks at the other photo, the one of Samuel and Margaret. He has the same rounded features, the same determined eyes as the young man in the photo. They are unquestionably both photographs of Samuel, taken decades apart.

But it isn't the same woman, that's for sure. Even odder, Samuel shows a smile with those dimples that is at once mischievous and alive. Charli is no expert on love, but she knows these two are enraptured by one another. A longing to know a love like that presses down on her. Though Charli has been a skeptic of true love for most of her life, she's secretly hoped that it might be out there. And this photograph feels like it's proof that it is.

Charli flips the photo over to find some faded writing. It takes her a moment to make out that it reads: *For Miles.*

The handwriting looks feminine but not neat.

"Who is Miles?" she asks out loud. Maybe he's not the same man as the first photo. She scrutinizes the photo again. It has to be. Could the inscription mean *I love you for miles*? Samuel was born in London, which could mean the picture was taken somewhere in England, probably not London considering the rural setting. They certainly didn't use miles. Was it the metric system? Phone in hand, an internet search sends her down a rabbit hole. She determines that she's mistaken. They did use miles as a measurement, but not the same miles that are used now in the United States. A mile is eight furlongs, whatever those are.

"I love you for eight furlongs," she says in a silly voice. She puts herself into the skin of the girl in the photo. She imagines herself saying to Samuel, *"I love you for miles and miles."* Perhaps that was their form of love talk.

Or . . . was this photo a gift to a guy named Miles? She leans toward the latter assumption, then thinks back to the constellation in Costa Rica. Who was the angry man who stands in the way of her green lights? Purportedly he was the original cause of the Hall family's doom. Samuel doesn't look like the kind of person who could be that angry.

She dials her aunt. "Kay, yes, I made it home safe, thanks. I'm going through these photos and found one hidden behind the photo of Samuel and his family. But it says, *For Miles.* Does that name ring a bell at all?"

"I don't think so. Miles. Nope."

"Okay, just trying to figure things out. Do you happen to know when Samuel immigrated? He was born in London. I'm wondering if this photo was taken here or over there."

Considering there is no record of his parents, Charli has a hunch that she needs to fill out Samuel's side of the tree. It's the obvious place to start. Besides, she is pulled to him, as if she knows him. It's more than the fact that they share the same blood.

"You know what you can do?" Kay says. "Check the Ellis Island records. He probably came through there. How many Samuel Halls could there be?"

"That's a great idea, thank you."

It takes her a little while, but Charli's soon searching immigration records at Ellis Island. Hundreds of results come up for Samuel Hall, but the birth year matches for only two, and those Samuel Halls both arrived too late to be hers. She's mashing the keys harder now, getting frustrated. She thought she was making progress. She tries the name Miles Hall, also to no avail, but then gets a break. She reads that not everyone came in through Ellis Island, as it only opened in 1892. Before that, there was Castle Garden. She looks for him in the immigration records on Family Search.

There he is.

She can't believe it.

Well, it could be him. According to the records, he arrived on a boat from Southampton and reached Castle Garden on September 30, 1881. She eventually confirms what she thought: he was eighteen. He must have come with his family. But they aren't on the records, or at least not tied to him. She searches for the last name Hall. No other Halls came on the boat. Did he travel alone?

"What in the world is going on?" she says, tasting the edges of a desperate curiosity. And how about the woman in the photo? Was that taken before or after Samuel left England? Did she come with him? Or did he meet her shortly after arriving in the US?

Giddy with that feeling that every detective must get when they find a solid clue, she goes back to the family tree. Samuel's wife, Margaret, was born in 1870 in Maryland. She died in 1927. Samuel surely met her in America, after he immigrated in 1881.

Charli rubs her eyes and realizes her brain is fried. Taking a step back before she quits for the day, she writes out what's on her mind.

Who else could I talk to in the family?

Search newspapers. There has to be an archive online.

Find out more on Miles. Find his family. Check records in London.

Track down more information on Margaret and her family.

⁓

Charli wakes early on Monday, two days after visiting Kay. She walks Tiny and still has thirty minutes before she has to leave for work. More research on Sunday led her to believe that she might find answers from the City of London. Once she has her recently found information splayed out in front of her on the dining room table, she calls the London Metropolitan Archives and introduces herself.

"I'm calling from the US and trying to locate more records of my third great-grandfather. All I've found is that he arrived at Castle Garden Depot in September of 1881. That's it. Nothing I've searched on your site or anywhere is showing his name. Can you help?"

"I'm so sorry," the man says. "We don't provide service over the phone." Charli has to try hard to understand, due to the heaviness of his accent coupled with a robotic overtone. "To be quite honest, we don't have the majority of our information online yet. You'd be much better served coming into the office on Monday through Friday, nine to four."

And here's a red light, she thinks. "That's a long journey from Boston. It said on the website that you have staff who can help."

"Not over the phone, I'm afraid. We certainly have staff who can help on-site. You might be interested in our bimonthly starter sessions. They're the best way to learn how to search here. We've millions, if not billions, of archives."

"What do I do if I can't come to England?"

"Well, I suppose . . . I . . . quite, I don't . . ." He's apparently having a system error. Finally, he spits out something coherent. "I suppose you could hire someone?"

"Hire someone? Like a private detective. I can't afford that."

"Not a PI, more a professional genealogist."

"Ah, okay." She thanks the man and hangs up with a heavy hand.

She cuts wedges out of a grapefruit and pops them in her mouth as she searches for professional genealogists. A few come up in Boston, but she realizes she's best to hire one in London. Otherwise, she'll have to pay for the genealogist's travel expenses.

She finds a slew of information on professional genealogists in London, more than she could ever possibly contact. She doesn't even know where to start but tries the office that owns the top of the Google search. A woman with a British accent answers quickly. Charli introduces herself and explains her situation.

"Sure, that's what we do."

Charli smiles. "Can you just tell me about price and timing and all that . . ."

"We're taking clients for early next year. The cost is based on exactly the depth of information required. Can I take down your name, and we could put you on the list?"

"Yeah, that would be great." Charli's already given up on this one.

She makes ten more calls, and it's more of the same. Months of waiting. She doesn't want to wait.

During lunch, she contacts several local genealogists who quote outrageous prices and can't make any promises. That's the thing that frustrates her. Thousands of dollars, and they may not even be able to find anything more than what's on Ancestry.

The next few days go by, and she's fighting hard not to give up. A side of her knows it would be so easy to let it all go and return to the way things were. Still, though, the fight in her is not going away.

⁓

Charli heads over to William's house at six on Thursday, and she tries to stay chipper but is doing a bad job at it. Seeing the way her father is kills her, and as she hears the tone in his voice and sees the glimmer of doom in his eyes, it feels like she's losing him.

After letting Tiny run, they go into the kitchen. William slips an apron on and starts braising lamb shanks. He's more quiet than usual. She takes a seat on a stool around the island and watches him as the smell of rosemary wafts through the air. She pours them each a glass of wine. He takes a sip and leans against the counter with the lamb sautéing behind him.

"Are you going to make me pry it out of you? I want to hear more about Costa Rica. Sounds like an adventure."

"You could say that."

Appreciating his curiosity, even if he might be faking it, Charli fills him in and answers all his questions. She can't bring herself to say that it's him! It's mostly *him* that's the reason she's doing all this. It's a total long shot, but it's the only idea left.

As she's wrapping up, she says, "I'd like to figure out what happened. Or what all this means. You have to admit, there is some serious darkness in Mom's family. And I want to escape it. I also understand if you think that it might be time to stick me into the schizo program at Mass Gen."

She gets a smile out of him. Sometimes it takes a departure from politically correct to stir the soul.

He crosses his arms. "No, I don't think I need to check you in anywhere. Look, Charli, I'm all out of answers. You might have figured that out. If you have an angle that I haven't tried, I fully support it. Understanding where you come from is an important part of growing up. Even if you're not proud of who or what you find."

She wants to explain more, but she could potentially make things so much worse by shining a spotlight on her worry about him. His sigh and facial expression show a father who hates hearing his daughter wrestling with such heavy challenges.

"It's freaking hard, Dad. All of it."

"You're telling me." He dips his chin. "But I'm here for you."

But you're not, she wants to say. He's fading away right in front of her. She presses her eyes together. She's suddenly ten years old and hiding in the closet, crying.

She can barely look at him as a heavy weight of sadness settles in her heart. William goes to her and pulls her in as the tears come. She cries into his neck.

When they pull away, she sees that he's crying too. "What are *you* crying for?" She reaches for his tears.

Her dad cries like an old man, his body shaking. "I don't know, honey. I . . . I can't stand to see you hurting."

"I feel the same way about you," she says. "I don't know why *you're* hurting. I mean, Mom, I guess, but that was a long time ago. I don't know what's going on with you, selling the boat and everything."

Both wet with tears, they look at each other until they share the same thought as the smell of carbon wafts up into the air.

He cracks a smile. "The lamb chops are burning."

She laughs despite the tears. There's nothing that makes her feel safer than seeing his lips curl upward. He gets up and tends to them.

"I'm glad that I can still make you laugh," Charli says, "even if it is at my expense."

"You have a way with delivery," he says over his shoulder. "I think you could make a living doing stand-up of the self-deprecating variety."

"Right, I'll add that to the list of potential new careers to fail in next."

He sets down the tongs and turns to her. "You know what I think . . . I think you should go to England yourself. Take this picture and a name and see what happens."

"My boss won't give me any more time off." She's too ashamed to admit how she lied to get the time off for Costa Rica.

"From what I'm hearing, this job is not as important as what you're doing now. Your boss sounds like a jerk, and I'm not seeing the work as being exactly satisfying."

"That's not true. I adore poring over poorly written advisory reports for porta-potty rentals and car washes. I feel like I'm doing what I was put on this planet to do. I'm saving the world, Dad."

William drops his head and seemingly fakes amusement. What Charli sees through his mask is serious concern. Does he feel like he's the one to blame for the disaster that she's become?

He goes to her with a face that melts with sadness. Putting his hands on her shoulders, he stares into her eyes. "You're exactly the person I want you to be. I'm so proud of the woman you've become."

They both know he's lying. Or, at least, pushing the truth. That's what you have to say to your daughter, just like how Kay must have felt obligated as an aunt to say something similar when Charli had visited her in Lowell.

"I'm serious," he says, letting her go. "You turned into this miraculous young lady despite how much I screwed up. And I . . ." His voice cracks. "I . . . I'm sorry."

She can barely get out, "You did your best, Dad."

Tiny senses Charli's pain and comes to her. She finds comfort in petting him. It's not fair that her dad is apologizing, as if what happened could ever be fixed.

William wipes his eyes, reaches for his daughter's hand, and flashes a weary smile. "I'm so proud of you for doing what you're doing. You don't ever let up. Quite frankly, it's inspirational. Makes me want to raise my fists a little."

"Well, you should, Daddy. You're too young to give up."

He's the one to look away this time, and that's when she knows for sure. He's not going to raise his fists. He's completely given up.

That's why she has no choice. She'd do anything for him, even chase ghosts from the past with a baseless hope that she might be able to alter his outcome.

~

Friday morning, Charli's editing a report for a company called Wish and Wash that's been growing throughout New England, and the words are blurry. She's determined to somehow convince Marvin to give her another week off. Just one week to save the life of her father. One week to save her own life. Then she'll return to this shithole with unwavering enthusiasm and gusto, the likes of which Marvin has never seen. She'll get back to her car wash reports as if she's been tapped on the shoulder to save the entire human race—with her *astounding* car wash advisory reports.

Because car washes are a big deal. And we must keep them in business. The section she's editing now has to do with the wasted overtime pay due to a lack of depth on the employee roster. Seriously, what is more important than trimming the fat and making sure hourly wage workers don't make one more freaking dime than they're supposed to? Overtime is a killer, and it's wasted on people who oddly like to work more than forty hours a week. Don't they have anything better to do?

Charli takes a pause to lower her head. No, not drop it like her father sometimes does, as if he's been beaten. She lowers her forehead all the way down to the keyboard and feels the keys press against her skin. Nonsensical text is surely muddying up her report, and she cares one iota less than zero.

"A little morning nap there, Charli?" a voice says. Marvin's voice. He must always be watching her. Are there cameras?

Resisting the urge to be snarky, she pops up like she's the most chipper person since Julia Child. "Oh, no, I was just brainstorming about Wish and Wash, making sure we've dotted all the *i*'s. You know, crossed all the *t*'s." Clichés are the worst, and they seem so fitting when she refers to the life-changing work she's doing.

He second-guesses her look but eventually nods in satisfaction. She looks down the row at her coworkers. There's a steady chatter coming from the army of keyboards in this room. Marvin rarely stops to talk with anyone else. She's apparently the chosen one.

"Listen, I wanted to ask you something . . ." She can't believe she's doing it, asking for more time off. The Costa Rica request felt like she was asking if she could have Marvin's left kidney.

"Ah, yes, Charli Thurman needs more from me. I don't know whether to be honored or afraid."

She ignores him and presses on with everything she has. "I need some more time off."

He cocks his head toward her, then jerks it right and then up and down, as if she's caused him to self-destruct. Finally, he says, "I don't think I heard you correctly. More time off?"

"That's right. My mother's not doing well." She can't remember what kind of cancer she gave her mother in the first excuse, so she goes garden variety. Was it cancer at all? Had to be.

"The cancer looks like it's gone," she says, "but during the surgery, she picked up an infection. She's on heavy antibiotics, which she's allergic to . . ." Charli wonders where she came up with that, but she's on a roll and keeps going. "So she's bedridden and swollen and has no one to take care of her."

Marvin looks at Charli like Hercule Poirot stares at potential suspects, as if he's searching for any hint of a lie. "Firstly, I'm sorry about your mother. But let's consider everyone in this room. They all have things going on. Trust me, because I hear about them. Every single day. What if I let everyone take more time off. We'd go out of business."

Wouldn't that be terrible, Charli thinks. We must stay in business so we can protect companies from overpaying employees who barely have a pot to piss in already. Heaven forbid they get a few extra dollars for working hard. Then it occurs to her—all while Marvin continues his soliloquy—that she's become a part of the evil machine.

When he's done, Charli says, "I totally get it. And I feel awful asking, but"—this is when she turns on her charm—"she's my mother. Despite having a difficult life, she gave me her all. And now she's quite possibly dying. This is *my chance* to pay her back for all that she's done for me." Charli almost laughs but is reminded that none of this is funny. "I don't have a choice. But I do like this job, and I will come back after a week ready to give it my all. No more time off the rest of the year."

Marvin is wide eyed. "You're good. You know that? You're really good."

Charli is on the verge of tears. And it's not because she's faking. Real tears are coming. Maybe because in this desperate plea she created the mother she wished she'd had.

One tear actually escapes, and that's when she knows she's won. Who could say no to this pity party?

"Okay, my God," Marvin says. "Don't start crying on me. And don't cause a scene." He leans down. "You can have another week. One last week. But you need to take your computer, and you need to be available."

Charli wipes her eye and feels like Pinocchio when he sheds his first tear. Maybe she's a real human with real feelings after all.

"Thank you, Marvin. You're a good man."

That seems to satisfy him. "You're welcome." He extends his hand and briefly touches her leg, causing her to cringe. She resists thrusting a knee up into his crotch. She's gotten what she needed, and now she doesn't have to see him for a while.

Chapter 10

THE OTHER SIDE OF THE POND

The Monday-morning fog hasn't even burned off when Charli climbs into a black cab at Paddington Station in London. She slept only a few hours on the overnight flight but has two cups of coffee running through her. Settling into the back seat, she tells the driver the name of her hotel. He knows exactly where it is, explains that cabbies in London are required to know the city backward and forward before they can get behind the wheel.

She picked Notting Hill for no other reason than she adored the Hugh Grant and Julia Roberts film. Even if that kind of love doesn't exist in real life, it's nice to see it on the screen. Her take on relationships is more squarely planted in the camp of how it exists on *The Bachelor* and *Bachelorette*. Even *if* they find their soulmate, and that's after testing the prowess of several contestants in the fantasy suites, they almost always find their way to a messy divorce sometime after the show. Just like her parents' experience, love is a honeymoon and a sinking ship, all aboard one long tragic cruise. Is it any surprise she likes to get off one port before the sinking?

As she takes in the sights, she recalls the last time she'd visited London—a father-daughter trip ten years earlier. They caught a couple of West End shows and visited the National Gallery to see works by some of the greats. She'll never forget first setting her eyes on the Paul Delaroche painting called *The Execution of Lady Jane Grey*. She was mesmerized by it, heartbroken, torn to pieces, and yet she couldn't *not* look at it. All that darkness. Of course it was her favorite painting. She still remembers the story of a teenage Lady Jane, who was queen for only nine days in 1553 before an executioner chopped off her head. But all the way to the end, Lady Jane holds a look of resolve, as if she knows something they don't. Perhaps that touches back to Charli's view of faith. Perhaps she doesn't have faith, but she wants to have faith, which is maybe the first step. She wants to believe that she's not the waste of flesh that she feels like now. She wants to have faith in the idea that maybe she does matter, that she's somehow part of the grand design out there in the cosmos.

But for right now, she is the metal scraps of an old satellite stuck in a far-off orbit in which she will never escape.

It's not only Lady Jane's resolve that stuck with Charli since she was last here. It was also the way the painted woman looked so comfortable in the darkness. Charli can relate. Perhaps that's why she's attracted to mysteries. She's utterly unbothered by even the most gruesome of scenes. She recalls Herman, the angry man in the constellation, or Letícia, the Brazilian woman, falling to the floor. Charli would not be surprised if what she learned in Costa Rica is true, that murderous DNA swims in her blood.

It could explain a lot, like her bleak view of the world and the guilt she often feels. She's cut from the cloth of a killer, so what could anyone expect?

Nevertheless, the fate of her family is in her hands. What's worse is that this holistic mission to right an imbalance in her family isn't a science-based methodology. She's having to rely on her faith that there's something out there more powerful and possible than what she currently knows, and she's been pretty short on faith for the majority of her life.

Walking into the lobby, Charli guesses her boutique hotel has about forty rooms. The smell of sausage and eggs and pastries wafts over from the restaurant where guests are having breakfast. A porter takes her bag and leads her to the front desk, where a woman in a turban gifts her an early check-in.

By booking through the hotel directly, Charli landed a decent rate with an open-ended reservation, as she's not sure she needs to stay all the way to Sunday, which was only a guess. For that reason, she'd coughed up the extra hundred for a changeable flight too. Not that she'll stay longer, but maybe she'll go home earlier to save money.

Her room on the fourth floor looks out over a busy street. She's directly across from a Chinese take-out place. When she cracks the window, she instantly smells sweet-and-sour chicken and gasoline. She takes a hurried ten minutes to unpack and make herself presentable before rushing out the door to get started.

⌐⌐

The London Metropolitan Archives is located in the parish of Clerkenwell and housed in a dull brick building with windows that look like they'd come right out of an American high school in the eighties. Yet the magic of this place shows like the tip of a bookmark poking out of a page, and she becomes eager to pin down the truth of Samuel's life.

The LMA has just opened, and she files in with the other early birds to begin her research. There's so much red in there: the red chairs that push up to the desks with computers, the red shelves that line the walls. She finds the red information desk and waits in line.

A few moments later, a woman younger than Charli—perhaps midtwenties—invites her to sit. Charli feels like she's applying for a driver's license.

"Welcome, my name is Anna. How may I help you?" She's likely new to the job, has this youthful vigor to her, like a starter plant that hasn't been transferred from the greenhouse to the garden yet. Thankfully she's not wearing red.

"I'm visiting from Boston to find out more about my family, specifically a grandfather on my mother's side. I think his name is Samuel Hall, at least that's what my family has always called him. I found records of his immigration to the US from London, landing at Castle Garden in 1881. The trail kind of stops, though. It looks like he came over without his parents, but I can't find any records. It's like he didn't exist before the boat. I can't find a middle name, which makes it even harder. My family tree on Ancestry goes back to the fifteen hundreds and sixteen hundreds with every other line, but nothing comes up for him."

"Oh, dear . . . well, you're in the right place." Anna speaks with so much enthusiasm that she might as well show all her teeth and give a thumbs-up. Charli almost feels bad that this woman has met her match: a jaded near-thirties pessimist who has seen too much to smile like that.

Charli doesn't even pretend to match the energy. "I tried to get some help over email and the phone and wasn't able."

"Yes, we're quite busy. But let's see what we can do for you."

"And I have this." Charli opens her backpack and extracts the photos of Samuel. They're in sleeves of plastic for protection.

Anna eyes them. "Oh, he's a handsome one, isn't he?"

"He is." Looks might be the only good trait passed down through the man, but she doesn't say that. "I can't tell if that was taken before or after he came over. I'm pretty sure that's a beech tree, which grows here and there. But he was on a ship out of Southampton on September 16, 1881. The manifest said he was eighteen."

Anna scrutinizes the photo as if her entire life depends on finding this man. "It does look a bit like the English countryside, doesn't it?"

"I'm not familiar enough to know," Charli says. "But you can obviously see that he didn't marry the woman in the photo. The other one is him with his wife and their kids."

Anna stares back and forth between the two photos with a frown. "Someone was heartbroken, I can guarantee that. What a cutie."

Charli lights up. "That's what I thought. If you flip the one of the younger couple over, you'll see another clue."

The woman does and says aloud, "For Miles. Who's Miles?"

"Exactly what I'm wondering. Maybe a nickname? Or the photo was a gift to someone named Miles? Or maybe it means something like, 'I love you for miles and miles'?"

The woman shrugs. "Don't know that that's a very British saying."

"Right," Charli says. "That's what I was thinking. But I know him as Samuel Hall."

One of Anna's eyebrows rises. "Intriguing, isn't it? Wouldn't be the first time we've seen a name change. Family history is so much like playing telephone. A misheard word here, a misspelling there."

"Yeah, I know what you mean. Do you think we could find some other records of him? I can show you what I have from Ancestry, but I'm not sure it will help. The trail goes cold afterward. Maybe his original birth records will show his parents. The only reason I know he's from London is that it said it on the manifest. That's where I want to start. And to see if he had any siblings. Just seems so weird to me that every other branch of my tree was easier to figure out."

"Indeed," she says, staring at the younger Samuel. "Don't you wish he could speak from here? He looks like he has so much to say."

"That would make it easier."

Anna hums a brief but jolly melody. "I've seen miracles happen in this building. It takes some work, you know? Do you have a few days?"

"Just a few, yes," she says quickly. "I fly out Sunday."

"And I'm sure you've tried what we have online. Did you search the BNA files, the British Newspaper Archives?"

"I have. I've done everything I could from Boston, and nothing is turning up. Well, I have found lots of Samuel Halls, but nothing that I can pin down to my family."

"You don't have a lot to go on, do you? A name that's possibly not accurate, paired with two photos. Not even a middle name."

As Anna states the obvious, Charli's hope sinks. She flew all the way here for what? For fish and chips? There's a good chance she'll be going home without a shred more evidence. "I know the likelihood of finding anything is slim, but I have to try."

"I wouldn't give up yet. If you have the persistence, you might get lucky. How about I get you started, and my staff and I will be available to help along the way. Come with me."

Charli follows Anna toward the red desks with computers. "Samuel Hall is quite a common name," Anna says over her shoulder. "Miles Hall, perhaps not so much. What I might suggest is the process of elimination. Let's knock out the easy avenues first. On one of these computers here, you can access the census records. We've uploaded everything since 1841. Let's assume that the age on the manifest is somewhat accurate. You'll be able to search by potential birth years. And print out a list of any matches."

"How could I possibly narrow it down from there? Let's say I have fifty Samuel Halls."

"I don't know that you'll have fifty. See what you come up with. Then we can take those names to search further. I can show you how to use the microfiche machine to search through both the civil and parish records. There can be a great deal of overlap, but you never know. I've seen someone almost give up when they found a baptism noted in the parish records for a child whose birth wasn't even recorded in the civils. Can you believe that?"

Charli pretends she's floored with a face more stretched than her mother's. "This could take the rest of my life."

"You'd be surprised what you can come up with in a few days of looking. We also have quite a few hospital records and wills that I can lead you to as well. What we want to do is get a full list and start eliminating. Who died before they were eighteen? Who died here in England? Who has their family trees populated all the way down?"

Charli sits down at one of the computers. "And what if I don't have his name right?"

Anna blinks. "Oh dear. Then you're trying to find someone with a photograph. That becomes much harder. You might have to dig deeper in your family. See what else they might have. Perhaps a long-lost uncle who remembers hearing something. I think you're in the right place to get started, that's for sure. I'll be here if you need me. Don't forget to drink water and eat on occasion. I've seen folks forget both for days on end."

"Noted." Charli pulls out her notebook and pictures and sets them out in front of her. She writes down *Search Miles and Samuel Hall, possible birth dates from 1855 to 1865, keeping the dates broad so as not to miss something. Consider other name variations. Start with census records, then civil and parish records via microfiche. (Should have paid attention during high school library visits, as I have no idea how to read microfiche.)*

That out of the way, she takes a moment to center herself by looking at her mysterious third great-grandfather. "Show yourself," she says. "Wherever you are."

Trying not to consider her odds, she starts tapping at the keys. The database returns twenty-two possible Samuel Halls, which is promising. Each entry shows the full name, date of birth, and the borough in London. Maybe Samuel did have a middle name, but it wasn't recorded. An idea strikes. Could someone further down the family tree have been named after him?

Opening up her own computer, she pulls up Ancestry.com and studies the names of his children and their children, all the way down to Georgina. Then she scrolls through the list, hoping for a match.

"She's right about that," a voice says from a few desks down.

A man of generous proportions sits back and waits for her to respond. His belly protrudes out of a thick blue cardigan. His red cheeks and youthful smile make him look disarming enough that Charli is at least cordial as she returns a smile.

"What was that?" she asks.

"Drink your water. What Anna said. I sometimes forget."

"Oh, yeah. I can imagine." Charli twists back toward her work, thinking there's no time for chitchat.

As she clicks on the next Samuel Hall, he asks, "Just getting started, are you?"

Charli once again pulls away from the computer and says politely, "Yes."

"You sound American?"

"Yes," she says, allowing more annoyance to slip into her tone than she intends.

He gets the message. "Well, welcome. Let me know if I can help."

This time she puts a little extra effort into offering thanks and then goes back to work. Her search for a middle name she might recognize proves fruitless for both Samuel and Miles, the latter of which drew only three entries. Returning to Anna's plan, Charli exports the lists and prints them out.

She walks away from the desk and goes to find Anna. It's time to try the parish and civil records. Anna is so gracious with her time and teaches Charli how to work her way through the file systems, which are organized by borough and year, and then analyze her findings using the microfiche reader. This work will be a time suck because she has to search all thirty-two boroughs and doesn't have a way to export and print the results, which means she must transfer the information to her notebook by hand.

Once she gets the hang of it, she moves faster, but it's still a slog. What drives her mad is that she might be searching for a false name. She tells herself not to even go there until she's eliminated every last Samuel or Miles Hall.

With jet lag nibbling at her, Charli spends the rest of the day searching microfiche, adding new Samuel and Miles Halls, or subtracting when she can. The middle names and birth and death dates found in the civil and parish records help tremendously, and by the time the LMA is closing, she's narrowed it down to twelve potential people.

Exhausted at the end of her long day, she collapses into the chair of a pizza spot and has a glass of wine, a salad, and a slice. She's too tired to even pull out her computer and allows herself to take the rest of the night off. Knowing she has to stay up to settle into the new time zone, she walks through the West End, checking out all the shows playing, and then recalls that the National Gallery is right around the corner.

Walking into the museum as most people are leaving, she takes in a few pieces that call out to her. Being there among such magnificent art snaps her out of her funk and gives her some energy. Great art is like great fiction, she thinks: telling and transporting.

When she finds Delaroche's painting, she's floored by how big it is, how it takes up almost an entire wall. She'd forgotten that. But she hadn't forgotten why she was so captivated. The painting depicts Lady Jane in a beautiful white gown. A white cloth has been wrapped around her eyes, no doubt to keep the others from having to see her so intimately as she faces her death. Despite her eyes being covered, her face and posture seem to show her acceptance of her fate. She's being led toward the wooden stump where she will lay her head by the lieutenant of the tower. To her right, her ladies-in-waiting grieve. To the left, the executioner, a well-dressed man in scarlet tights, leans on the axe.

It's a chilling painting, and Charli finds herself staring at it for a long time, staring at the axe and at the face of the executioner, a man seemingly unfazed by his mission. Some people have a darkness in them. Is it always passed down? What if she was doomed from the day she took her first breath?

~

The next day, Charli wakes and, while still in bed, searches for details on her twelve potential relatives online. She signs up for Ancestry.co.uk, which is England's Ancestry version. She's able to find the family trees of seven of them, all of which eliminate them as possibilities.

Upon opening time at the LMA, she enlists Anna's help. "I'm down to five, but I'm clueless as to where to go from here. I can't find any death records, which means they could have immigrated."

All the while, Anna is nodding thoughtfully. "Okay, so you have five names, including middle names. And birth dates, I'm assuming. One could be your third great-grandfather." Anna swings her arm across her body. "Let's go deeper. I doubt we'll find much luck in tax records, but we've a few tricks up our sleeve. Let me show you how to search the cemetery and coroner records. In the meantime, did you search your leftover names on BNA? How about Ancestry?"

"And Family Search. I even went back this morning and checked the Castle Garden manifests for any other Halls on any other boats within a few years of his arrival. Nothing. You know what I was wondering. Since he's school age, do you have any school records? Or yearbooks?"

"Wouldn't that be nice. I suppose you could go to every school in London and see if they can drum up the appropriate yearbooks for you. Not a bad idea, actually. Especially since your photo is the only thing we know for sure is real. Of course, you'd have to visit every public and private school in all the boroughs. Doable but challenging."

"There have to be other options."

"I think you might have to take it outside of these walls. You have names, middles included. You have two photos. You have their boroughs, their dates of birth."

"And for a couple, I have baptism and christening dates."

"Ah! Go to the churches. They might have more information, including photographs."

Charli pinches the bridge of her nose. "This is not work for the faint of heart, is it?"

"Not at all, but all the more rewarding that way. Let's check those cemetery and coroner reports first, just so you can eliminate any last ones."

"Will do. Thank you, Anna."

⌒

Two hours later, Charli's brain is fried. She was able to eliminate one Samuel, as he was buried in Hackney in 1894, according to the cemetery records. She's down to four but can barely see through her weary eyes.

She stands from where she'd been sitting for the last hour, stretches, and looks around. The man from the day before sits in a chair against the wall, seemingly staring off into space. He wears the same cardigan as the day before.

Feeling bad for shrugging him off yesterday, Charli walks up to him. "Hitting a roadblock?"

"You could say that."

"Do you work here? Seems you know your way around."

"No, though one might think so, considering how much time I spend within these walls. Now that I've retired, I've tasked myself with becoming the family researcher. Why? Is there something I could help you with?"

"No, no. I was going for a water, per Anna's instructions, and thought I'd offer to buy you one."

He returns a bright smile. "Oh, that's so kind of you. And yes, I'd like that. Let me see if I have the—"

"Please, it's on me."

"Are you sure?" He reacts like she's given him a fifty-dollar bill. "My name's Monty, by the way."

"I'm Charli."

"Hello, Charli. What are you working on?"

"Oh, gosh. I traveled here from Boston in hopes that I might find the roots of my third great-grandfather. He's proving to be a complete ghost."

"I have a few ghosts in my tree as well."

"At least you know what you're doing. But I'm getting closer maybe. I basically came here with a possible first and last name and two pictures."

"Did you try the facial-recognition software?"

Charli about drops to the floor. "They have that? Why didn't anyone tell me?"

"No, they don't. I apologize, that was a rather crude joke. May I see the photos? You know, sometimes there are clues."

She takes off her backpack, takes out the photos, and hands them to him. She's sure he can't help, but he's about as nice as someone can get. Not enough of that in the world.

Monty puts on his readers and stares at the older picture first. "That looks like American architecture in the background."

"That's right. That one was taken in the US. Then the other, I'm guessing here."

He flips to the picture with the younger version of her third great-grandfather. "Ah, now that's England if I've ever seen it. I wonder what river that could be. Down south, if I had to guess." He points with his free hand. "I'm sure you know that's a Winchester College tie, correct?"

"What?" Charli takes the photo back from him and looks. She stares at the tie, for the first time, really. Being in black and white, she can't tell the colors. "How do you know? I've never heard of Winchester College."

Monty rests his crossed arms on his belly. "The angle and the thickness of the lines. My neighbor a few years back was a Wykehamist, which is what they call the men of Winchester College."

"You're sure?" Charli's head is spinning.

"I'd say so. Worth a look anyway."

Charli finds his eyes. "Thank you. You have no idea how helpful this is."

He offers a smile that's as soothing as a cup of chamomile tea. "Glad I could help."

"What is Winchester College anyway?" Charli asks. "Where is it?"

"It's in Winchester, of course. A hobnobby place. Seems your Samuel was of a higher class. Sunak went there, you know."

"You mean the prime minister?"

He unfurls his arms. "That's the one."

Charli fades into her thoughts. She has to go there. She's found the clue she's looking for, and if she wasn't such a pessimist, she'd call her feeling exhilarating. Since she is, though, she might play it down, go with her English roots, and say she's *rather enthused*.

"I wonder if they have some kind of records there," she says.

"They have a wonderful set of archives, my dear. A museum even. It's a stunning place, Winchester. First capital of England. One of the finest cathedrals in the UK."

Charli thanks Monty again. "I can't even express my gratitude." She stops just before she admits that his warm and generous demeanor has taught her something she won't soon forget.

"Good luck to you, Charli."

She rushes toward Anna, the woman who originally helped her. "You won't believe this. The tie in my third great-grandfather's picture. The man over there says it's from Winchester College."

"Oh, how about that! Look at you. A little hard work pays off, doesn't it?"

"I don't know that I did that much." Charli's in tears. She knows she's onto something.

"Showing up is half the battle," Anna says.

"I guess so."

After getting Monty his water and giving him a big hug, Charli leaves the LMA and races back to her hotel room in Notting Hill. She calls Winchester College in a frenzy of excitement that the *rather enthused* part of her can't believe exists. Anticlimactically, they've already closed for the day. Finding a Hildon sparkling water in the fridge, she sits in the chair in her tiny room and reads about Winchester. It's only an hour away, which means she's going to Winchester first thing in the morning. That's for sure. She tries searching for Miles and Samuel coupled with "Winchester College" but comes up dry.

Eventually, she calls her dad. "You won't believe what happened today."

"I'm all ears."

"The clue was the tie."

"What?"

She goes on to tell him everything, all too aware how uncharacteristically cheerful she is. What if she could truly make a difference in their lives?

Chapter 11

A Second Encounter

Winchester, England
October 28, 1880

Miles watched her through the newly polished window of the inn. She held a content look on her face. He said her name, his heart warming as the word leaped off his tongue. "Lillian."

As beautiful as a lily picked in a field, he thought, but she was far from a fragile flower. She carried herself with a seasoned power and possessed a commanding presence at the bar. Even the most intoxicated treated her with respect.

"Lillian," he whispered again. Was it possible to love a woman whom he barely knew? It had been two weeks since he'd first encountered her, and they were the longest of his life. He'd have returned sooner, but the housemaster had taken ill and could be heard wandering the downstairs of the boardinghouse late at night.

Miles found it nearly impossible to focus on his studies. His professors' words would fade away as Lillian's velvety voice tickled the ears of his imagination. Even in the depths of his algebra book, he sketched her face. He could see her smile as if it had been painted on the ceiling above him while he slept. Her face had been etched into his soul.

After sliding a beer down to a patron, Lillian happened to lift her gaze, and she caught sight of him. Miles stood proudly and tipped his hat. She raised a finger to tell him to wait a moment. He resisted a smile, as the cat-and-mouse game was certainly afoot.

She came out from the bar a few minutes later, snapped the door shut, and tugged a shawl over her body. It was chilly out, the winter winds coming early this year. Being a Thursday around eleven, High Street was crowded with diners having finished their meals and beggars hoping to take advantage of their liquored-up generosity.

Miles stepped toward her, resisting an urge to reach out and touch her—a gesture most assuredly inappropriate even with her class. Instead, he dipped his head and said quite formally, "Good evening." He surprised himself at his own amplified confidence, but then again, that was one of the reasons he was attracted to her. She brought the best out of him.

Lillian was confident herself and held his gaze as she said, "So you're back for more business, I see. And what business was it that brings you to Winchester?"

He felt his dimples cave inward. She could see right through him and had properly called him out. "I suppose there's no reason to continue a facade. You were correct the first time." He held out both hands. "I am indeed a Wykehamist."

She smiled at him with satisfaction. "I knew it."

"Which is why I haven't returned sooner. It's risky business sneaking away."

"I imagine so," she said. "But not risky enough to keep you from being here tonight."

"I suppose nothing would have kept me from at least trying to see you."

She blushed at his forwardness. "Ah."

If she only knew the risk, he thought, trying not to imagine the consequences. "I'd like to ask . . ." He stumbled over his words in this slightly awkward space they created. He finally let out, "Would you do me the honor of accompanying me on a walk?"

Lillian glanced back at the bar. "I suppose so. I have about ten minutes before my father wonders of my whereabouts."

Miles pivoted in the opposite direction. "Then let's not waste a second of it."

They strolled side by side down High Street, very close to one another. He didn't want to be recognized—as his father would be livid—so he suggested they take an alley that would lead them away from the city center. With his family so well known, he never knew whom he might encounter.

"So how is it that you were able to sneak out?"

Miles smiled. "I leave a window open and wait for everyone to fall asleep."

"And what would happen if you were caught?"

He sighed. "I don't rightly want to think about it. A good caning, that's for sure. Detention. Suspension."

She had worn a subtle smile since they'd left, but it stretched wider. "You risk all that just to see me?"

"I'd risk far more than that to see you."

"An assured statement from a man who doesn't even know me."

He stopped and she stopped with him. The clouds had broken enough to show a patch of stars above her head. "Then tell me about you," he urged.

She darted her eyes from his eyes to his nose, then lips, as if she were deciding which of the desserts behind the glass she might try. "You're a bold man, aren't you, Miles?"

"Not always, but I can't waste my ten minutes."

Lillian liked the way he spoke to her; he could tell. Most likely because he was absolutely sincere, and she knew it. She effortlessly stoked the boldness in him, causing him to feel less trapped in the prison his father had constructed around him.

They started walking again, passing a stretch of food shops, a fruiterer and butcher, that were closed for the night. "As I might have mentioned, my family owns the inn. That's my father in there with the beard, if you saw him. I've worked there since I was little. And by no means am I worthy of a Wykehamist."

Miles stopped again and touched her arm. It was the first time he'd made physical contact with her. "I'm not sure what you mean."

"Of course you do. Tell me . . . about your life. Who is your family? What privilege do you have to attend the college?"

"You're right; my father is a gentleman and a member of the House of Lords. But none of that matters to me." He felt the hardness that took over his expression.

"But to him?"

"That doesn't matter either."

A boisterous laugh came from one of the carriages passing by. They both turned and realized it had nothing to do with them.

"What do you want from me, Miles? What is your last name, by the way?"

He said almost shamefully, "Pemberton."

"You're a Pemberton?" She laughed. "And you're attempting to court me?"

He liked the sound of him attempting to court her. That was indeed what he was doing, all else be damned. "Why not?"

She looked up at the night sky, watching the fast-moving clouds glide by. "It's like making a wish on a star that was never there."

He stepped toward her. "I don't like the sound of that."

"I know my place in the world, Miles. And I could only imagine the trouble you'd bring into it." She suddenly looked deflated, as if she'd decided this wasn't a bright idea after all.

Miles was ready to put up a fight. Though his desire to act on the stage had brought to the surface his need to break free, it was this woman here before him who gave him the courage to truly consider disrupting the order of his life. "Yes, that's possible. But how about let's not talk about the potential barriers to our becoming something that we're not yet. I want to be here with you now."

She didn't reply, so he spoke his mind. "I should have told you that I'm a salesman in town from London."

She diverted her eyes down the street, where gaslight illuminated another pub. "I'm not sure a lie is the best way to build on anything, even if we're meant for doom."

Miles stepped even closer. "Meant for doom? Aren't you the cynic."

She twisted his way and shuffled her feet on the dusty road. "I'm a realist."

Whatever she was, he wanted more of it. How could he possibly explain to her the life he'd been living, the one draped in facades and expectations? Had he barely known anything real at all until this moment? He'd been living like a sheep at the mercy of his father, the shepherd, and now she'd given Miles a taste of what it was like to be shot up into the heavens.

"What if I told you I don't believe in the systems that I've grown up captive in? What if I told you I didn't care about my family name or my path to Oxford or even the gown and tie of the college that I attend? What if I told you that love matters more to me than the duties of my family?"

"I'd tell you that you're a fool." But he could see that her words did not reflect how she felt inside. She didn't really believe that he was a fool. In fact, he might take it one step further and call her a romantic, just like him. Desire certainly glittered in her eyes, despite her attempting to hide it.

"I'm a fool of your making," Miles said. "It's as if I've stepped through a door, and now it's locked, so there's no turning back."

She chuckled to herself, clearly enjoying the flattery. And then taking on a playful manner, she said, "Sadly, your ten minutes is up."

"What a tragedy that is."

Their eyes locked, and it was Miles who eventually turned away. He pinched his chin and looked back down the street. "May I walk you back?"

"I'd like that."

Miles shortened his stride, attempting to prolong their time together. She knew well what he was doing and seemed amused by it. He asked about her family, and she told him of her mother and father and then her brother, Arthur, and his pregnant wife—all of them very close and working well together at the inn. Miles could not imagine what that would be like.

"What is it you want to do, Miles Pemberton? If you don't want to follow your father's design?"

Miles appreciated the question. "You mean if I didn't attend Oxford?"

"If you did what you wanted to do," Lillian reiterated. Her soft skin glowed in the moonlight, toying with him and beckoning him.

"I'd find someone to love," he said, "and I'd give her all of me."

Of course, his choice would be to chase his stage dreams, but he found such pleasure in expressing these other feelings that stirred inside him, feelings that he'd not ever known before making her acquaintance. And she didn't seem to shy away when he pressed, which made it even more enjoyable.

Her incandescent eyes widened, and the pitch of her voice lifted in good fun. "Oh, you'd let a woman determine your future?" She knew exactly what he was doing, adding an extra scoop of sugar to his words.

Her going along with it caused him to smile. "Not just any woman."

"Well, surely whoever this lucky lady is, she'd want you out of the house all day, so she could enjoy some time alone." She could be an actor herself with such delivery.

"If that is her wish."

"What is it you would do? Where would you go? Where would the money come from?"

Though he detected a serious note in her curiosity, he kept his course. "It would be a shame they wouldn't pay me to enjoy her beauty all day."

"She won't be beautiful forever."

"Oh, I doubt that. I think she grows more beautiful by the moment."

Her eyes went to the dusty road. "I see."

They took a few steps in silence, and he thought she might be questioning his sincerity. "I don't mean to make light of my feelings," he said. "It's only that I enjoy the banter between us. And I don't exaggerate much. You cause me to rethink everything in my life."

"After a brief walk?" she asked.

"I feel that we've known each other for far longer than the time we've actually shared. Perhaps in a past life."

She shrugged.

"To return to your question, though, I suppose I'd finish this school year and then go to London and become an actor."

"An actor?"

He let his jaw fall in a gentle display of his dramatic sensibilities. "Yes, is that so hard to believe?"

"You'd be the first Wykehamist ever to grace a stage."

He waved a hand in the air. "Not true at all. We're doing *The Merchant of Venice* in the Shakespeare Society."

"I would love to see that. Why don't you recite a few lines for me?"

A bout of shyness ran over him. He glanced over at the inn, which was now only a few steps away. Though he wasn't ready to say goodbye, he wasn't ready to recite Shakespeare either. She seemed as sweet as a fig, but she came with a level of intimidation.

He offered a sly smile. "I'm afraid we've run out of time tonight."

"Ah, I see. Well played, Miles. I suppose I should thank you for risking your life to see me again."

"May I return?"

She bit her lip and looked him over once again, as if she were inspecting him. He wanted to assure her that he was a good actor and that he could make his way to the West End to find work, but he wouldn't dare show her the weakness and worry that lingered around such a dream.

Finally, she whispered, "I am here nearly every day and night, should you return to High Street."

He felt his dimples cave in again. "I'll take that as a strong urging to return."

"Take it as you will." With that, she kicked up her chin and whipped around.

But she stopped to deliver one more message. "Though I admire your confidence, it's your shyness that is your finest quality. The red in your face is a feather in your cap."

He found himself lost for words as she nodded to him and disappeared into the pub. In that moment, he believed that he could do anything his heart desired.

He'd not beamed so brightly in his entire life as he had on the walk home along the river. If she was not careful, Lillian could set his world on fire. He strolled if there ever was a stroll, slow and steady steps that allowed him to feel the ground underneath his boots. He could hear the whisper of the water, the call of the moon, the breeze of his future stirring up forbidden dreams of a life of his own.

Manners makyth man, he thought as the school came into view, only a few gaslights showing the way. *Manners makyth man,* the school's slogan. Indeed, the decisions he made now would make him whom he would become. Should he continue on his current path, Miles could lose his chance to be with a woman who was far more important than any other facet of his life.

He liked his classmates and his teachers, despite the difficulties, but he had never felt like he'd belonged at Winchester College. The same would occur at Oxford and even as he returned home to live the life of a gentleman. He would never belong, especially now, as Lillian had set something free in him, as though she'd opened the gates to the corral where he'd been penned all his life.

If she would allow it, he'd rush back to the pub and sweep her off her feet and take her somewhere for a new start, a place where they'd be free of their chains. Alas, he had no money and was unsure how he might ever succeed. Though he adored acting, did he have what it took to be the next Henry Irving? Or would they laugh at him and send him back to Winchester with his head down? If so, what would he do then?

Judging by the moon, he thought it must have been an hour past midnight when he finally reached his boardinghouse and hurried in the darkness toward the lavatory window. Miles took a deep breath and launched himself up on the sill and slipped inside. All was quiet as he came into the main hall.

Eerily quiet.

A match struck, and the room became visible in the faint light.

Miles turned to stone, fear barreling over him. His insides churned at even the thought of what hell he'd invited into his life.

Housemaster Warren stared at him from a seat in the corner. "Thought you'd go wander about, did you?" Though the man wasn't particularly daunting in stature, he was frightening, nonetheless. He had sallow cheeks and penetrating eyes that carried punishment enough when he shot them your way.

"I . . ."

"Don't you bother talking, young man." He fired a finger at Miles. "You'll never do this again, I can assure you that. Now get up to bed, and we'll deal with you in the morning."

"Sir."

Miles didn't hesitate and rushed up the stairs and removed his shoes before sneaking through the bunks to find his own. He slipped into bed, that rock-hard cot, and spent a long time staring at the ceiling.

It wasn't the repercussions coming to him that were on his mind.

No.

He thought of one thing and one thing only.

Lillian.

Whatever was coming tomorrow, he'd welcome it a thousand times over to share another conversation, to stare into those eyes, to taste, to *finally* taste what it was like to love.

Chapter 12

To Winchester, She Goes

Present Day

After guzzling down an Earl Grey tea, Charli takes a cab to Paddington, the Tube to Waterloo, then the South Western Railway to Winchester. Though it doesn't come without some stress and confusion, she is proud of her ability to navigate this foreign land. On the train, she listens to the Zac Brown Band and stares out the window, considering the idea that this is the land of her people.

Walking out of the station, she's almost hit by a motorcyclist, as she's still not used to people driving on the wrong side of the road. Well, they don't consider it the wrong side, do they? She carries her backpack with the photos, her notebook, and her iPhone and charger. There's also her trusty Kindle loaded with Louise Penny. She's determined to finish the entire Inspector Gamache series before the next one publishes.

According to the website, the college opens at nine. She'd found that they did indeed have an archivist, a woman by the name of Sarah. Charli emailed her but hasn't heard back. She figures the best thing to do is be there when they open and see what she can find out. Following the GPS on her phone, she hikes up a quiet residential road and bears left on High Street.

She finds herself at the top of a hill, walking down into the city. Unfurled before her is all of Winchester. Charli's awestruck by its beauty and instantly feels as if she's been pulled back in time. She removes her earbuds to take in every sound, the lyrical lilt of everyone's accents, the rush of energy, the laughter, the conversations.

It's a walk down Diagon Alley from the Harry Potter series, all these gorgeous and old brick and stucco buildings cascading down High Street, its cobblestones busy with a flurry of handsomely dressed pedestrians with their waxed jackets zipped high.

This must be what London had once looked like before the city became a cultural melting pot. This . . . this was England. Her grandfather generations back had once walked these streets, and now she was here, and she was going to figure out what made him tick. And what he'd passed on that was so painful that she'd feel the aftershock more than a century later.

At least, she hopes so.

It's either the buzz of the Earl Grey still lingering or the feeling of getting closer to the truth that sends her nearly skipping down High Street, brushing by stylish men and women starting their days. There are pubs everywhere, with names that catapult her back to a time when Oscar Wilde posted up to the bar for a pint of cask ale and fish and chips. And the boutiques. Had she not had a mission, she could spend all day looking at clothes.

But she does have a mission and follows the directions on her phone to the college. Swinging right through an alley that features a bakery wafting out yeasty goodness, she comes upon her first look at the cathedral. She'd read that a Norman bishop had spearheaded the start of construction in 1079, but it had taken five hundred years to complete. Nothing could have prepared her for this moment. Her eyes wander up and down. Never has she seen something so beautiful and daunting and commanding as this Gothic masterpiece. She recalls Ken Follett's *Pillars of the Earth*, the novel she recently gifted her father that details the build of a vast cathedral. Having read it twice, she feels privy to some of what it took to create such a jewel. How strange the timing is that she happened to give her father the book recently, but it must be a coincidence.

Passing by a host of tempting restaurants, she walks straight toward the cathedral and imagines a far-gone time, long before cars and electricity. She can barely stand not going inside, but she presses on, following the GPS and winding around the cathedral to the back side, where she finds a gate that leads her outside the city walls. There must be no more magical place on earth than Winchester, and she's there in March, before leaves have even sprouted on the trees, before the warmth has brought back the flowers and the green in the grass. She breathes in the air of her ancestors, wishing to tap into them.

Then she sees it . . . Winchester College. And her delirious rush of enthusiasm falls away, leaving her suddenly overwhelmed by her task. She's out of her element and also surely incapable of exacting any sort of real change in her family.

The college appears to be a fortress, raised outside the city walls, buildings of brick and stone and stucco that fit together like patchwork and evoke a scholastic dominance that grinds her to a stump of inferiority.

She walks down College Street toward what looks like the entrance, too distracted to do more than glance at the bookstore she's passing. Two buildings down, she notices a sign on the wall of a small house: Jane Austen spent her last days here.

She comes to a halt. "What?" She's read all her books, of course. Who hasn't? And she loves them so much. Well, she might prefer the darkness of the Brontë sisters, but for a woman like Charli who has spent a lifetime reading, it's dazzling to stumble upon such a magnificent treasure. And how did she not know this existed until now?

For a moment, she's not even thinking about Samuel or Winchester College or her struggling father back home. She's the nerd she's always been and nothing more. She never would have made it through life without books, and how many of her favorite authors had been inspired by this one woman, this otherworldly talent that lived here? *Right* here.

Charli spends ten minutes recalling Austen stories and peering through the windows and wondering what Jane was like, what her life was like. How was it that Jane could do such great things in her time, changing the world, and Charli couldn't even open a bookstore?

She eventually pulls herself away and walks with trepidation to the entrance of the college. A student in a gown passes by her as she enters, and Charli kicks her thoughts away. In their stead, she imagines Samuel wearing such a gown, walking these same steps. Then what? Why would he be alone on a boat to America at such a young age?

Through a door to the right comes a woman's bouncy voice. "Here for the tour?"

"No, I don't think so. I was . . . I was hoping to connect with Sarah."

"Do you have an appointment?"

Charli shakes her head. Of course she should have made an appointment. She could have called this morning and spoken to someone as opposed to waiting for an email reply.

"No."

The lady's earrings rattle as she speaks. "Let me ring her, but I suspect you might need to set a time with her. She's busy right now with the alumni weekend coming up."

Charli's heart sinks. "If you could tell her that I'm only in town a few hours and that I've traveled all the way from Boston and need her help."

"Yes, I will do that."

Charli can't stop pacing as she waits.

A long three minutes later, the tour guide returns and says, "I'm so sorry. She's unavailable right now, but if you email her, she'll get right back to you."

"I did already. Did she get it?"

Her earrings dance about like wind chimes. "I don't know, but she's on top of things."

Swallowing an urge to lunge past the woman and race up the stairs to find Sarah, she asks, "Would you let her know that it's an incredibly important and time-sensitive matter?"

"Yes, of course."

Charli adds defeatedly, "But I guess I would love to do a tour if that's available."

"We do have a couple of spots. Be here in twenty minutes."

Charli walks back by Jane Austen's place to the bookstore she'd passed. There was a time when she could wander a bookstore's aisles for hours, but now they feel like heavy reminders of her own inadequacy. Still, she's too curious not to walk inside. She browses the various books on Winchester and falls into a conversation with one of the staff.

"I didn't even know Jane Austen was from here," Charli says.

"Oh, yes," the man says jovially. "She lived next door and shopped here, found the last books she read in her life on these very shelves."

Charli looks around respectfully, imagining Jane thumbing through the books, seeking inspiration. It's nearly too much to imagine her third great-grandfather and Jane, who came before him, both sharing the same space.

"She's buried in the cathedral, you know. Certainly worth a visit just to be close to greatness."

"I will make that happen." She shakes her head in awe.

Charli joins the Winchester College tour at 10:00 a.m. A lively woman in a black gown speaks with dramatic flair. "Welcome to Winchester College. I'm delighted to share some of the secrets of this fine school. We'll start right here. To the left of the Porters' Lodge, this building that is now the library featured what every school should have: a brewery! Up until well into the twentieth century, the men of Winchester College drank beer all day. No water at all."

She sticks her pointer into the air. "Why, you might ask. Because there was no proper sewage, so the water was tainted and made you ill.

Gave you typhoid fever, among other things. Day and night the men—as the students are called here—drank their beer, even before class. Isn't that the way to do it?"

She points toward an archway. "Only the warden who lived up there got the good stuff, though. High-alcohol beer and the finest cuts of lamb. The men, meanwhile, ate rotten mutton and stale bread. Though they go on to become leaders of our country, they are raised with a firm hand." Charli can almost taste the bread as she imagines her ancestor becoming a man within these walls.

The guide takes them under the warden's quarters and into the courtyard. She talks about how only the scholars live on the grounds, that most men lived in boardinghouses outside the school walls.

"Up until only recently, after strong protest from the students and parents, there was no heat in the building. And that meant no hot water either. Can you imagine waking up with a cold dunk every morning? A firm hand, I tell you."

She beckons the crowd to follow. "*Manners makyth man.* That is the slogan for Winchester College, and that is what our man William of Wykeham created. He believed that it didn't matter where you came from, who your parents were. All that mattered is what you did with it . . . how you contributed to society."

"Sounds like a great man," one of the tourists said in a Scandinavian accent.

"Indeed he was."

Charli wonders what Samuel thought of such a saying, how *he* went on to contribute to society.

After the tour, she returns to High Street to find something to eat. She hasn't seen the river Itchen yet, so heads that way, farther down the hill. She almost stops for a poke bowl but doesn't like the look of the avocados. She continues on and comes across a charming pub called the Smythun. The pubs in England all have such an inviting look, mouthwatering food specials scrawled on chalkboards, polished windows with nothing but happiness and pints inside. It's barely twelve, and she already sees an army of mugs on the tables.

Inside, the beams supporting the ceiling are uneven and weathered, like old train tracks. An iron chandelier hangs from the center. The windowsills look like they've been painted over time and time again. A fire crackles by the bar, giving the air a smoky odor. On the mantel are burning candles and photos that could be hundreds of years old.

A plaque reads: FOUNDED IN 1524. How is that even possible? They were still building the cathedral! Impressive brass tap heads stand atop a wooden bar that is a piece of art itself. How many men and women had bellied up to it to find comfort on their worst days? Five hundred years' worth of broken hearts and abandoned dreams. High above, empty mugs hang in lines. She sees names on the bottom of each and knows these are the vessels of every local in town. The patrons wear shiny shoes and scarves and prim-and-proper dresses. They are joyous beings, all laughing and making Charli feel like she doesn't belong.

She takes a seat by the window at a two-top that looks out over the hustle of High Street. On the table is a bottle of Sarson's malt vinegar, Heinz ketchup, and a menu on a clipboard. She looks it over and settles on a super salad with buffaloumi, which she guesses is Halloumi cheese made from the milk of water buffalo.

Having been to more than one pub since she arrived, she knows to go up to the bar. She leaves her jacket and bag to claim the space and makes her way past a couple busting up over a joke. It's the first time she's noticed someone behind the bar.

Charli stares him down, thinking she does need to eat.

He finally turns.

Poof, her whole world goes numb for a moment. She doesn't know what is happening, but she likes it. He's handsome—no, gorgeous—and she's never seen anyone like him before and *why is she feeling this way?* and her brain is starting to come back to life when he steps forward.

"Hello."

"Hi."

His voice is calming and low, resonant. Her nerves settle, and she says again, looking up to find his eyes this time, "Hi."

The guy smirks, almost like he's used to being noticed and knows all too well how handsome he is. He wears a pressed white shirt with the sleeves rolled up. A tasteful watch with a caramel-colored band clings to his wrist. His forearms are muscular. His chiseled face reminds her of a man she saw in an advertisement in the airline magazine. He's a treasure, truly. Charli doesn't remember the last time she's studied a man, especially with him standing a few feet away, but she does so now. He has cobalt-blue eyes that are kind and gentle and yet strong. He wears a well-trimmed beard, light and blond. And his hair is cropped close to his head.

"Where ya coming from?" he asks. "You look like you're a long way from home." It's loud in there, and he leans down to hear her answer.

Charli is upping her game by the second, sitting up straight and suddenly wondering how she looks. She hates and loves that he's doing this to her, and she wants to scream, "How dare you?" Instead, she answers calmly, "I'm from Boston. In the US."

"Ah, thanks for the clarification." He gives a smile that could get a woman in trouble. "I thought it might be the Boston in Uruguay."

She rewards his humor with a sliver of a smile. He's a naughty one.

He scoots right along. "What'll ya have?"

"What's good?"

"I like the partridge. But you'll need a beer first."

"What do you recommend?"

"The Alfred's Saxon Bronze will do right by ya."

"Okay."

"And the partridge?"

"How about the super salad, with the buffaloumi?"

"Yeah, that'll do too."

"What's your name?"

"Charli," she blurts.

"Charli. I'm Noah. A pleasure to meet you."

He sticks out his hand. She takes it and feels the ceiling bend as a surge of energy rushes through her. It's so powerful that she has to step away. But she does so with all the cool in the world. Well, now that she'd already given up her name and blushed a bit. "I'm right over here." She points to the table.

"I think I'll find you."

His accent is to die for, she thinks, as she turns away and returns to her table. She looks out the window for a moment, pretending to enjoy the view, but in truth taking stock of what just happened. He blew her skirt up, and it won't come back down.

She slides her eyes back, and he's looking at her. Not even slyly either. He's pulling a pint and staring right at her. He offers her a smile, finishes with the beer, and walks over to a man with his legs crossed, reading the newspaper. She opens her bag and pretends she's doing something, but she's not doing anything at all. She feels almost postcoital. Good thing there's not a pack of cigarettes on the table.

Finally, she sits back and looks at her phone. She remembers why she's here and looks at her email. Sarah has written her back! Charli reads enthusiastically, glad for the distraction. Sarah says that she's got some space tomorrow, but today is stacked up.

Frustration sets in. "Oh, c'mon." She stabs out a quick response, then sits back and thinks that she should have checked out of her hotel so she could stay a night. She should have anticipated some issues. And depending on what she finds, she might need another day anyway. Good job, Charli, figuring that out after the fact.

Noah comes her way, sets down an amber beer in front of her, and takes a seat. He's as casual as could be, as if they're best friends. He's about to ask her out.

"What brings you to Winchester?"

She takes a sip of beer; it's a good one. "I'm researching my family."

"Ah, one of those."

"There's more than one of me?"

"I run into one of you about once a week. You're in town for a while then?"

"No, just the day. I had a meeting at Winchester College that was delayed until tomorrow, so I'm going back to London in a bit."

He sets his elbows on the table and rests his chin in his hand. "Not to intrude, but if you need to stay, we are an inn. Happen to have a room available upstairs."

A tingle runs from her feet to her spine. And elsewhere. Maybe he's just being nice, but she's no fool. If she stays the night in Winchester, let alone in this building, things will happen—*not* that she's opposed.

"Yeah," she says. "Probably not. But thanks, though."

He shrugs, like he doesn't care either way.

Which drives her *bonkers*. It's a card she should have played. She almost tells him he's a little brash for his own good but resists.

"Anyway," he says, "your food will be right up."

He stands and returns to the bar, and she picks up her phone to try to lose herself. But she can't stop thinking of him, lifting her eyes to him. He's magnetic, the way he's drawing her in. Does he take a seat with every woman who walks into the bar?

She drinks her beer and stares out the window, then at her phone. If he's not careful, she'll have to douse the fire by dumping the beer on her lap.

Sarah finally responds. I'm so sorry. I don't have a minute. Charli takes a handful of hair and pulls at it. She doesn't want to ride all the way back to London, but she hates the idea of wasting money on two places. And she doesn't even have a change of clothes.

He's back in front of her. Noah sets down a salad that looks too good to come from the kitchen of a pub, these gorgeous veggies and cuts of cheese lined with grill marks. She'd assumed she'd be living off boiled potatoes the entire trip but has been thankfully mistaken.

"Bon appétit," he says, and then walks his firm derriere back to the bar.

She returns to her dilemma regarding the college. The other option is what she should have done in the first place, asked Sarah over email if there was a Samuel Hall that attended. Or a Miles Hall. Maybe they could do it all without meeting. But Inspector Gamache wouldn't leave it to email. And neither will she.

Charli searches her phone with tingly fingers and discovers five stars and rave reviews for both the pub and inn. The rooms are nice. What's stopping her? If it came to it, would a fling in a foreign land really be so bad?

She looks up at Noah. He's chatting with another customer, laughing again. He's so friendly. Is he actually dangerous? He couldn't be that dangerous with a smile like that.

Her bowl is clean, and her beer is almost empty when he returns again. "How'd you like it?"

"I loved it. Great food."

"I know."

They share a look, and another electric current runs between them. They both give a slight laugh at the same time, showing that they're on the same page.

She could stay here, take him up on his offer. A round-trip train ticket wasn't cheap. And what could be the harm? He is cute. No matter what happens, she's gone tomorrow.

"About that room. Maybe I will take you up on it."

He smiles like he knew she'd come around. She hates to be a foregone conclusion and decides that she's going to make him work for it.

Chapter 13

A Handsome Distraction

"Hope this'll do," Noah says about thirty minutes later. She'd followed him around the bar and up two sets of green-carpeted stairs to one of the rooms.

"Yeah, I'll survive," she says sarcastically. It's more a suite than a room, with a cozy sitting area facing a fire, a beautiful four-poster bed decorated with elaborate pillows. Gold-and-purple wallpaper creates a sense of royalty in the room. A tall mirror wrapped in a gold frame hangs by one of the windows. She could squeeze her hotel room in London into this space three times over.

She hasn't asked the cost of the room, but it would be mortifying to ask now. "I have to say . . . the pubs here continue to surprise me."

"We've figured out a thing or two in the last thousand years. You'll find some earplugs by the bed, in case you go to sleep early. We have a few that like to get rowdy on the weekends downstairs."

Even then, Charli can hear the commotion of lunch down below. "I don't sleep that well anyway."

He checks the heat on the radiator. "You and me both, Charli. I'll need your passport and email address, but I'm not going to charge you for the night."

Her brow furrows. "No, you can't do that."

He steps closer to her, which forces her to lift her chin higher. "It's my inn. I can do whatever I please."

"No, really, I insist on paying." She still doesn't want to ask how much, but she certainly can't let him pay. Can she? And why is he even offering?

"Suit yourself. We'll get your card at breakfast." He turns away.

"I'm serious. I'm paying."

"Okay, then." He finds her eyes. "Anything else I can do for you? Need any recommendations for the day?"

"I'm going to poke around," she says, "see what I can figure out on my own."

"Great." He walks to the door, stops short. "You won't let me buy you a room. Why don't you come down about seven tonight and let me buy you dinner. I'll take good care of you. And you'll like the menu."

She appreciates his persistence and smiles into his charming eyes, wondering where the two of them are headed and perhaps even slightly eager to find out. "Yeah, okay. That's nice of you."

After he closes the door, Charli looks around. Kicks her shoes off and lies down on the bed for a while, considering how she can make the best of her time. Let's say her third great-grandfather Miles/Samuel did attend Winchester College, which is what she's betting on, then what else can she do while she's waiting on Sarah? She pulls out the picture of Miles and the girl and stares at it, as if there may be more clues. She could have been looking at the wrong set of archives. The LMA only included London.

She searches the internet and finds that the Hampshire Record Office is nearby. It closes at four, so she'd better get on her way. Out the door fifteen minutes later, she hikes up High Street, making a mental note of a couple of boutiques she'd like to swing by on the way back. After all, she doesn't have a change of clothes. As if she needs an excuse.

The Hampshire Record Office is in a building built with no regard for art. She's amazed at how much it reminds her of the place in London, though this one is much tinier. She finds people waiting in chairs like they're in an American DMV office. She takes a number and waits her turn.

A half hour later, she's called back and follows instructions to a door marked with the number seven.

"C'mon, yeah," a wily young man with a puffy nose says as he waves her in.

Charli takes a seat opposite him. "Hi there, how are you?" She's doing her best to be kind, the whole get-more-bees-with-honey thing.

"Lost on the lotto last night, but other than that, I'm surviving," he says. "And you? What can I help with?"

Charli starts by recounting her visit to the LMA and tells him about the tie. "I'm hoping that you might have something that can help. You don't have facial-recognition software, do you?"

The guy runs a finger under his puffy nose and then: "You're joking, right?"

Charli shows her teeth, thinking that she's starting to get British humor. "I was hoping that maybe you could search some names for me."

"Happy to." He tries Miles and Samuel Hall and even throws in Shamuel for good measure. "No one born between 1850 and 1880 with that name. Let's stretch it out a bit, see if this old computer can keep up." He types away. "There's a Samuel Hall born in 1817. Could that be him?"

"It would make him one of the oldest living men in history, as he died in 1925. That's the only other piece of information I have. But maybe he was named after this one. What information can you give me on that Samuel Hall?"

He types for a while, then pauses to scratch his nose, making it even redder. "He was never married and no children. There's not much. Let me print it out for you. I'm sorry I can't be of more help."

"Thanks for trying," she says, as the printer kicks to life.

⌒

By five she's returned to the pub with a bag of clothes in hand. The lunch rush is long gone, and only a few patrons linger, sucking back cask ales and chatting boisterously with friends. Noah isn't there, but a woman slightly younger than Charli is singing along to an Eric Clapton song.

When she sees Charli, she cracks a grin. "You must be Charli. I'm Victoria, Noah's cousin." Curly red hair cascades down her back. Her striking emerald eyes have a confident way about them, as if she's exactly where she's supposed to be standing behind that bar. Even grateful to be there.

"He told me to take good care of ya," she says.

"I'm sure he says that about everyone." And before Victoria can verify that notion, Charli says, "You have beautiful eyes."

Victoria turns up a smile. "Thank you very much. Can I do anything for you? Looks like you found the good shops."

Charli holds up her bag. "That I did. And no, no thank you. I'll be back down for dinner."

⁓

Noah seats her by the crackling fire at seven sharp. He furnishes her with a menu and a bottle of sparkling water and disappears back behind the bar. They're already crowded, the only empty tables featuring RESERVED signs on them. Candles are lit up everywhere, and she wonders how this place hasn't burned down in the hundreds of years it's been around. She might have expected some *Riverdance* music from the speakers, ignorant though that may be, but instead she hears the familiar growl of Dave Grohl from the Foo Fighters singing about the wheels coming down.

Victoria appears next to her with a pad in her hand, ready to take her order. Her red hair is now pulled back behind her.

Charli points to the specials on the board. "I'll try the hake."

Victoria scribbles. "And a beer?"

"I'm all beered out. Do you have wine?"

"I know what you mean. Can you imagine growing up in this place? Of course we have wine."

Charli settles on a Chablis, which she knows is French chardonnay, and sits back in her chair, pulls out her phone, and connects to the Wi-Fi. Viv has texted with enough emoji to knock down a cell tower, followed by: I made partner!!!!

Before the pity party that appears on the horizon comes to full form, she tells herself that she wants to be the kind of person who can be happy for people—especially her best friend. And she is, in a way. Viv has worked incredibly hard since law school, and she's such a great person and deserves this. And Charli wishes her own reaction could be one of pure elation. But it's not.

It's mixed with all kinds of raw ugliness inside. There she is back on the sidelines again, watching everyone else do their thing. She's not sure what's worse, the fact that she's not doing anything great in her life, or that she can't seem to find enough joy in her heart to feel happy for her best friend, who achieved her career dream. Yeah, the second part is worse, she decides. What kind of monster makes it about themselves in a moment like this?

But damn right, she's going to at least respond, and then she'll beat herself up the rest of the night for being a bad friend. Maybe her own arsenal of emoji will make up for it. She launches perhaps her strongest emoji campaign to date and follows it with: I'm so happy for you!!! Can't wait to celebrate as soon as I get home. Let's talk tomorrow.

She mindlessly thumbs through social media as she further mulls over how disappointed she is at how her life has turned out. Maybe there is some reason. Maybe she does have murderous blood running through her veins. Does that let her off the hook, though? She pauses to consider her life expectancy. She's twenty-nine now. If she's lucky, she'll die in her seventies. And she'll be pissed if she makes it to ninety. Either way, she's looking at fifty more years of letting people down, including herself.

As if she hasn't had enough, her Insta feed knocks her down even lower. According to this repugnant picture she's looking at, her friend Alice is pregnant with number three. Look at her disgusting smile while she pats her belly in this shot that her happy husband is photobombing. Alice doesn't have to work, because she married an entrepreneur who has started an app of some sort. She already has two boys that look like mini Greek gods. She has a nanny, so that she can continue to go to the gym every morning—or prenatal yoga or whatever—followed by spa day and mom day and whatever-the-fuck-else day. Alice can go walk into traffic. And Charli would happily tell her that to her face.

Then there's Melissa, doing her thing on TikTok. She started a business at the same time that Charli was going to open up the bookstore. But they chose two different paths. Melissa opened a food truck. A food truck! All of a sudden there was a second and third and a fourth truck in her TikTok videos, where she's showing off her generous chest while she pretends to cook all the food herself. Charli bets she can't even spell *spatula*. Now her feed is covered in inspirational quotes by Brené Brown and the *Atomic Habits* guy. Ugh.

The sad truth is Charli can't see herself ever having some sort of success story. Maybe that's why she pulled the plug on the bookstore after the debacle with the lease. Her failure was already written in stone.

Charli knocks back her first glass of wine. "May you all have minor traffic accidents."

Another glass of wine in, and she's successfully numbed some of the pain. When Noah appears with her food, she's ready to eat . . . and that means more than the food.

The fish is smothered in a lemon caper sauce. The veggies are a sautéed mix of spinach, green beans, and purple cabbage. The sliced and roasted potatoes look to die for. And the handsome bartender looks like he could go down easy.

Charli gestures toward her place with confident flirtatiousness. She feels at home in these early stages of a relationship, where she can turn it on for a while. Dare she even call it fun.

"Definitely not the boiled-potato-and-ham dinners I'd imagined on the plane," she says.

"You might be thinking of the Irish," he says. "We definitely know what we're doing here."

She lifts her eyes to him. "You do, don't you?"

"Anything else for ya?"

"This is great. Thank you."

He nods, almost says something, then walks away. She goes about enjoying her food.

Noah returns after her last bite, almost like he's been watching her. The rest of the tables are full, and he's been running around trying to keep everyone happy. His staff seems to know what they're doing, though. He sits across from her, like there's no one else in the whole place.

She finishes chewing a bite and dabs her mouth with her napkin. "Oh, just have a seat. Invite yourself right in."

"Well, it is my table, you know."

"Oh, you mean you own it?" Charli asks.

"I do. Well, partially. With the rest of my loony family."

Charli reaches for her chardonnay. "We have that in common."

"Don't we all?"

A pause fills the space, but it's nothing strange.

"Wanna go have a drink somewhere?" he asks.

"I don't know if I need another one right now. Two glasses of wine are about all I can handle." She hears a slight slur in her words.

He's not giving up, though. "Okay, then, wanna come watch me drink? Or we can take a walk."

Charli looks at a few of the tables, notices the servers moving quickly. "Aren't you busy?"

"It's my pub. I can leave if I want. Besides, Victoria can run this show by herself."

"Yeah, she seems like a good one to have around."

"You have no idea. What do you say?"

She pauses long enough to make him sweat. "Yeah, okay."

"Superb, let me make sure the place doesn't burn down while I'm gone."

After going back to work for a while, he reappears while pulling on a green waxed jacket. "You ready?"

"I didn't settle the bill . . ."

"I told you, it's on me."

Okay, nice guy or not, he's clearly making a move on her. Which doesn't *exactly* feel threatening? Charli thanks him and leaves a few pounds on the table for the server. He holds the door for her and follows her out into the night. Helps her with her jacket as a wispy cool breeze rushes by. It's quiet out, only a few people passing by, talking in whispers.

"Kind of empty for a Thursday night," she says.

"Aside from the pubs, it's a sleepy town. Early to bed, late to rise."

Charli senses he's about to ask about her, so she deploys a distraction. "What's Victoria's story? She seems like a good person."

"Oh, she's great. Kind of the light of our family. Well, despite some tough times growing up. Her mother, my aunt, died young, and her father turned to the bottle. My parents basically raised her. She's been working the bar almost as long as I."

"Pretty much a sister, then."

"That's right."

When Noah and Charli find their stride, he asks, "So what's the meeting at the college about?"

There he goes, starting to dig. "I'm trying to track down my third great-grandfather. I think he went there." For one wee second—they say *wee* in England, right?—she almost tells him more but decides she doesn't want him to think she's a kook. In fact, she wants to glaze right over this topic.

"Ah, gotcha." She sees something pass over him, a thought that pulls him away from the present. He recovers quickly. "You seem a little young to be into genealogy."

"You're into pigeonholing me, aren't you?"

"I love this about American women. You don't hold back, do you?"

"You're aware that you responded with yet another stereotyping statement?"

He cracks a smile that is so genuine that she knows he's doing his best to flirt with her. "For a pretty girl, you sure are sharp."

She lets her jaw drop dramatically. "Do you want to be smacked on the left or right side?"

He touches his left cheek. "Please forgive me. I'm being silly."

She lets him off the hook. For a moment. "So how many young American women researching their families have you bought dinner for this week?"

"I've not bought dinner for a woman this year."

It's the first time she sees him as truly human and wonders if he's more damaged than she originally thought. Taking the upper hand, she hits him with a few surface questions. He's nice to talk to. Sweet without being boring, and smart without rubbing it in her face. He mentions that he lived in the US for a while, and she pushes for more. This is the part she's good at, those first few dates when she's getting to know someone. She enjoys the back-and-forth.

"I attended Pepperdine, then moved to San Jose to work in tech in the Silicon Valley world."

And the layers peel back . . . "Oh, look at you. What did you do?"

"I worked for Oracle first and then joined a start-up called KComm that was helping small-time investors develop apps. I was a liaison between the coders and the salespeople, spending a good bit of time on the road, trying to get the company off the ground. I met a girl and almost got married. But now I'm back."

"What happened?" she asks, feeling more confident by the minute. He sighs as if the answer will require more than he has in him. But he tries. "My family has owned this place since the first beer was poured in the fifteen hundreds. You might have seen the plaque on the wall. I grew up there, worked there long before it was legal. It's all I knew, and I wanted something else. Built a somewhat American life in California, got hypnotized into buying an engagement ring, and then my father got sick."

"I'm sorry," Charli says, feeling like a monumental jerk. "Is he . . . ?"

"Oh, he's still kicking. I'm not sure the whole Russian army could take him down."

"Is that saying a lot?"

They share a grin that can only exist between allies. "Anyway, he had an ugly fight with cancer, though. My family has this amazing way of throwing a leash around me and keeping me close. But that's okay. I'm accepting my place here. I'm needed, and that's always a good thing."

She goes thousands of miles away for a moment, thinking about her own father, hoping that he's hanging on. And she's trying not to even go to the fact that she'd used a fake cancer excuse to get here . . . what an awful thing to do.

"What happened to the girl?" Charli asks, returning to the moment.

Noah swallows, and she can see some past pain flare up in his eyes. "Turns out she was sleeping with my business partner—and friend."

How nice it is to have someone to tell war stories with. "That's awful. How'd you find out?"

"They were perfectly fine not telling me. I suppose we might have gone on with the wedding had my dad not gotten sick. But when I asked her if she'd move to Winchester with me so I could help him with the pub, she broke off the engagement. A few days later, after she'd moved out, I found a poem he'd written her. A very shitty poem. I confronted them and got out the truth. Wasn't too hard to go back home after that."

"I'm sorry," she says. But what she wants to say is, *This is* exactly *why you have to be careful.*

"I'm just glad we didn't get married and have kids before I figured it all out. Anyway, enough of that. Let's pop in here."

He opens the door of a seafood restaurant and guides her in. Chefs in white work behind the bar in an open kitchen. He knows everyone and introduces Charli before they finally take a seat near the window. "You sure you don't want a drink?"

"Maybe in a little while."

They fall into easy conversation. She likes talking to him. But it doesn't take him long to start prying into her life, so she raises the deflector shields.

"Are you on vacation from work? How long are you here?"

She answers the easier question first. "Fly back Sunday." A wave of shame hits her as she says, "I edit advisory reports . . . that are not interesting."

"Ah."

"Yeah, that's enough of that. It's hopefully a bridge to something else. There was a time when I was going to open a bookstore, but it fell through in October."

He puts his focus on her, leaning in. "What happened?"

Part of her wants to share, as she hasn't talked with anyone about it in a while—maybe this year. "My landlord got into some legal trouble, and I lost the lease. I was devastated and pulled the brakes on the whole thing before we even opened the doors. The writing was on the wall, you know. If it wasn't the lease, it was going to be something else."

"That could have been the right call, you never know. Maybe it wasn't the right time; or perhaps you're meant to be doing something else."

"Yeah, I suppose."

"What did you do with all the books?" he asks. "Had you already ordered them?" He comes off as truly curious, and it's certainly cathartic to talk about, especially with a stranger.

"The shelves were about half-full. Thankfully I was able to return some for a refund. Others I sold and gave away to charity. There are stacks in my apartment. I play a little game sometimes. I grab one and try to find the perfect person to give it to on the street." A twinge of joy rises in her, thinking about some of the people she has surprised.

He gives her a look of far too much admiration. "That's kind of . . . incredible."

She shrugs and looks away.

He draws her back in. "You like books then? I can't ever find the time."

"It's all about priorities," she says. "I read two or three a week."

"Two or three a week?" he says incredulously. "That's impressive."

"It's not something I have to work at. It's just . . . what I love to do."

He stares into and through her eyes as if they are windows. "I can only imagine the places you've gone in your imagination. I suspect that much reading teaches you a lot about the world."

He's saying the right things, and she's pretty sure it's not an act. "I think it's nice to dive into other people's worlds, see how they think. If anything, I'm maybe more open-minded than some."

While pondering her response, he has a lightness about him, as if quenching his curiosities couldn't be more satisfying. "If you're not careful, you're going to reignite my love of reading. What would you put in my hands if I was a stranger on the street?"

Her eyes go wide. "Oh . . . I . . . you have to let me think on that one."

He crosses his arms. "I'll be right here."

"Oh, now?"

"Yes, now. Put a book in my hands."

"Fiction or non?"

"Fiction."

She closes her eyes and wanders along the shelves that occupy her mind. Alice Hoffman comes up, but she shakes the idea away. This is a guy who doesn't read anymore. He needs something easy, a book that appeals to males, probably a male author. And a story that will carry him away as if he's watching a movie.

Titles flash by in her mind. She could easily suggest some espionage—a Daniel Silva or John le Carré. But no, they're not quite right.

This is fun, she thinks, almost forgetting that Noah is on the other side of the table, waiting. He'd love *Shantaram*, but it might be too daunting of a tome for his first book in a while. Same with *Kane and Abel*, another that she'd recommended dozens of times.

"Okay, I have questions," she says. "Do you need guns and car chases? Are you a sci-fi kind of person? Horror? Mystery? And if mystery, noir or cozy?"

"I'm open. I will read whatever you suggest."

She stares at his face and then around his head, as if the answer is in his aura. It's like she's back in one of the bookstores where she worked, and just like back then, she wants to get it right. There's a certain pride when a returning customer tells you that your pick was spot on.

"Okay," she says. "I got it. Chris Whitaker, *We Begin at the End*, about a guy who returns home after decades in prison. It's fast moving, yet thought provoking. What was the girl's name, the outlaw? Oh, Duchess Day Radley." Charli beams as she recalls the character. "She's one of the most interesting characters created in the last ten years."

He's smiling, but she can tell that it's not because she's picked the perfect book for him. It's likely because he's just seen who she really is. Now that she's back in the real world, it's embarrassing.

"Sorry, I get carried away."

"Don't you dare be sorry."

Charli thinks she feels the temperature rise.

After a long staredown, he asks, "What's next for you then, Charli? Genealogy?"

She takes a moment to recalibrate. "Uh, no. I'm not showing much promise in that department. The bookstore thing killed me. I'm afraid to take another chance." She never shares this much information, but the fact that he's history starting tomorrow makes him extremely safe territory.

"You can always try again," he says.

"Yeah, I suppose. I don't know."

"You know what my father used to say? Failure is a step in the right direction."

Charli laughs out loud. So much so that it feels like the entire restaurant turns to them. "If he's right about that, I'm a whole lot of steps into the right direction."

When their smiles tame down, he says, "I, for one, can't wait to hear what you do next. I'm expecting big things."

She's pretty sure that's the nicest thing anyone has ever said to her, and every bit of her below the table squirms.

"What was the name of your bookstore going to be?" he asks, showing incredible persistence.

What the hell, she might as well tell him. "The Iambic Inkpot . . . is what it was supposed to be."

He repeats her words. "Are you serious?"

"That's what I wanted to call it, but I was outvoted by my family and friends."

"What in the world does it mean?"

"I'm a big Shakespeare fan, and he wrote in iambic pentameter. You have the unstressed beat followed by a stressed beat, which mimics the human heartbeat. To be, or not, to be." She makes her best heartbeat sound. "*Duh dum, duh dum.* Of course, there are variations, and you can break the rules once you have mastered them. It has this beautiful cadence to it."

He's looking at her, and she doesn't know what he's thinking, but this feels like it's happening too fast, even if their time together has a short expiration date.

He finally says, "What'd you end up naming it?"

"The Merchant of Boston."

"Ah, after *The Merchant of Venice.*"

"And I thought you were just another pretty face."

His cheeks swell with . . . what is it? Joy? Is he really having that much fun? She's pretty good at first dates, but he has a way of making her feel even more confident than usual. He's definitely not the only one having fun.

He's first to say something. "You're amazing. You know that, right?"

"Ehhhh. You're catching me on a good day." Her hands become clammy.

He's not finished. "You're amazing and you don't even know it. How endearing."

"Anyway, that's a pretty tall cathedral over there."

He gives a light chuckle. "All right, all right. I get it. So, first time to England?"

"You've overcorrected, Noah. We don't need to keep it all surfacy. But I don't do the mushy stuff either. Can we meet in the middle?"

He nods and grins as if he's accepting the challenge. "Tell me about your favorite book."

"We don't have to keep talking books. But I will."

"Then let me have it, your favorite of all time."

She feels like someone has just asked her to sprout wings and fly. "No one can have a favorite book. I don't believe in that."

His head kicks back. "Is it something you have to believe in?"

Just like that, they slip into the pocket of what Charli finds to be more truly enjoyable conversation. They talk a long time, barely pausing to take a breath. It's as if they've both been craving to find someone to talk to, and now that they have, there's no stopping them.

They talk and laugh for two more hours, all the way until they're the last people in the place. Walking back, she asks, "Where do you live, by the way? Not above the pub."

He shakes his head. "No, I don't think I could do that. I'm down by the river. Charli, you should hang around after your meeting tomorrow. Let me show you the city, help you with your research. I'll take the day off."

She waves a hand through the air. "That's nice of you, but I have to get back."

He nods kindly. Knows exactly when to push, when to let go.

"You're something, Charli. Offer stands if you change your mind."

When they get back to the pub, she's expecting a kiss . . . or something. This kind of sexual tension doesn't happen every day.

"I enjoyed it, Noah. Definitely better than watching the BBC back in my room."

"Yeah, I hope so."

Wait, isn't he going to make a move? He looks like he's holding back. Should she do something? Inviting him up seems like a bad idea, considering it's his pub. And she can't bear the idea that he'd reject her. No, if he wants her, he needs to be the one to make the move.

The three feet between them seems to grow as they stare at each other. What is going on behind those eyes? Is he really done? Had she read way more into this than she thought?

"Anyway," he says. "I'll see you for breakfast, yeah?"

"Yeah, I think . . ." Her forehead crinkles. "I think so." He's going to walk away? So much for her little foreign fling.

He raises a hand in the air and gives a quick wave. "G'night."

She watches him turn and wants to throw her purse at him. How dare he? Is he playing her? Is he hoping she'll run after him? Well, he's got another think coming.

Charli turns and heads upstairs, mesmerized that she can't even land a one-night stand. Probably because she got all squirrely when he was saying nice things. Why does she have to do that?

Once she's in her pajamas, she sits on the couch and turns on the fire. As it comes to life, she calls her father. "Hey, Daddy, just checking in."

"So you're in Winchester now. I got your message."

"Yeah, what a wild couple of days." She tells him about discovering the tie and how Sarah put off the meeting. "We'll see what happens tomorrow. At this point, I want to find his real name and who his parents might have been."

"Sounds like you're getting closer."

"We'll see." As she's speaking to him, she finds it once again ridiculous to think that what she's doing could have any impact on him whatsoever. How could she be so gullible?

"So how about you?" she asks. "How are things?"

"Oh, you know. Staying busy."

He can't even lie. That's how badly he's doing. A pang of sadness shows itself in her gut.

"Can I ask you something?" she says, unable to keep avoiding the question.

"Yeah, anything."

"Don't take this the wrong way, but have you . . . you haven't considered hurting yourself, have you?" As the words fall from her mouth, she can't believe she's asking them. She can't believe it's come to this, or that her sadness now fills every cell in her body as she waits for an answer.

"Oh, c'mon, Charli. You don't need to worry about me."

"You didn't answer the question."

He pauses long enough for her to get her answer. Her heart rate slows to a crawl.

"I'm working on things, okay?" he says. "I know I've been a little down."

"Hold on, Daddy. What I'm doing could be good for us all, and even if not, I'll be back soon, and we'll figure it out."

Another long pause. What's he doing? "Daddy?"

"Yeah, I'm here."

Yeah, but for how long?

"Daddy, just . . ." She doesn't know what to say. "We'll figure this out."

"Will you stop?" he asks with a dose of anger.

The last thing she wants to do is make it worse, so she nods to herself and whispers, "Sorry."

"Thank you for caring, honey. We all have our demons, don't we?"

"I can't wait to see you Sunday night. Let's go out to dinner, maybe Pammy's."

"Yeah, that sounds nice. But you need to go to bed. Big day tomorrow. Will you keep me updated?"

"You know I will."

Even imagining losing him makes her chest cave in. He might not have always been there for her when she was young, but he's tried. And she can't stomach the idea of a world without him in it.

Chapter 14

REPERCUSSIONS

Winchester, England
October 29, 1880

Miles was up most of the night, considering his plight. The dread of being caned was enough to stop his heart. How had he not taken the threat more seriously as he'd casually slipped out the window for his adventures? Even worse was the idea that he might not be able to make a life for himself without a degree at Oxford, the inheritance due to him, and the surname that he was born into. But such a life spared no room for a lower-class woman like Lillian. Soon he would have to choose, and both options promised dire consequences.

He woke on his hard wooden bed to the sound of the prefect striking a pan while marching up and down like the general of this army of young souls. No older than Miles, his name was Nicholas, and he'd been deemed a prefect for his exemplary behavior and excellent marks in the classroom. He had certain privileges, such as enjoying finer cuts of lamb on the weekends, but it came with certain responsibilities, too, including the wake-up call and carrying out much of the disciplinary action.

The men had twenty minutes to shave and shower in the arctic water before a quick breakfast of bread, cheese, and beer. The grub house on the ground floor was large enough for fifty men and the staff. The small windows offered a view onto Kingsgate, where early risers rushed toward the city walls. On one end of the rectangular room hung a portrait of the headmaster, his eyes always watching. A short bundle of sticks burning in the fireplace took on the daunting task of warming the air. A pot of water on the way to boil hung in the center. The chapel bells rang in the distance.

Miles sat at one of the long tables and reached for a piece of bread from the basket. He could take only a small bite, as his stomach was in knots. He could not find the courage to look over on the wall to the cane that would soon become the instrument of his discipline. The one thing he knew, though, was the torture coming would not elicit regret for visiting Lillian. She had settled in his heart and was giving him strength even now.

The men were all chatty, including Miles's friend Quimby, who was unaware of Miles's predicament. Quimby was making chitchat about a man who'd supposedly wet his bed when Housemaster Warren entered the grub house, the wrinkles that etched his face showing a man who did not tolerate rule breakers.

He cleared his throat, and it was the equivalent of firing a rifle as the chatter in the room came to an abrupt stop.

"You men are leaders," he said, his voice an echo, "and you are tasked with the responsibility of achieving greatness." His hand rose in a flash and came down even faster at the end of one of the tables. The plates all rose in unison and then came crashing down in a clatter of fury. If there was any noise left in the grub house, his act decapitated it.

"I will not tolerate insubordination," he said through gritted teeth, and Miles swallowed back fear. "The rules of Winchester College and of this boardinghouse exist for a reason. And if one of you chooses to break these rules, you will be punished severely."

Warren shot his angry eyes at Miles. "Mr. Pemberton chose to sneak out of the house late last night for a wandering. You shall stand before me now."

Miles's legs felt watery and kept him from standing.

Warren hammered the table again with so much force that several of the beers nearby spilled. "Dammit, boy, stand before me!"

Miles scurried away from the table and rushed toward Housemaster Warren. No room in all of England could have been more silent.

Warren called out for the prefect. "Nicholas, take the cane off the wall and deal this man his blows."

As if commanded, all eyes snapped toward the infamous cane hanging by the fireplace. Like Housemaster Warren, it wasn't exactly a threatening sight without context. It was a bamboo cane with a leather handle at the end. Its flexibility allowed it to cause greater damage than a rigid cane when brought down on an unruly student. He could still hear the screams of the boy who had been caned the previous year.

Housemaster Warren returned his attention to Miles and told him to remove his shirt. Miles did what he was told, feeling the sting of the cold air pass over his flesh. Nicholas came over with the cane held out in front of him like a sword, his eager desire to use it clear on his face.

Warren dragged a chair from the closest table to a clearing and told Miles to place his hands on the back of it. As Miles did so, doing everything he could to keep from shaking, Warren instructed Nicholas. "Ten strokes. And let this be the last lesson I must teach this year." He gazed upon the room of men who were not yet men at all.

Miles set his eyes on the wall, where the portrait of the headmaster stared him down. He made sure he wasn't biting his tongue, and then he closed his eyes and steadied himself for the first stroke.

When it came, the bite stung hard, shooting fire across his body. But Miles would not fall and not gasp either. He refused to be beaten down. No matter what happened in this room today, his father had dealt him far worse, and Miles had learned to find pride in how he handled his pain.

The second swing came, the cane sounding like a whip making contact, and he lost his breath but bit down hard so as to not let out a cry. Pain shot up his back. His cheeks quivered as a tear escaped.

The prefect hit him again, calling out, "Three!"

Miles squeezed his face tight, doing everything he could not to scream. A warm liquid that he knew was blood seeped down his back. He recalled the reason for his beating, and he let himself escape to the memory of the previous night. As if he had wings and was floating above High Street, he could see himself looking at her through the window.

Lillian.

Her eyes . . .

"Four!" *Whack.*

She could take the pain away from any man, and that was what she'd done.

"Five!" *Whack.* Blood. Tears. His legs nearly buckling.

Miles wished himself to London, his bride sitting in the front row, enjoying his performance of a new Shakespeare production. The audience cheers this newfound English treasure known as Miles Pemberton.

"Six!" *Whack.*

By the tenth stroke, Miles could barely stand, and his back was bloody, his face smeared with tears. One more strike, and he surely would have fallen to the hard floor.

And yet he'd found strength through Lillian, and he knew now what had been building since the moment he'd first come upon her on the bridge.

He would do anything to have her in his life.

Miles thought it amazing that his father had no time for his son unless something went wrong. Eyeing the carriage from the boardinghouse window, Miles knew his father had been summoned, and a sharp blade of fear cut through him. Hadn't he suffered enough? He could barely walk, let alone sit, from the caning. It hadn't helped that rumors of his punishment had spread quickly, and every man had gawked at him all day, whispering about what he'd done to earn a beating.

Dressed sharply in all black, his father traipsed down the steps of the carriage and motioned for Miles to walk his way. James stood there in his suit and hat and polished shoes with fury on his face. Their coachman sat with his eyes fixed on the horses. He knew as well as every other servant at Elmhurst that one was better off avoiding contact with Lord James Pemberton when he was on the rampage.

"Get in," James snapped.

Miles did so, sitting across from his father, still feeling the searing leftovers from his earlier beating. He kept his eyes on his shoes, terrified of what was to come but determined to salvage his dignity and stay strong.

"Carry on," James ordered to the coachman.

They moved along College Street at a slow, bouncy pace. His father's breath was an angry steam engine climbing a grade. They passed through town and then by the sports fields before breaking into open country.

Ten minutes later, his father thumped on the ceiling of the carriage. "That's enough."

The carriage stopped, and Miles waited for a fist to come his way.

His father's words came out in a growl. "You have one task in your life, and that is to uphold your duties as a man of this college, as a man of this family, and as a man of England. Look at me, dammit."

Miles looked up to see his father's jaws trembling as he spoke. The man didn't realize that Miles carried his own anger inside.

"What if I have no interest in upholding my duties?" Miles asked, saying it while well aware of the potential consequences.

James paused, bit down on his own teeth, as if holding himself back. "You have no choice. You were born into this family, and you will *not* embarrass us."

Miles held strong. "I have no interest in being your subject, a doll that you can throw around and tell what to do." He knew what was coming. "I don't care about your . . ."

His father's hand came up so fast that Miles barely had time to blink before he was backhanded so hard that he suddenly tasted the iron of his own blood. He reached for the pain, feeling his jaw shaken by the blow.

"Whether you like it or not, you are my son. You are my firstborn son. And you will fall in line. Your childish desires have no place here."

"And that is the problem!" Miles spat back to him. "My desires are far from childish, and I have every right to entertain them."

James was clearly holding back his attack. "You were born into a privilege that you do not deserve, but there's nothing I can do about it. Here your younger brother is doing exactly as he should. *He* is the example you should follow."

"He's a bloody fool," Miles said. "Your soldier and nothing else."

Another swing from his father, a backhand that drew more blood and humiliation and fear. But he could not falter. "I will not let you beat the life out of me," he said, thinking of Lillian, hoping desperately that he had the resolve to withstand his father's wrath.

With an eye on his father's rising fist, he said, "I am my own man, and I will do what I choose with my life. I will marry whom I choose." Miles heard the lack of strength in his tone as his bladder gave way. Urine dripped down his legs, taking all the man out of him, making him feel once again like the prisoner he'd been all his life.

Miles's defiance shook loose something dangerous in James, and he lunged at his son. Miles held up his arms and tried to protect himself, but he was no match for the fury of James Pemberton. The man screamed obscenities as spit flew from his mouth, and he proceeded to grab Miles by the collar and swing at the side of his head until Miles nearly lost consciousness.

"Goddammit!" James yelled as he finally backed away from his son and sat down on the bench. "You force me to punish you!" He panted in exhaustion.

Miles fought hard to keep his head up. Anger soared through him, but it wasn't only anger directed at his father. He was perhaps even more angry at himself, as all that he'd told himself about no longer taking these beatings, taking this abuse, had fallen to ashes under attack.

Chapter 15

CIRCUMSTANCES CHANGE

Present Day

On the plate in front of her is the makings of a semitraditional English breakfast: roasted tomatoes and potatoes, baked beans, two poached eggs, and vegan sausage. And bread and butter and jam, which she knows is homemade. Everything they do at the Smythun is so well thought out and particular. Even the tea is the best she's ever had. After giving her best attempt, she'll spread the rest out on the plate to make it look like she did better, as she doesn't want to hurt his feelings.

Then again, he left her and her libido on the plate last night by not making a move. Maybe she should make a point by showing her own lack of appetite. If he's not going to eat her American dessert, she'll snub his English breakfast. She rolls her eyes at herself. Thank God no one can read her thoughts.

Checking her email, she finds one from Sarah at Winchester College.

> I'm so sorry, but I've got to push the meeting to Monday if you can. I've taken ill and won't be coming in today. Might we connect Monday?

Charli drops her head. "What the hell," she mutters. She sighs and looks around, unsure what to do. Marvin would be furious if she asks for another day.

Noah seems to pick up on her mood when he returns to the table. Only one other table is taken, a German couple studying a map.

"You don't like my breakfast?" he asks.

"Oh, no, it's not that. It's just . . . I'm so full from last night."

He nods. "Everything else okay? You seem a little less charged than earlier."

She looks up into his cobalt eyes, finds so much comfort there. "Ugh, I got an email from Sarah at the college. She's sick and can't meet me till Monday."

"Monday? Great, you'll stay the weekend?" He lets out a smile that makes her feel so wanted.

"No," Charli says. "I can't stay the weekend. I have a flight home Sunday. And work on Monday."

Noah leans in so close she can smell the menthol of his aftershave. He's still wearing a light beard, but he cleaned it up this morning. "Guess you'll have to change it," he says. "And push off work for another couple of days." He gestures toward the ceiling to the room above. "You can keep your room."

She considers the offer. Of course she'd be willing to spend the extra money and/or be fired if what she's doing here can save her father. "But all my stuff is back in my hotel in London."

"Then we'll go get it."

What is it with this guy? He doesn't even try to kiss her, but he wants to ride back to London with her? "You have an answer for everything, don't you?"

He raises his hands. "Look, Charli. I'm not pushing you. Do what you want. But if you're here to find more out about your family, I'm happy to help. If not, go do your thing."

"It's not that easy," she says. "I've already maxed out my vacation days."

"Call in sick, then." Brazen as ever, he slides into the chair next to her and scooches it up toward her. He reaches for her hand under the table; she doesn't pull away.

"Stay through the weekend," he says. "I'll help you find your grandfather. We'll eat some good food. Do some walking."

She can't imagine calling Marvin and asking for even two more days off. Then again, why not? She can't leave now. Her father is far more important than her waste of a job, and she's *this* close. Even if it's the most far-fetched and desperate attempt ever made to help someone, she can't stop now. Would a weekend with Noah be the worst thing in the world? How nice it would be to let go and have a no-strings-attached fling. What else is she going to do?

"I can see your pretty little brown eyes wandering about," he says, "your mind churning over the idea. C'mon, Charli." He's fiddling with her hand, running his thumb over her skin.

She's unable to pull away from his gaze. He's got her right where he wants her.

He leans even closer. "Shall I beg?"

She pulls her hand away and falls back in her chair. "Oh, jeez, Noah. We met yesterday. I could be a serial killer, for all you know."

He doesn't laugh at her stupid joke. "I'm willing to take the chance, Charli. I don't understand it, but it feels like . . . I don't know, like our paths crossed for a reason. What is the harm in spending some time together?"

Now hold on, she thinks. *Let's not start getting cosmic again.*

"Don't you feel it?" he asks.

"Again . . . we met yesterday."

He sits back. "Okay, sorry. I get a little excited sometimes. All I'm saying is that if you walk out that door with your bag this morning, I think we'll both wonder why we couldn't have given each other the gift of a few days. That's it. A weekend." He smacks his hands together. "Then you can be done with me. Chew me up and spit me out."

She swallows, tasting the sweetness of the idea. Having booked a flight that allowed free changes makes this decision so much easier.

"Forget all that anyway," he says, going in for the kill. "Let me show you around Winchester. If you tell me a little bit more about your search, maybe I can help. I happen to know people."

She wonders if he's playing her. Either way, she could use some help.

"What do you say? And if it turns out that you're a serial killer, I'll show you where I'd bury me."

It's her turn not to laugh.

He takes her hand again. "Don't make me kidnap you."

"That's not funny."

"Wait, you can make serial killer jokes, but I can't be a kidnapper?"

"Fine," she says.

"Fine, what? I can be a kidnapper or you'll stay? If it's the kidnapping, I promise I'll only tie your hands loosely." Noah wiggles an eyebrow in jest.

She smiles at his ridiculous humor, and in that instant, they both know . . .

She's staying.

"Let me call my boss and the hotel. I'll see if they can check me out and store my bags. I left it open ended. Then I'll change my flight, and we'll go from there."

"That wasn't so hard, was it?"

She sneers at him, albeit playfully. "I'll probably be fired."

"You're better than that job anyway. Let's meet outside in an hour, and you can tell me what you're working on regarding your family."

Upstairs, she successfully extends her flight to Tuesday and convinces the hotel to pack up her things and check her out. The call to Marvin can wait, as it's too early back in the States.

Right on time, she finds Noah standing in a sunny spot on the cobblestone street. He's holding two cups of coffee. "Care for one?"

She takes it and thanks him, shoving away what his chivalry does to her. "Okay, so are you ready to hear about my family?"

"Absolutely. Let's go take a seat."

They find an open bench on the sidewalk. "Okay, Charli Thurman, tell me all about why you're here. Let's see if we can crack the code."

She's decided that she doesn't need to share everything with him, especially the constellation. Instead, she gives him only what he needs to know to help her. As she takes the two photos from her purse, she says, "I've successfully populated most of my family tree going back to the sixteen hundreds, save one branch, and that's this man." She shows him the picture of her third great-grandfather when he was older, the one with his wife, Margaret. "We, meaning his family, know him to be Samuel Hall. He had kids who had kids, who eventually led to my mother."

Charli explains more, including the clue of the tie, and then hands him the second photo. "This is him when he was younger. My guess is that it was taken before he came to the US."

"Oh, I'd say so. I think I know the spot."

Her head perks up. "Really?"

"Possibly. We can head over that way."

"Um, yes, please." She's not sure what she's going to do when she gets there, but the prospect of finding the actual setting of the photo seems like a massive break. "If you flip it over, that's the only other clue."

"For Miles," he says.

"So maybe he's Miles, maybe he's Samuel. That's what I'm hoping the college can help with."

Noah stands and drops his coffee cup into the recycling can. "Let's head that way, and we'll go from there. First, though, you still haven't been inside the cathedral, right?"

"No, but I'm not sure what that has to do with finding my ancestor."

He makes a face that says, *How could you ask that question?* "You can't come to Winchester without going inside the cathedral. Let's pop in; then we'll continue past the college to the river."

Charli starts to protest, but he's already leaving. She pours out the rest of her coffee and recycles her cup, then follows him down the street. They pass through a gate that opens up into the vast lawn that surrounds the cathedral, and she looks up in awe. It's a marvel, a stone cacophony of arches and towers that radiate with power. Perhaps her search can wait a moment.

"You know that show *The Crown*?" Noah asks. "They were filming up until yesterday. It was a bit mad."

Noah guides her through the entrance and says hello to his friend working the front desk. A minute later they are standing over Jane Austen's bones. Imagining the literary power that must fill the entire city, she reads the epitaph.

"I can't believe I'm this close to greatness."

Noah grins. "Well, they say she might have been scooted over a little bit to here. When they ran heating, a guy had to go through the floors."

She cocks an eyebrow.

"That's part of the insider's tour."

After he shows her the rest of the cathedral, surprising her with his historical knowledge, they walk through the West Gate, and he points out Cannon Street, which used to be the red-light district.

"So close to the college?" Charli asks.

"It was a different time, wasn't it? I'm sure the students were forbidden to even think of passing through there."

Noah soon leads them away from town, and they follow a dirt path until the river Itchen comes into view. Planks are set out over the muddy patches to help people cross over them. Swans float by. Locals in their waxed jackets and muck boots walk their spaniels and Labradors. In the distance behind a weary fence, a flock of sheep grazes. Beyond the river and open field, the terrain rises up into a series of green hills topped with clusters of trees.

Charli pulls out the photo with a gasp. "You're right. It has to be somewhere over here."

He leans in to look with her. "I don't recognize the tree. But it could have been chopped down. Either way, you at least know now that you're in the right spot. These two lovebirds were right around here one hundred and fifty years ago. How about that?"

She's seeing the picture in a whole new light now. Her grandfather must have been experiencing his first taste of love. She can nearly feel it. "How sad," she says. "Something must have happened between them. I wonder if they were still together when he left for the States. It must have hurt so badly. But why did he leave? His parents weren't even with him. I wonder if he was running away."

"I suppose it's possible," Noah says. "You know, the students at the college are typically born of a high class, unless they're on scholarship. You must come from strong stock."

She turns to him. "It's been watered down through the years."

"I don't believe that for a second."

Charli tries to find the exact spot of the photo by examining the trees. "It's not quite right. Maybe around the bend."

They look together to where the river winds into the forest. Some wire fencing stops them from going much farther. "Can't go that way, but let's keep following the path. The river winds back around. Perhaps we'll find something there."

Charli takes another look and slips the photos back into her purse.

Moving along again, Noah glances at her. "You know John Keats, right? The poet."

"Sure."

"He used to make this walk every day. Wrote one of his most famous poems here, 'To Autumn.' 'Season of mists and mellow fruitfulness, close bosom-friend of the maturing sun; conspiring with him how to load and bless with fruits the vines that round the thatch-eves run . . .'" He stops. "Something like that."

Charli bites her bottom lip. "Did you just quote Keats to me as we walk through the Winchester countryside?"

"What's wrong with that?"

"You're good," she says. "You realize it's in iambic pentameter, don't you?"

"I wish I could say I did."

Duh dum, duh dum goes her heart, and it scares her some. No, it scares her a lot. The *duh dum* turns to air-raid sirens as she considers what he's doing to her, making her feel this way. Perhaps for the first time she realizes leaving him Monday might hurt. What is that all about?

Noah crooks his arm out. "I want to show you something."

She laughs to herself. "Another detour from our search?"

"We're close. Trust me." He continues to hold his arm out, waiting on her.

What the hell. She slips her hand in, and they walk in tandem for a while.

"How about your family?" she asks, jumping in before he's the one asking questions. "What are they like?"

"I've a sister, Marianne," he says, as church bells chime in the distance, "who is a complete loon. And I love her with all her flaws. My brother, Wesley, is . . . he's still trying to find his way, let's say that. My parents have been running the pub together for forty years, my grandmother before that. There are aunts and uncles and cousins spread all over Winchester. Small town like this, I'm related to just about everyone." He shares a few of their stories as they go deeper into the country.

They come to a section where the plank has sunk into the mud. Noah holds out his arms. "May I help you over?"

Charli can't say no. He lifts her like he is carrying her over a threshold, and as he navigates the mud, she feels a flurry in her chest.

"Thank you," she mutters, appreciating the gesture.

Soon an old church with several sprawling buildings attached comes into view, surely the origin of the chiming bells from earlier. "This is the Almshouse of Saint Cross," he says. "For as long as it's been around, travelers have shown up for the Wayfarer's Dole. You've heard of someone on the dole, like on the take. It's a handout . . . of beer and bread. I thought we'd stop in."

Charli is intrigued and allows him to continue distracting her from the reason she's here. "Wait, they still do it?"

"Every day," Noah says. "Shall we?"

How can she not go with the flow a bit? *Fun* is not an emotion she knows or does well, but she's certainly getting a taste now. They pass through a corridor and stop at a heavy wooden door. "It's in the gift shop now," he says.

"The gift shop? So they get you with the free beer and bread but push a T-shirt on you once you're there."

"Yeah, I suppose it's more of a novelty these days, but there was a time when a stop here was the only way someone could get by."

They walk through the doors, and a heavily tattooed woman Noah's age says, "Hello, Noah."

He makes introductions—she's an old friend—then says, "We're here for the Wayfarer's Dole. Long journey to get here, you know."

"Can't have you thirsty and hungry now. Give me a moment."

Charli glances around at the books and trinkets. No T-shirts, though. The lady returns with two cups of beer and two thick slices of white bread.

"I didn't believe you," Charli says, taking her share.

"I would never lie to you," Noah says.

Oh, but I'd lie to you, she thinks.

Walking back outside, they both sit on the same side of a table—very close to each other, facing the expanse of the courtyard, where the grass is turning green. A monk does tai chi in the far corner.

She takes her first bite of the bread. "That is as bad as it looks." She sets it back down on the plate and reaches for the beer.

"It's a bit stale, isn't it? I suppose this is an example of what English food tasted like back in the old days."

"The beer isn't so bad, though," she says, tasting the hops as it goes down.

"No, I think we've gotten that one right since the beginning. My father often talks of the holy trinity: God, family, and good ale."

"What's he like?" she asks.

He crosses his arms. She's so close she can smell the beer on his breath. "He's a simple man—not in a bad way. He adores living in Winchester and is quite sure it's the center of the universe. I find myself a little more curious of what else is out there."

He glances at her lips before continuing, and the gesture leaves her wondering what might come.

"Don't tell me it's too late."

"No, it's not too late." He rubs the stubble of his beard. "But I do have an obligation here." With that, he turns to the monk doing tai chi and takes a sip of beer.

She takes in his side profile, his sharp features. What a handsome man. And a good one too. "You seem like such a sweet and loyal guy, taking care of your family. But I hope you're not putting your life on hold. People like you deserve the world. You should make sure you're realizing your potential." She can't believe the words leaving her mouth.

He turns back to her with a cocked eyebrow. "People like me? What does that mean?"

She thinks about how to answer. "I don't know. Honest, genuine. Selfless. Kind. Worldly."

It's his turn to blush, and he does so wonderfully. "No offense, but I don't get the sense that you throw out such compliments that often."

She'd be mad if he wasn't so spot on. "No, I don't. But something tells me you need to hear them."

He takes a peek at her lips again before saying, "I'm flattered. Thank you."

The heat is a little much, so Charli brings them back to her question. "Seriously, there's nothing wrong with working in a pub. At all. Look at Victoria. She's so happy there. But are you? You're very good behind the bar, but is it quenching the thirst inside of you?"

Appreciation glows in his eyes. "I can find a way to be happy anywhere."

"That's slightly, kind of . . . sort of . . ." She stops, amazed by how hard it is for her to say it.

"Sort of what?"

"I don't know. You make me see the world a little differently. I appreciate that."

A quiet moment bubbles up to the surface as their eyes lock.

"I hope you'll come back," he says, inching toward her.

"Oh, yeah? Why's that?"

He gently places a hand on her thigh. "Because England looks good on you." He plants a kiss on her lips that rattles even the most brittle parts inside her heart.

⌐

They take a different route on the way back but are unable to find the exact spot where the photo was taken. Charli accepts that the passing of time has made finding it nearly impossible. It's okay, though. How would it help her cause? She is also starting to accept that there's not much more she can do right now, so she leans into simply enjoying the moment. It's not only for herself either. Noah seems to have needed their time together too.

As they stroll back through town, Noah asks, "How did your love of books come about?"

"You keep going after my Achilles' heel, huh?"

"I'm simply curious."

"Don't worry, I can talk books all day."

Charli finds herself amazed that she is both being honest with him *and* that she wants to share so badly. "I mentioned my mother to you. I had a tough childhood, and books became my escape. I taught myself to read and burned through young adult books when I was five or six. I love stories, love curling up somewhere and disappearing into another world."

He casts a glance over and then returns his eyes to the busy sidewalk. "The way you talk, it makes me want to get back into it."

"You should."

"I know. But television is so much easier, isn't it? Especially football."

"Yeah, but books are so so *sooo* much better."

Charli talks about the authors that changed her life—Alice Hoffman, Alice Munro, Pat Conroy, Ann Patchett—and Noah reciprocates by taking her to some of his favorite places in Winchester: the Great Hall, the city mill, a couple of cemeteries. They occasionally dip into a pub for a pint. She always drinks a half pint, because she can't keep up with him. They stop in a boutique so she can dress herself for the rest of the weekend. He's patient with her, sits on a couch in one place, a cracked leather chair in the other, and happily critiques her as she models potential purchases from the discount racks.

Before they know it, it's close to dinnertime. He takes her back to the inn so that she can call Marvin and change for dinner. After drying her hair, she dials her boss's number and is more than thrilled to leave a message.

"Listen, Marvin, it's Charli. I know you're going to be mad at me, but I need two more days. It's just my mom . . . I can't leave her yet." Charli lets some sadness rise out of her, which isn't hard to do when she's talking about her mom. "I have my computer if you need anything while I'm away. Thank you for understanding." She ends the call, confident she's made the right decision. Noah had said she's better than her current job. She doesn't know about that, but she's where she needs to be right now. She takes her time writing a follow-up email, restating the message she left on voice mail. At the last minute, she decides to copy Marvin's boss, as it might better her chances of him treating her more like a human being. A twinge of guilt hits her as she presses send.

Charli puts way more effort in than she usually does, starting with a bra and panties that she quietly bought in the boutique. She's not sure he's going to see them, but she's thinking odds are in his favor. She slides into a velvety red dress that flares at the bottom, then uses the mirror to tastefully apply makeup.

At seven, they walk arm in arm to a restaurant called the Chesil Rectory. She wears a cashmere scarf to fight the wind. He's drummed up a jacket and has to be the best thing going in Winchester.

The outside of the restaurant is the kind of place where Bilbo Baggins might live, featuring a thatched roof and exposed beams that show through the cream stucco. They have to duck to squeeze in through the entrance. Once they're inside, it's a fairy tale of a restaurant, with ancient timbers holding up the ceiling. Candles burn atop every table. The flames of a fire lick the charred brick of a chimney. Odors of grilled foods drift in from the kitchen. Servers in white shirts snap to attention as Noah and Charli pass by.

The hostess leads them upstairs to a cozy table tucked away from the others. As they wait for drinks, Noah says, "Queen Elizabeth owned this building back in the sixteenth century. When she married at the cathedral, the marriage nearly bankrupted the town, so she gave this place to the city. It eventually found its way to these guys, who make some of the best food in England."

Charli looks at him with admiration. "How do you know so much?"

"Comes with the territory of being an innkeeper, I suppose."

"You say I'm the one who doesn't realize how amazing I am. That's . . ." The words get caught in her throat, but she has to finish. "I'll tell you this . . . whatever your ex is doing now, she's missing out. I'd bet the world on that."

Another blush that he does so well. "You're nice to say so."

"I mean it. And I do hope you chase your own dreams, whatever they are. It's so admirable what you're doing for your family, but at some point you have to break away and quench your own thirsts." She's good at giving advice when she sees someone who actually deserves more than they're getting out of life.

"We'll see," he says, and the way he says it makes her feel a little depressed.

In fact, the intimate quiet that follows yanks her out of the moment. She let her guard down more than she should, and there's something brewing between them that seems like it's going to be hard to shake.

When the bread comes out, Charli eats her feelings. And it's the best sourdough she's ever had in her life. They serve it with a homemade butter and a side of dukkah spice. They share a smoked trout next, pulled right from the river Itchen. It's served with flake almonds, braised raisins, and grilled gem hearts. For the main, she has a veggie plate that brings tears to her eyes, to-die-for butter beans, black garlic, crisped artichoke, and pureed cauliflower. He goes for the scallops and prawns with a champagne and squid ink risotto.

"Are you kidding me?" she says, after her first bites. Focusing on the food lessens the fear that crept up earlier. "I'm still wondering why people think England has bad food."

"I think the French started that rumor."

They share a laugh.

After dinner, he walks her along the river. Deciding he will indeed get a peek at her underwear, she stops and peers into his eyes. "Don't you live around here?"

Noah smiles. "I wasn't going to say anything."

"Oh, you weren't? We just happened to be in the area."

Grins and smiles and flickers of a craving rise up into the air.

He lives along the river in a small apartment building that was once a mill. Funny how everything here was once something else. Not that architecture is even a blip on her radar. They push through the doors, and she barely takes notice of his space. They're tugging at each other, hitting counters, stumbling over chairs.

"Is it possible to extend your flight out a few months?" he asks, as they collapse onto his couch.

"Don't push your luck," she says. And she means it. He's about to get lucky unless he starts talking about a future again.

Chapter 16

FAMILY TIES

Charli's eyes snap open and she lets out a smile. She can't wait to tell Viv about her tryst. For a moment there, it was getting dangerous, but she has it under control now. Noah needs to be watched, as it's clear he wants more. He's like a dog that needs to be corrected from time to time. Sorry, Noah. There's no more to be had starting next week. Get it while you can!

She turns to touch him, but his side of the bed is empty. His off-tune whistling drifts in from another room. Pulling the sheet off the bed, she wraps herself in it, then passes through the hallway. He sits shirtless at the living room table, staring at a puzzle. The box shows the entirety of it, a variety of license plates.

She can't help but smile. "A man who does puzzles . . ."

He turns, bathing her with good-morning charm. "I enjoy a good puzzle. In fact, I'm wondering who that woman is I woke up next to."

"Yeah, me too," Charli admits. "I really put up a fight, didn't I?"

"In spirit, you put up a great fight."

"Whatever that means. You got lucky this time."

"Hey, I'm the one feeling a little cheap and easy right now." He stands, puts his hands on her waist, and kisses her. "I feel taken advantage of," he says as their lips pull away.

She sees right through him this time. "Oh, do you? You poor thing. Trust me, I'm not that easy. And I know that you've probably been told that before by some girl standing naked in your living room—probably another American—but I'm really not. It's just that your . . . your . . ."

"Yes?"

"It's your stupid rugged charm, and your quoting of poetry in iambic, and your historical facts, and . . ."

Oh, he's grinning big-time now. As long as she can manage the heat, it's nice being in the throes of it.

"Well, it was pretty wonderful," he says.

"I suppose." She's messing with him and can't hide her smirk.

"You suppose? Maybe I need another shot."

"Not a chance." Though she instantly pivots to hard to get, he's probably going to get another shot. Why not?

He turns so glum, his lips turned downward, that he becomes the eighth dwarf in *Snow White*. She'll call him Mopey.

Taking on a sinister grin, he tugs at the sheet wrapped around her. She playfully smacks his hand.

"There's a get-together at the pub for my granny Helen tonight," he says. "She's turning one hundred. I want you to come. I want you to meet my family."

Everything comes to a halt. Her heart. Her brain. The flow of blood in her vessels. "Meet your family?" She thinks back to how it was attempting to meet Patrick's mother that was the death blow for their relationship. "You don't want me meeting your family, trust me."

He backs up. "They're easy. You'll have a lovely time. And then Sunday, we'll see where it goes, maybe a roast dinner followed by a hike."

"Oh, for Christ's sake, Noah." He's gone and ruined it, hasn't he?

"What?"

"You don't get it." She hates how she's speaking to him, as if he's done something wrong. Something horribly wrong. It's only that he's stomped out the flame. "What's the point? Are you going to get down on one knee tomorrow too? Tell me I'm the one."

"I might," he says, and he's most likely joking.

Noah tries to tug off her sheet again. Instead of a fun smack of the hand, she gives him an aggressive push.

"That was a bit harsh," he says.

She turns away from him and says, "I have to get back. Last thing I want to do is get caught in a walk of shame." It's her best excuse for an escape.

"A walk of shame?" He follows her. "Who do you know in this town that's gonna shame you? What's there to shame anyway? I'd be happy to walk you back to the pub . . . and right through the bloody door."

Charli dresses while managing to keep him from seeing any of her lady bits.

"What is going on?" he asks. "I saw all of you last night, and now you're hiding from me? Because I want you to meet my family?"

"It's fine," she backpedals. "I'm happy to meet your family. I think I'm a little worn out."

No surprise, her mother's voice is in her ear. *That's right, Charli. Run away. That's what you do. Probably for the best anyway, though. You know he deserves far better than to get tangled up in your toxic web.*

Finally dressed, Charli sits on the bed and laces up her boots. She hates herself for feeling this way.

He comes to face her. "Look," he says, careful not to touch her, "I don't sleep with people like that either. But you know what, it was pretty damned good. I don't know what the future holds, but it makes me sad to think about. That's what I was puzzling over at the table. Damn this world for finally putting an amazing woman in my life who lives a world away." He unloads his frustration with an exhale.

"Let's catch up in a little while, okay?" That's all she can seem to say, and she stands and starts out of the room.

He backs off. "Yeah, okay."

She darts down the steps and goes out into early-morning mist. The river glides by dreamlike, full of poetry and romance. The moss on the terra-cotta roofs on the houses around her glistens with dew. And she wants to take it all and rip it to shreds and burn it to nothing.

Slightly unsure of where she is, she reaches for her phone. Only to discover that she doesn't have her phone. "Oh, crap," she says to herself, turning back to the old mill where he lives. She goes to the entrance but doesn't know which apartment to ring. It was the second floor, but there are two options.

She's beyond mortified and is tempted to leave it there and buy a new one when she gets back to Boston.

He appears at the downstairs door, dangling her phone like a carrot. "Forgot something?"

She doesn't want to reward his smile by offering her own. She barely looks at him as she snatches it back like he's stolen it. "Thanks."

"So will I see you?" he calls out to her as she makes her second getaway.

"I'll text you in a bit, okay?" It would be nice if she could have a fun fling with a handsome Englishman and go home and laugh with Viv about it. But no . . . she couldn't even make it two days without messing it up. What's worse is that he's just a nice guy and a gentleman.

It's a sleepy town; Noah was right. A few people are out getting their morning exercise. A homeless man sips coffee and sucks the last life out of a cigarette. Most places are closed. She finally sees an open bakery and pops inside, taking momentary refuge in a cappuccino and a croissant at a corner table. She needs a game plan. Is she making a mistake? She can't bear the idea of returning with an apology. She'd surely mess it up a second time.

Checking her emails for the first time of the morning, she sees Marvin responded while she was sleeping. She takes a calming breath and reads his message. Family is most important. We can cover for you a few more days. Please keep us posted. Well wishes to your mother. —Marv

Charli reads it again and again, making sure she didn't miss something. Apparently copying his boss made all the difference.

Ignoring the time, she texts Viv next. You wouldn't believe what I did.

A response comes a minute later. Charli, it's early. What'd you do?

I had a thing with a hot guy and then deliberately blew it up.

Wait, isn't that what you always do?

Charli feels better for a moment—validated even—as she types: Hahaha. At least she's consistent. She catches Viv up.

Her friend finally texts: Sounds to me like you like him. You should see where it goes.

Oh, I know where it goes. I ended up fast-forwarding the whole thing.

You're impossible. Nothing I could say would change your mind.

You're a lawyer.

Not even the best lawyer in the world can convince you to do something when you're against it.

He wants me to meet his family.

Charli, I can't with you. You've met a guy that you like. He likes you back. And he wants you to hang around. Why in the world wouldn't you?

189

It's complicated.

> Sounds like the most uncomplicated situation in
> the world.

Charli can't possibly explain what's going on inside her, how she can already see the future. She can already feel the pain of what it would be like to disappoint him. Like with Patrick but worse, because maybe she is even more attracted to Noah.

⌒

Charli lies in bed above the pub most of the day, trying to read but mostly tossing and turning. She texts back and forth with her father for a while, making sure he's okay. She tells him she's in a holding pattern until Monday, and he suggests that she try to enjoy herself. She is in Winchester, England, after all. There are worse places to be, he texts. And it sounds like this Noah character is worth getting to know.

Maybe her father is right. And yet it would be so much easier to return to London for a couple of nights, or to even switch hotels. The guy has some kind of superpowers to make her feel this way. Patrick had certainly not infested her thoughts in such a way. She can't stop thinking about what it was like sleeping with Noah. It was like a fuse had been lit when they'd first met, eventually winding its way up the stairs to his apartment . . . and then . . . *Bam!* She's never had sex that good in her life.

At one point, she literally eyes the window and considers dropping her bag down and jumping and making a run for it. If she weren't worried that she might break an ankle, she'd do it. Then she's talking to herself. "What would be so wrong with a couple of more days running around with a cute guy?"

Finally, she relents and texts him. See you tonight, okay? I think all the travel caught up with me. She takes a long hot bath, shaves her legs.

At six, she's trying on outfits and putting on makeup while psyching herself up to go downstairs.

By seven, the party is hopping below her. Down two flights of stairs, she enters through the back to find the pub packed. It smells like beer and good food and a burning fire. Night has fallen outside, and the streetlights cast an orange glow on the cobblestone street.

"You're Charli, aren't you?" a voice asks.

"I am." Charli offers a smile and regards the older woman staring at her. She wears a cardigan over a white blouse. A part equally divides her short hair, which is dyed the hickory color of Charli's floors back home. No doubt Noah's mom. The two of them share many of the same features, though worry lines have worn into hers.

"I'm Robin, Noah's mother. He's told me all about you." Her accent sounds exactly like how Charli envisions someone of royalty to speak, incredibly proper and sophisticated. More evident, though, is that Noah has told his mother about Charli.

Robin makes friendly conversation for a moment and then opens her arms toward the bar. "We can't have you going thirsty."

Charli finds Noah pulling a cask ale. Victoria is on the other side of the bar, making a round of Irish coffees.

"Don't you say a word," Charli whispers to him.

He stays focused on his task but smiles wider. Those big bright whites sparkle in front of her. "I didn't say a thing." He finally takes a peek at her and then goes back to finishing the beer. "What can I get you?"

"Anything but beer, please."

"No beer, coming up." He slides the beer across the bar to a patron. "Enjoy, mate." He then inches toward Charli and reaches for her hand. She lets him take it. "Did you have a nice day?"

She shakes her head at him. Apologies are not easy. "I'm kind of complicated, if you haven't figured that out."

"It's my favorite part about you. How about a chardonnay?" He allows a cute grin. "You Americans love chardonnay, right?"

"How about whiskey?"

"Ah, there you go."

He pours her an Irish whiskey and drops a cube in it. "Take two of these and call me in the morning."

The first sip calms her. She starts to say something but stops and takes another swig of whiskey.

"Are you gonna hang around a few more days?" he finally asks.

"I guess so."

He nods. A woman joins them, and Noah says, "Charli, meet my sister, the ever warm and always cordial Marianne."

Charli turns to find a younger version of Noah's mother. They share the same scowl. A freshly applied coat of fire-engine-red lipstick demands attention. Large gold earrings that match the gold of her dress dangle from her ears. And she looks like she's a complete mess. Charli doesn't know why, exactly, other than she sees so much baggage in those eyes, and in the way she's looking at Charli. Perhaps it's like looking in the mirror.

"Hi, Marianne. So good to meet you."

Marianne looks at her in a way that says, *Is it nice to meet me? Or are you afraid of me?*

Charli's heard enough Marianne stories to know some of the baggage. The ugly divorce, the painkiller phase, the church phase, now the healing phase. At first glance, Marianne certainly lives up to Noah's stories he's shared during their time together.

"I love your earrings," Charli says. She never compliments someone on their earrings, but she's scrambling for conversation.

Marianne doesn't flinch. She lets out a grunt. "Uh-huh."

Thank heavens Noah throws a buoy into the icy water. "Marianne, could you be sweet for one moment?"

She looks at her older brother. "What would be the fun in that?"

"Oh, I don't know. The sweet taste of civility. The embrace of kindness."

Marianne looks at Charli and rolls her eyes, like Noah is the unstable one. "He exaggerates, if you haven't noticed. Believe me, he's not all he's cracked up to be. If I were you, I'd be on the next train back."

"Oh, I'm not here for him. I'm tracking down some missing pieces of my family tree."

"Ah, that's right," Marianne says.

"And how about you? What do you do?"

Marianne goes colder if that's even possible. She could dive into the river and turn it into ice. "You're looking at it. I run the books around here."

Marianne and her mother back on the Cape would love each other, absolutely *love* each other. "Ah, you're the smart one."

Marianne seems to like the compliment for a short second but then lets skepticism rule. "I'm the one who doesn't like people, so I'm best hiding out in the office."

"You and me both."

Marianne drinks her wine, and Charli drinks her whiskey.

Noah says, "You two would like each other. Charli, Marianne is a lot of fun when she climbs off her broom."

"Oh, I'm a witch, am I?" She extends her middle finger.

"Yeah, but you're also my favorite sister."

"I'm your only sister, asshole."

"I love you, Marianne."

Marianne makes an ugly face and gives him another birdie. At least she knows she's difficult. It's like she keeps her middle finger on speed dial.

Charli notices a flash of gray hair in the center of a group of men bellying over with laughter. "Is that your grandmother?"

"That's her," Noah says. "Let me introduce you."

As Charli says goodbye, Marianne takes a moment to use her sincerity gauge. "You seem okay, Charli."

Honesty kicks into gear. "I'm not."

They both snicker.

He guides her toward Helen, who is laughing mightily with a half pint in her hand.

"Granny, I want you to meet someone."

Helen turns away from the three men she's entertaining. "Ah, Charli."

"You know my name?"

Noah shrugs. "I may have talked about you some today."

Helen touches Charli's cheek. "You're spectacular, aren't you?"

"Thank you. And happy birthday. Are you sure you're one hundred today? I'd have put you closer to sixty." The woman is sharp and spry.

"All that sugar'll get you everywhere with me." She takes a sip of her beer. "So tell me about yourself, Charli . . ."

Charli meets close to fifty other people throughout the night, including Noah's father, who is not the healthiest man—looks beat up, even—but he's charming, too, in the way he makes fun of everything. He's the most self-deprecating man she's ever met.

Around eleven, the guests clear out, and Noah's family pulls together three tables and falls into hilarious conversation. Charli's never seen a family interact this way, tossing aside their differences and coming together like best friends. Even Viv's family has issues.

Noah's father is telling a story about how Noah used to call antelopes cantaloupes, and everyone sitting around them is busted to tears, including Charli. It's a family roast, where everyone's participating and everyone's a target, but no one is offended.

"Charli," his father says to her, "what can we do to keep you sticking around for a while?"

Everyone laughs.

"Oh, I'm leaving Monday. Sadly."

"Would you take him with you?"

"I don't have a big enough bag."

He brushes off the excuse. "We'll put him in the luggage hold with the dogs. He'll be fine."

"And how long would this place last without me running it?" Noah asks.

"Yeah, we'd run it into the ground," his father agrees. "Guess that means you've got to stay here, Charli. What's keeping you in Boston?"

Charli sits up. "Now hold on. You're making some big leaps, Mr. Armstrong. I've only just met your son."

"It's more than that," he says. "I've not seen him glow like this in a long time."

Charli tenses up, as if she's walking alone at night and hears footsteps behind her.

"Oh, c'mon, Pop," Noah says. He looks at Charli. "He'll say anything to embarrass me."

Charli fakes a smile.

Mr. Armstrong gives a chuckle that shakes his belly. "Well, I do hope you find a way to stay. You're welcome here as long as you like."

"Thank you, Mr. Armstrong."

"Please call me Andrew. And know that I mean it."

This man is the genesis of Noah's charm, and it feels like they're all trying to woo her in, as if they're collaborating to convince her to stay. They're wasting their time.

Chapter 17

The Christmas Ball and Winter Blossoms

Winchester, England
December 22, 1880

The Christmas Ball was an elaborate affair, created to raise money for the Hospital of Saint John the Baptist but most certainly more so to groom the young men and women of high society Winchester toward grand couplings that would perpetuate strong lineages established by their forefathers. At least, that was how Miles saw it.

All he could think of was Lillian, and yet here he was, listening to his father woo the Thornhill family in the center of the hall on the top floor of the main building. The musical ensemble played a slow Christmas ballad between dances, a rather sad melody indeed. It perfectly punctuated the feeling Miles had as he listened to his father speak.

"It's raucous right now in London," James said, enunciating with such volume that surely even the man holding the trumpet on the other side of the hall could hear him. "I dare say I'd be fine not returning after the summer, had I not my duty." He was referring to his position in the House of Lords, the one Miles was supposed to inherit upon his father's death. "The streets are by far the worst I've seen in my lifetime. You can barely take a breath without retching. The city simply can't handle this influx of people, especially those of meager means."

That could be me before too long, Miles thought. And nothing his father said could extinguish his love for London and the possibilities it harbored within the city's borders.

"Oh, I do agree," Lord Thornhill said. "I remember a day when the Thames ran as clear and clean as the Itchen, but now it's a sewage pit."

"I'll resist the urge to point the finger at your railroad," James said. "I must say I'm enjoying the ease of travel these days."

"Well," Lord Thornhill said, "it's not mine anyway. I simply climbed aboard to enjoy the financial fruits."

The men snickered at one another, as did Miles's mother and brother and also Lord Thornhill's wife and daughter, Etta. James had been urging Miles to court Etta Thornhill for years. She was a striking young lady, and Miles had come to know her well through such events. They had a mild friendship, but he'd not once felt more strongly than that. Of course, his father would say such feelings were irrelevant.

"You choose your wife with your brains, not your root," he'd say, then follow it with, "Lord Thornhill made a second fortune in the railroads, but he comes from a long line of good blood that would be a fine blending with ours. You understand me?"

Miles would nod because any other response might draw a strike from his father's vicious right hand.

Now that he'd met Lillian, though, he'd decided that no amount of persuasion, be it physical or monetary—or any such threat his father might devise—could sway him from following his heart. He'd not seen Lillian since the night he'd been caught, though an hour had not passed without her on his mind. He could still hear her velvety voice and warm laugh. So he wouldn't forget her face, he would close his eyes and imagine each feature—the round cheeks, the bright eyes. He'd gotten out of school for Christmas only the day before, so he'd not had a chance to find her. Not until tonight.

When a lull came in the conversation between his father and Lord Thornhill, Miles seized the opportunity to excuse himself. He'd seen his grandmother near the giant Christmas tree. She stood alone and looked like she needed company.

Eleanor Stewart—a woman Miles respected more than any other person on earth—was mother to Miles's mother. She'd lost her husband to typhoid and now lived alone in her manor in Twyford off the road to Southampton. Miles's parents had tried to convince her to move in with them at Elmhurst, but she'd declined. It was no secret that her reasoning had to do with Miles's father. She'd never liked him and would certainly never live in the same house as him. Needless to say, Miles loved that about her. He loved a lot about his grandmother, who had always encouraged him to be himself. Only one other person in his life had done that: Lillian.

Eleanor smiled as her grandson approached. "Ah, you look sharp in your new suit, young man."

"Thank you, Granny. And you're exquisite as always." She was seventy-six and had fought off two illnesses to make it that far. Though she was a little slower than she used to be, she possessed a youthful vigor and was determined to make it to eighty. Miles thought that if anyone could, it would be her.

"How does it feel to be one step closer to graduation?" she asked.

"It's as if freedom is within my grasp."

She nodded knowingly. He'd spent many a night at her house during his breaks between terms, and he'd come to know her well. His favorite thing about her was that he could say just about anything, and she'd not judge him. Theirs was a relationship of authenticity and honesty.

"You know, you will like Oxford, my dear boy. Your life will be very different."

"I can't imagine, quite honestly. Is there somewhere in this world where I can break free of the leash of my father?"

She dipped her chin. "Oh, I assure you there is."

Miles nodded as he looked beyond the band to James, still standing there with the Thornhills. "I have feelings for someone," Miles blurted out. And it was the most exhilarating moment he'd had since coming upon Lillian on that October night a few months ago.

"Is that right?" His grandmother looked keenly interested. "The Thornhill girl?"

"Etta? No." Miles resisted for only a moment, long enough for him to remind himself that he was safe to say whatever he wanted around his granny. "It's a girl who will not please my father."

Eleanor took on a sinister look. "Then I like her all the more. Who is she? Do I know her or her family?"

"She's not of our class," he admitted. "She's the daughter of an innkeeper."

Her eyes grew wide. "Oh, I see." Miles was pleased to see no judgment, only surprise. She looked at him differently now. "Is that love twinkling in your eyes?"

Miles felt his face redden. "I do think so, Granny. I've never felt this way before."

Eleanor smiled. "That makes me happy. But what a challenge you've stepped into."

"Yes, indeed."

She seemed to consider his predicament. "I'd like to meet her one day. You should bring her to visit."

What a bump to have someone on his side. "Yes, of course. I'd love that. And thank you. Thank you for understanding."

She blinked. "Do you remember how your grandfather and I met?"

"I don't believe so."

"We were destined to be together. The only argument we ever had was your mother marrying your father. I'm sorry to say that, but it's true. For some reason, Franklin was quite sure it was the right fit. He always tried to find the best in people, to a fault at times. Yes, your father was charming. But I could see the evil in him. Almost as if it was caged and waiting to get out. However, that is not my point. What I want you to know is that I was sure from the very day I met Franklin that I'd been born for him, and he for me. When you know that you've found true love, it would be a crime not to realize it. Don't you think?"

If only the rest of his family were as supportive as his granny. "Of course."

They spoke until the dancers were called over, and Miles found himself waltzing with Etta Thornhill. Though he had no intention of marrying her, he wouldn't dare avoid their moment on the dance floor. All he had to do was make it a few more months, and then he could do whatever he liked. The couple barely spoke as she giggled shyly.

After breaking away from the dance floor, hoping anyone seeing him disappear out the side door would think he sought a lavatory, he dashed down the stairs and out into the street. He'd not taken his coat, as it may have aroused suspicion, so it was a chilly walk up High Street to the Smythun under the light of a waning moon. Not that it bothered him too much. Inside, he was melting.

Carriages and single riders passed by, kicking up dust due to the lack of rain lately. A man holding a Bible and a bottle preached to a small group standing around him. Someone whisked by on a bicycle. A woman who looked suspiciously like a prostitute seemed to have strayed far from Cannon Street.

Then he was there, standing outside the pub, hoping with all of him that she would be there tonight. He looked through the polished glass of the pub and saw happy patrons eating their dinners in the amber light of the gas lanterns on the walls. His stomach dropped as he pushed open the door to hear a bell ring above him. No one turned, though. All were welcome here, or that's how it had always felt.

He saw the back of her first, in her dress that was so less fancy than the one adorning Etta. Yet even from his current vantage point, even though she was in the midst of scrubbing a table clean, she was more striking than any girl at the ball.

Stepping inside, he wound his way to her position and cleared his throat. "Lillian."

She froze, and he wondered if she'd been waiting for him, worrying over his return. It had been two months since they'd last seen each other.

She dropped the rag in the bucket and turned to him. "Ah, you're still alive." Her smile nearly made him fall to his knees. What torture it would be to say goodbye to her again.

"Barely," he said, removing his hat. "I'm so sorry I didn't come back to see you. I was caught sneaking back in."

"No." She pretended to be afraid for him but couldn't smother a grin.

"I was . . . ," he said, mirroring her. "It was no laughing matter either. I was caned in front of my mates. I'm just getting over the bruises."

Lillian showed a look of concern. "Oh, I'm sorry."

"I'd do it again a hundred times . . . to see you."

His bluntness forced her to turn away. "I'm sorry . . . I didn't mean to be so . . ." She turned back. "It's nice to see you. I wondered . . ."

Having reached a pause, they looked at one another. He bathed in her beauty and felt, all in the span of a few seconds, like he'd found his life's purpose. He couldn't hear the noise of the bar. All he could hear was his heart, beating for her.

He lowered his voice to a whisper. "I've snuck out once again. I'm attending the Christmas Ball at Saint John and popped out to see you. I only left school yesterday, and I'm headed back home tomorrow. Do you have a few minutes to take a walk?"

She looked around and shook her head. "No. I don't, I'm afraid. It's busy tonight."

Miles nodded in defeat.

"But I'd like to see you again too," she said, lighting the fire of his resolve.

"How can we make that happen?"

"When are you back in town?"

Her encouragement was all he needed. "My father is leaving for the city in two days' time. I can ride into town then."

"Are you sure? I don't want you to get punished again."

"Quite sure. Do I find you here?"

"Always."

A smile stretched across his face. He didn't dare even attempt to hide it. "I'll see you then."

—

It didn't take much to sneak away from his house for the day. When Lord James Pemberton went to the city, Cora would often stay in her room for hours at a time. How she passed her time up there he did not know, though he guessed that much of it was spent sleeping. Miles's brother, Edward, had gone to see his friend in Sparsholt, and so the house was quiet. He'd asked the coachman to have his horse saddled, that he was off for a ride, and it was as simple as that.

At a strong gallop, it took him under an hour to reach Winchester. As the city came into view from the South Downs, he found his heart fluttering again. He was finally free to see her, to actually have a conversation during the day. As long as he was not recognized by someone who knew his family, he'd be fine.

He left his horse at a stall on High Street and first stopped at a jewelry store that he'd spotted when his family had come into town for the Christmas Ball. The kind gentleman standing behind a counter of dazzling necklaces welcomed him.

"Hello, sir, I'm looking for something for a girl."

The jeweler inclined an eyebrow. "A girl. How special of a girl?"

"The most special."

"Ah, I see."

Once he'd found a gift that pleased him, Miles walked up to the Smythun full of renewed hope. It was empty, aside from one man breaking his fast by the window.

"Hello?" Miles called out while removing his hat.

Lillian came out from the back. She was dressed much differently than he'd last seen her. A white dress with her hair in a bun.

"You make me smile every time I see you," he said.

"You're easy to please," she replied.

"If only that were the case."

She raised a finger. "Let me tell my father I'll be leaving. He's upstairs."

"May I meet him?" Miles said quickly, an idea that became terrifying only after he'd suggested it.

She stopped with a puzzled look on her face. "You want to meet him?"

"Of course I do," he said. "If I'm to court his daughter."

She smiled at his brazen advance. "Suit yourself."

A moment later, he heard footfalls coming down the stairs. Lillian appeared with her father, a chubby man with round cheeks and a thick mustache. "Miles Pemberton," he said, thrusting out his hand.

"Yes, sir," Miles said, the sound of his own last name giving him pause. He'd not considered that their fathers might know each other.

"I'm Tom Turner. Welcome to our pub."

"Thank you, sir."

"We're going for a walk, Father," Lillian said, "and I thought we might go by to see Arthur and Sadie."

"Ah, yes, of course." Miles knew that Arthur was Lillian's brother. Tom nodded for a moment, taking Miles in. "I don't need to tell you what kind of trouble the two of you might cause. And I think you know what I mean. I know *of* your father, and I'm quite sure he would not be keen on you visiting my daughter."

Miles simply nodded.

"But I am not a man who stands in the way of two people who are developing feelings for one another. What is life without love? All that I can say is that you should be careful." He looked over to Lillian. "That goes for the both of you."

"Sir," Miles said.

They left her father and the pub.

"Where shall we go?" Miles asked out on the street.

Lillian walked a safe distance from him. "I have a place."

As they left High Street, he said, "Your father is a kind man."

"Yes, he is. And he must like you too."

"I'll do my best to live up to that honor."

They broke free of town and came to walk along the river. The trees were naked of leaves, and only a few birds had not flown south for winter. Their escape into the woods soothed Miles's worry of being discovered, and it also sent his mind to wonder if he might have a chance to kiss her.

He thought it rather rebellious and even courageous that Lillian was fine being alone with him. Any woman at that Christmas Ball wouldn't have dared stroll the city streets without a chaperone, let alone disappear into nature.

Miles slowed. "I'd like to give you something, Lillian."

She stopped with a smile that was the true gift. "You would?"

He drew from a pocket the hair brooch that he'd purchased from the jeweler. It was in the shape of a sunflower; a shiny emerald rested in the center.

As he handed it to her, she lost her breath. "You can't give that to me."

"Why not?"

"Why not? Because it's . . . it's too expensive."

"There was nothing worthy of you in the entire store. But I hoped that this might do."

She looked like she might cry. "Are you sure?"

"Of course I'm sure."

Lillian took the brooch from him and admired it, glazing her fingers over the design. She gathered her hair in her hands and pinned it down with her brooch. "How does it look?"

Miles took her in, her stunning figure, her dazzling eyes, her thick wavy hair, and the brooch. Never had he seen a woman more captivating.

"Like it was meant for you," he finally said.

"Thank you, Miles. You certainly flatter me."

"This is more than flattery."

They began to walk again. Miles placed his hands behind his back and looked over to her. "Are you sure you're not cold?"

She shook her head. "I'm quite fine," she said. "I come out here all the time."

"By yourself?"

"Yes, why not?"

"Oh, I don't know. I'm not accustomed to ladies with such freedom."

She chuckled. "You're in a different world with me. I can't dance but I have my own things."

"No doubt," Miles responded. "Wait, you can't dance?"

"Not as you do."

"What is it that you do outside of working then?"

"I very much like exploring the wilderness, taking these walks, breathing the clean air. I can't wait for the spring, for the trees to come alive, the flowers to bloom. The birds to return."

There was her lovely voice again, teasing him into a dream. "You sound like a poet."

She shook her head. "No, just a happy girl when I'm out here. How about you?" she asked. "What blows your kilt up?"

Miles smiled. "You do."

"Quite forward, aren't you?"

"My time always seems so limited with you. I don't want to waste a moment."

She stopped. "Then why haven't you kissed me?"

Miles couldn't believe she'd said it and felt like he'd been struck in the chest. In the best way possible. "I . . . well . . . I didn't want . . ."

"But our time is limited, is it not?"

Miles licked his lips and stepped toward her. "I hope not." He leaned his face close and touched his lips to hers in what felt like finding the answer to every question he'd ever had. She placed a hand on his chest and then pulled at his shirt, kissing him harder.

As they broke away, he regarded her beautiful face and the slightly curled lips that he'd kissed. This was the woman he would spend the rest of his life with, no matter the odds. "I like you, Lillian Turner."

"And I like you, Miles Pemberton. Yet we have so many obstacles between us, don't we?"

"Nothing that will stop us," he said almost too seriously.

She nearly laughed out loud. "What would you expect between us then?"

"Well, marriage, of course. Children. A life together."

"Don't you think you're getting ahead of yourself?" She asked the question in a playful way, as if his bold statement hadn't scared her in the slightest.

"No. I don't believe so at all."

She held his gaze, grinning as if she couldn't agree more.

They walked farther into the moors, and he fell deeper into her spell with each step. Stopping in a spot by the river, they lay in the grass and came to know one another, pausing on occasion to share another kiss.

He thought it remarkable that she spoke so much of her family, telling him of how her parents had fallen in love as teenagers and how they still danced together, and speaking so fondly of her brother and his new bride, who was expecting their first child.

In turn, Lillian asked him about his family, and he was honest with her, talking about his father's anger and abusive tendencies, his mother's submissive behavior and feeble demeanor, and his clueless brother's desperate desire to conform.

"I envy what you have," Miles said, lying on his side, facing her.

She touched her chest. "And my heart hurts knowing what you've told me about your family."

He stroked her cheek. "I suppose I've been given a glimpse of what to avoid in creating one of my own."

"And that is perhaps what I adore most about you, Miles. From the moment that I met you, I could see that you are so kind and caring and wise—far more than other boys your age." She took his hand. "Now that I know your story, I can see that it's the challenges in your life that have made you such an extraordinary person."

Her words were as comforting as the warmth of her skin against his. "You leave me speechless," he finally said. "Thank you."

Eventually they stood and walked hand in hand to another spot, and then another. He wanted to know everything about her, and at the same time he felt a desperate need to share his own hopes and fears and dreams. Hours passed in a breath.

Returning to the city, they knocked on the door of a row house with the number 7 etched into a metal plaque and were welcomed by Arthur and Sadie, who were anything but intimidating. In fact, the warmth of her family made Lillian all the more intoxicating.

Arthur wore simple clothing and a mustache that nearly connected with his long bushy sideburns. A bump protruded from Sadie's faded purple dress. Lillian had told him she was two months away from becoming an aunt.

Sadie's jaw fell open when she noticed the brooch. "Where did you get that?"

Lillian beamed. "Miles gave it to me."

Jaw still lowered, Sadie turned to Miles. "My heavens, Miles. You must like her."

"No doubt about that."

Arthur disappeared into the kitchen, and Sadie invited Lillian and Miles to join her by the fire. In this small home that was warm and comfortable, they sipped their tea, munched on biscuits, and got to know one another. Her older brother, Arthur, was clearly Lillian's protector.

When talk of the baby came, Lillian rose from her seat and knelt next to Sadie.

"May I?" Then she pressed her hand to the woman's belly. The look of delight that rose to her face warmed the air. "Ah, he's kicking."

"Yes, he is, isn't he?" Sadie agreed.

Lillian pressed her ear to Sadie's belly and listened for a while as she giggled. "I can't wait to be your auntie. I'll be the best of any in the world."

Miles knew that she would be the best mum in the world, too, and he was desperate to leap forward to a life that they could share together. Forget Oxford. He could not leave her that long. Besides, it would get him no closer to gracing a stage in London.

"And you two," Sadie said, as though she'd read Miles's mind. "Is there a future between you?"

"So bold," Lillian said, pulling her head from Sadie's belly.

"Well, you do make a lovely couple."

"Yes, I think we do," Miles said, dropping another cube of sugar in his tea.

Arthur took his chance to be big brother, clearly the spit of his father. "How do you propose to make your lives together? She'll live with you at Elmhurst? You'll make a lady out of her?"

"I'm sad to say my father will not likely approve of our relationship. I will need to find another way to make a living."

"How so? What trades do you know?"

Miles didn't dare mention his dream of acting. "I will have to learn, but I am certainly capable of finding a way to take care of my family. The fact that I'm a Wykehamist will only help."

Arthur conceded that truth with a nod. "These are bold plans for two people who barely know each other."

"It feels like we've known each other a long time, though."

Lillian touched his back. "Yes, it does."

"Just be careful," Arthur said.

"Your father told me the same thing."

"Yes, I suppose he would. It's good advice to follow."

"Indeed." He wasn't sure how to be careful, though. His father would never approve. They'd live at a stalemate. But Miles had no choice. There was no turning back from the way he felt about Lillian Turner or his desire to carve out his own path. There would be no compromises.

Chapter 18

THE EASE OF GOODBYE

Present Day

In the morning, Charli wakes to find Noah nestling up against her. It's slightly invasive, but she allows it, like a judge might allow a prosecutor to ask an impertinent question while prodding a witness. "I'll allow it," the judge might say, "but this will be your last warning."

But she does pull the sheets up over her exposed breast.

The memory of the night flows in, how they were the last to leave the pub. She's never craved a man so much in her life, and they'd gone after each other with a rabid intensity once they were behind closed doors.

She remembers something and chuckles.

"What?" he asks.

She finds his eyes and looks lower. "Your Donald Duck boxers. I can't believe you have Donald Duck boxers." She remembers sliding them off the night before while poking fun at him.

He looks down and then pulls the covers over them. "They seemed charming when I found them at the store."

"Oh, they certainly are."

She bites her lip. He really is stunning, even in the morning.

He reads the tea leaves, proverbially speaking, and turns toward her. Starts to pull the sheet from her. She grips it tighter, and he smiles. "Are you off limits this morning?"

"I'm undecided," she says.

"Ah, I see. So do I need to go about convincing you?" He moves closer to her, slides a hand under the sheets to find her hip.

"I'm . . ." She feels his touch and closes her eyes.

He tugs at the sheet with his other hand, and she lets him expose her. Then she lets him have her.

Later, they sit up against a stack of pillows. He wraps his arms around her, and she lets him do so. Their narrowing time together allows for such intimacy.

"For a guy who claims not to indulge in trysts like these often, you sure know your way around a woman."

He chuckles with his mouth closed. "It feels natural with you, almost like I keep a map of you in my wallet. A treasure map."

She grins. "You're certainly close to the gold."

"I'll keep mining then." He twists to her, and his foot grazes against hers under the covers. "How do I know you don't go all over England taking advantage of men like me?"

"It's a possibility," she whispers.

"Why don't you stay longer?" he asks, dragging a finger up her chest and neck to her lips. "Even my father wants you to. That's high praise."

"You get me for one last day."

"That's not long enough."

"You'd better make the best of it."

He grows serious. "I know you're being funny, but there's some truth in there. Why do you keep me at a certain distance?"

She starts to answer but bites it back. Though he's crossing a line, he deserves more than her shrugging it off. "I have to get back. I have a job and a dog waiting for me. And my dad, who needs me. Let's face it. I've been hurt. You've been hurt. We know where this is headed." That last part is about as real as she's going to get.

"What if we tried to make it work? What if I came to see you? I like you, Charli, and I don't want to let you go."

Don't want to let you go. She wasn't expecting that; no one has ever said such a thing, even her father.

"Let's enjoy today. I like you, too, Noah, but . . . but trust me, you don't want anything long term with me. Especially long-distance long term. I'm not good at either."

"Maybe this is different. For heaven's sake, what are you afraid of?"

She retreats into herself. Slightly annoyed, she sits up and reaches for her clothes. She starts to dress, and she can feel him watching her. It's making her embarrassed.

"Don't do this again. What is it with you and the morning? You can't be mad at me for bringing up a possible future. It's like I go to bed with one woman and wake up to another."

She snaps her bra clasp and turns to him. "Sometimes it's best to enjoy the moment and not let the future trample on it."

He nods slowly. "Is that a passage in your new book, *The Wisdom of Charli?*"

"Could be."

"Well, it's a negative-feedback loop that you're caught in. The future doesn't have to trample. You're scared, and it sucks, to be honest."

Charli pulls on her shirt and stands. "This is all I have to offer. We don't have to hang out today if you don't want to, but I'm not looking for something past tomorrow."

He climbs off the bed and stalks into the bathroom, closes the door. She hears the shower come on. She goes to the window and fights off a cry.

~

Hours later, they're back at the Chesil Rectory, sitting at the exact same table under wooden beams that had been holding up the ceiling for nearly a thousand years. As she's learned, the English celebrate Sunday by having a roast dinner. And it's not even noon yet, so "dinner" doesn't feel like the right word. She opts for the vegetarian nut roast, and it's exquisite. And there are potatoes and onions, the same bread she had the night before, and Yorkshire pudding. She imagined something else from Yorkshire pudding. In reality, it's basically a popover. And it's jaw-droppingly good.

Charli's had time to recover and is back to the person she's good at pretending to be. And Noah is being a good boy, accepting the inevitability of their separation.

"You look happier than you were earlier," he says.

"This is the best meal I've ever had in my life," Charli says honestly, content with putting all her attention on her plate.

"You said that last night."

"They've outdone themselves." The food is helping keep the demons at bay.

She's no good at apologies but forces herself to say, "Sorry about earlier. I must have been hangry."

"Yeah, you certainly surprised me."

She eyes him. "Please don't rain on my parade while I enjoy this meal."

"Fair enough."

It's almost as if her mother is watching, because Charli's phone buzzes in her purse. Georgina has texted. Call me back!!!!!

Charli turns the phone over and pushes it away. "Sorry, that's my mom."

"Everything okay?"

Charli scoffs. "I don't know that anything is ever okay with her." Her mother has managed to kill her good mood.

214

After the meal they walk up a hill, where they enjoy a breathtaking view of Winchester and the rolling hills that surround it. The air seems thinner up here. He leans against a tree and gestures for her to join him. As she does, he asks, "So talking about us at all is off limits?"

With his simple question, she tightens. "Do we have to do this again? Nothing's changed. We live thousands of miles apart. Why set ourselves up for failure?"

"That's such bullshit. I promised myself I wouldn't push you anymore, but I can't help it. How do you not see what we have?"

Charli shrugs. Why can't he leave it alone? "What, I come see you once a year? Then you come see me? You're a nice guy. I like being with you. But you have to take logistics into the equation."

"Why put rules on it? We just see what happens."

"You must have been desperate before I came to town," she finally says, deciding not to take him seriously. "You're the one who says there are no women here."

He sighs to the clouds. "Don't make a joke out of this—don't do that. Please stop your unbearable attempts to mask how you feel with humor."

She doesn't like to be psychoanalyzed. Just ask her therapist. "Trust me," she says. "I will let you down. That's what I do." She can't believe how her negativity can go from zero to sixty in a second.

He picks up a stick and tosses it in the grass ahead. "Whatever it is you're running from, it's not me."

Her mother starts laughing in her head. *Told you so, Charli.*

"Sorry, Noah."

"So that's it," he says. "You're going to leave tomorrow, and we never talk again."

"We can text sometimes."

"We can text sometimes? How bloody great. I'm so glad we met, Charli. More so, I appreciate that you're opening up and being so real with me. Here's a hint. I like you even at your worst."

"You haven't seen my worst," she said with a nearly venomous hiss. "Trust me, this . . ." She makes a circle around her body with her finger. "This is the best of me. It falls apart from here. I'm saving you a whole lot of trouble."

Her mother is going after her now. *It's your father's fault, sticking me with a brat like you. I told him I didn't want kids, but he kept nagging me.*

Noah raises his hand. "Look, let's head back. I'm not going to spend the entire day living some kind of lie between us. If you want this to end, let's cut it off now."

"That's exactly what I've been trying to say." She springs to her feet, ready to head home. "Thank you for finally listening."

He shoots her a stubborn and frustrated glare. His jaw is tight; his head shakes.

As with a rotting limb, it's better to cut it off now.

Not a word is shared between them as they descend the hill and return to town. When they reach the river, they cross over it, and then he looks at her. "I'm going to head home. Don't worry, I'll stay out of your way until you're gone tomorrow."

"Thanks," she whispers.

He starts and stops a few more times. She wishes he'd give up.

"It doesn't have to be this way," he finally says.

He's such a nice guy, and she wishes she could be more compassionate right now. She doesn't want it to end like this. But she doesn't know how else to say goodbye. This one is going to hurt no matter how they do it. The sooner it's over, the better.

It's all she can do to say: "Goodbye, Noah. If I don't see your family, tell them thanks."

He finally breaks eye contact and turns away. She watches him walk down the hill and along the river. When he's gone, she turns and breaks into an unbearable cry. He's shattered her and doesn't even know it. And she hates herself for ruining it, for not letting them enjoy their last day together. She hates herself so much for ruining everything she touches. And for letting her mother win. She's twenty-nine years old, and her mother is *still* winning.

Chapter 19

THE ARCHIVES

It's Monday. Noah is true to his word and stays out of her way the rest of her stay. She doesn't even bother eating breakfast, worried that he'd be there, but as she's walking out with her bag, he's nowhere in sight. She sneaks out the back and beelines it to Winchester College. Doesn't even take a moment to look at the cathedral one last time.

The mirror told a sad tale today. Lines of a fifty-year-old crease her forehead. She's barely slept. The only thing that offers any light in her life is that she's finally going to get somewhere with her search. At least she hopes so. Any thoughts of Noah she tries to cast away, setting them on fire and letting them burn, burn, burn. If anything, she's been reminded through the whole thing with him that not only is it her father who needs help; it's her too.

Charli checks in with the front gate and says she has an appointment. The same person she's spoken to before tells her to hold on a minute. Charli is relieved when she sees Sarah come through a back door. She's a little older than the photo on the website, perhaps fifty or so. She wears red-framed glasses and looks kind of like . . . well, an archivist.

"I'm so sorry about pushing you off," she starts out, sticking her hand out for a shake.

Charli takes it. "No, no, I'm sorry for stalking you. How are you feeling?"

"Oh, I'm much better, thank you. Just one of those winter colds, you know. Don't worry, I slathered myself in sanitizer. Anyway, I'll never get used to that chill that comes through sometimes. You're from Boston, though. I'm sure this is a summer day to you."

"It's certainly a little warmer here."

"So you've done the tour. Shall we walk upstairs to my office and have a chat then?"

Charli follows her up a set of spiral stairs that must have been built a thousand years ago. Sarah opens a door into a magical library of archives. Books fill the built-in shelves that stretch all the way to the ceiling, which explains the ladder next to the window that looks over the roof of Winchester. The cathedral rises high and holy over the city wall.

In the center of the room is a long wooden table; at the end is Sarah's desk. Her computer has two screens. Sticky notes cling to every available spot.

"How long have you been doing this?" Charli asks.

"I'm a bit new, actually. Started last year, still trying to find my way around."

"Why does a school have an archivist anyway? I've never heard of such a thing."

Sarah looks shocked. "I'm sure Harvard does as well. Many of the older schools in England do. We even have a museum. I'm sure you've seen it."

"I have."

Sarah sits and invites Charli to the chair by the window. Sarah swivels around. "There's nothing like history to help us raise money, and that's so much of why I'm here. The alumni appreciate our legacy."

"And then people like me looking for information?"

"All the time. I just had a novelist visit the other day. I think his name was Boo, if I'm not mistaken."

"Boo who?"

"I can't quite recall at the moment."

Charli plows ahead. "Well, I know you're busy. I don't want to take much of your time . . ."

"I'm happy to help, but you're right—let's jump right in. I got your messages . . . all of them." She laughs, and Charli does too. Charli's emailed and phoned a few too many times. "But why don't we start from the top? You believe your grandfather attended."

Charli opens her purse and extracts the photos, hands the first to Sarah, and explains what led her here.

Sarah takes the second photo and examines it. "He seems taken by her, that's for sure."

"Right?"

"He's a looker. Both of them are."

Charli sits at the edge of her seat. "I have this weird feeling that he loved this woman a great deal. And he still had the photo after all those years—kept it hidden behind another frame."

Sarah points. "And there's the Winchester tie."

"Is it for sure?"

"Absolutely. That's it."

Charli almost thrusts her fist in the air in a victorious chant. "Flip it over."

Sarah does and says, "For Miles. What does that mean?"

"That's exactly what I wondered. I'm thinking that it might be a nickname, though no one in my family had ever heard of it. Or is it her name? Kind of an odd girl's name."

Sarah shakes her head. "Wouldn't be her name."

"So here I am, and I was hoping that you could help me see if we can find him."

"We don't have a lot to work with, though we can certainly search by name. Do you know how old he was when he died? We can work backward and get close to the year."

"He was sixty-two when he died in 1925, according to Ancestry. com. I'm guessing he was here in the late seventies, early eighties. Of the eighteen hundreds, of course."

Sarah swings around to her computer and hammers the keyboard. Her finger occasionally goes to the screen to help her follow a line.

After about five minutes, she turns back to Charli. "I don't see a reference to Samuel Hall. So why not try Miles Hall, right?"

Sarah's back at it before Charli has even dipped her chin for a nod. Another round of typing and searching before Sarah says, "Nope, nothing under Miles Hall."

"Ugh, that's so maddening. I was sure there might be."

"We could search first names or last names, but it won't be as easy. Of course, Samuel is a very popular name, so we'll have to sift through quite a lot. We might get luckier with Miles."

Charli hopes Sarah isn't done with her. "Do you have time?" she asks hesitantly.

"Oh, I love a good challenge," Sarah says. "Why don't I start pulling up photos?"

"You have class photos?"

"For most years."

Charli is elated.

Sarah goes back to typing, and then they're both looking at a black-and-white photo of about twenty-five boys standing in a courtyard. Charli squints. "They're not as crisp as I hoped."

"No, it's not a perfect science, is it? Photography was just getting underway."

Twenty minutes pass. They search every year, every grade. It's not only the official class photos she has. They pore through any associated shots with the search year, including those of sports teams and clubs.

"Wait, that could be him," Charli says with far more excitement than she usually exudes. She holds up her photo next to the screen. "I'm pretty sure it is." Chills run all over her; she's done it! She's found him!

"I am in agreement," Sarah says.

"I can't believe it. What's his . . ." Charli's afraid to ask. Something tells her to be cautious. "What's his name?" she finally gets out.

Sarah leans in to make out the text. "Miles Pemberton," she whispers.

"Miles Pemberton." She says his name again and again as she stares at her relative. "I had the first name right, but why did he change his last name?" Thank goodness she came to Winchester as opposed to chasing down the remaining leads she had in London.

This is the break she's been looking for, and her mind turns to scrambled eggs as she races through thoughts of how he could fit into the constellation in Costa Rica. Was he the evil one in the constellation, the man who seemed to murder the woman who fell to the floor? He looks so . . . so innocent.

"Oh, name changes happened more than you would think," Sarah answers. "Especially if he went to America. Misspellings are quite common, though Pemberton is a long way from Hall. He could have simply wanted a new start."

It's more than that, Charli thinks. "What can we learn about him? I mean . . . do you have any more information?"

"Let's see."

Sarah reads from the screen. "His parents were James and Cora Pemberton. Looks like James was a Winchester alum. Oh, he also had a younger brother who attended: Edward. And let's see . . ." She hammers away at the keys. "Not a ton of information, but I see a reference to him here, in the *Wykehamist* magazine."

"What's that?" Charli's still holding on to the fact that not only has she found Miles, but she's found his family. Which means she's found her family too. And this giant step gives her hope that maybe this wild-goose chase isn't one after all. If she isn't careful, she might call this fun.

"It was a monthly publication. More of a pamphlet, but it caught people up on the goings-on. Something to share with parents and alumni. Seems he was in the Shakespeare Society, part of a performance his senior year."

She hears the Bard's name and nearly chokes on the information. "Wait, I'm huge into Shakespeare. I wonder if he's the reason." She holds her hands out in front of her, looks at them as if she can see his blood running with hers. "I feel so connected to him."

Charli remembers Sarah is there and says, "Sorry, just got excited."

"They did *The Merchant of Venice* that year."

The hair on the back of Charli's neck stands up. "That was the name of my bookstore! Well, I didn't open it, but I almost did. It was going to be called The Merchant of Boston. Before that, it was going to be the Iambic Inkpot, but . . . long story. What are the odds?"

"How special. And he rowed for the crew team. Did you as well?"

Charli smiles. "No, no crew team."

"I must warn you," Sarah says, "I do have an eleven. But we have a few more minutes."

"Is there anything else?" Charli asks, frustrated that they're running out of time. She can't even take a minute to relish Miles's and her connection with Shakespeare. "Can we know where he went after graduating?"

"This is all that's showing up. I can look up more this afternoon and tomorrow, but our database from that time period should be up to date. We're still collating earlier records." She turns. "But you have a name."

Charli nods. "Yes, I do. I'm so grateful."

"What I'd do is go up High Street to the Hampshire Record Office. Do you know—"

"Yes, I was there the other day."

"Now that you have names, you can find all sorts of stuff. Of course, the British Newspaper Archives. See what you can find out."

Sarah gives her a few more ideas; then Charli rises to leave. "Please let me know if there's anything else you can think of. Thank you so much."

"My pleasure."

~

Charli takes the long way to High Street so she can avoid getting close to the inn and risking running into Noah or his family. She hurts to the core, this emptiness that she wants desperately to go away. The dumbest thing is that she doesn't want to call her aunt or her father to break the news. She wants to call Noah.

Back at the Hampshire Record Office, she takes a number and a seat in a far corner away from everyone else. She opens her phone with the annoying hope that Noah has texted her again. Perhaps he's still fighting for her. Alas, no such luck. She types one out to him. I'm sorry, Noah. I know I could have handled it better. I guess I'm just afraid. And a realist. I know where this is going.

She deletes all of it and tries again. About to board the train. Great meeting at the college! Thanks for everything.

Thank God she stops herself at the last second from sending that inauthentic awfulness. He knows her too well for that one.

She could stay. Of course, she'd have to tell him why she's in Winchester. He doesn't have all the facts. And maybe he wouldn't care. *Of course* he wouldn't care.

Charli can still feel his hand in hers. She can hear his laugh, taste his kiss. She chuckles when she recalls a joke he told. It seems the entire records office looks over at her then, and she whispers, "Sorry."

When her number is called, she walks down the familiar hallway and into the office with the number 14 on it. "How can I help you?" the man sitting at his desk asks. He has a mild twitch in his left eye.

"I'm American; well, I'm sure you can hear that. I'm trying to find out more information about my family," she says, putting a cork on her inner dialogue.

"Oh, that's not what we do here."

Her eyebrows crinkle. "But I thought . . ."

"You're looking for the McDonald's down the street."

Charli tilts her head. "Are you joking with me?"

He shows a crooked-toothed smile. She can see he's harmless, too, and she grants him a laugh in return. "That was a good one," she says dutifully.

"Let's have a look. What's the name?"

"Pemberton. Miles Pemberton. And his parents James and Cora. I know he was born in 1863, so . . ."

"Let's start with James and Cora Pemberton."

His typing is a tortoise on Xanax compared to the archivist's. After what feels like forever, he says, "There's one James Pemberton in Hampshire that's coming up, and he was a landowner and member of the House of Lords."

"As in a member of Parliament?"

"Technically, he's a peer, not a member, but yes." He's typing again. "Oh, oh yes. There's still a Pemberton in the House of Lords. His name is Steven Pemberton."

"What? I'm confused."

"The House of Lords used to be an inherited position. They got rid of most of those positions recently, save a few. Now you must be voted in. Pemberton is still active as a peer, though." The man swings his screen around. "Looks like we've got James and Cora right here."

Charli can't believe it. Her fourth great-grandparents are looking back at her. James stands beside his wife, one elbow out, his fist resting against his side. Neatly cut gray hair protrudes out from under a black top hat. Under a sharp nose, he wears a bushy mustache twisted at the end. He has a look of annoyed arrogance. If Charli had to guess, he's bothered by having to pose for so long. Though dressed fancifully, Cora is not an attractive woman, and she doesn't look any happier than her husband. Her eyes are set far apart from each other. Her rounded nose tips upward.

The two look no different from Miles and his wife, Margaret, in their picture, or William and Georgina in the photos Charli had seen of her parents. How could she possibly have been born happy and smiling when she comes from this stock?

Once he's given her sufficient time, the man pulls the screen back so that he can see it. He starts to type. "What was the other one you mentioned, their son?"

"Miles was one of two."

"Miles, yes." More typing. "Wait," he says. His face contorts into worry. "Is this . . . that's right. Oh, dear."

"What is it?" Charli could never guess in a million years.

The man sighs and pulls off his glasses. Sets them down. "I'm sorry, this is rather sensitive."

"What is it?"

"Your man Miles. He was convicted of murder in 1881 . . . and sentenced to hang."

Chapter 20

THE GIFT OF FOREVER

Winchester, England
April 10, 1881

Spring term came to an end in April. Only one more before graduation in July. Miles was desperately eager to see Lillian, as in the four months since he'd last seen her, he'd only strengthened in his want to chase his own dreams, and she was very much a part of them. It was nearly agony to wonder if her feelings had grown as well during their time apart.

Even as the coachman drove Edward and him back to their home at Elmhurst, west of Winchester, Miles was devising ways to escape the clutches of his family.

"Dammit, it's bumpy," Edward said. He hit the ceiling of the carriage. "Marlowe, can't you find a smoother path?"

"Sorry, sir. I'm doing my best."

"You're a coachman and can't even run a carriage without nearly knocking the wheels off."

Miles chuckled to himself. No boy had ever been more of a spit to his father than Edward. They barely spoke a word together on the drive.

As they drew closer, gunshots echoed across the estate. James stood next to another man near a visiting carriage. He had a special relationship with his guns and had been collecting them for longer than Miles had been alive. Surely, this was one of the firearms salesmen who frequented the estate.

The coach moved swiftly down the long drive, and the house in which Miles grew up came into view. Elmhurst had been in his family for generations. Spring had sprung, and an army of gardeners and landscapers were busy prepping the estate for a season of entertaining. Two men flanking each other pushed mowing machines across the lawn that had turned green since Miles had last seen it. Their estate was a revolving door for dignitaries, his father always angling to establish his place among the elite.

Elmhurst consisted of nine bedrooms upstairs and a series of living quarters for the servants down below. The stone building featured a tower in the center where Miles's father kept his office. Miles and Edward stayed in two separate rooms on the opposite end of the house from their parents, who enjoyed an entire floor to themselves. Miles and Edward had not been on their parents' floor since they'd stopped nursing as babies. James was a private man and did not want his boys messing about with his belongings.

The exception was with guns. Miles had never shown any interest and felt nothing when he saw his father holding a new gun. Edward, however, leaped from the coach to join the excitement. Miles followed well behind.

His father was dressed in hunting attire, had probably been out shooting grouse, and now inspected a gun that he would likely purchase. He'd once overheard one gun salesman say to another as they pulled away from the estate: "Pemberton is a sure bet if you know what he's looking for."

The back of the visiting carriage was open to reveal a multitude of gun cases, including the one at hand, which was propped open, revealing several shells and a cleaning kit. The gun salesman barely looked at the boys.

"Welcome home, sons!" James was a different man around others, the father Miles wished he was. He clapped Edward on the shoulder with his free hand and handed over the opulent rifle with joy—a look reserved only for guns or a Whig victory in Parliament.

"Take a look," he said.

Edward took the rifle, examining with his own form of rare glee the elaborately etched metal and the exotic wood. Edward and Miles had spent years shooting with their father. "Walnut?" he asked.

"The finest walnut specimen in England," the gun salesman replied.

"May I give it a go?"

"Why not?"

Miles could see the pride with which his father watched Edward cock the gun and shoot it into the air, and it grated against him.

"He's got a keen eye for targets too. What do you say, Edward? Should we purchase it?"

Edward examined it again. "I think so, Father. I love the weight."

"Indeed."

Their mother came out the door, welcoming her boys back with kisses on the head. Even she could put on a jolly look around guests.

"How was the term?" she asked them both.

James brushed her question away. "Let's save it for the meal, Cora." He looked at the salesman with a shake of the head, as if they both could understand the impractical nature of women. "We'll take the rifle."

⌒

The first three days were busy with entertaining. His father invited wealthy families from around Hampshire and Wiltshire to dine with them. He'd drink his French wines and tell stories that made them laugh, and if they had a daughter of the appropriate age, he'd slyly suggest that their families should unite. Miles tried to be civil to the young women who would accompany their families, but he had no interest in any of them.

It was the most unbearable when the Thornhills visited with their daughter, Etta. She was his father's first choice of a wife for Miles. He was polite without indicating any interest in a future with her, and though she seemed to get the message loud and clear, the fathers seemed oblivious. Or more truthfully, they simply did not care.

Miles wasn't able to get away to Winchester for three days. But, finally, their guests were gone, and he said he was going fishing at a spot toward town. He rode his horse at a near gallop and arrived in Winchester before lunch one morning.

Lillian stood in full concentration in front of a stack of shillings, counting away. When she came to a pause, he said, "Hello there, Lillian."

She gasped with surprise and emitted a luminous smile when she realized it was Miles. "I thought I might not see you again."

Relief set him down gently as it became clear how much she missed him. "You said that last time."

"It's true. How many months was it this time?"

"Nearly four, which is four too long." He didn't care whether the patrons at the tables or at the bar knew his name or his desire to court her.

Lillian wasn't able to get away, so Miles ate lunch there, a trout from the river with boiled beans and cabbage. He stole bits of conversation with her and her parents, and he conversed with her brother Arthur too. Miles was continually surprised by their kindness, despite their warnings to be careful. He left that day thinking that Lillian's family wanted only her happiness.

Upon his departure, Lillian followed him out. "When will you return?"

"As soon as possible, I assure you. I have things I need to say to you."

"Very well. But I want to know, exactly, when I will see you again."

Miles smiled. He liked being wanted. "I'll be at the cathedral for a christening on Sunday—ten o'clock. I can steal away afterward. My father will be traveling to Paris from there. Will you be here?"

"As always. So I can expect you directly afterward?"

"You seem uncharacteristically concerned with time."

She shrugged. "I can't stand around and wait on you all day every day now, can I?"

"Of course not. But . . . I know you well enough by now. You have something up your sleeve."

She revealed a devious look. "You'll see what's up my sleeve soon enough."

How bold of her, he thought. Was she speaking in metaphors? He couldn't have hidden his sinister thoughts for a thousand pounds. "I certainly hope so."

She shied away.

"Was that a blush I see?"

"Not at all." She turned back with those same devious eyes. "Not at all."

Miles glanced at her rosy cheeks. "Then I must be color blind."

"Clearly."

He wanted to kiss her, but he sensed curious eyes from those in the inn, and he did not want to upset her family. Instead, he removed his hat and bowed. "Until then, Lillian."

She gave him another smile that he tucked into his memory. As he walked away, he grew increasingly desperate to know what she had in store for Sunday.

"It isn't fair, you plotting something without my knowledge," he said, shortly after she'd joined him on High Street two days later. Church bells rang in every direction.

"It may not be fair," she said, "but I thoroughly enjoy seeing your curiosity pique."

He still wore his coat and tie from church. He'd told his mother the night before that he would take his own horse, as he and Quimby would be joining a game of rugby at the college sports fields. She'd been perfectly fine with it so long as he returned by dark.

Lillian was as striking as ever in a simple dress. Her comeliness outshone any of the young women who visited Elmhurst. Though her appearance was plain with regards to the standards of his own class, Miles could see that she'd put more effort than usual into her look today, as if whatever she had planned required it.

It became a guessing game for Miles as they meandered down the hill, walking as close as socially permitted. He barely considered the idea that someone who knew his family might come upon them.

"Is it a Sunday roast somewhere?" he guessed. "Or another church service? Or perhaps a concert? Or are we off to the theater?"

She laughed at his attempts. "You're wasting your breath."

Soon he realized they were walking toward her favorite spot along the river. Perhaps she'd planned a picnic of sorts. He took a few more guesses, which drew another round of giggles.

Once they were safely alone in the woodlands, Lillian stopped and turned. She rose onto her toes like a ballerina and kissed him.

"What was that for?" he whispered, wanting never again for her lips to stray from his.

She smiled and raked the hair from his eyes. "I love you, Miles Pemberton." Her words were a song to his ears.

"You love me?"

"Yes, I do. What's wrong with that?" Her eyes searched him, tugging at his heart.

"There is nothing wrong with that," he said, allowing himself to fall fully into this intimate moment. "It's only that . . . that I've wanted to say the same to you since the moment I first saw you on the bridge."

"It's only my looks that you love?"

"You've captured me with far more than your looks, Lillian Turner. I can't quite put a word to it, though. It's as if I've found a missing piece of myself."

Her smile grew wider.

"And the more I've come to know you," he continued, "the more I've grown to love you—if that's possible."

Lillian kissed Miles again and placed a finger against his lips. "That is why today is special. I wanted a way to mark this time we're sharing, the days when we fell in love."

"How might we do that?" His legs quivered in anticipation as his imagination overflowed with possibilities. Whatever it may be, he was certain it wasn't another church service they'd be attending. In fact, God may need to avert his eyes.

She tugged his hand and led him around the bend of the trail. To Miles's surprise, a man in a wool suit sat on a stump by the river, smoking a pipe, the smoke floating up over him. Miles at once felt guilty, as if he'd been caught. His family would certainly not approve of him strolling through the woods unchaperoned, especially with an innkeeper's daughter.

But the man offered a kind smile as he pulled the pipe from his mouth. "Hello, Lillian."

"Hi, Daniel. Thank you so much for being here."

It took only a moment for Miles to interpret the situation. Next to the man stood a camera on a stand.

Lillian took Miles's hand. "Daniel is a frequent guest of the inn and a particularly fine photographer. He's very famous in London."

Daniel stood and brushed off his trousers. "Well, I don't know about that."

The two men shook hands and formally introduced themselves.

"Daniel has been offering his services to our family for a while," Lillian said, "and I finally found a reason to take him up on it."

"It is quite nice out, isn't it?" Daniel said, taking in their surroundings. "And I do like the light today. We got lucky with a few clouds."

Miles looked at Lillian. First, Lillian had confessed her feelings for him and now this . . . this extraordinary gift. "Somehow you caught me in my suit, though I'm not sure I'll wear the tie."

"Oh, you must," she responded earnestly. "I think the tie makes you look terribly handsome."

"It's my father's, though. From his days at the college."

With no mind to Daniel, Lillian said, "Today it is your tie, and I'd like you to wear it."

Miles glanced at Daniel. "The lady wins this one."

As the sun moved through the sky, the photographer took his time setting them up in various poses and taking shots. Each one required that they stand motionless for a while, which proved to be difficult amid all the laughter.

Afterward, Daniel promised that he'd deliver his favorites within a few days. As he watched the man leave with the camera under his arm, Miles thought that she'd given him the perfect gift. He would cherish the photos and never let himself forget this day.

He stepped toward her and touched her hip. "That was special, Lillian. Thank you."

"You're welcome." He could see that she was so proud of what she'd done for him.

"That kiss earlier," he said. "Are there any more of those on offer?"

"I suppose there might be."

Where she was once perhaps suspicious of his motives, she seemed to have shed them now. She took his hand and raised it to her breast, and Miles fought not to lose his footing.

Though their clothes stayed on, Miles and Lillian explored each other's bodies in ways Miles had never done before with another girl. He wanted to go further, but she'd rightly slowed him down.

⌐

Later, they lay together by the river in the grass. A kingfisher watched from its perch above. The sun occasionally broke free of the clouds, bathing them in a welcome warmth. Other than their voices, only the river and the birds made any sound.

"I've decided not to go to Oxford," Miles said, stating what had been on his mind for months. "And I'm not quite sure I can leave you that long anyway. You have me, Lillian, all of me."

Worry creased her forehead. "You must go to Oxford."

"And why is that? Do you not feel the same way as I?"

"Yes, of course I do, Miles, but what do we do? Your father will disown you. I don't want to derail your life." Her worry for him was evident in her tone.

"Lillian, if you didn't want to derail my life, you'd best not have been crossing the river that night. You'd best not have drawn my attention or said a word to me when I entered the pub. There's no turning back now. Tell me . . . am I wrong?"

She closed her eyes and seemed to go away for a moment. In the silence, he could feel her being pulled in two directions. "No, you're not wrong. I love you, Miles. But I don't want you to suffer."

"The only way I would suffer is a life without you." He sat up. "Let my father disown me. He certainly will. I will find my own way. Only because it will behoove me to call myself a graduate of Winchester College, I will get through the last term and then tell him of my plans."

She sits up, too, and wraps her arms around her legs. "And what are these plans? Is this the one in London, where you are an actor?"

"You doubt me?"

She exhaled a long breath and took her time answering, as if she was coming to peace with their trajectory. A firm determination suddenly flickered in her eyes. "Not for a minute."

His heart shot up into the sky. "Yes, the one in London where I am an actor, and you are my bride. I'm certainly not naive to the fact that I don't have much experience, and what little I do is more reading than performing. Nevertheless, I believe that I can be good with the proper training."

Even if he could not make it as an actor in London, he could be happy carving out a simple existence where he could have a family so different from the one he currently had. He might be perfectly happy as a blacksmith or a baker, so long as he woke to her every morning.

"I believe that you're capable of anything, Miles Pemberton."

He offered a close-lipped smile. "And I, you."

"What will your family say to that?" she asked, reaching for his hand. They clasped fingers.

"I don't need their permission."

"Are you sure?"

He looked deep into her eyes, losing himself in the blue, diving deep into her soul, seeing the future of the two of them. "I've never been so sure of anything in my life." He kissed her again, and this time she pulled him in for a long hug. Breathing in the scent of her hair, like lilies in the spring, he never wanted to leave this place, never wanted to return to his old life.

"Have you ever thought about leaving Winchester," he asked, as he let her go, "and going to London?"

"Of course."

"Then let's go."

She considered the question, the excitement of his proposal lighting her face. "It's quite a proposal."

"I know it would be hard to leave your family, to leave your work."

"It would. But my parents have always said they wanted more for me."

"What an extraordinary family you have." Miles felt a rush of exhilaration. "And what would you do in London? Would you like it there?"

She lifted her gaze to the sky. "Of course. Perhaps I could eventually own my own inn."

"I wouldn't want you to work for long," he said. "As soon as I can find a way to make a living on the stage, you'll be set free."

"But I have no qualms with working. I quite enjoy my duties at the inn. It would be nice to run my own place in London."

"By all means. I'm simply saying that you wouldn't have to, that I can take care of you. That is why I must finish the school year. A diploma from Winchester College will no doubt give me a leg up. I turn eighteen in May. The last day of school is the first of July. Then we will go start a life together. You give me the courage, Lillian, to seize my life. And I thank you for that."

She nestled closer to him, her delicate smell dizzying him. "I enjoy seeing the fire that I stoke within you. How could I not follow you to London and see what we are capable of together?"

"And this is one of the infinite reasons I love you, Lillian. What other girl would be spontaneous enough to join a man she's only just met on an adventure to the city?"

She kissed him and left her lips to linger on his cheek. "If you weren't so devilishly handsome, I might not be so spontaneous."

They were a pair, indeed. "I'd like to introduce you to my grandmother, if you'd allow it."

"Really?"

"She says she'd love to meet you."

"She would? It makes me rather nervous."

"Oh, no, not at all. You'll see. She's the exact opposite of the rest of my family. In fact, she's my only hope for turning out right, and I pray nightly that her blood is strong in mine. Would you come with me to have lunch with her before I return to school?"

"I suppose so. If you're sure."

Miles felt a glimmer of excitement. "Someone in my family must get a chance to see what I see. Besides, I think she might have some wise words to share regarding our plight."

Lillian sat up. "Our plight?"

"Yes," he said. "The one where the whole world is against us. Except the whole world isn't enough to keep me from loving you."

She placed a hand on his arm. "You know exactly what to say, don't you?"

"Lillian, my darling, all I have is the truth."

~

Miles would have loved to usher Lillian to his grandmother's estate with grand affair, but he couldn't take the risk. So three days later, they rode alongside each other on horseback toward Granny's estate in Twyford.

Lillian rode sidesaddle in her dress. He could see by the way she handled her horse that she'd likely been riding all her life.

"Are you still nervous?" he asked her.

"To meet Lady Twyne? Yes, I am."

"She'll love you."

He'd stayed with Granny the night before, and she'd offered her wisdom. "It is quite a decision to abandon Oxford for young love and a small chance in the West End," Granny had said. "But you are indeed gifted in the dramatic arts, and I certainly can't blame you for eschewing a life at Elmhurst with your father. I do look forward to meeting Miss Turner. She must be quite special."

Miles held on to her encouragement with a tight grasp as he rode.

When they stopped to let their horses take a drink from a brook, Lillian pulled something from her bag. "I brought you a gift." She handed him a photograph protected by a frame. "This one was my favorite. What do you think?"

He'd been a part of several photographs with his own family, but he was still mesmerized by the invention, seeing their faces captured with such detail. What pleased him more was the joy that seemed to rise out of the photograph, and he felt it like never before.

Miles caressed Lillian's face and kissed her. There was new confirmation of their love in every touch. "I adore it more than you could know."

~

His grandmother waited at the door after they'd tied up the horses. "Miss Turner," she said warmly. "It's such a pleasure."

"For me as well, madam," Lillian replied, accepting Granny's hand with trembling fingers.

Over a cup of tea, they took their time reaching any serious discussion. Granny could talk about the birds for an hour if you let her. Miles steered the conversation toward the future he hoped for with Lillian. "We'll take any jobs we can find and sleep wherever we can until I have a successful audition. And if it doesn't work out, then I'll find other work."

Granny set her cup down. "Perhaps I could lend you some money so that the two of you could at least sleep in a decent place until you establish your footing."

"I would pay every pound back," Miles replied.

"I've no doubt. And you, Lillian . . . you're equally enthusiastic in such a pursuit?" Miles loved how receptive his granny was to the idea.

"Would you believe I've never been to London?" Lillian said, appearing more comfortable by the moment in Granny's welcoming company. "For me, it's as far away as Paris and Rome—or even New York. So, yes, London does sound appealing—especially with your grandson."

Granny looked over at him fondly. "He is quite the young man."

"And I intend on contributing money as well," Lillian continued. "My father taught me to save when I was young, and I have enough to feed us for a while."

As their conversation continued, Miles was so proud listening to Lillian speak. She carried herself well despite her nerves, and he had a feeling his grandmother saw exactly what he saw in Lillian.

"Granny, I mentioned the wonderful gift Lillian gave me. Having the photographer meet us. Would you like to see his work?"

"Yes, please," she said enthusiastically.

Miles retrieved the photograph from his satchel and handed it to his grandmother. "I thought you might keep it if you don't mind. You know what could happen if I kept it at Elmhurst."

Granny sat back with a smile, as though the photo reminded her of when she'd first fallen in love. "Look at you both, a perfect couple if I've ever seen one."

Miles beamed. The two women he loved and respected most in the world sat there with him in the same room. What an honor to know them both.

Eventually there arose the topic of dancing. Granny was speaking of her own wedding and of the dance, and that was when Lillian said, "I've never learned."

"You don't know how to dance?" Granny had said it a little harshly and backed off. "Of course you don't know. Let me tell you that I don't always love the life that I was born into, but I do love a good ball. It would be my great pleasure to teach you, if you'd like. I think you'd enjoy the waltz."

Miles had seen lovely smiles rise on the surface of Lillian's porcelain face, but none like the one she showed then. He felt even more proud to see how his grandmother did not let their social divide hamper their connection. In fact, she seemed undaunted by any obstacles, rules, or regulations.

Granny took Lillian's hand and showed her the first steps. "Arms up. Shoulders straight. That's it. Eyes on mine." It took a few moments, but Lillian finally got it. Miles let out a joyous grin and clapped as his grandmother and Lillian spun around the room in delight.

"I wish I had a violinist," Granny said. "Perhaps I'll arrange one for next time. Miles, your turn."

Miles sprang up. He'd never been quite as fond of dancing as his grandmother, but he welcomed the opportunity now. He took Lillian's hand and swept his eyes over her face, the joy so evident it could have made him cry. He was so caught up in it that he couldn't quite remember his steps and nearly tripped over himself.

"Oh, dear, my grandson might be the one who needs the lesson," Granny said.

"She causes me to feel dizzy, Granny."

"I do say!"

Miles wished everyone would see Lillian the way Granny did, but he knew better than that.

Chapter 21

YELLOW LIGHT REVELATIONS

Present Day

Charli runs a hand through her hair in shock. The man at the Hampshire Archives is being kind, offering to print out whatever it is he's looking at, but she's finding it hard to answer him. She's the descendant of a murderer. The notion is no longer a possibility. It's a fact.

Not only that, but the reason she's here, the constellation. It wasn't a bunch of woo-woo.

"Looks like he was sentenced to swing and—" the man starts.

"Wait, who did he kill?"

The printer comes to life, and he reaches down to take the paper. "Take a look for yourself."

Charli takes it from him, and her eyes go straight to the drawing of a young man sitting in court. Her throat tightens. The image is faded and grainy, but there's enough detail to see that it's him, her third great-grandfather.

Though she's befuddled by Miles's predicament, she can't help but think about how her father would be so proud of her for following through, and she can't wait to tell Frances and even Aunt Kay. She still doesn't know the details, so she sets her eyes to work to make out the grainy text.

It's a newspaper clipping from the *Hampshire Chronicle* from September of 1881. She breathes in some clarity and reads the copy.

Hampshire Man Sentenced to the Gallows

In a speedy trial that has caught the attention of all of England, Miles Pemberton was sentenced to death today for murder. As has been previously reported by this newspaper, he caught the victim stealing a necklace from the estate of his family, his father being Lord James Pemberton. The victim, eighteen-year-old Lillian Turner, is the daughter of Tom Turner, owner of the Smythun Inn & Pub. She was involved romantically with the . . .

Charli skids to a stop. "The Smythun? That doesn't make any . . ." She pauses to sift through the information. The man across from her is talking, but she's not listening.

"No," she says out loud. The fact that she was staying above that exact pub doesn't feel like a coincidence, but she can't make sense of it. Her relative was a murderer, and he murdered someone from the family that owned the Smythun. Wait, Noah had said his family had owned the inn for hundreds of years. But his last name isn't Turner; it's Armstrong. She supposes that is easily explainable with a change of name through marriage. She's sure she heard him right. Which means her third great-grandfather murdered someone in Noah's family tree.

Her mind is blown. Her heart pounds. Her brain shuts down.

"I . . . I need to . . . think through this . . . thank you." She stands and stumbles out of his office and the building. The train station is close by, and she heads in that direction. It's all too much, and she wants out of Winchester, out of England. She buys a ticket for a train that leaves

An Echo in Time

in twenty minutes, then goes to the small store to get another bottle of water.

On the other side of the tracks, she finds the end of a bench available. She drinks her water and starts to sift through the information that's whirring about in her head. A murderer in her family, the victim of whom was a Turner. What's mind-bending is that she somehow walked into the pub that the Turner family owns. That wasn't a coincidence. What it is, is scary. Terrifying.

Is someone toying with her? Charli's not sure what her relationship with God is, but it feels like he's having a good laugh at her expense. It's like she's been given a glimpse inside the universe, seeing how it all works. She can't even bring herself to look at the piece of paper that's now folded up in her back pocket.

She catches herself mumbling and glances over to see an elderly woman with shaky fingers looking at her. Or is it Charli who's shaking? The distance between her and home seems so vast at this moment, and she's wondering if she's having some sort of episode, a mental breakdown. Her head starts spinning again as she looks around and sees all these foreign faces. The English accents sound so foreign, too, despite this being her homeland. She's terrified that she's going to faint and wake up in an ambulance.

A train roars by without warning, and the wind blows her back. A man comes over the intercom and says something indecipherable to Charli that suddenly causes a stir among the other travelers. They pull out their phones and stare with worry. Charli's anxiety skyrockets. A group swarms a man in uniform, who tells everyone to settle down. She stands up and leans in to hear the specifics of the issue. There's a strike that's causing major delays for trains heading into London.

Charli feels trapped.

With a kick of fear, she realizes she left her bag on the bench and turns around.

It's gone.

She races over in a panic. "Where's my—"

"Are you okay?" someone asks.

Charli looks over at a girl dressed in a school uniform. "Someone took my . . ."

Then she sees it. She was at the wrong bench. Once it's looped around her shoulder, she sits and tries to calm herself. She can't make any decisions while she's losing it. She closes her eyes and tries to shut out the madness around her, the people frustrated at the delays, angry that they're missing meetings or their reconnections with family.

Charli's not sure what to do. She can't sit here on this bench all day.

She decides to go to the bathroom so she can splash some water on her face. She follows the signs, but there's tape on the door. It's out of order.

First she can't get home, and now she can't even use the bathroom. Why is everything blocking her way? "What is going on?" she asks herself.

Her forehead is sweaty; her head still hurts. She wants to be back in Boston, back in her bed, holding Tiny. She wants her dad and wants to call him, but she'll make him worry. She sees the tall stairs that will take her back across the tracks and thinks she has to get out of there. She climbs the steps, checking constantly to make sure she has her phone and wallet. Her thoughts are bumper cars running into each other.

Once she comes down the other side, she's totally unsure of what to do. She finds another man in uniform, who is smoking a cigarette.

"Excuse me, I'm sorry. I know you're probably . . ."

"How can I help you?"

"I'm so far out of my comfort zone right now, and it seems like my train is canceled. How do I get to London?"

He studies his phone, surely used to foreigners scrambling to make sense of the chaos. "Yeah, looks like the strike is going to make it hard today. You might catch the 12:15 toward Leeds, but I suspect that might get canceled too."

Charli feels like she's stuck in the Matrix with the weird robotic worms chasing her. "Where's the bus station?"

The guy is so calm and collected as he says, "Bottom of High Street. You might hurry, though. They're probably booking up quickly." He takes a long drag, then politely blows smoke up and away from her. "Are you okay?"

"I hope so. Thanks for your help."

She exits the train station and starts walking. She's sweaty and has to go to the bathroom and . . .

"Pull it together, Charli," she tells herself. "You've got this."

She stumbles upon a coffee shop, buys an Americano so she can use the restroom. Or toilet as the barista calls it. Charli walks out feeling better. She tells herself that she's safe. She doesn't have to be anywhere. And she has money. She can just get a hotel.

But what she wants to do is call Noah. He's so close, and she wants to be in his arms. She can't believe she's thinking such a thing, but she wants him to protect her. Of course, he's the last person she can contact.

There's a park a couple of blocks down with a bench that's free of people. She sits and tells herself she's not moving for a while. A bus sounds awful, but she doesn't want to take a taxi or Uber all the way to London. The cost is too high, and she'll be carsick the whole time.

She sets her coffee down, as the caffeine is already making her predicament worse, amplifying it. She folds her head into her hands and pulls at her hair, feeling the sting of it. She needs to see it all written out on a whiteboard, all the facts. Samuel Hall is not even a real person. It's Miles Pemberton. And he killed a woman named Lillian Turner, who must be a relation to Noah. Of course she is. Her father owned the Smythun.

Charli's mind starts to come back to her, and her curiosity comes alive. How had she not even googled Miles's real name yet? She couldn't have imagined he'd be in the papers for a murder. She takes out her computer and connects it to her phone's hot spot. A Google search for Miles Pemberton leads her to multiple articles. According to an article in the *Hampshire Chronicle* dated July 3, 1881, Miles shot Lillian in the chest with a rifle.

She eventually finds a drawing of Lillian Turner.

"Wait . . ." Charli's mouth turns into a flycatcher.

How could she only now realize? The girl in the photo. The one with Miles as a young man. It's her, Lillian! She tears through her bag to find the shot. It has to be. That's the way her life has worked since she originally found the photo, all these coincidences that are not coincidences. So he killed her? If there's an opposite of wanting to kill someone, that's how he looks, what with the way he's smiling, almost laughing.

She's unquestionably the exact young woman in the photo. Miles killed her. But why?

The murderous side of Charli comes alive as she imagines him becoming fitful with a rage that can only be quenched by . . . hold on, why?

Charli feels like she's been dumped into an Agatha Christie novel and wonders how she can possibly piece together all the facts of a case without going berserk.

And the constellation! How had Charli not realized it until now? She's just figured out who Herman and Letícia represented. Charli is suddenly back in Frances's studio looking at Herman standing over Letícia, who is curled up under the blanket.

"Herman is Miles and Letícia is Lillian . . ." The idea is almost too much. Total strangers had somehow acted out a murder that they knew nothing about.

Noah pops into her mind as if he's pulled open the door. How did she end up staying at that pub? What are the odds? She thinks back to how it happened, how she felt drawn to it. Was that it? She was waiting for more information from Winchester College and then . . . she met Noah, and she'll never forget the power of their first exchange, as if atoms had split when their eyes met. It was as if they had to meet, as if it was destiny.

"How is this even possible?"

Waves of information crash down on her, and she hops on one and rides it.

"Miles was sentenced to hang," she says out loud. "He didn't hang, though. He somehow found his way to a boat to the US, then changed his name. What happened?"

It's all impossible. But considering the constellation's accuracy and how she slept with Noah all weekend, maybe anything is possible.

She's reminded quickly of another apparent fact. That Miles's father was in the House of Lords. An internet detour teaches her a few things about what that means; how, for instance, he's referred to as a peer due to his inherited position. She searches for the man who is quite possibly her relative: Steven Pemberton.

Lord Steven Pemberton lives near Stockton at his estate known as Elmhurst. She looks at the picture of him, studying his face for any similarities to her own. Or with her mother. She's not quite sure she sees it, though her mind is definitely playing tricks on her. She finds him on a list of members of Parliament and even finds his email address.

Charli composes a quick note to him: My name is Charli Thurman, and I'm researching my family history. Looks like I might be related to you. If you're not too busy, I'd love to connect via phone or email.

When she's done, she sits back and takes a moment. A stone fountain gushes water in front of her. Across the street, there's a school, and a herd of children pour out to the playground. She wonders if the red lights are gone now. She's done exactly what she should do; she's found the truth. But she doesn't feel any different.

Charli forgets that she's decided not to drink the Americano, and it's empty. Her mind is a frenzy now, ideas ping-ponging back and forth. She reads everything she can, finally coming across a piece talking about how Miles had escaped prison.

"So that explains it," Charli says to herself, her face contorting as she puts more of the pieces together.

She reads on. He escaped in September of 1881. A prison not too far away from where she is sitting now. But it says he was declared dead shortly afterward.

"Oh, I don't think he was dead," she says. "Unless he'd gotten her pregnant first." A rare feeling of pride is rising out of her. Has she done this, come all the way to England to find answers and actually found them?

She can't go another minute without calling her dad. When he picks up, she says, "You won't believe what's happening over here, Dad."

"Well, good morning. No, I guess afternoon for you. Tell me. I can hear it's good from the tone of your voice."

"It's good, I guess. More to the point, I'm getting somewhere. Seriously, I came here with so much skepticism, but you wouldn't believe the pieces falling into place. I know all this sounds absurd to you, but I'm starting to think it's not absurd at all. I'm starting to think that Viv's guru knows exactly what she's doing."

He laughs, which is like a pacifier for her ears.

"It's not pretty, though. The truth. Samuel Hall . . . was not Samuel Hall. His name is Miles." Charli goes on to tell him everything, and he's listening and asking questions and making her feel even more proud of herself. "The thing that I don't even believe, or what is really blowing my mind. Noah. The guy I spent some time with this weekend—it's his pub."

"You've got to be kidding me."

"I know. I know, Daddy. I can barely process all this, but it's happening. It feels like I'm supposed to be here, like I'm onto something. And maybe, just maybe, this curse or whatever it is that's hanging over us, maybe it will go away." She hears what she's saying and knows he's as skeptical as she'd been. "I know it doesn't make sense."

"It does. Sure. More importantly, I like hearing you so excited about something. You know when I heard you like this the last time? When you told me you were going to open your bookstore."

Her eyes turn watery. "Yeah, it kind of feels like that. So how are you doing? Tell me you haven't sold the boat."

"Nope, haven't sold the boat."

"Good. I'll be home soon; it's kind of a moving target. But I can't wait to see you. I love you."

"I love you too, kiddo. And I wish I could tell you how proud I am of you, how much I love this fighter inside of you. You stay as long as you need to, okay?"

"Thank you."

After hanging up, she calls Frances and leaves a desperate message. "I'm onto something, Frances. And I need your help. I have all this wild information and not exactly sure what to do with it. Please call me when you get this."

She has one more phone call to make before she gets back on the trail. She calls Viv and congratulates her again on the promotion, then catches her up on the goings-on in Winchester.

"Hey, I don't doubt it," Viv says. "I told you. Frances is changing my life. I don't doubt a thing she says."

Charli's head swivels back and forth. "I'm excited but a little creeped out."

"Yeah, well . . . there are big things happening out there, Charli. That's what I keep realizing. We sometimes get stuck in our own little worlds, but things we can't possibly fathom are happening all around us. I'm a believer, honey. What we don't know is infinite."

"You're so not a lawyer anymore."

"I know, right."

~

Hunger pangs eventually get her, and Charli walks down the street and finds a Thai place. She'll be happy if she doesn't see a pub the rest of her life. While she eats tofu and vegetables, she goes back to her biggest problem at the moment, which is her inability to get back to London and her lack of a place to stay. Something is keeping her here, is that it?

She's ashamed to do it, but she calls Frances three more times. This is an emergency that warrants phone stalking. Charli has no idea what to do with all this information. She's come this far. She's onto something. What little bit of her still holds hope for breaking through the red lights is telling her that she's not done, that she's close. She's just not sure what to do next.

The truth is out there, and it explains so much. But . . . what now? Fly back home knowing this fact and hope for a life of green lights ahead? Will the truth really set them free? Or is there more to it? Surely she needs to do something with the information.

"What am I supposed to do?" she says out loud, drawing the attention of the server.

"Do you need something?"

"No, sorry. I'm talking to myself." Well, she does need something, but it's not on this menu.

She pays the check, or bill as they call it over here, and goes out the door as directionless as before. Perhaps even more. She walks aimlessly for a while. Her backpack and bags are getting heavy.

Sure, she's found a vital truth, but there has to be more to it. She nearly snorts as she imagines that maybe she has to write these truths down and then burn them in some sort of spiritual act. Another constellation could be necessary. She has no idea. This is why she needs to talk to Frances.

Another idea visits . . .

Does she need to make things right? Is there something to make right? Noah barely knows about the murder. It's not as if his family is struggling like her own. Or are they?

Her phone rings.

Chapter 22

DO YOU BELIEVE IN DESTINY?

It's Frances calling from Costa Rica! A bus passes by and it's loud, so she races across the busy street and goes toward a patch of trees.

"Hey there," she says, "thanks for calling me back. Sorry to stalk, but you won't believe everything that's happened. Well, maybe you will."

"Slow down," Frances says in a pacifying tone. "I've got time."

"Sorry, yeah." Once she has a clear head, she gives Frances the lowdown. It takes about five minutes.

As she reaches the river, she catches herself rambling again and asks, "You still there?"

"I am . . . and listening," Frances says.

Charli follows the path along the rushing water. "I wonder if I have to do something to make up for what my family did. I did sleep with Noah—a few times—and it was great, but I'm not sure it was make-up-for-murder great."

A barely audible laugh comes through the phone from Frances. "I'm not sure that's the answer . . ."

"But I can't imagine that me figuring this out is going to do much good."

"It's early to tell, but you're bringing your family's pain up to the surface. It could be guilt that's leading the way. Miles killed a woman and then went on to have a long life. He got married and had children. Was he consumed by guilt? Was he even aware of it? This is exactly the sort of occurrence that can knock a family system out of balance. Miles's guilt could be affecting everyone, like your mother making you feel so small. I'm sure you feel guilt, too, even if it manifests as something else, like self-loathing."

"Uh, yes to the guilt . . . and self-loathing. I want to sentence myself to the gallows as we speak."

"Don't be so harsh on yourself. Part of restoring the balance is accepting that you've done nothing wrong, that your mother's behavior, or anyone else's in your family, doesn't have to affect you the way it has. You get a fresh start. You are not bound by genetic determinism of any kind."

"It sounds a lot more complicated than simply finding the truth."

"In some cases, it is, but I'm sure the shift is already happening."

The path diverts away from the river and winds into marshy terrain. Charli glances at a board that reads: WINNALL MOORS NATURE RESERVE. Under it is a trail map and a local-birds poster. Focusing more on the conversation than her direction, she keeps going.

"You're not even surprised by my whole story, are you?"

Frances gifts her a laugh. "As you alluded to, there's a reason you met Noah. I'm not sure it's because you owe him something, but I can't say that for sure. Every journey is so different. Some are easy; this one's not."

"You can say that again."

"Suffice it to say, I don't think you should leave Winchester."

"Well, I can't, so . . ." Charli's thinking of the train strike when Frances drops the hammer.

"You need to go see him, tell him the truth. That's a good place to start."

"Please don't say that." A flurry of paradoxical emotions tug at Charli like she's being drawn and quartered. She wants to see him again, but it would be awful to have to tell him why she's here and what she's discovered.

"Noah aside, what do I do now? I have the truth. Maybe things are shifting, but I guarantee that if I call my dad right now, he's not going to be doing jumping jacks, if you know what I mean."

"I think that if you quiet your mind for a while, you'll know what you need to do. But you've had a *huge* day. Find a place to stay and take some time for yourself. Be patient. Seize this sense of courage and confidence that you're finding. Believe in yourself."

Charli never wanted to be the protagonist in her own mystery novel. She enjoys the safety of being able to close the book if things get weird. Well, things have certainly gotten weird.

"I am so confused by the idea of Miles being a murderer," Charli says. "All I see is an innocent boy who reads Shakespeare and rows crew and likes—maybe even loves—a girl with curls who is not exactly of his class. I don't know what happened between them, why he killed her, or even *if* he killed her."

"Sounds like there's still more to uncover."

Charli's arms tingle. "I guess so. You keep telling me to trust my intuition. I don't know if I'm doing it right, but something tells me he's not guilty."

"Listen to that voice, Charli. Allow it to keep speaking to you. And you know what my intuition is telling me? Perhaps you owe Lillian this journey. Think about it. You might not be alive had Lillian not died."

"Whoa." Charli processes the suggestion. Had Lillian lived, Miles might never have immigrated to the US, might never have changed his name and married Margaret and had children.

"You could have a life debt to Lillian," Frances says.

"What does that mean?" Charli knows, though. That's why she does have to make things right.

"If you listen, she might tell you. Maybe find her grave. Could you do that? Or a place that means something to her. Go see her, talk to her, see if she talks back. And, meanwhile, hand back the guilt to Miles. You don't own it. You have nothing to do with it."

"I don't know how to do that."

"You're doing it, Charli. You might not see it, but you're getting somewhere. Do you remember what I told you? Your destiny is to break the generational pain that has encapsulated your family since this murder. You, I believe, have the opportunity to set your entire family free of what happened. If you're right and he didn't do it, then who did?"

"This is not easy."

"Keep following the pieces," Frances says. "Take it all the way home. And I'm sorry to say, part of the truth that you must uncover is coming clean with Noah. About your feelings, about why you're there."

Charli shakes her head. "Why?"

"You already know the answer to that."

"But I don't. Not really." Charli's head is spinning around, and she's terrified of even the idea of facing him, let alone telling him the truth.

"My mentor used to share a quote with me, and it took a long time for me to figure it out. But once I did, I found it to be profound."

"What is it?"

"I can't remember who first said it, but it goes like this: I went searching for a cure for my sickness, but it turned out my sickness was the cure."

"What in the world is that supposed to mean?"

"You might have to sit with it awhile. You're trying to fix all these things to reach a point of healing, but the healing is already taking place by you being on the journey."

The way Frances says it this time does make sense. If only because Charli knows she's changing. Even if she returns to the struggles from which her family continues to suffer, she will see them in a different light.

"There's a reason you came to see me. And now you have to finish what you started."

Charli's shaking her head with frustration when she comes around a bend and nearly drops the phone. She stares in dead silence as the setting registers in her mind.

The grass is tall along the shore. A dead tree stands by the river. Everything about the scene seems familiar.

Then it hits her.

"You won't believe it," Charli says, looking around. "I'm in this park called Winnall Moors, and I think I'm where they took the picture, the one with Miles and Lillian by the river."

Charli pulls out the photo and studies the tree; it's definitely a beech tree. She compares the shape of the mossy trunk and sees some of the same knots.

Her heart charges out of the gates like a horse at the Kentucky Derby. "Yeah, I'm looking at the same tree. It's wider and a little taller . . ." She gazes up at the gnarly old branches. "There's not one leaf. "And dead," she adds, "but it has to be the same tree. This is it, Frances. The *exact* spot. What is going on? I'm losing it."

"No, you're not. I think it means you're on the right track."

Charli can't deny it. "What's going on, Frances?"

"This is called setting yourself free, Charli. You're doing it."

The words hit her hard. She *is* doing it, whatever *it* is.

Charli has to get off the phone to process what is happening. Frances tells her she'll make herself available. Charli barely hears her and drops her phone into her backpack.

Aside from the how of it all, she's wondering, *Why? Why* has she ended up here of all places in Winchester? On the day she's trying to get back to London. How is it possible that she discovered it?

Charli hears movement and whips around. It's only a bird perched on one of the dead limbs of the tree. As if someone has possessed her body, she walks over and puts her hand on the crumbling bark of the tree and closes her eyes. She feels Miles's presence and lets his energy run through her. It's like a drug of which she can't get enough.

When she opens her eyes again, she lifts her gaze and follows the knobs and knots upward. Then she sees it, a carving above her head that's barely legible, as if it was done many years ago. She stands on her toes and tries to make it out; something is telling her it's important.

The weather-worn characters come to life: *M P + L T*.

"No way," she mumbles. Her eyes water as the initials register. Miles Pemberton plus Lillian Turner.

The letters have been stretched by years of growth, but she can still make them out. Chills wash over her as she reaches tall and runs her fingers along them. She can feel Miles and Lillian's love, and it pounds inside her.

Retracting her hand, Charli looks at the photo again, now with a much better understanding of the love shared between the two. She stares into Miles's eyes. "You didn't kill her, did you?" If only he could speak back.

Eventually, she stands and snaps a picture of the carving so that she'll know for sure she wasn't dreaming. She lies back against the tree and tries to find her bearings. Her conversation with Frances returns to her. *You might not have the whole truth, Charli.*

"What if Miles didn't do it?" Charli says to herself, considering the possibility. "How could someone feel that strongly and then take it away?"

The constellation in Costa Rica becomes a chessboard in her mind. Letícia, the woman who fell to the ground, had certainly been representing Lillian. But what about Herman, the man who represented the red lights in Charli's family. The murderer . . . he couldn't have been Miles.

Or could he? What if something happened? What if Lillian broke up with him? Or cheated on him? Miles could have lost his mind. That notion seems possible. Love brings out the worst in people. The thought is sobering. Her intuition and all these feelings are one thing, but she could be wrong. Miles could have snapped like her grandfather and Georgina snapped.

If that's how it happened, what does Charli do? Maybe she does need to make it right. But to do that, she would need to determine exactly how Noah's family was affected. And if Miles didn't do it, she needs to figure out who did.

It also means she had better change her flight again, so she calls the airline and puts it off until Sunday this time. She can always change it again. Next, she taps out a quick message to Marvin, saying that she'll know more in another day or two, but she'll be back by Monday at the latest.

Then she sets her mind on finishing what she started. There's only one way to get to the truth . . . by stepping back into the lion's den.

Chapter 23

A Brother's Envy

Winchester, England
July 2, 1881

"How does it look?" Miles stepped back to see his handiwork. He'd carved their initials in the tree that grew where they'd taken the photograph.

Lillian slipped her fingers into his and whispered, "Our spot forever."

He'd graduated the day before and now felt freer than he ever had in his life. Without even asking his parents, he'd woken up this morning and made the ride into town to find Lillian. She'd only moments before confirmed that she was ready to go with him to London, so he would return home tonight to pack his belongings and tell his family at breakfast in the morning.

"Can you reach the inn by noon tomorrow?" she asked. "My parents want to host us for lunch, a sort of goodbye and celebration."

"How wonderfully kind of them. And they're not bothered that we're leaving without being married?"

She considered her answer. "They know it will come in due time."

"Indeed, it will." Miles was in awe of the support her family gave her. "Sounds like a far more positive response than what I expect from mine tomorrow."

"There were a few tears," she said. "But I've been working them up to it, giving them clues. They know how I feel about you, and they know that I must get out of Winchester."

"And we can return any time you like to visit. I'll need to come back to ask your father for your hand in marriage soon anyway."

A smile sprouted on her face like one of the wildflowers growing around them. "He would expect nothing less."

Miles nodded. "I'll have our driver bring me by carriage. We'll usher off to the train station from there." Even saying it felt liberating. "I'm still in shock that we're making it happen."

"As am I."

He breathed in her scent, the flowery essence of her, and tasted the sweetness of her lips. She gently raked her nails across his cheek. Shivers shot up from his toes and cascaded up his legs and across his body. As long as she was close to him, he could do anything in this world.

"Where will we sleep tomorrow night?" she asked, her face lingering close to his.

"I feel confident we'll find a place, perhaps a hotel near the West End. My granny has lent me some money that we'll put to good use. A fine dinner, hopefully a visit to the theater, and a good night's sleep. The following morning, after waking up next to you, I will find a job and secure acting classes."

"Both in the same day?"

"Why not? And what will your first day be like?"

Excitement leaped from her eyes. "Oh, I can barely stand the idea. All the tall buildings, the people rushing about. The restaurants, the theater. I can't believe it's happening either. I'll find work, as well. Something I like."

He touched her cheek. "Don't worry, we'll find a nice place to stay. I won't have my bride living in squalor."

"I like the sound of being your bride." Her joy was nearly tangible, as if it occupied a cloud above her head. "And I have faith that we will find our way."

"God willing," Miles said.

He pulled her in and ran his hands up and down her body as she kissed his neck and cheek and ear, sending a fresh round of shivers that made it hard for him to stand.

"We should go swimming," he suggested with choppy breath, their lips a blade of grass apart.

"Swimming?" Lillian replied, pushing back enough to find his eyes. "In my dress?"

Miles shook his head. "You don't need your dress to swim, do you?"

"You shameful boy."

"Boy?"

She nestled her cheek to his and whispered into his ear, "You'd rather me call you a man?"

Her breath made him tingle and sent him floating. "I'm eighteen. And I've found my wife. What more makes a man?"

"You sure you've found your wife?"

Miles moved his head back to look into her eyes again. Was she doubting him? "It's the one thing I am sure of, Lillian."

"And I as well."

He cracked a grin. "You've found your wife? Who is she? Do I need to worry?"

Lillian playfully hit him on the chest and let him enjoy his retort. She stepped back and said, "Let me look at you." She lowered her gaze to his boots and raised it up along his trousers and shirt all the way to his forehead.

He stood there, slightly shy and exposed, but still warm and comfortable, too, the way only she made him feel.

She steadied herself with her hands against his chest. "I've certainly found my husband."

All the love in the world passed through him, and he found the courage for Shakespeare. "Not did I wonder at the lily's white, nor praise the deep vermilion in the rose; they were but sweet, but figures of delight drawn after you . . ."

Her expression bloomed with delight. She kissed him again and moved her hands to his shirt buttons, undoing the top one. His shirt gave way as he closed his eyes. Pleasure like he'd never known before roared through him. It was a sense of being utterly vulnerable yet comfortable, feelings he never could have imagined before he'd met her: a desperate taste for her, a need to nearly consume her.

"I want more," she said.

His cheeks swelled. "Fine." He drew in a breath, attempting to keep the swarm of bees in his chest at bay. "Love is a smoke raised with the fume of sighs; Being purged, a fire sparkling in lovers' eyes; Being vexed, a sea nourished with loving tears. What is it else? A madness most discreet, A choking gall, and a preserving sweet."

She seemed to bathe in his words as though they were hot springs. She was indeed his Juliet.

Another button, and then another. The breeze came off the river and blew against his bare chest as she pulled off his shirt and placed a soft kiss on his collarbone. Then another, lower down. A sense of urgency washed over him, and he tried to go for her dress, but she wouldn't let him.

"No, no," she said. "It's my turn. I want to see all of my future husband."

She pulled at the laces of his boots, and he aided her in kicking them off. As he stood there barefooted, she rose and placed her hands on his trousers, unclasped his suspenders. His heart throbbed like his stallion at a full gallop. She held his gaze and pulled the belt free from its straps. Miles barely blinked as he lost himself in the moment, in her eyes and in her touch. He could see that any part of her that had once been hesitant was now gone, and she was always and forever his. He could have cried he was so full of life and joy.

Setting him free, she lowered his pants ever so slowly and guided them off his legs and ankles. Rising, she stepped back again and looked at what she'd done, at Miles in all his glory. He might have felt embarrassed had he not seen a craving for him swimming in her own eyes.

"Yes," she whispered, stepping again toward him. "You are no doubt a man. The most man I've ever known."

With that she touched him in places where he'd never been touched, and he had to work hard to control himself, to pace himself.

"And when is it my turn?" he asked in a moaning mutter, the words spilling out of his mouth in a desperate plea to remove her dress. Never in his life had he wanted anything more than to see her nude.

Lillian whispered into his ear, "I am all yours."

Naked and eager, he tugged at the belt that wrapped around her waist, and he reached for the bottom of her dress. He'd never undress her for the first time again in his life, and he wanted to treasure this moment with all of him. As she raised her arms to aid him, their eyes locked. Miles imagined the water of the river rising, the grass in the meadow standing taller, the clouds parting. He began to lift the dress over her head, a tad bit at a time, his breath escaping him and then rushing back in as he gasped for it.

He set the dress to the side and looked at the beauty that was the love of his life. She stood there confident and gorgeous in her cotton undergarments. Her legs, oh, her legs, they'd been shaped by God's sculptor, so feminine and smooth and tempting. Her décolletage made his mouth wet. He removed her undergarments and pulled her into him. They fit together like two bodies never had before.

"Shall we go swimming?" she asked.

Butterflies filled his stomach. "I had other things in mind now, but . . ."

"We have time," she said, taking his hand. She guided him into the water, and he studied her silky bare back, wanting her more than he'd wanted anything in his life. They slowly slipped into the water, the chill of it taking their breath away. He pulsed with a nearly uncontrollable craving and held her tight in the cold water.

"Is it too much for you?" she asked, as if she swam in this river every day.

"Cold? Holding you, I'll turn this water to boiling."

She kissed him again, more passionately this time, her tongue sweeping into his mouth and finding his, while wrapping her legs around his waist. He stood there with his feet in the soft grass under the water and felt the river rush by them, wrapping around them like her legs.

"I could stay here for the rest of my life," he said.

As her lips parted in reply, something caught her eye, and she shouted, "Who goes there?" Miles thought she might be attempting to be funny, but she let go of him and said again, "Who goes there?"

He turned his head to find his brother standing under the shade of a tree with a wry smile on his face. Miles's hands tightened to fists, and rage collected in his cheeks.

"What a show you put on!" Edward called out.

"Bugger off," Miles said.

Edward seemed not to shy away at all as he put his eyes on Lillian, who'd wrapped her arms around her breasts.

"What are you doing here?" Miles thrust his finger in the direction of town. "You need to go."

Edward didn't move, only kept his eyes on Lillian. "I might wait until you get out so that I can enjoy one more look."

All the energy that Miles had directed toward Lillian at once turned to fury as he scurried out of the water.

"Who is it?" Lillian called desperately, clearly full of fear.

"My brother." Miles cared not at all that he was unclothed. Dripping wet, he pulled himself up to the shore and rushed after Edward, who turned and started running.

"How dare you disrespect me!" Miles shouted. Briars and branches cut the skin of his bare feet, but he did not let it slow him down.

His brother, however, stayed ahead of him.

As Miles's head cleared from the anger, and he started to lose his breath, he realized that his brother was now in on a secret far more dangerous than carnal knowledge.

"Edward!" he shouted. "I must be the one to tell Father!"

His brother let out a cackle, stopping only long enough to say, "You know what Mother says about secrets."

Miles chased his brother until the houses near the river came into view. He stopped and yelled one last time, "Edward!"

He was seething as he returned to Lillian. She'd climbed out of the water and slipped back into her dress. Her hair and dress were wet, her face heavy with concern.

"I'm so sorry," he said, panting as he located his own clothes.

"He's sick," she said.

"Unquestionably so." Miles pulled on his undergarments, then his trousers. "I fear that he'll tell my father immediately."

"How did he find us?"

Miles began to button his shirt. "He must have followed me." The idea of someone breaching their intimate moment was unforgivable. It might be best that he hadn't caught Edward, as he damn well might have killed him.

Miles went to her once he was dressed and took her hand. "I'm so sorry."

"You've nothing to do with it."

He saw the love swimming in her eyes, but it wasn't enough to quell his anger. "I couldn't hate my brother any more than I do. I loathe that I share their blood."

"Don't worry, my love. We'll be gone soon enough."

He let go of her hand and looked west through the trees. "I think I should go now, to break the news to my parents."

"Are you sure?"

"Best to get it over with. Depending on how they take it, I may have to stay over at my granny's tonight."

"I want to go with you," she said.

"To Elmhurst?"

"If we are to marry, then they must meet me. Even if they don't approve, they should know who I am."

She was right.

"And perhaps they will tone down their reaction in my presence," she added.

"I would not count on it. But yes, let us go together. You have a horse available?"

"I'll need only a few minutes to saddle her. I do wonder if you can keep up with me, though."

He let out a welcome smile. "Let us find out."

Chapter 24

RIGHTING WRONGS

Present Day

Charli draws close to the Smythun Inn & Pub, thinking that she might understand why her attraction with Noah was so volcanic. It's a long shot, but in the world she's living in right now, anything seems possible.

When Miles lost Lillian in 1881, a tear in the fabric of the universe had presented itself, and something about this present-day encounter had begun to close the gap, to repair a love lost. Never mind the gender reversal, Charli had recognized the feelings she'd been having about Noah in how Miles loved Lillian. Did she and Noah somehow dredge those ridiculous feelings up?

She laughs to herself as she cuts down an alley of High Street. Einstein said energy cannot be created or destroyed. If they inherited the feelings, then it's clearly not real anyway. She and Noah are simply puppets acting out what Miles and Lillian had, much the same way the representatives of the constellation in Costa Rica had done.

Charli reaches the pub at three p.m. and stops well short of it. The lunch rush has slowed. She doesn't see Noah inside and wonders if he might have the day off. She once again considers staying somewhere else, at least maybe for a night, but that thought grows cold as she reminds herself why she's here. She needs to get to the truth, and that means jumping right back into where she'd been.

Shoving away her hesitation, she pulls open the door and first sees two older men watching soccer—or football, as they call it. They pay her no mind as she looks around to see who's working. She knows everyone by now.

Victoria comes out from the back, carrying a glass rack, and hits her with those emerald-green eyes. "Oh, hello, Charli. Did you forget something?"

A lot of things, Charli thinks. "I . . ." She doesn't know how to respond, hasn't gotten this far in her head. "I can't seem to pry myself away," she finally admits.

Victoria sets the rack down; the beer glasses rattle. "Noah will be happy to hear it."

"Is he working today?"

"He's not; he's got the day off. Shall I tell him you're looking for him?"

"No, please don't. I think I'll surprise him."

Noah's sister comes around the corner as Charli is turning to leave. "Ah, she's back for more," Marianne says, twisting her hair into a ponytail and assuming her place behind the bar.

"Hey there . . . how's . . . how are you?" Charli is less than thrilled to see her, only because she has to explain herself now. Victoria goes to the opposite side of the pub and busies herself cleaning tables. It seems obvious she's getting out of the path of Hurricane Marianne.

Marianne looks at her curiously, suspiciously. "I'm . . . fine?"

"Good, that's good."

"What brings you back?"

"The good food?" Charli can't even say it with a straight face.

Marianne chuckles darkly. "Right. Look, I think you've had your fling, and now it's time to let it go." And the prickly one rears her head.

"Trust me," Charli says, "I know we don't have a chance in the long term."

She nods in what feels like a distrusting way. "Can I get you a drink or something to eat?"

"Maybe a water would be great." Come to think of it, Charli does have a headache.

As Marianne fills a glass, Charli asks, "How is it that your family gets along so well? I'm sure you butt heads, but you seem to all find a way to get along, to have fun. Know what I mean? You're not all perfect, but you're far more perfect than my broken family."

Marianne slides her the water. She doesn't bother putting a lemon wedge on the rim, per the usual treatment of guests. "Yeah, well, we make a good show of faking it sometimes. You have to in a small town like this."

Charli hates that she's bending the truth, but she's good at it. "I swear, sometimes I think my family is cursed. Like something bad happened long before me, and we can't seem to recover." It's like she's chumming the water and seeing if Marianne smells blood. Sure, Charli will soon talk to Helen, as she probably has more answers, but Marianne is a good place to start. The trick is not sounding like a journalist as she probes for not only the truth, but a way to possibly make right the wrong set in place so many years ago.

Marianne's suspicious eyes beam a little harder at Charli. "We all have our family secrets, don't we?"

Charli can't stop herself. "What kind of secrets could you guys have? Noah mentioned that something happened a long time ago. Was it to Helen's grandmother or great-grandmother?" She's neck deep in lies now, no turning back.

The question goes out into the air and lingers for what feels like hours. Charli can't even bring herself to look into Marianne's eyes.

A boisterous couple comes rushing through the door. The woman is half in the bag, and if she's not careful, she's going to snap one of those long heels. The husband in his fine cashmere scarf approaches the bar and asks if they can take a table.

Charli sits on a stool to wait, that question still hovering in the air.

"Anywhere you like in the bar," Marianne says to her new guests. "We start serving food again at five."

"Thanks," the husband says. "Let me do a pint and what do you care for, wifey? Never mind, let's get you a water."

"As long as there's vodka in it," she slurs.

The husband looks at Marianne. "A water for her, no vodka. Maybe some chips if you have them."

"Yeah, sure," Marianne says, unfazed by these people.

As the couple surrounds a table in the corner and falls back into their lively conversation, Marianne says, "What were we talking about?"

"Oh, just families and history." Charli's not sure she can ask again about Lillian's name and what happened; it was too much the first time. Marianne is not dumb.

She calls out to Victoria, "See if you can drum up some chips from the kitchen." As she starts on the drink order, she says to Charli, "Helen's great-great-aunt, Lillian, was murdered by her lover. And then Lillian's brother—who was Helen's great-grandfather and obviously my grandfather a few times back, tried to get revenge and was killed too."

"Get out of here!" Charli is genuinely surprised. She knew nothing about the brother's death. What a tragedy.

"True story," she says as casually as if she's reading off the latest specials. "I've been rather fascinated with it since I was a child. She fell in love with a kid from the college who lured her back to his house and shot her."

Charli's telling her heart to settle down. More than anything, she now knows that there is far more to be discovered. She wishes she could pull out the photo and ask, "Does he look like the murdering type?" Marianne's making it sound like he's a predator.

That being said, she does feel the darkness inside her. Like her, maybe he looks far more innocent than he is.

Charli pries. "Why would he do that? Did he go to jail?"

"You know . . . a well-to-do brat with too much money. He was arrested and then escaped before his necktie party."

"Necktie party?" Charli asks, but the reference makes sense.

"That's what they called a hanging."

Charli can't imagine the boy in the photo facing the opening of a noose. A rope slips around her neck and tightens as if it's her own necktie party. She stops breathing for a moment before she realizes she's sitting at a pub in the present.

She clears her throat. "What happened with the brother?"

"Arthur was his name. He went after the family years later, attacked their carriage up the hill on High Street. He shot the brother in the shoulder but was killed in the process."

Charli's getting somewhere. "It probably takes a family generations to get past something like that."

"Maybe that explains our malfunction," Marianne says.

Charli would have loved to come clean and say, "Exactly! I think it explains my family's, at least!" But outing herself will make it all but impossible to forge ahead and figure out exactly how to restore the imbalance in her own family.

Still, she's getting somewhere, and Clarice Starling would be proud.

Charli shoots back the last of her water like it's whiskey. "But you guys seem so happy."

"We've got you fooled. I suppose we've learned to be happy despite the struggles." Marianne seems to shed her skepticism and opens up like a flower—or maybe a Venus flytrap. "Is it any wonder that I won't marry again? I'm surprised my husband didn't shoot me either. I fell for the same tricks and married a rich man. No surprise, he turned out to be a terrible person."

Compassion softens Charli's face. Perhaps there is some fallout in Noah's family from the murder. "But . . . I'm sure there's someone out there for you."

"Oh, are you sure, Charli? What do you know? How old are you, twenty?"

Charli fends off the barb. "Almost thirty," she says calmly. What is she supposed to do, help Marianne climb out of her own shit? Is that how she brings everything back to normal?

Marianne wrinkles her forehead. "Yeah, talk to me about love when you're forty. I'll be right back." She takes the couple their drinks. The inebriated woman is complaining about her water not having vodka in it. Marianne plays it like she's grown up dealing with drunks. Considering she'd been working in the pub most of her life, she certainly has.

"Finish that one up, love, and then we'll find you something with more bite. Deal?"

"Deal," the woman says with a pacified satisfaction.

When Marianne returns, Charli asks, "How did your ex lure you in?"

"Like they all do. With good looks and flowers. A few one-liners. You can't be too picky in this town, so I let myself fall in love."

"Can you actually let yourself fall in love?" Charli asks. "I think it just happens—not that I'm an expert."

"Apparently you're right. Because I sure as hell don't love him now. What about you? Ya falling in love with my brother?"

Charli prepares to deflect but can't find the words. "What? I . . . it's . . . it's complicated."

"Yeah, it always is."

No, it really is in this case, Charli says to herself. More than you could possibly understand.

Marianne sets her elbows down on the bar and clasps her fingers in a dominant gesture. "Yeah, well, you best not think you can take him away from here. He's where he belongs."

"Yeah, I get that."

Marianne doesn't move a muscle. "What are you really doing here?"

So much for Charli's stealthy questioning. They hold eye contact, and Charli decides that she's got to stop lying. "I wish I knew, Marianne. But I do know that I'm here for a reason and that I need to see him again."

His sister laughs. "Well, don't say I didn't warn you. This family doesn't want him leaving again." She goes cold after that, standing tall and turning away. "Victoria, where are those chips?"

Charli stands too. "I'm gonna go see if I can find him." The words barely escape her mouth. Marianne has successfully intimidated her.

"Okay, you do that," she says without even glancing back.

⌒

Charli reaches the entrance to Noah's building and texts him. I'm down-stairs. Can we talk?

A window opens above and his head pokes out. "Charli?"

"Don't tell me you weren't expecting me?"

"I wasn't." He flashes that smile of his, and she knows he's glad she's back. He stares down at her for a while, clearly attempting to charm her.

"Aren't you gonna let me in?" she hollers up to him.

"You're like a yo-yo, you know? Up, down, up, down. It's a good thing I'm long on patience."

That's not the only thing he's long on, but she doesn't say that. "I know, and I'm sorry. Believe me, I grind on my own nerves way more than anyone else's."

He stares down at her, probably wondering what to do with her. If he was smart, he'd shut the window and wait until she's gone. Instead, he looks past her for a moment and then raises the volume of his voice and says rather dramatically, as if he's performing Shakespeare, "Dear lady, what are your intentions?"

Her mouth falls agape. She turns to see what he'd seen. A tour group of seven people is walking by. He's trying to embarrass her. Is that punishment? As silly as it is, it feels like flirting to her, and she kind of likes it. Either way, she's not going to let him win.

"Oh, wouldn't you like to know," she shouts back.

He smiles, apparently pleased she's not shrinking away.

The tour group draws closer. Noah is still looking down at her, his smirk frozen on his face.

Charli finds a little mojo and calls out loud enough for the people back on High Street to hear, "I think you were still wearing my panties when I left. Mind if I get those back?"

A round of giggles rises from the tour group.

Noah shakes a finger at her. His eyes say, *Two can play at this game.* He shouts back, "I'm missing my wallet. Did you run off with it?"

More laughter from the group passing by. They've slowed to enjoy the exchange.

Charli will do this all day. Below the surface, she appreciates that this is his way of letting her off the hook. Never has she met a man so patient with her. "I didn't even realize you had a wallet. You've stuck me with every bill."

"Ouch." His voice echoes against the other buildings. He takes his time coming up with something else. "I suppose I do owe you something then."

"I just want my panties back."

"Yeah, okay, I'll let you in."

She hears a buzz and is smiling all the way up the stairs. He's standing in the hallway when the doors open. He's shirtless and wearing sweats.

"Oh, you dressed up for me."

"I'd no idea you were coming."

The lingering surprise on his face corroborates his statement, and she's glad she'd broken from the mold of being a foregone conclusion.

"What brings you back?" he asks, staying at a safe distance away. He's keeping it light, but he's definitely annoyed, justifiably so.

If only she could tell him the truth, but she will not. At stake is her father's life, her own life. Perhaps the life of everyone in her family. She must keep their relationship surface level and get down to the truth. Figure out exactly what happened and how she can make it right. And, of course, there are worse things than spending a little more time with him in the process.

"The strike with the trains didn't help."

"Ah, so you *couldn't* leave."

"It's more than that," she says.

"Yeah?"

"I'm sorry, Noah."

"There it is. But does she mean it?" There's more of that frustration he should be showing. For a moment, he'd become something of a milquetoast.

"Seriously, I'm sorry that I walked away. I'm not good at this kind of thing, which I did forewarn you about."

"I'm sorry that I ignored your disclaimer."

Warning, she thinks, he should still heed the disclaimer. Guilt comes crashing down on her. She's doing this, taking advantage of him. What an awful person she is. But she did warn him. And her father comes first.

For good measure, she says, "I'm back for a few more days and would love to see more of you. But the disclaimer still stands." She can't help herself from injecting some humor. "Besides, I don't have anywhere else to go."

He takes a step back toward his door. "Ah . . . so now you're using me."

"You wouldn't want me to sleep in the street, would you?"

He fakes a smile that shows his anger.

"Look," she says. "I really am sorry. I'm trying here. I don't want to leave with a bad taste between us. But I'm not looking for anything serious."

He's searching her for sincerity.

She shrugs. "That's about as good as it gets with me. And if it's not enough, I can turn around and leave you for good right now. Believe me, I would not blame you." Though she's working him some, her honesty surprises her.

Distrust creases the skin around his eyes. "I suppose we can take this inside."

A football match plays on the television. Or *telly* as he calls it. The commentator sounds like he's about to have a heart attack. "Ramon kicks it to Alejandro. But *heeerrre* comes Piña from behind and . . ."

"Who's playing?" she asks, following him into the main room.

"Do you really care?"

She side-eyes him.

He bites his lip and steps toward her. "I don't know what to do with you."

"That makes two of us," she admits. "And that's why we go day by day." She turns fully toward him and takes his hand. "We have no chance of survival, so we accept that and enjoy a few more days before I go back. We're like kitty cats trying to survive in the wilds of Zimbabwe."

Meanwhile, she thinks, I will be simultaneously searching for facts in a cold case from 1881 while also infiltrating the depths of your family to assess exactly how I might make up for my grandfather killing your great-aunt. Even thinking the idea is absurd, but this whole trip has revealed a world that allows for the absurd. The unbelievable keeps happening.

"Kitty cats in Zimbabwe . . . ," he says. "Has anyone told you you read too much?"

"My mother did. All the time."

"Well, I guess I'll take what I can get right now." He holds her cheeks and kisses her. They could have saved a lot of headaches if he could have had that attitude from the beginning.

The commentator on the telly yells, *"Goooooooaaaaaall!"*

Noah smiles into her lips and she smiles back, and they press into one another.

"They scored," he whispers.

"Yeah, I kind of figured," she says, feeling him grow against her. She reaches down. "Are you jealous of them?"

He shivers as she touches him. And he tries to speak, but only a gasp escapes. Looks like they're going to score too.

~

Charli's lying next to him later. They're chatting. The football match is still on in the other room. The announcer is going wild over something. Charli is less thrilled herself. As much as she wants to come out and say exactly why she's back, it would be easier if she actually knew what that was, but she's hoping—with giants heaps of skepticism—that her intuition will guide her.

Does she have to help every one of Noah's family members? If she starts with Noah, what would that be? Encourage him to leave the pub and chase his dreams? She's not exactly equipped with motivational-speaker skills. It's certainly not a *Sleeping Beauty* kind of thing where a kiss will set him free. That train has already left the station.

Or is there some other issue in his family that will soon reveal itself? The Armstrongs seem normal enough to her—far more normal than her own family.

Which sends her back to considering Miles . . . if he didn't kill Lillian, then the truth has been suppressed. But, seriously, how is she going to figure out who killed her? If the stakes weren't so damn high, if her father's life wasn't on the line, she'd allow all the doubt floating in her mind to win out. She keeps forcing herself to revisit all the ser-endipitous things that have happened, most recently coming upon the *exact* spot where the photo was taken—and where they'd carved their initials. It might not be fairy-tale stuff going on, but there are forces at play that continue to blow her hair back.

If only she could come out and tell Noah what she's thinking. And she will, soon enough. Her darn intuition is bucking like a feisty bronco, telling her that the lies must stop.

But not yet. "I ran into Marianne at the pub when I was looking for you."

Half of Noah's body is covered by the white sheet of the bed. His head is propped up on his hand. "Oh, yeah?"

"I'm not sure she's a Charli fan."

"If she spoke to you, she likes you."

"She seems afraid that I'll take you away."

He lets his head fall back on the pillow. "I suppose it's nice to be wanted."

Charli seizes the opportunity to ask, "She told me about what happened to your . . . who was it? Helen's great-great-aunt?"

He glances over and asks with a strong dose of curiosity, "How did that come up?"

Charli decides that she has a lot to learn before she opens her own PI business. "We were just talking. It came up when we were chatting family stuff."

Noah seems satisfied by her explanation. "Yeah," he says. "She has always been interested in it."

"Aren't you?"

"Not really, to be honest. You and Marianne must be alike in that way, curious about the past."

We're alike in more ways than that, Charli thinks. "I wonder if my grandfather knew your family. He surely ate in the inn at some point."

"Yeah, could be. Funny to think about. How'd the meeting go, by the way?"

"A dead end so far, but I'm going back tomorrow." She keeps on with her curiosity. "Why would someone murder her?"

He blows out a breath of air. "No idea. I can't remember. Why are you so interested?"

"Well, it's an unsolved murder. I'm into mysteries. I almost opened a bookstore, remember?"

That seems to quell his suspicion.

Charli sits up and reaches for her underwear. It's stupid, really, the idea that she can make things better. What is she supposed to do? Help Marianne find love again? Restore Noah's faith in love after his failed engagement? Noah's brother, Wesley, is a mess—tied up with some bad people—but Charli can't help with that either. She's in way over her head.

The one thing she does know is that saying sorry doesn't quite cut it. *Oh, Noah, I'm a descendant of the man who shot your relative. Sorry about not telling you earlier. While I'm at it, sorry about him shooting her. Will you forgive me? Or us? Actually, I don't think he did it anyway. Oh, why's that, you ask? I don't know. A feeling.*

Chapter 25

UNRAVELING A MESS

On Tuesday, Noah makes breakfast while she takes a shower. Charli uses his razor to shave her legs. Her mind is ablaze with revelations. After thinking that her idea of making right a wrong from 1881 sounds pretty ridiculous, she's back to the other consideration, that Miles didn't kill Lillian. Is that the piece that Frances says is missing, the truth that is yet to be unraveled? Could that be the puzzle piece that sets her family free? If so, how in the world could she ever figure out the answer? Though she likes a good mystery, she's no Miss Marple, especially when it comes to cold cases from the Victorian era. To that end, she's no Sherlock either.

Her self-doubt sprouts wings, and she can hear her mother laughing at her. *Charli, you dumb shit. All you are is a pile of excuses—just like your father.* Her mother slapped her face only a couple of times, and she feels one of those strikes now, but it's the blunt force of her mother's disappointment that hurts even more.

The razor drops to the shower floor.

Charli presses her eyes closed and turns the water hotter, hoping to burn her mother's energy out of her. When she pulls her head away, she sucks in a breath that tastes like courage. "Go away." She touches her cheek and shakes her head with the fight that she knows she has in her. She's getting somewhere in her journey and can't let up now.

She puts her focus back on why she is here. As she dries her hair with a hair dryer she found under the sink, her mind goes to the constellation in Costa Rica. She'd like to draw it out, and maybe she will when she gets some more time alone.

At the beginning of the constellation, she'd been tasked with choosing someone who represented herself. She'd picked the woman with the Chinese characters tattooed on her neck—Millie—and it was she who originally faced Herman. Later, Frances had asked Charli to replace Millie/Charli with a representative of who was really standing there: Lillian. Was that the life debt that Frances mentioned? Somehow, Charli had assumed Lillian's spot in the constellation, facing Herman, ultimately facing the same red lights.

If Herman wasn't Miles, though, who was he? Who is the murderer? Miles's father? His pictures don't evoke feelings of warmth, to say the least. And what or who is the source of his frustration, as represented by the guy wearing the Lionel Messi uniform? Could that be Miles? Did he upset his father so much by falling in love with a woman of a lower class that his father shot Lillian? It's a stretch, but she can't deny that she feels a connection to the angry man.

Charli remembers saying that it felt like Letícia was protecting the guy in the Messi uniform. "So Lillian was protecting Miles from his father? Is that it?"

A waft of simmering bacon fills the air, and she's reminded of how kind Noah is being, how accepting of her. And here she is playing him for a fool. But she has no choice. Her father's life is more important than her own integrity.

A curious seed planted earlier blossoms in her mind. Flipping open her computer, she searches the British Newspaper Archives and reads an article from the *Hampshire Chronicle*, dated October 11, 1921.

Arthur Turner, owner of the Smythun Inn & Pub, was shot dead after an attack on Lord Edward Pemberton, who was also shot and is recovering at his

home of Elmhurst. It is believed that the attack was
Mr. Turner's effort to avenge the death of his sister,
Lillian, who died forty years ago at the hand of Lord
Pemberton's brother, Miles. Mr. Turner leaves behind
his wife, Sadie, and son, Joseph . . .

Charli finishes the article and lets her mind wander, imagining
what it must have been like for Arthur to lose Lillian and then for his
wife and son, who were left to run the inn after Arthur's passing. What
a tragedy. Maybe that kind of trauma *was* powerful enough to set their
family constellation out of balance as well.

What's even worse is that Miles went down in history as the one to
blame. If she's ever going to prove otherwise, she needs to dig deeper.
She has to find a way to have a conversation with Helen, but she doesn't
want to force it. And what if Noah's family doesn't have the truth? What
if she's been barking up the wrong family tree?

That's when an idea strikes.

The taxi costs her fifty pounds, but she's okay with it. What's on her
mind as she travels through the Hampshire countryside is that she's
about to knock on the door of a family she didn't know she had.

Accepting that Lord Pemberton wasn't going to write her back,
she'd committed to finding the address of the house that had been
in the family all this time. She'd read mention of Elmhurst multiple
times. Turned out the estate was included in the National Heritage List
for England, and she found a brief description. The Pemberton family
originally built the house in the year 1630, and it has been in the family
ever since. It took Charli only another few clicks to find its location.

They wind through country roads over rolling hills. Classical music
creeps out of the taxi's speakers, the cabbie tapping his finger on the
wheel to the beat of the timpani. The first flowers of spring bloom

purple and yellow. Baby leaves have begun to decorate the trees that collect in clusters in the valleys. Long wooden fences keep sheep and cows from crossing into the road.

Cresting a hill, the cabbie says, "I think that's her."

Charli isn't quite prepared for the grandness of the estate. Tucked at the end of a perfectly straight driveway that cuts through a lawn big enough to land an airplane stands a magnificent country manor that is surely fancy enough for a visit from the royal family. Statues and mature trees line the drive. Several chimneys rise like steeples from the house's roof. It must take a team to keep the place running.

The idea that she came from such magnificence is inconceivable. All the way from this apparent royalty to the runt of the litter known as Charli Thurman. The degradation of the family tree could not be illustrated any better, and it's a triple reminder that there will be no babies filling her womb. She can at least spare the world that. Another few generations of procreation and they could devolve to rodents.

At the bottom of the hill, the cabbie turns onto the drive. Straight away stands a large iron gate. ELMHURST is carved into the stone wall that flanks either side. Just below that is an intercom system with what looks like a video camera.

"I guess this is as far as we go," Charli says. "Give me a little bit. I don't even know if I can get inside. I wasn't expecting a gate."

"Looks like you could walk around it if you like."

"Probably not the best way to introduce myself to my long-lost family. Let's try this first."

He comes to a stop, and Charli climbs out. She peers through the iron gate and imagines her people coming and going over the years, by foot and horse and eventually automobile.

She presses the button with a jittery finger, and it rings with a chirp.

A high-pitched British female voice comes through the tiny speaker. "May I help you?"

"Hi there," Charli says. "I know this is wild, but I'm looking for the Pembertons. I'm family visiting from the US."

A crackle. "Family?"

"That's right."

A pause. "Do they know you're coming?"

Charli deduces that she is not talking to a family member. "No, I didn't have their number."

There is a pause. "I'll be right out."

Charli waits a moment and then sees a hefty woman come out the front door and waddle her way along the driveway. It must take her three or four minutes from the front porch to the gate. She's dressed in black with a white apron. A mole protrudes from her chin. She's breathing heavily and does not look happy about the interruption or the long walk she had to make.

She squints, and her face scrunches together. "You said you're family?"

"My name is Charli, and I've been researching my family tree. Lord Pemberton is a cousin of mine."

The woman sighs, as if she gets genealogy cuckoos every day. "Well, I'm sorry, they're not here, and they don't like visitors."

Charli's head kicks back. She understands the want for privacy, but there's no call for the surly attitude. "I just wanted to . . . do you know how I could get in touch with them?"

"They're in London."

"Oh, his wife and him?"

She replies by giving a skeptical look toward the taxi.

Charli tries to be as kind as possible. "I wrote him with an email I found. This is all so new to me, but I would love to say hello. I have some incredible stories and have just learned how my side crossed the Atlantic to eventually settle in Boston."

The lady crosses her arms. "I can tell him that you emailed. I'm sure that's fine. I must get back to—"

Charli puts her hand on one of the iron bars. "Could you share with me his telephone number? The email could have gone to spam."

"His telephone number?" The woman chuckles, her body jiggling. "I'm not going to give out me boss's telephone number to some strange American claiming to be kin."

"Fair enough. Could you let me write out a note and make sure he gets it? I know that's asking a lot, but I do think he'd find the whole thing interesting. Does he have children? I couldn't find that information. I could reach out to them."

"A note is fine." She doesn't bother addressing Charli's last question.

Charli doesn't have a paper or pen. "I don't . . ." But she doesn't want to make the woman walk all the way back. Lord knows, she's not getting through that gate. "Let me ask if the driver has something."

Charli runs to the cab and gets a piece of scrap paper and a pen. On the hood of the car she writes a quick note, saying that she's family with an interesting story to tell that may explain what happened to Miles Pemberton. When she returns, she says, "Thank you for doing this." She hands the note through the iron gate. If only Charli could describe through the gate how high the stakes are in her mission to liberate the truth.

Since it can't hurt to ask, she says, "Is there any way you could share their address in London? I'm going back there in a few days and could find them."

"I'd say this is enough," the woman says, waving the paper in the air.

Charli's not surprised. "Yeah, yes, of course. Thank you for passing it along. I promise I'm not looking for anything other than putting some puzzle pieces together." In hopes of sounding more real, she adds, "I'm almost thirty now, and family has started to mean more to me."

She shoves the paper into the pocket of her apron. "I'll make sure he gets it."

Charli keeps a smile on until the lady turns away. She might not be Miss Marple, but she can lie like her.

On Wednesday morning, Charli sneaks in a question to Noah about where his family is buried. She's sly about it, telling him that she wants to be cremated and eventually eases the conversation into his family. He doesn't seem to give it a second thought as he replies, "There's a whole swath of us buried over at the Brighton Cemetery. I've got a spot waiting for me."

Once he goes to work, she tracks it down. A light rain falls, and Charli holds an umbrella over her head. It's a modest cemetery flanked by a movie theater and a Verizon.

Ten minutes later, she finds it. The gravestone reads: LILLIAN JANE TURNER, TAKEN FROM THIS LIFE ENTIRELY TOO EARLY. MAY SHE REST IN PEACE. FEBRUARY 27, 1864–JULY 2, 1881. A fresh wound arises as Charli considers how much pain Miles must have felt losing her—at losing anyone who means a lot to you. She tries not to think about her father, but his body stretched out on the floor flashes before her.

Then there's Noah. She can't quite figure out his part in all this. Why did he happen to be behind the bar the day they met? Why did she choose that pub anyway?

Next to Lillian lies her brother. The stone reads: ARTHUR HENSLEY TURNER, LOVING FATHER, HUSBAND, AND SON. REST IN PEACE. JANUARY 7, 1860–OCTOBER 10, 1921. Charli imagines how absolutely devastated he must have been to lose her. So much so that forty years later he was *still* holding on to it so tightly that he decided to avenge his sister by going after Miles's brother.

She sits facing Lillian's gravestone and says a few words, forcing herself to take the action seriously and not get caught up in the doubt. After all, she's about to talk to a dead person.

"I don't believe that Miles killed you," she says to Lillian. "I don't know that I can prove it, but . . . Frances says I owe a life debt to you, that I wouldn't be alive had you lived. Please know that I'm trying to get to the bottom of things, but don't hold your breath."

She snickers. "Well, I guess you can't do that anyway, being dead and all. But let me tell you that I'm not the best person to owe you a life debt. If I were you, I might have gone after someone with a better track record for getting things done."

Charli laughs at herself but doesn't want to leave it like that. If there's any substance to what she's doing, she can't make a joke out of it.

"Sorry, I have a bad habit of doing that. It's serious, though. I feel like I'm a phone call away from finding out my father killed himself. And my mom is no better." The reality of what she's saying tugs her down. "I'm not sure *I'm* much better. But I want to be. I want to wake up and be excited about the day. I want to stop hearing my mother's voice. I want to have some level of confidence. Would it be so bad if I liked myself?"

Her eyes water, and for some reason she keeps talking, telling Lillian about her life, everything from her childhood to the Bookstore That Never Was.

"If all this family constellation stuff is true, then maybe a lot of this is guilt. My bet is that it's Miles's dad who killed you. I wish you could give me a little help here. Whether it was Miles or him, they're my relatives, and I guess I do feel the guilt of what they did. Maybe that's ultimately what's been drowning my whole family. I'm here trying to figure out how to make it right, Lillian. I don't know where to go from here."

She shrugs. What else can she say? "For the record, we have suffered. I mean, generations of pain, possibly all tied back to the moment you were killed. Isn't that enough? Why can't it stop with me?"

In the following silence, a slight breeze stirs, giving Charli the chills. As impossible as it seems, the movement feels like a response to her plea. Once again, Charli finds it hard to doubt the unseeable magic in her mission. Lillian is there with her, urging her along.

Charli stands and whispers, "Thank you, Lillian."

⌒

Back at Noah's place, while Noah's still at work, Charli sends Marvin another email assuring him she'll be back Monday. Then she updates

Viv and Aunt Kay. Despite feeling like the answers are not coming as easily, she does taste this sweet flavor of possibility, and that's what she tells them on the phone, that this trip has been good for her, one way or another. Last, she calls her father.

"Daddy."

"Everything okay?"

"I don't even know where to begin." She shares some details. "More importantly, how are you?"

"Charli . . ."

"Yeah?"

"Will you stop with all this worrying about me?"

"Will you stop with giving me reason to?"

"Hey, I'm fighting like you are. That's about all I can say."

Nothing is changing. And why would it anyway? Because she stood over the grave of a dead woman?

"I want to say . . . that I love you." With that she cracks, breaking into a million pieces, and she pulls the phone away so that he won't hear her.

She hears his reply. "I love you back. And I should be asking if you're okay."

Her phone back to her ear, she puts some pep on her voice and says, "Yeah, Dad. I'm really good. Hoping that I'm getting closer."

"I'm sure you are. Hey, Charli."

"Yeah?"

"I'm proud of you."

"Thanks, Daddy."

She ends the call before he knows that she's crying . . . and then she lets it all out there, sitting on Noah's couch. She folds into herself and becomes consumed by the dark void that's swallowing them all.

When the tears have dried up, she makes herself a sandwich and tries to figure out what's next. She needs to get a moment alone with Helen, who seems to be her last hope, but it's not easy. She can't outright call or track her down at home. The stealth of this operation still seems paramount, as they surely won't tell her a thing once they know who she is.

That night, while she and Noah are watching TV, she casually asks Noah if his grandmother is still involved in the family business.

"No, not really. The buck stops with my father, though even he's not involved that much anymore."

Charli tries to find an angle. "But she still eats for free, right? I mean, does she still have ownership?"

"Oh, yeah, she still has her part of it, though she's given half to my father. He'll get the rest when she passes, and then on to us."

Charli is prying but dares ask one more push. "I haven't seen her in a while. She's doing okay?"

"Oh, yeah. She'll be in tomorrow. She still has a desk."

Having to return to London in three days to fly out Sunday morning, she hopes that she can finally make some headway.

Charli goes into the pub for lunch on Thursday. She takes her laptop and stays for a while. Helen is in and out, and when Charli gets the chance, she suggests they have tea. Helen looks slightly surprised by the invitation but politely agrees.

They share a pot of black tea, and Helen raves about tea with immense passion. Her age doesn't seem to be a burden at all. She explains that they're drinking a first flush Darjeeling from West Bengal, India. Charli is so wired after a cup that she's asking all sorts of questions about Helen's life. The woman is incredibly interesting and wise and passionate.

"You are an inspiration," Charli says about fifteen minutes after Helen sits. "What's the secret to aging so well?"

"Oh, you folks will all live to one hundred. What with all the technological advances. Can you believe electricity was only becoming a thing when I was a little girl? We didn't have it at the pub until 1936.

And now we're talking to each other on screens. By the time you're my age, can you imagine?" She lets out an infectious laugh. "You'll be half robots."

Charli sees a way into the conversation she wants to have. "I think I would have preferred to be born when you were. The Roaring Twenties."

"Oh, I don't know how much they roared here in Winchester. It was a nice time to grow up, I suppose, but . . ." Her voice and words trail off.

Charli seizes the moment. "Noah told me about what happened to your . . . was it . . . great-great-aunt? I bet even your generation was affected by such a thing."

She takes a moment to wade through the years. "Well, yes, of course. I suppose it had been fifty years by the time I was old enough to hear about it, but the sadness of it lingered in the pub like a ghost."

"I can imagine."

She seemed to be engaged in the memory now. "My grandfather was born the same year of the murder, so he was always connected to it, talking about it, throwing out his theories. His father had told him that his aunt Lillian used to talk to him while he was still in the womb."

A chill travels down Charli's neck. She swallows and says, "That's so much of why I admire your family. You've been through a lot but somehow manage to be the happiest family I've ever met."

Helen smiles. "Yes, the recipe seems to be lots of family time, even if we don't always see eye to eye."

"That would be a recipe for disaster in my family. I don't know if Noah told you, but I'm a big mystery buff and so interested in what happened to your aunt. Do you mind talking about it? I'm curious."

Helen pours the last of the tea. "I don't know that it's a mystery. She was murdered, and they caught the man."

"But they don't know where he ended up? Noah said he was declared dead. They didn't find a body, did they?"

Helen stares into her cup, as if the Darjeeling has all the answers. "My grandfather claimed that they'd declared him dead so that his brother could step into line to inherit his position in Parliament. What was his name? Edward, I think. No one truly knows what happened to Miles Pemberton."

"It's the makings of a documentary."

"I suppose it is." Helen sits back. "It would certainly be nice to know that poetic justice eventually found him, wherever he ran. You know, his family was and still is, to a degree, rather powerful. It was said that Miles's father turned him in."

"What kind of father would turn in their own son?"

Her bony shoulders incline. "Who knows? But I will say that my grandfather once mentioned that he thought it might be Miles's grandmother who helped him escape. I don't quite remember why he said that."

"What a story." Charli wishes she could go into the details of the constellation, but she worries she'll be chased right out of Winchester. Not feeling like she's getting any closer to proving Miles's innocence, she does her best to draw out more information. She tries her other angle.

"How do you think Lillian's murder affected the family? The reason I ask is that I read a book, can't remember the name, and it was talking about how trauma can be passed through the generations."

Helen tilts her head, and her pupils dilate.

Charli waits for a response while the flames of guilt burn at her insides. The irony of lying to get to the truth is not lost on her, but she douses the flames.

Helen lifts her hands from her lap and smooths them together, as if it helps her journey back into time. "I could see some truth to the idea. According to my grandfather, Lillian's brother, Arthur, nearly ran the pub into the ground. He was devastated after losing his sister and never quite recovered. After he was killed, my grandfather, Joseph, took over and saved it. He was not without his hard times, though. He and his wife lost three children as babies before finally having my father, John. Then John hanged himself when I was a little girl."

"Oh God," Charli says, at once knowing that Noah's family has indeed struggled too. "I'm sorry. This isn't my business."

Helen nods. "You asked. And now I'm afraid I must excuse myself. My cat will turn naughty if I don't check on him."

"Sure, yes, of course. Please let me pay for the tea."

Helen waves a finger. "It's my pleasure. Would you care to walk me home?"

"Yes, I'd like that." Charli admires this woman so much and wishes she had someone like her as a mentor, to show her how it's possible to find so much light in the darkness.

They stroll a few blocks at Helen's easy pace, and she points out places that have meant something to her over the years. When they arrive at her house halfway down a skinny street, she says, "This is me."

Charli looks at the brick row house with white shutters. The chafed door is so old it looks like driftwood. A tarnished plaque indicates the address: #7. A strand of ivy that has climbed up to the second window is coming to life.

"You grew up here?"

"At one time, it was me, my parents, and my grandparents all under this roof. Before that, it was Arthur's place."

"Right, Lillian's brother."

Charli can almost see Lillian coming through the door to visit her brother. Pieces lock into place, but she's still so far from the truth.

She turns to Helen as she approaches her door. "Thank you for today. I enjoyed it."

Helen presses her key into the lock of number 7 but turns back. Her eyes shrink. "From where does all this curiosity stem? If I were to guess, you have more than a passing interest in my family."

Charli looks away but fights hard to twist back to Helen. "I . . ." She doesn't want to lie.

Helen waits patiently for a reply.

"I'm trying to make sense of my own life, and it seems like I've come across your family for a reason. Once I know for sure, I'll tell you. Can we leave it at that?"

Helen's forehead crinkles. She searches Charli's eyes. Then lets her off the hook. "You do right by my grandson, you understand?"

Charli breathes for the first time in thirty seconds. Guilt pours over her like a waterfall as she barely lets out, "I'm trying."

Chapter 26

Unraveling a Life

It's later in the afternoon after Noah returns from work. The lovemaking is mechanical. Charli's not quite motionless, but she's having a hard time getting into it. Not that Noah's performing poorly. Not that he's not everything. It's just that she's being eaten alive by shame and doubt and an overall self-loathing that never strays far enough away. How could she possibly love someone else when she feels this way about herself?

What is she doing here anyway? She's certainly not going to disprove Miles's guilt—*if* in fact he's not guilty. Even if she does, what's really going to happen? Her dad is suddenly going to spring to life? Her mom is going to escape the clutches of her own imprisonment? Will these truths somehow absolve her mother of all the terrible things she's done, the way she treated Charli and William? Is it going to erase the responsibility that Georgina has never owned up to anyway? And is Charli suddenly going to be floating around with the glee of Mary Poppins?

No. Not a chance.

She's on top of him, straddling him. His clothes are on the floor.

He stops, right in the middle of things. One moment he was moaning and then nothing. He waits for her to look at him. When she does, he asks, "What's going on?"

Looking at him is a chore, the hardest thing she's ever done. Their eyes meet, and she pulls them away as quickly. He tugs her down to his side and wraps his arm around her. She usually feels safe, but she now feels like his betrayer.

She's still not ready to confess, though. The pit in her stomach is killing her, but she knows it will be even worse once she tells him. *Please, please, give me a little while longer before I tear it all apart,* she begs to whoever is listening. Because it's going to hurt—she knows that. She knows that now more than ever. These feelings seem more real than any she's ever had before. Noah allows her to be herself, even when she's not her best self. Of course, he still hasn't seen her at her worst, which is the part she knows will eventually tear them apart.

Noah maneuvers so that he's on his side and facing her. She sits up and wraps her arms around her legs. Her eyes squirm left and right. She's never felt such push and pull in her life, the need to grab hold of him like he's a lifeline while also wanting to run, run, run out of there like she's trying to break an Olympic record.

"Someone in there?" he asks.

Charli turns away from him. She's ten years old, and her mother is shaking her finger at her, demanding to know who spilled the orange juice without cleaning it up. Charli can't bring herself to turn back to her mom, to face her.

"Tell me what's going on with you," Noah whispers.

Even *now,* as he's showing her that he's there for her, she can't seem to be the person she wants to be.

"Hey, hey," Noah says, sitting up and petting her. "I can't help if you don't let me in. Is this about us?"

She can't answer. Tears well in her eyes, and she attempts to blink them back.

He's so patient with her. "Charli, you gotta let me in."

She can't turn back to him, like she couldn't face her mom. "I can't," she mutters.

"Why not, dammit? I am trying to be patient, but you make it hard sometimes."

"Oh, don't I know." She's heard that before a thousand times.

"Tell me what the hell is going on."

Charli finally turns halfway toward him. "I told you. I ruin things." He sits cross-legged, facing her. "Why would you say that? You're in control. There's no one else steering you. Make this one different." He's getting angry with her, and she welcomes it. This is more like it, giving her what she deserves.

She looks away again. He can't understand. Even if she comes clean now, and even if one day he forgave her, she'd screw it up again and again and again.

"I love you, Charli."

Those three words smash into her chest. She can barely reply. "Don't say that."

"Oh, I'll say it a thousand times. I've never felt like this before, and I never will again."

"I'm not who you think I am."

"Stop," he says. "And look at me."

She won't. She can't.

"Charli," he whispers. And then he waits.

When she finally twists back to him, he says, "What is all this negative talk? Why do you let yourself believe this stuff? What happened to you that you can't let yourself love anyone? What happened to you that you don't believe you deserve this?"

She tries hard to hold his gaze this time. Where to even begin?

"I want a chance with you. I think I'm falling in love with you."

The word *love* catches her like a sharp blade in the side. "No, you're falling in love with the part of me that I've shown you," she says, squeezing her legs tighter. "Not the rest of me. Trust me, you do not love the little girl inside of me that's still so fucking damaged by her childhood.

The little girl whose mother told her she should have thrown her away. Whose father was so focused on work that he barely noticed."

Charli jabs a finger at her own temple. "I still hear my mother's voice every day. I see her smashing my dolls because I wasn't . . ." Charli loses her breath. "Because I was such a sorry excuse for a child. Trust me, you don't love that, and you don't even want to try. You don't want to bring me into your life, let alone your family's."

Noah raises a hand. "Stop. Dammit, stop." He pauses to make sure Charli's listening. "That is not your call to make. I'm sorry to hear about your parents—"

"It wasn't my father. I didn't mean to say that. It's . . . my mother . . ." She wipes a tear. "She had this extraordinary ability to make me feel small. She did the same to my dad, too, tearing into us. I was always one slipup away from her launching into me. The things she said . . . they were bad. The kind of bad that I can't get past."

Noah scooches back and leans against the headboard to give her space.

"I know you see this pretty girl who knows how to have fun. Make conversation. Maybe even make you laugh some. But trust me, that's me trying. That's me doing my best not to let you see the other me."

"Geez, Charli." He starts and stops. "Don't you see that I don't need you to be perfect? I'm certainly not. There's nothing that you're hiding from me that I'm not ready for. You had a hard life. Mine wasn't always easy either. I don't know that anyone's life is gravy. So we move on and find people that we love and that love us, and we do our best to be our best. But we're not always going to be. Love is about being there for someone at their worst. It's easy to be there when things are good."

She wants to rip her heart out and throw it into the garbage. He has no idea of her worst. "I'm different."

"You're not."

"Noah, I've been down this road before. Maybe not this exact one. And to tell you the truth, I do care about you. A lot. That's what makes this worse. I know I'm going to ruin us, and you don't deserve it."

She's caving, her heart and soul. He's looking at her and through her, and he must see that she's dying inside. "You don't know that you will ruin us. You're afraid to try."

"Do you want me to prove it?" she asks.

"Prove it? What kind of childishness is that?"

"It's facts, Noah. I am saving us, saving you." She can't take it anymore. "I'm not who you think I am."

His head falls back, accidentally hitting the headboard. "If that isn't a cliché."

"I'm serious." She gathers her thoughts, hating herself for what she's done. "A couple of months ago, I connected with this woman named Frances . . ."

Charli tries to tell the story as best as she can, taking him to Costa Rica with her. "I'm not one to believe in such stuff, really. I'm not the person who believes in miracles or happy endings . . . or even true love." She feels how that hurts Noah but plows on. "But this constellation shifted something inside of me. You know those moments where you think you have it all figured out. For a second there, I did. Somehow, some way, Frances helped me figure out that someone in my family a long time ago did something bad, and maybe that had trickled down to me. All that guilt I'd been feeling, the self-hatred, the way I felt cursed, she claimed that it was because someone in my family committed a crime."

Noah is silent and showing a thousand shades of perplexity on his face.

"Turns out they did. Someone in my family did. That's why I came here, to find out the truth. That's why I'm researching my family."

His brows curl in curiosity. "What?"

"The only thing I've ever done right is raise a dog with the love that I never knew. That's it. I've hurt almost everyone I know. I've failed at everything I've tried. And I didn't know it when we first met, I swear, and I don't know how it is that we were brought together. It scares the shit out of me, honestly. But it was my grandfather . . . well, my third great . . ."

She blows out a blast of air that slaps the corner of the sheet. "His name was Miles Pemberton, the man accused of killing your great-aunt several times back, Lillian Turner. You know the picture I showed you of my grandfather and the other girl? The one where we came close to finding where it was taken? That was them."

"Wait, let me get this right. That photo . . . you're saying the girl was my relative?"

She nods. "With my relative, who was accused of killing her."

"What in the . . . ?"

"Yeah, I know. The reason I'm here is because I was trying to figure out what happened. I thought that making sense of it would help me feel better. Of course, it's only destroyed things."

She could not be more disappointed in herself. "I should have told you the moment I knew, but I didn't. Because I tell lies, Noah. I'm bad. Just a bad person, like the man who murdered Lillian. I think it was Miles's father who killed her, not Miles, but that's a whole other thing. And like my mother and probably everyone else in my family . . ."

Noah shakes his head in bewilderment. "You're telling me that you're here because . . . I don't understand."

"Because I wanted to find the truth . . . and fix it if I could." She fumbles around the story for a while, attempting to make sense of something that she herself has lost faith in. Her self-disgust comes with a dose of relief. Finally, she doesn't have to pretend anymore.

Noah's disappointment in her looks a lot like Patrick's had, and a line of exes before them. "And you've stayed with me why?" he asks.

A bout of sadness catches in her throat. She doesn't want to lose him. It's a passing thought, and it's too late now. "Anything I say is going to make me sound unhinged."

"Might as well get it all out . . ."

Noah's right. What else is there to lose now? "I found the spot in the woods, Noah. It was in the Winnall Moors Nature Preserve. Like the exact spot, and I found a carving that they'd made with their initials in it. When I touched it, I felt their love. And I knew then that he didn't kill her."

He's trying to be patient with her. "You walked into the woods and felt their love from more than a century ago? And then what? Decided to take advantage of me? What in the hell are you doing here?"

Charli can't bring herself to look at him. But she finally does. "According to the constellation work, I needed to find out who did this bad thing in my family. I know it sounds crazy, but I had this hope that maybe I could remove some of what was going on with us. Mostly my dad. I was out of options, and there was a woman telling me that finding the truth could restore the balance in our constellation. So that's what I was doing. And I had another idea that maybe I needed to fix what had happened, like repay your family for my family's crime."

Noah holds her gaze for a moment, then climbs off the bed. "This is all too much, Charli. I don't even know where to—"

She wishes he could understand, but he's long gone. Another one bites the dust. "I know, I know. That's why I didn't tell you."

He makes a face like he's tasted sour milk. "You know what? It's not even that you were keeping the truth from me. Or that you do sound a bit batshit. It's this push and pull between us. I'm exhausted. Your omitting the truth is just the breaking point."

Charli seeks some warmth in his eyes, but he looks utterly exasperated by even her appearance. She can't stand to look at herself, either, so she gets it.

As he gets dressed, he says, "I'm going to leave now. I think it's clear that whatever we had is tied up in a lot of baggage."

She can't bear to lift her head.

He goes to the bedroom door.

"I warned you, Noah," she whispers. "You said it yourself. I'm a fucking yo-yo."

"You warned me? That's what you have to say? I need to go." He turns and goes down the hall.

Charli falls back against the bed and mashes her eyes shut, trying her best to run away from this awful world.

~

His scent is almost too much to take as she goes around to collect her things. She wishes she'd never kissed him, never slept with him, certainly never ever *ever* let him tell her he loved her. She wipes her eyes in the bathroom as she crams all her belongings—including the clothes she bought—into her backpack and heads toward the door.

There's a pen and a pad of paper on the kitchen counter. She walks over and scrawls: *I'm sorry. I was just trying to do something right for once.*

The ink isn't even dry when she crumples it up and drops it into the trash can. Worried he'll discover it, she digs it back out, folds it, and jams it into her pocket.

She tries again. *I'm sorry. You deserve better.*

She gets rid of that one. Tries five more times.

Accepting that she can't write her feelings, she leaves the apartment without leaving a letter at all. The abandoned letters weigh heavy in her pocket.

The wind has picked up even more and blows her hair in her face as she hikes up High Street, headed toward the train station. She has no idea when one leaves and doesn't care. She wants out of this town. And if there's a strike, she'll take a taxi back to London. If there are no taxis, she will take a bus. If there are no buses, she'll walk.

She buys a ticket for the eight-o'clock train, then buys a caprese sandwich and finds a place to wait. Though a tiny part of her feels like she hasn't done what she came to do, she doesn't care anymore. It all feels like a joke. *She*, who can ruin anything. *She*, who thought she might be able to make right what Miles did wrong.

But she only made it worse. She can feel Noah's pain right now, as she knows that he loves her.

Or *did* love her.

He never loved you, you dumb shit. What's it been, a few days? You're stupid, Charli.

"Stop it," she says, but her voice lacks any fight at all. And in this moment, she knows exactly what being unlovable means.

Chapter 27

Love Rising

Winchester, England
July 2, 1881

Two hours after leaving their spot in the moors, Miles and Lillian reached Elmhurst. It was a fine day outside, a jeweled-blue sky—the perfect recipe for a day worthy of celebration. Gardeners pruned a row of hedges along the approach to the house. Their family had owned the land as far as Miles could see for nearly as long as the cathedral had been standing, but he had no issues with giving up his rights. He'd never been more sure of a decision in his life.

A stableboy came out to take the horses. Miles introduced Lillian and then asked, "Is my brother back?"

"Yes, he returned about an hour ago."

The secret was surely out. He led Lillian by hand to the front door, where a servant waited.

"Hello, Nathaniel," Miles said to him, having known him since he was a boy. "Meet Miss Turner."

Nathaniel nodded with his dimpled chin. "A pleasure, miss."

"How do you do?" Lillian said to him.

They entered the house, and Miles straightened his back, ready to stand up to the man who had stood over him since the moment he'd taken his first breath. True freedom was only moments away.

"Father?" he called out into the house.

Silence echoed back.

"Father, are you there?" Noticing her timidity, Miles pulled Lillian closer.

Footsteps and the smack of a cane on wood announced Lord Pemberton's presence. The hat that seemed nearly permanent was removed from his head, revealing straight gray hairs that couldn't quite cover his baldness anymore. The sight of his eldest son elicited only frigidity. The sight of Lillian evoked contempt.

His eyes narrowed to Miles. "What is this?"

"Father, meet Miss Lillian Turner."

He glanced at her briefly, avoiding eye contact. "Yes, the girl Edward told me about. I asked him to follow you this morning. Had a feeling you were up to no good."

Miles found strength in his love for Lillian and his hope for their future, and he squeezed Lillian's hand tighter, hoping she felt it too. James lowered his gaze to the connection of their hands, and his eyes squinted in disapproval.

"Where is Mother? I'd like for her to be here as well."

"What for?" James asked.

"Where is she?"

James looked up the stairs and back at Miles. "Your mother is not feeling well."

Miles knew what that meant. He'd seen it since he was old enough to understand, how she'd probably been struck by her husband and was hiding from the outside world. He wanted her to be there, but then again, it was James who was in charge. Miles wondered where his brother might be, but only for a moment.

He looked at his father with all the strength that he had in him and said, "May we talk?"

"What about?"

"My future. Let's walk into the great room."

Miles wasn't asking, and he led Lillian past the stairs and into the massive room that featured views of their estate. He asked Lillian to take a seat on one of the sofas. Miles waited for his father to follow and take a seat.

But his father entered the room and said, "I am fine standing."

"Very well."

At his words, Lillian sprang up and stood next to Miles on the rug that stretched across half the room. Only five feet away, James wrapped his fingers around the lion of his cane and waited for Miles to speak.

He swallowed, ready to protect himself if need be. He'd been hit enough by the man to know that it was a possibility now. "Never have I loved someone before. Never have I known love . . ."

James snickered coldly. "I thought that's what this might be about."

"Let me speak."

"Do so."

"I am in love with Lillian and plan on making her my bride. And I know that love is not your first concern, but I am not you."

"Oh, I certainly know that." He gave Lillian another glance. "Who is this girl, anyway? She's dressed like a bloody house servant."

Miles's jaw tightened as he let go of Lillian's hand. "You prove my point well. Again, her name is Miss Lillian Turner. Her father owns the Smythun."

James's face contorted as if he'd eaten a rotten piece of trout from the river. "The cesspit on High Street?"

"How dare you," Lillian said.

His father let out a cackle, not even acknowledging that Lillian had spoken. "And you think you're going to marry her. I have to say, you show tremendous bravado to even joke about such matters in front of me."

"There is no joking here," Miles snapped. "I have come here—*we* have come here—to ask for your blessing before we leave for London tomorrow."

"You think you're going to London together? I'm sure you know you've wasted your time."

Miles stood even straighter. "I thought I would give you the opportunity to redeem yourself. I certainly do not need your blessing. I am a man now and will do as I please."

"Ha. You will certainly not marry this . . . this hussy. How dare you bring her into my house."

Miles stepped forward. "You will not speak of her this way!"

Lillian sensed what might be coming and stepped forward as well. "Mr. Pemberton—"

"Lord Pemberton, dammit."

"Lord Pemberton, I know that I am not who you might have hoped for your daughter-in-law. It is true my family does not have the wealth or status that you would like, but if it is of any consequence, I can love your son more than any other. And take care of him."

"Take care of him? With what? You'll put him to work behind the bar. Pouring beer. My son?"

"He can do whatever he likes, and he will be great at it." Lillian stayed impressively calm, smiling at Miles in a way that made him believe her words.

"His future is already written," James said, his pupils narrowing to darkness, "and you're not in it."

Miles stepped forward. "Do not speak to her that way, Father."

James moved his hard eyes to Miles. "You're wasting your time. Take this person back to Winchester and report back to this house instantly."

"That's not the way it works. We are leaving here together and will be on our way to London tomorrow."

James looked even more surprised. "You're threatening me? My little eighteen-year-old is threatening me. What would you do in London? Entertain me with that answer."

"I will be an actor."

"Ah, I see. The dream of being Henry Irving again." He nodded for a while, the smirk on his face turning Miles angrier by the moment. "And if it doesn't work, I'll become a teacher."

"A teacher? My son?"

"Yes, why not? Or a writer, or a butcher. The world is endless with possibilities." He glanced at his love. "We can figure it out."

James brushed a dismissive hand through the air. "I've had enough of this. I will have Miss Turner driven back into town."

Miles stood his ground. "You have heard my stance. She will not be leaving here without me. I wanted you to know our plans. So that we're clear, I am not asking."

James used his cane to move forward. The strings of his neck stretched. "You will not threaten me in my house. You will do as you're told and go up the stairs at once. I will deal with this whore who is trying to get at our money."

Miles cast a quick glance to Lillian. Rising anger glowed in her eyes, stoking Miles's own fury and resolve. To his father, he said, "You will apologize to her this instant, you bastard."

"For calling your whore a whore?"

Though his body tensed to a near breaking point, Miles resisted every urge to hit his father. He did not want to be like him, resorting to violence. He'd done what he needed to do, and he was ready to leave.

Turning to Lillian, Miles said, "Please forgive him. I am ashamed to be his son. We've done what we should do, and now it's time to—"

James swatted at Miles with a heavy right hand, nearly knocking him to the floor. Lillian let out a scream.

The rage that had been simmering inside Miles for all these years erupted, and he lunged at his father. James lifted one hand and his cane to protect himself, but it was too late. Miles barreled into him, knocking him up against a chair before bringing him to the ground.

For the first time in his life, Miles swung back at his father, smacking him in the mouth. "You will never disrespect her again."

Though his father had an injured leg, the man had a strength that allowed him to roll Miles over and get him into a headlock. Miles felt his father's arm go tight around his neck, and he grew dizzy as he lost his breath. No matter how hard he fought, he could not take in any air, and his limbs grew weak and . . .

Lillian appeared above them and dropped a vase down over James's head. It shattered into a hundred pieces as it drew a deep cut of blood on the side of the man's head. He howled in pain, weakening long enough for Miles to escape his grasp. Miles sucked in air and felt himself come back to life.

He threw several punches that didn't land, and the two men wrestled on the rug, the thump of their hearts and the smack of their bodies on the floor shaking the room. Screaming obscenities, Lillian did her best to pull James apart from Miles, but he pushed her away. James's aggression toward Lillian only incited Miles more, and he finally landed a strong punch to his father's mouth.

"You are dead to me," his father spat with blood-coated teeth. "You and the whore."

"Get off him!" a voice growled from behind them.

Gasping for air, Miles glanced over his shoulder to see Edward standing there pointing a rifle at him. Edward's eyes carried a lifetime of hatred for his brother.

James pushed Miles away and wiped the blood from his face.

Lillian stood frozen with her hands in front of her in a fighting position, her face showing more fight than fear. She looked from the gun to Edward to Miles. As their eyes met, Miles thought that all they had to do was escape this madness, and then they could move on with their lives. They were so close to escaping their prison.

"Stand up," Edward barked, stepping over the broken vase toward Miles. "I've no qualms with shooting you."

Miles turned back to his brother. Deciding it best to defuse the situation, he fumbled up to his feet, his whole body hurting. "You don't need the gun. We're leaving."

Edward pointed the gun at his chest while James reached for his cane and attempted to push himself up off the floor.

Something about the malevolent twitch that suddenly arose in Edward's eyes convinced Miles that he would shoot. He could feel the eagerness of his brother's trigger finger, his propensity for violence. He had to do something.

As he prepared to launch at Edward, a flash of movement caught his eye. Lillian rushed forward, charging for the gun. Miles raced to stop her, but it was too late.

Edward diverted his aim to Lillian in a quick motion and pulled the trigger. Lillian crashed hard to the ground with a smack. Rivulets of blood splattered onto the floor.

"Noooooo!" Miles raced to her side, sliding next to her on his knees. A pool of blood gathered on the tile as he scooped her up.

A cavity of emptiness manifested in his gut as the prospect of losing whom he cared for most in the world presented itself.

"Lillian," he said, begging for her to be all right, his whole body swelling with agony.

Her lips moved and relief flooded him. He was too shocked to be angry, so shocked he could barely hear his brother shouting, "She had it coming!"

"I love you," Lillian whispered with blood on her tongue. In her eyes, he saw her unshakable spirit, and yet the rest of her grew weaker by the moment. The color in her cheeks dissolved. Her lips quivered.

"You're not going anywhere. You're just fine." Tears pricked his eyes; his body went numb.

A beautiful and loving smile crossed her face. One of pure awareness, as if she'd seen God. "I love you," she said again.

"I love you too," he said, breaking apart inside.

Refusing to lose her, he searched for the wound. She was hit in the chest, above her right breast. He pulled back the fabric to see blood pouring out. He pressed a hand against the wound, her warm blood spilling out through his fingers.

"Call a doctor," he said, but the words came out as a croak.

He looked up to find his brother standing like a statue, the gun still smoking.

"Call a doctor, dammit!"

Edward didn't acknowledge him. Miles twisted to his father as the blood coming escaped the sides of where he held his hands. "Father, call a doctor."

With one hand resting on his cane, James stared back blankly.

Miles returned his attention to Lillian. His overdriven brain scrambled for answers. As he looked into her fading eyes, he sensed her life leaving her body. And then it happened. In one second the love of his life was there, and then she wasn't, her soul vanishing into nothing. Her eyes were wide open, but she wasn't there.

"No . . . ," he said. "No, don't go." Loss cascaded through him, tearing at what was left of him like vultures. He gathered her head in his arms and searched her eyes for signs of life. "Lillian, stay with me. Don't go . . ."

With one hand still covering the wound, he felt fruitlessly for her breath. She was gone, and every part of him knew that.

But it didn't stop him from yelling, "Call for a doctor!"

A door opened, and the valet came rushing through. "What happ—" He stopped in his tracks when he saw Lillian lying there dead.

"Send for the doctor," Miles begged, but it was too late. The hurt in his heart was like nothing he'd known before, a cavernous loss that pummeled him over and over like his father's fists.

With a racing heart and blurry eyes, he reached up and pulled her lifeless body onto his lap. Blood soaked his clothes. Her face had already begun to turn purple, but he took her in, all of her, in a flash seeing the times he'd had with her—the times when he'd felt the most alive in his life. He stared into her eyes, wishing her to come back, but she wasn't there at all. Her spirit, her laugh, her thirst for life . . .

All gone.

He slid her lids closed and held her there for what felt like a long time, what felt like forever, and in those agonizing minutes, he lost her over and over again, the life of him being drained out, his body going numb.

When a smidge of clarity returned to him, he twisted his head toward Edward. "You will swing for this."

Edward looked past Miles to James. "Someone will."

Footsteps sounded behind him, and Miles turned. The last thing he saw was a flash of gold from the lion's-head handle.

Then nothing.

Chapter 28

STUMBLING INTO THE ABYSS

While on the train, Charli tries to move her Sunday flight earlier, but there is nothing available. She gets back to her hotel in London around ten p.m. Checking into a new room, she showers and then lies on the bed in her robe and berates herself for treating Noah so poorly, let alone for failing her mission.

The minibar is too tempting. She pours herself a glass of wine. It goes down so well that she takes another and goes numb.

When she tries to remember why she's here, she can't. Not for a while. Something about trying to help her family, help herself. Well, she's not solving any murders from 1881, that's for sure. Frances would say that the truth is still waiting. What's the truth going to do anyway?

Like everything else she does, she wants to give up. Even thinking about the idea of going back home and returning to Tiny and her tiny life gives her peace. She texts the dog sitter and asks how he's doing, asks for more pictures. She gets some back pretty quickly and lies back on the bed with her alcohol buzz and stares at Tiny, missing him so much.

Three more days and she'll be home.

It takes her until the morning to realize she is experiencing something unfamiliar. She's worked her whole life to protect herself from this particular emotion.

Heartache.

It's a hole so empty that she could cave in at any moment. She's barely eating, getting down only enough to keep her stomach from hurting.

In the bathroom, Charli's afraid to look in the mirror. She never likes what she sees. But something forces her to take inventory of her appearance, and she rests her hands on the counter and looks at herself. Her hair is all over the place, her skin pale. Her Costa Rica tan is a distant memory. And her eyes.

Her eyes.

The eyes of her mother.

Charli turns away but then goes back to them, stares into them, the irises opening up to show her soul. She feels so weak and empty, but there's something else in her too. The remnants of a fire, that small cinder burning, the one that's been burning even brighter since the constellation. What else can she do for her father? That's what's on her mind now. What an epic waste of money and time this trip has been. And now she's returning to exactly the same issues: her father, who is giving up; her mother, who is lost; and her own life, which is hopeless.

But she got so far . . . she proved that she was capable of far more than she ever thought. She tracked down so many clues and tasted what it was like to be hopeful. Maybe the money *was* worth it. And is she right in leaving? She can't take another week off, can't afford it even if Marvin was okay with it. And even if she did, she's out of ideas.

Deciding that she needs to pull it together either way, Charli dresses in her running gear and goes out the door. It's eight in the morning, and people rush by on their way to work. She runs past them without any destination, just trying to shake loose the demons clawing at her.

Up ahead she sees Hyde Park and goes that way. A late-winter mist conjures up memories of all the Jack the Ripper books during her true-crime phase a few years ago. That's all she'd read for months. Though it isn't exactly warm outside, the park is crowded with people exercising, groups practicing yoga and Pilates, others running sprints. Police officers ride by on horseback, their eyes sliding left and right. Couples hold hands.

A girl catches Charli's eye.

The girl looks like Charli did when she was that age, maybe seven. It's not only that they share the same features—the skinny frame and dark-brown hair with eyes a shade lighter—she also exhibits a look of being alone, of being afraid and alone and lost.

The girl sits cross-legged in the grass. Her straight hair was recently brushed. She wears a fleece sweatshirt and blue jeans.

"Are you okay?" Charli asks.

The little girl looks up with teary eyes; she doesn't say anything.

"Where are your parents?" Charli asks sweetly, looking around, not seeing anyone directly in the vicinity.

"I lost them." A front tooth is missing, causing a lisp.

Charli's protective instincts take over. "Oh no. Can I help you find them?"

The girl nods sadly.

Charli offers her hand and helps her up. "I'm sure they're right around here. Where did you last see them?"

"I was chasing those ducks, and when I turned around, they were gone." Her missing tooth makes it hard for her to say so many words.

Charli looks through the mist that is slowly burning off the park. A raft of ducks drifts out toward the center of the lake. She's not exactly sure what to do. She doesn't want to walk too far and leave this place. Where is that pair of cops on horseback she saw earlier?

Recalling exactly what it felt like to be lost, Charli decides that comforting the girl is the most important thing she can do. The rest will take care of itself.

Charli takes a knee. "You stick with me, and we'll find them, okay? Worst case, we'll find the police, but I think we're going to get lucky. How does that sound?"

"Good," the girl responds in short.

They start to circle the pond. "What's your name?"

"Lucy."

"Hi, Lucy, I'm Charli. I'm from Boston. Do you know where that is?"

She nods. "Near New York?"

"That's right. Are you from London?"

"Norwich."

"Oh, gotcha. So you're just visiting?"

The girl nods and her shoulders droop.

"I remember being your age," Charli says, surprised at the buoyancy of her tone. "You know what I liked more than *annnnnything* else . . ."

"Lucy!"

Charli whips her head around to see Lucy's mother running for her. She wears a leather jacket, and her hair is pulled back into a ponytail, revealing all of her worried face. Mother and daughter embrace, and Charli witnesses something so different from what she knew growing up. She sees a mother loving her daughter more than it seems even possible to love someone. The mother sheds tears, and she lifts Lucy up high and squeezes her so tight, so beautifully and lovingly tight.

Instead of berating her for getting lost, the mother takes a knee, brushes her hair from her face, and showers Lucy with apologies. "I'm so sorry I lost you. I turned around and you were gone."

"It's okay, Mommy. It's not your fault."

Charli can barely take it, and a memory gently washes over her. She was five or six, sitting on her parents' balcony in Boston. They had one right outside their bedroom. She remembers hearing them laugh as she stood up on a flowerpot and leaned over the railing to watch a bird. That was right before she tumbled over, screaming as she landed hard on a bush. It couldn't have been longer than a second before her father came over the railing after her—like a superhero might. He leaped down and swept Charli up into his arms and squeezed her tight, just like this woman was holding Lucy now.

Sometimes, it's as if she's forgotten those moments, those exemplary showings of love from her father . . . and others. Her mother's volatility often eclipses the memories she should hold on to, but it's just a veil—a veil that Charli can remove. A veil she must remove.

The mom looks at Charli. "Thank you for checking on her. Oh my God, I was freaking out."

"I can only imagine. She's such a sweetie."

A man races up wearing Clark Kent glasses. His eyes are darkened with fear but brighten with each step he takes toward his daughter. "Lucy, my God. Are you okay?"

He wraps her up in his arms, and Charli feels his love as if . . . as if it were her own father, and Charli was the lost little girl. The dad presses his eyes closed and squeezes his daughter with so much love that it seems to brighten the color of the evergreens beyond them.

Her ribs rattle as the air leaves her lungs. She is loved like that, she realizes.

The mom says to the dad, "This kind young lady found her."

The dad lifts his gaze. "I'm so grateful."

"You've got a brave girl there." Charli smiles and waves. "Bye, Lucy."

The girl looks over her father's shoulder and peers at Charli with eyes that are so wise that they seem to be the eyes of a sage. "What was it?" she asks with her lisp.

"What was what?"

"The thing that you liked more than anything else."

"Oh." Charli falls back through the years and answers with a rush of warmth. "My father holding me like your dad is holding you." Love fills her heart.

Lucy smiles knowingly. "Bye."

Charli turns and senses her eyes darting around, trying to put together what has just happened, what has just occurred to her. She looks back over her shoulder and sees the family of three squeezing each other. Instead of feeling like she missed out on that part of her life, Charli realizes what a gift this moment has been.

She's been given the most perfect glimpse of what has been holding her back all these years. Therapists have told her this, but it never seemed to matter till now. Charli's twenty-nine years old, but there's a younger girl inside her that still feels lost and alone and abandoned. She's been letting that little girl lead the way. She's been letting that little girl keep her from living and loving the way she is capable.

Maybe she can't find out who killed Lillian. Maybe she doesn't want to learn that Miles did it. Maybe she can't change the luck of her family. But it's time for her to take some accountability. It's not the truth of what happened to Lillian that will change her life. It's Charli and Charli alone. She must seize life and quit feeling sorry for herself. She has to stop letting her mother win.

Georgina's voice comes alive in Charli's head, but it's not as venomous as it once was. It sounds weak and raspy, as if she's dying. Charli can't make out what she's saying. What she knows, though, is that she's done being a victim to her mother. She's done allowing that voice to permeate her life.

And she's not alone anyway. That's the irony. She has people who love her. Maybe not her mother, but her father sure as hell does. She knows it now more than ever. Viv does. Aunt Kay. And Noah.

Noah.

It might be young love, but love it is, for sure. And she loves him back. She's been afraid to let herself love him because that little girl inside her keeps getting in the way. But no more. Charli's going to love with all of her, even if that means opening herself up to be vulnerable. Especially so! All this information is blasting at her like it's coming from a high-powered fan, but it's all settling into place.

Charli starts to run, setting free the little girl inside her and taking the freaking reins of her life. Her mom will not get in the way anymore. Tough luck, Charli didn't get all the face cards in life. She didn't have a mom and dad who cared like the couple she'd just seen. But no more making excuses. No more beating herself up.

She realizes she's picked up the pace, and she's smiling. Because for the first time in her life, she feels free from the wounds of her youth. *What is it that's gotten me here?* she wonders. She hasn't found the total truth, certainly not proved it, so why does it feel like she's made a difference by coming here?

The constellation springs to mind. She thinks of each person and who they represented, wondering the role—if any—the constellation therapy has played. She'd flown to Costa Rica seeking green lights, and now she feels like she's finding them. Amid all this chaos, she feels like she's breaking through.

"It's Noah," she whispers as she slows down to consider the possibility. She nods to herself. He's her green lights. Or at least one of them. A very big one of them. Love came and smacked her on the head, and she'd totally missed it. She spent the last week and a half pretending it was nothing more than a vacation hookup.

If she'd get out of her own way, she could let it be more than that. God bless Noah for being so patient with her. He'd given her all the space in the world to be who she really was, to make her mistakes, but it still hadn't been enough. How lucky she is to know such a man. And she *loves* him.

She loves him so much she'd commit to him, marry him, even have a child with him. Wait, what?

What were those thoughts that just spilled out? She'd marry him? She'd have babies with him? She's full of surprises today. For a moment, as she crosses a street, she imagines what it would be like to give birth and for Noah to be standing there next to her, holding her hand. She imagines them raising this girl or boy and playing Santa Claus and being there when he or she struggles. Being there when he or she succeeds. Charli wants to be a parent, she does. She wants to prove that she can break the cycle. That she's capable of all kinds of love.

But what about the curse—or whatever it is? It's one thing to stop playing victim, to take ownership of a life, but what if that life is bound for a destiny of troubled times? No, no, no. That's not how it works. Even if her morphic field is wrought with pain and bad fortune and awful events, she can overcome it.

A clarity seems to settle inside her. She has no idea whatsoever how to go forward, how to break free, how to stop the lying and self-sabotaging, but she knows that she has to.

And she knows that it all starts with going back to find Noah.

He may hate her, he may regret knowing her, but she must apologize and express her feelings for him. It's terrifying, the idea of returning to Winchester. He's probably told the whole family everything by now. Frances talked about how the truth would set her free. Maybe she'd not ever find the truth of what happened in 1881, but she could at least share *her* truths. She could go back to Boston knowing she'd left it all on the table.

Not ready to return to the hotel, she runs for what seems like forever, stopping at crosswalks and jogging in place, getting lost in the city. She's not running away from anything, she's going toward something. Toward something real. It's so clear now that she's been running away from so many of the things in her life that matter, like Noah, and love, and even opening the bookstore. She could have gone through with it. And she still can!

She still can.

Her whole body feels like it's radiating with awareness. If anyone is watching her, they're surely considering committing her someplace. She's going between bouts of crying, laughing, and smiling, and she's talking to herself too. She's playing Sherlock again, thinking about the constellation, seeing the people standing around her, wondering if she'd gotten everything right, wondering if there was anything missing.

Forget the woo-woo. Maybe all of this was a way to snap her out of it. Perhaps Frances is a little bit cuckoo, as was this idea of finding the truth. But no matter, because the fire burns inside Charli like never before.

As she takes in her surroundings, she sees she's made it to the river Thames—its color far darker than that of the Itchen. An empty barge slowly passes under the bridge ahead. To the left, standing tall, is a site she knows. But she's not sure exactly why or how.

It's a formidable building, taking up several city blocks. Tall towers rise from it, one of which has an enormous clock that looks like Big Ben.

Wait, is it?

Yes, it is. And this is the Palace of Westminster, the home of Parliament. Where Steven Pemberton attends the House of Lords meetings. *Is he there?* The ghost of her family's past brushes by her in the form of the chills.

Could she find him?

A bell rings—it's Big Ben telling the time. The sound reverberates across the city and throughout her body, and she realizes it's speaking to her. Well, it feels that way, at least. What other signs does she need to know that she's doing something right?

With a determination that she's never known before, she marches toward the building and seeks the entrance, which is on the opposite side from the river. As it's nine on the nose, people in suits are pouring in. She wonders if Lord Pemberton is among them. If she can find him, she'll tell him the truth. Isn't that part of what she's learned this morning? That she can't lie anymore.

A police officer rests his hand on the handle of a machine gun that's strapped to his chest. Charli walks up to him with some hesitation. "Sir, may I ask you something?"

He's in near head-to-toe black. His cap has a polished visor; a black-and-white-checkered band wraps around it. A bulletproof vest covers his trunk.

He's caught off guard but is nice enough to nod a yes to her question.

Charli tries not to look at the gun. "If I were hoping to get in touch with one of the members of Parliament, how could I do that?"

His threat level appears to lower as he pulls his hand from the gun to point. "You can go right through the doors. No one's stopping you."

"I can go inside?"

He eases even more, saying kindly, "Absolutely. And you can ask a visitor assistant at the desk to deliver a note to the peer, notifying him that you'd like to speak with him."

"Is there a dress code?" she asks, realizing that her sweats aren't exactly her best foot forward.

"No," he replies.

"Will he be in there?"

"Who is he?"

"Lord Pemberton. Steven Pemberton."

The police officer squishes his lips together and gives a subtle head-shake. "I can't know that. They don't always attend. I'd check the order sheet inside and see what's on topic in the next few days. If you know what his specialist subjects are, you'll have a better chance of finding him."

"His specialist subjects?"

"His interests. The wars he likes to fight. The military, affordable housing, that sort of thing."

"I did read that he's into the environment."

"There you go."

"Thank you," Charli says, unable to completely wrap her head around how easy this feels, as if she's meant to be here. Is this how life is supposed to be, a current moving in the right direction? Would Frances even believe it?

Yeah, she probably would.

Chapter 29

The Peer

Charli enters through a set of giant wooden doors and passes through a security checkpoint, which includes stepping through an x-ray machine and having her photo taken. Now with a pass hanging on a lanyard from her neck, she walks onto the fancy tile floors of the main lobby. As far as lobbies go, this one deserves all the awards. The vaulted ceiling is as high as that of Winchester Cathedral. An enormous chandelier glows with yellow lights in the center. Statues of what look like past kings and queens stare down at her. Beyond them, mosaics line the walls.

Feeling out of place with her so-very-American accent, she approaches the information desk and finds a man with uneven side-burns, looking up at her. "How may I help you?"

"I was hoping to have a note delivered to a peer? I was told that was possible." Charli waits for him to laugh at her.

"Yes, sure."

Charli can't believe her luck. "Great. Do you know if Lord Steven Pemberton is here today?"

"I do believe I saw him this morning, yes."

Charli's jaw falls like an anvil. "Really? May I borrow something to leave a message for him?" If she's going to keep playing detective, she'd better start traveling with a notebook and pen.

She writes out a quick note in her best cursive, briefly stating that she is a relative from the United States and would love to say hi. To hook him like a good writer, she finishes with, *Did your family ever wonder what happened to Miles Pemberton, who I think would be your great-uncle a few generations back?*

As she hands it over, she asks, "How long do you think it'll take?"

"I'll notify you of his response within thirty minutes or so. Depends on if he's in chambers."

Charli sits on a chair with a green velvet cushion and decides that she is the most underdressed person in the building. Before her, constituents shake hands with their representatives; tourists eyeball the impressive architecture; two visitor assistants laugh almost uncontrollably over something one has said.

Eventually, she locks her eyes on the doors through which he could come out and imagines what it would be like to see him in person. It's probably a good time to work out what she is going to say to him. *Hello, Lord cousin Pemberton, are you familiar with the murder your uncle several times back committed? Well, he didn't do it! How do I know? Because he loved her. How do I know that? Because . . . because I feel it in me, that love.*

It takes every bit of thirty minutes for the visitor assistant with the distracted barber who forgot to line up his sideburns to return with an answer. He seems to realize only now what she's wearing, and he does a double take at her sweats. She'd be offended, but she was busting his chops for . . . well, having uneven chops!

She bites back another smile and says, "Any luck?"

"I'm sorry, he's unavailable."

"What does that mean?"

"He must have meetings. I'm not sure. There was a decline from his office."

"A decline. Hmm." So much for green lights. She recalls what the police officer outside had said. "Could I at least go to the public gallery?"

He nods. "I can escort you. And I'm sure you wouldn't, but please do not attempt to contact him while he's in chambers."

"I wouldn't dare," she says, but in truth, she would. If that's her only option.

He gestures for her to follow him. "The House of Commons usually has a queue, but you'll have no trouble getting into the House of Lords. I can't say that he'll be in attendance—maybe only ten to twenty percent usually are at any given time, but you might get lucky."

Charli follows him through a set of doors, down a hall, and up a flight of stairs. He walks her into the public gallery, where a group of everyday people sit on benches looking down over the proceedings. Heads turn as she quietly takes a seat and looks down from her place on the balcony to find Parliament in session.

She's seen pictures, but it's an impressive sight to behold in person. The ceiling is as elaborate as was the lobby. A structure resembling a church altar stands against the back wall, its polished gold sparkling under the bright lights from the pendants swinging above. Men and women dressed in their finest business suits sit on red benches, all facing two men in wigs who reside at a large square desk in the center. Charli needs to brush up on her British politics, but she imagines the members sit with their respective parties.

Also at the square desk are two podiums, one on either side. A man with a red tie is making an impassioned speech. He's an advocate for whatever bill or policy is under debate. He smacks down his fist. "We must act now before it's too late."

Charli bounces her eyes from one member to the next, hoping to recognize Lord Pemberton. She's studied his picture enough by now. As she starts to lose hope, she acknowledges that there's no way she's going to grab his attention. She'd have to nearly yell, and then everyone in the chambers would look her way. She'd probably be dragged out in cuffs.

Her mind is wandering ten minutes later when a door in the corner opens. She watches with hesitant anticipation as a petite woman in a black suit shuffles in, followed by a man in gray who is straightening his collar. As she's about to give up and the door is closing, a hand appears to catch it.

It's him.

Lord Steven Pemberton follows the other two into the chamber. His facial angles are sharp enough to cut something. He has curly hair the color of gunmetal. He takes a seat, crosses his arms, and listens quietly.

Did he really see my note? she wonders. If so, is he intentionally avoiding her? Surely, he's heard by now that she's hunting him down.

Charli watches him as Big Ben chimes another passing hour. He claps, he stands, he nods, he takes notes. She hopes she can catch his eye, but he never once lifts his gaze upward to the balcony.

An hour later, he stands to leave. She seizes the opportunity and hopes to find him in the hallways. But a man in blue and green is there on the other side of the door and escorts her back to the lobby.

On the edge of giving up, she exits and wanders around the building. Perhaps he's taking a lunch or smoke break. She notices a car park directly across Abingdon Street. Is that where the members park? Or perhaps they take the Tube.

Deciding that it's a good opportunity to change, she hops a taxi back to her hotel. After a shower, she folds her hair into a towel and sits back on the bed, phone in hand. It's time to call Noah.

His voice comes over on voice mail, and it's like a balm for her heart.

"Noah, it's me. I . . . I'd like to talk to you. I have so much to say, and I . . . I'm sorry. Would you call me? Can I come see you? I could come in the morning."

She sets down the phone and brings her attention back to Lord Pemberton. Even if she can get him to talk to her, it feels like a long shot that he would have any additional information. But she's in a leave-no-stone-unturned kind of mind.

～

Back at the Palace of Westminster, it's four thirty, and she thinks she's figured out which door the members use. While leaning inconspicuously against an iron fence across the street, she watches the door open and close. At five fifteen, people pour out. She crosses the street and stops by a tree growing out of the sidewalk. She pretends to use her tube of lipstick as a vape pen.

The rush slows, and the door snaps shut. She's frustrated and doesn't know what to do but hangs around a few more minutes, scrolling through her phone, chatting with Viv and her father and the dog sitter, smiling when she sees new pictures of Tiny.

The door opens and closes several more times, but it's never him.

Until it is. Lord Pemberton jaunts out the door while tightening his scarf. By now Charli's given up on stealth and goes straight for him.

"Lord Pemberton!"

He looks over with alarm.

"Yes?"

Charli reaches him and sticks out a hand. He doesn't shake it. Instead, he looks like he's about to lift his arms in defense.

"I've been trying to reach you. I'm a relative from Boston, and . . ."

He raises a hand, suddenly looking terrified. "I'm sorry, I must go."

"I'm not a scary person. I'm just . . . I'm into genealogy." Her statement comes off more as a question.

"I must go," he says again, and rushes past her with almost comical speed.

No, she's not losing this opportunity. Catching up with him, she says, "Just a moment of your time. I'm . . . I don't even know how to explain, but I'm investigating something that happened in our family. A murder in Winchester."

He stops.

She knows that he knows exactly to what she's referring.

This is her chance. "I have reason to think it didn't happen the way it was written in the paper," Charli says, approaching cautiously. "I'm talking about Miles Pemberton . . . your direct relative. I think he would be your third great-uncle. This means a lot to me, trying to find the truth, and I'd so appreciate it if you'd sit down with me for a few minutes. Or we can keep walking. I have some questions, and I'd love to explain more of why I'm here."

She guesses he's going to come around and be nice, but he cuts a mean look at her. "I don't know what you're talking about, and you're making me quite uncomfortable. I'll ask you to walk away now."

Charli looks at him with pleading eyes, but he doesn't seem to care.

"Sir, you know what I'm talking about. We are family. I just want to . . ."

She sees a war he's fighting in his head, and if any part of her is a detective, that part of her is screaming at her, telling her to get the truth out of him.

"What do you know?" she asks.

He spins around and raises his hands in the air, palms up. "I've no idea what you're talking about. I must go."

Charli looks at him now with more anger than anything else. "Why have you been ignoring me?"

"I don't know who you are, young lady."

"I'm a woman from Boston who is related to you and asking for your help."

"I'm afraid I have nothing to offer you. Now, excuse me."

He pivots and speed walks across the street toward the Tube station. Once he disappears, Charli sighs. What could he possibly know anyway? It was almost one hundred and fifty years ago. It was a silly hunch.

⌐⌐

"It felt like he did know something," Charli says to her dad as she faces a plate of Indian food. Not simply Indian food—the *finest* Indian food she's ever tasted. She's halfway through a plate of *saag aloo*, and her mouth is on fire, but in the best of ways. "I don't know. I could be reading into it too much."

"I think your gut has proven to be right lately. Don't ignore it."

"Yeah, well, what am I going to do? Take him hostage? Tickle him until he confesses that he knows what happened?"

"Please don't do that."

His lightheartedness summons a slight smile, as she can sense the lightness in him, perhaps hiding behind a veil. "Dad, can I talk to you for a minute? Like really talk to you."

"You know you can, Charli."

Does she? She's been holding back for years. "I think I've been harboring some resentment toward you. About you always being gone when I was younger. And how Mom treated me."

"Charli—"

"No, Dad, let me finish. Do you remember when I came down hard on you about not protecting me? When I blamed you for how Mom treated me? Back in high school?"

She knows he remembers because she'd never been so ugly to him, but she waits for his response.

"I do."

She pauses to get it right. "I'm sorry for saying that. It's not true. You were out there making a living and supporting us, fighting through your own grief after losing my brother. You didn't know what Mom was doing. You were trying so hard to be a good husband and a good dad. And I know you loved me. It was all her, and I'm realizing that. And before you say anything, I realize that I've been stuck since then, believing all the stuff she told me. Believing that you guys would have thrown me away if you—"

"You know that's not true," he says, his voice cracking.

"Yes. Especially in your case. And with Mom, I'm not going to give her excuses, but she has them. She comes from a long line of troubled people, and I believe with all of me that trauma travels through the generations in a multitude of ways. There's been a momentum of bad building in our family since Lord James Pemberton and possibly before that. There's no way to know when it started. But I know where it stops."

He lets her finish.

She drops a fist onto her leg. "With me. I'm not going to let my experience with her dictate the rest of my life. What I'm going to do is hold on to all the love you've shown me and move on. Daddy, I haven't even let myself be in a relationship because I thought that I wasn't good enough. I didn't want people to find me out. It's so stupid. What am I hiding from? I'm human."

"Aren't we all?"

"And that's what I really wanted to say. Something happened to you. I remember you being so bright and full of life years ago, and you're letting life beat you. I didn't tell you this, but one of the main reasons I came here was that I had this wild hope that I could somehow turn you around. Somehow keep you from . . . giving up or hurting yourself. And you don't need to tell me what was going on with you or tell me if I was right, that you were thinking about it. I want you to tell me that you'll join me in trying to climb out of this hole together. What do you say?"

The following silence isn't so scary.

"Yeah," he finally says. "I can do that. I can definitely do that."

She smiles into the phone.

"Sounds like this adventure was all worth it, huh? I'm hearing some fire in you."

"Yes, for sure. You know, it's funny. I came here following Frances's instructions. I got to the truth. Not sure I set the truth free, but I think I've at least found it. Is that why I feel so much better? Or is it because . . . just because I'm finally growing up. Either way, coming here has changed me."

"I can hear it, Charli, and I'm so proud of you. I'm not sure it matters how we exactly change, as long as we do. And I'm sitting here hearing you, and it's putting a smile on this old face. You make me want to fight too. I've told you that before."

Is that some fight she hears in his voice? "The only piece that doesn't make sense is why I had to finally fall in love—really fall in love—with someone who lives so far away. That doesn't feel right."

"You're young, Charli. Love can come around again."

"Can it, Dad? Do you believe it?"

"I don't know."

"Yeah." At least he's being real with her.

"Look, Charli. Please know that you're my everything. You're what keeps me going. And I love the way you're talking now. If anyone can lead this family out of the darkness, it's you."

His encouragement fills her up and makes her believe that he's right.

It's Saturday morning—twenty-four hours before her flight, and Noah still hasn't returned her call. There's a difference in her mindset today, though. Who could blame him? She messed up, and if he truly feels about her the way he says, then he's hurting inside. It's her turn to be brave. That's why she will not leave this country without telling him to his face that she loves him.

A cab takes her to the train station, where she buys a ticket back to Winchester. She's got about ten minutes before departure and goes to grab a croissant while she's waiting on the boarding announcement. Attempting to slow her speedy mind, she puts on her headset and plays Taylor Swift's newest album. When they flash the track number, she heads that way and climbs aboard a car toward the front.

She's casually checking her emails, scrolling for no reason, when a new one appears and makes her choke on her pastry.

He's written to her.

Lord Pemberton has written her.

She focuses and reads his note.

Miss Thurman,

I apologize for my hesitation in speaking with you yesterday. Your communication has caught me quite off guard. Upon further consideration, I'm willing to sit down with you and discuss this matter. Please let me know when you are available.

Steven Pemberton

Never has Charli moved so quickly in her life. She springs from her seat, races down the aisle, and leaps down to the platform just in time.

Chapter 30

BLOOD TIES

Eleven a.m. and gloomy. Lord Steven Pemberton stands alone on the path that runs along the river Thames. He wears the same scarf as the day before, neatly knotted at his neck. He holds a cup of coffee in his hand and is watching a man waving a metal detector over the small beach down along the shore.

"Lord Pemberton?" The formality makes Charli feel awkward. "Is that what I call you?"

He twists to her. "Steven. Please call me Steven." He shakes her hand. He's so much warmer now. "I'm sorry about the weather."

She glances up at the clouds. "I was told this was the norm."

He has the smile of a politician, one that's difficult to decipher. "It is. And it's quite normal to apologize as well."

Charli thinks he's made a joke, but she's not sure. "That's funny." There's a fading question mark in there somewhere.

He turns back to the river and nods toward the man with the metal detector. "You wouldn't believe what the mud larkers find down there. You'd think they would have picked it dry by now, but the river keeps turning stuff up."

"Turns what up?" Charli asks, stepping to get a better look at the man focused on his task down on the beach.

"Artifacts from centuries of life here. Pottery, wine jugs . . . murder weapons. Now they require permits, but in the old days, anyone could go rummaging along the shore. My son and I once found a Roman coin near the bridge over there."

Charli follows his finger to the arched bridge that crosses over the Thames. "You have a son?"

"A son and a daughter, yes. Nineteen and twenty-one, both attending school in Oxford. How about you, Charli? Do you have children?"

"No, it's just me."

Only then does he take a peek at her naked ring finger. "You're still young, though."

"I'd like to think so. Actually, I wasn't sure I ever wanted kids, but I'm changing."

He smiles warmly, easing her nerves. "They are the delight of my life. Anyhow . . . you seem quite interested in speaking to me. I have indeed received your communiqué, and I must say that you've caught me off guard. Are you sure that we are related?"

Charli crosses her arms and looks up into his green eyes. "Miles Pemberton, the man convicted of murdering Lillian Turner, was my third great-grandfather. That, I know. But my family didn't know him as Miles. We knew him as Samuel."

He pinches his chin. "How do you know they are one and the same?"

"I have pictures. Well, one picture from his life in the States, with the family he started there. Where I came from. And I have this . . ."

She reaches into her bag and first hands him the picture of Miles and Lillian. He takes it delicately and studies it. For a moment his eyes widen as he shuffles his feet. What had he seen?

"I found this picture hidden behind this one with his American family." She hands him the photo of Miles and his American wife, Margaret, and their two children. As he looks, she says, "A man at the London Archives pointed out that the tie in the first photo is a

Winchester College tie, so I visited the college archivist and found more pictures."

"Quite the researcher, aren't you?" He looks one more time at the photograph of the older Miles, then hands them back to her.

"I'm new to genealogy, but . . ." Where does she even begin? "As you can imagine, I'm intrigued. It seems that he escaped prison, somehow made his way to Boston, and created an entirely new family tree under the name Hall."

Lord Pemberton looks up toward the dark clouds. "It's been a question passed down through my family for a long time."

Charli's heart kicks. "So you're familiar with what happened . . . I mean, you . . . you know about the murder?"

"Of course I know about the murder."

"I just . . . it was a long time ago."

He chuckles. "I don't know that family murders are forgotten that easily."

"Fair point."

"And here you go, digging it back up as if it were yesterday."

"Yeah, it's becoming an obsession, getting to the truth."

"I can imagine."

"Look, Lord Pemb—I mean, Steven. There's more to it than me stumbling upon a photo. It's a long story, but I've become fascinated with transgenerational memories, both genetically speaking, and something perhaps even more . . . how do I even say it? Something more powerful than genetics. My family has been struggling a lot since Miles's generation. Suicides, early deaths, cancer, depression, and almost unfathomable bad luck. I've experienced it myself. Ever since I learned this idea of how transgenerational memories can affect us, I've been trying to get to the bottom of where it all started."

She wonders whether he's about to turn and walk away, referring to her later as his balmy American cousin.

"I know what I'm saying is hard to believe but—"

"I don't think it's hard to believe at all," he says.

"Wait, really?"

Steven draws a breath, as if he's not sure whether he wants to unlock this door.

"Forgive me, but I must ask you . . . are you wearing any kind of recording device?"

"What?" Charli says in surprise. "No, I'm not recording."

He chews on her response, possibly considering a search. After a moment he nods, as if he's okay with believing her. "I come from a long line of struggle. And it has everything to do with that day in 1881. Or at least I believe so."

"Are you for real right now?" Charli takes a quick inventory of what is happening. She's tracked down a relative, who happens to be in the House of Lords, and he's been thinking the same thoughts?

"I'm certainly for real. I suppose I'm a bit of a history junkie myself, and I've always wondered about the truth. All of us have. What happened to Miles after his escape?" He bites his lower lip. "Here you are, bringing the answer. What other details do you have?"

"Barely anything. It was such a long time ago. I'm afraid my cold case–solving skills could use some developing, and no one in my family has much to tell. He had two children, died in Boston in 1925, when he was sixty-two."

With a stifled smile, he reaches for something in his jacket pocket. As he's about to draw it out, his hand stops, and he lets his jacket close again.

"Do you know something that I don't?" Charli asks.

He hesitates, spinning his cup of coffee in his hand like it's a wineglass. "I'm not looking to drag up history, Charli. As far as legally so. In other words, what I'm going to tell you is not something I'll repeat again, but . . . but I feel that I owe you something for bringing to me this truth."

Charli loses her breath in anticipation. She hangs on his words.

"I don't believe Miles Pemberton was a murderer. I believe there was some kind of cover-up."

"Why do you say that?"

"While my father was dying, he called me to his bed. He told me that our family carried a dark secret and that I had to lead the best life I could if I was ever to escape it."

Steven reaches into his jacket pocket again and pulls out an antique silver hair brooch, shaped like a flower with an emerald in the center . . . Wait, Charli's seen it before.

When it hits her, she gasps. "That's the same one that's in the photo."

"I think so. His father had given it to him, saying to always keep it as a reminder that he has a responsibility in this life. He told me that what was written in the papers wasn't true."

Charli feels validated. "Miles didn't kill her, did he?"

Steven shakes his head. Not a word spoken.

She takes the brooch and runs her fingers along it, feeling the hum of the tragic memories associated with it. "I was right," she whispers to herself.

"You may keep it, as I think it's served its purpose now. Perhaps it's meant to fall into your hands."

Charli finds a certain pain welling in his eyes. "But what happened then?"

"Miles's brother, Edward, was my grandfather a few generations back. He, of course, once carried my position in the Lords. As you may know, he was shot by Lillian's brother but survived. Lillian's brother was killed in the gunfight. On his deathbed, Edward told the story of what had transpired that day and confessed to his son that he'd killed Lillian."

He sighs. "He said that in the years after being shot, he'd found God and sought forgiveness. He'd been responsible for Lillian's death and felt responsible for her brother's as well. He made his son promise that he would live a life that could redeem their family name. This has been a tradition all the way to me. My father gave me the brooch upon my graduation from Oxford and made me swear to live the life of two good men to make up for what our ancestor had done. The brooch became a powerful symbol in our family that I believe freed us from following in the footsteps of the bad men who came before us."

Steven looks up, as if searching for the heavens. "I have done my best to fulfill my oath to my father, but I do not want my children to know what happened. I don't want them to feel a murderer's blood inside of them. This is what kept me up last night, after you found me. I woke and stared for a long time at the picture of my son and daughter, wondering if I must pass this burden on to them or if I could end it with me. Perhaps it's time to let go. Perhaps you and I can finally set to rest this awful crime."

A sense of pride rises in her, knowing that she's found such a good man in her family tree. And she can't believe what he's saying. "So it was his own brother? Why would he do that?"

Steven presses his lips together in thought. "The details have faded as the story has been passed down, but I do believe his father, James, was a bad man. Abusive and angry. The story as it came to me is that James did not approve of Miles's courtship with an innkeeper's daughter. Miles refused to end the relationship, and on the day of the murder traveled to Elmhurst with Lillian to meet face-to-face with James on the subject. An argument ensued, and Miles and James began to fight. At some point, Edward attempted to break up the fight with a gun. Lillian got in the way, and he shot her in cold blood. Only later in his life did he realize the wrong that he'd done. I do believe his brush with death, and the good Lord himself, turned his heart."

"Wait, but . . . how did Miles get blamed?"

Steven nods, as if he knew the question was coming.

"It was James's design. He must have had a bad leg, as he walked with a cane. My father spoke of a gold lion's head as the handle. I've seen pictures of it since. James struck Miles with it, leaving him unconscious. He apparently had been forced to decide between his two sons in that moment, and he chose Edward. They devised a story that would send Miles to the gallows and allow Edward to take his place as the rightful heir to the estate and to the House of Lords. The only part that backfired was Miles's escape from prison. They always guessed it was Miles's grandmother who helped him, but nothing was ever proven."

Charli hasn't moved a muscle. She finally takes in a breath as she processes the information. She feels the betrayal that Miles must have felt when he realized what was happening. What a terrible, terrible thing that was done to him.

She finally looks back to Steven. "You're a good man," she says. "I appreciate you sharing this with me. It means everything. And, yes, I want what happened to go away. We've all suffered enough."

Steven nods. "I hope you'll agree that this crime does not need to be dredged back up, and I will not join you on some mission to clear Miles's name. We are a public family, and I have no interest in drawing the media further into our lives. They might even try to remove me from the Lords. But I felt compelled to tell you the truth, as I am ready for it to end. We, too, have struggled as a family, and life has been trying. I don't want to bring any more of that in. My children deserve to live without such a burden."

"I understand," Charli says. He's taken a big step, bringing her this brooch.

"Tell who you need to tell, family and such, I suppose. But keep the circle small. Absolutely no media, no books. I will deny we ever spoke." He takes a step back. "I must go, Charli. You now know as much as I."

"Understood."

He locks eyes with her, and she sees a man she admires very much. "You've satisfied a great curiosity in my life," he says. "Thank you for that. How terribly awful to be punished for a crime he didn't commit. I do hope he was able to find happiness again."

"I hope so too." Something else is already on her mind, though. "One last thing."

He stops. "Yes?"

"I'd like to visit Edward's grave, and perhaps James's too. For some closure. Do you know where they're buried?"

"I do. Everyone in our family has been buried in the West Hill Cemetery. The one up high on the hill near the hospital in Winchester. They're not hard to find, a whole cluster of Pembertons."

"Thank you. Thanks for everything. It's nice to meet you, Steven. If you ever find yourself in Boston, you have my contact info."

"Indeed I do." He looks at her one last time. "Farewell, Charli."

Charli sits by the window near the front of the train. The world outside passes by in a blur. The inspector is punching tickets. Across the aisle, a mother nurses her child.

Connected to the train's Wi-Fi, Charli scans photos of her family: of Miles and Edward and James. She can't believe she's finally gotten the truth, but even more, she can't believe what Edward and James did to Miles. What kind of people could do that?

Back in the British Newspaper Archives, she finds a grainy picture of James in a black suit and the top hat that seems glued to his head. She's not seen this one before. It's dated 1879, London. He sits on a wooden chair, one leg crossed over the other in a pose. He is scowling at the camera underneath the guise of his waxed mustache. He's no happier than that first picture she saw of him in the Hampshire Archives office.

Charli reads the copy below. It refers to him as an outspoken peer from the Whig Party who pushed to take away power from the crown. She looks deep into his eyes, or what she can see of them. What made him so evil?

Then she notices that he's holding on to something. Is that a . . . ? Charli uses the zoom feature on her computer, focusing in on what he holds in his left hand. It's a mold or a small statue. Or a . . .

It's the lion-head cane that Steven mentioned. She sees it instantly as a weapon and imagines this awful man—this man who is a part of her—swinging it at his son. He comes to life in her mind, how he surely was even more abusive than Charli's mother.

But why a cane? What happened to him?

"His leg," she says out loud. Back in Costa Rica Herman had said that his leg hurt and that he could barely stand on it. So Herman *was* representing James—and, of course, the guy in the Messi uniform represented Miles, who was the cause of James's rage.

Charli takes the idea in for a moment. If she had any last doubts about the constellation, how could she now? What Frances had helped her create in that room was exactly the dynamic that she discovered in coming to England.

What does it all mean? she wonders, unable to ever again question the validity of the constellation. She doesn't understand the science of it, if it can be explained by science at all, but what happened in Costa Rica was no joke.

But being realistic, she thinks that life can't be so easy as to restore an imbalance by solving a mystery. The hard work must be done to accompany it, and that's what Frances must have meant when she'd said, *You're trying to right the wrongs to reach a point of healing, but the healing is already taking place by you being on the journey.*

It's not a chicken or egg kind of thing, Charli decides. The constellation therapy will do its part while Charli does her own work to break the cycle. How many generations of bad people had led to that day when Lillian was murdered? And to Georgina and then Charli? It surely didn't start with James Pemberton. Like Georgina's past had shaped her into someone cruel, so it surely went for James.

There is some sort of dark momentum flowing through her blood and in the morphic field of her family, and it will take more than restoring balance in their family's constellation. It will take Charli standing up and taking action to make sure the momentum will not carry forward.

It ends with her.

Chapter 31

The Quiet

Winchester, England
July 2, 1881

Miles's body shook to the rhythm of the police wagon bumping up and down on the road. The back of his head burned. The handcuffs wrapped around his wrists were clasped so tight that they'd turned his hands blue.

He didn't care.

All he felt was emptiness and loss.

His eyes burned holes in the floorboard as he sat there in shock. There were no thoughts, only numbness. Perhaps this was what death felt like, all light fading, his soul detaching from his physical body.

The policeman sitting across from him said, "Taking the law into your own hands, yeah? What did she steal from you?"

Miles didn't respond, barely heard the man.

The policeman jabbed him with the billy club in the leg, but Miles didn't flinch.

"Yeah, where you're going it will be good to learn how to keep your mouth shut."

Miles stayed silent.

When they arrived at the prison, he looked up at the tall walls. His father had taken him by one time, proudly showing it off, as it was recently built. Never did Miles think he'd see the inside of it.

Prison guards pushed him around like a rag doll as they processed him, made him change into a foul-smelling uniform, and then led him to a dank cell that reeked of death. When they locked the doors with an unforgiving finality, Miles lowered himself against the cold wall, leaning back with his head dropped forward.

Silence. Pain. Loss.

The emptiness passed through him endlessly.

One image repeatedly played in his mind.

Lillian falling, her blood splattering the floor.

Over and over, he watched her fall, saw her struggling for breath, eventually going quiet.

Days turned to weeks. A solicitor spoke with him, someone appointed by the district of Hampshire. People probably wondered why the family had not hired their own attorney. Miles knew why, and resentment simmered in his heart.

The solicitor asked him questions to which he did not respond. He simply held his gaze on the handcuffs that bound his hands.

"If I am to defend you, you must tell me what happened," the solicitor insisted.

Miles had nothing to say.

"Dammit, Miles. You will swing for this."

The gallows seemed as welcome a place as any.

The solicitor returned four times, promising Miles he would do his best in court. And he did. He tried to say that Miles had gone mad, as there had been a theft of a precious item: a diamond ring that belonged to Miles's mother.

Miles never once looked at the judge. He hoped he'd be sentenced to death.

On September 12, 1881, the judge, a hefty man with a gravelly voice, asked Miles to stand. Miles did so, and then raised his head for the first time.

The judge swung down the mallet; Miles felt the tremor in his feet. "You are found guilty, and you will meet your death by hanging."

Miles felt nothing. No dread. Perhaps his one thought was that the rope would be a comfort around his neck.

Only as the day for his execution drew near did the numbness wane, allowing anger to step in. His family had stood there and watched him be sentenced to death, and they'd let it happen. They'd agreed upon a lie and had stuck to it. More to the point, his brother had shot Lillian dead, and his father had rallied around him. They would soon stand on Gallows Hill with the rest of the townspeople and watch him swing.

He would have been consumed by hate, but it was the guilt of what he'd done to Lillian that was the strongest. He should have taken her the moment he met her and run far away. Come to think of it, he should not have let her in at all. He shouldn't have allowed himself to love her, because he knew what trouble he was bringing into her life. This guilt would be the last emotion he felt when the noose tightened, for it wasn't his brother who shot Lillian. It wasn't his father who'd caused all this terror. It was he, himself. Miles Pemberton was the one who killed Lillian Turner.

Chapter 32

The Three Hardest Things

Charli hikes up Romsey Road on the western side of Winchester. The cemetery appears to her left, and beyond the lines of crooked and mossy gravestones stands the city in the valley below.

She enters through the gate and wanders along the path, searching for the name *Pemberton*. The information on some gravestones is barely legible, having endured decades, if not centuries, of English weather. She leaves the path and starts into the tall grass, where early spring flowers have begun to bloom.

One after another, she studies the names. At the far end, twenty minutes into her search, Charli finds what she came for. As Lord Pemberton had said, there are a cluster of Pembertons all buried under ornate gravestones, some dating back to the sixteenth century.

Chills run through her when she finds Edward Pemberton's grave. He died at fifty-seven years old. She stands in the grass above where his body lies and lets herself feel him, knowing that she is now at the source of much of her family's turmoil.

She studies the gravestones next to his and finds Cora's. How could she have supported these men in what they did? She must have been absolutely broken inside. Then Charli finds the gravestone of Lord James Pemberton. He lies on the other side of his son Edward.

Charli is standing above the bones of two men who destroyed generations. James lived until he was sixty-three, and Charli wonders whether, like his youngest son, he ever regretted his wicked actions.

Very possibly not. Not all bad men feel regret toward the end.

On the train, she was able to wake Frances in Costa Rica and get instructions for exactly what she needed to do. Charli sits on the grass between the two graves. Having smartened up enough to carry a pad and paper now, she draws the pad from her bag and reads the words Frances passed on to her.

"I am not responsible for what you did. None of us are. Your guilt is yours alone to bear, just as my mother's is hers and no one else's. I want to be set free from it. I want everyone in our family to be set free from what both of you did. The truth is finally out. Though we are bound by blood, I am no longer a part of your crime. No one else is."

Even as she says the last words, the weight lifts, almost as if she could float right up into the sky and fly over Winchester.

—

It's around three by the time Charli makes it to the pub. She can't know how Noah will respond to her finally expressing her feelings—it might be too late—but she's hopeful. The long-distance challenge seems insurmountable, but they don't have to make all the decisions in the world right now. One day at a time.

Hoping that Noah can sneak away for a chat, she pulls back the door to find a mostly empty pub. The lunch rush has cleared out. A man sits at the bar with a newspaper splayed out in front of him. His beer is half-empty.

No, half-full.

Victoria is behind the bar and waves. "Hey there, Charli."

"You never leave, do you?"

"I pretty much live here." She pauses. "Wouldn't want it any other way."

Though Charli has urgent business, she slows her pace and takes a moment to collect her thoughts. "Victoria, I hope you know that you're amazing. I don't know you, but you have this thing about you that makes everyone in your orbit feel good. You don't even have to say a word. It's such a gift."

It looks like even Victoria, fully content in her life, maybe needed to hear that today. "I appreciate you saying that. My mum used to say, 'You're only a smile away from being happy.'"

Charli lets a real smile surface. "She'd be proud, Victoria. I'm sure you know that already, and who am I to say so? But I'm saying it anyway."

Victoria whispers her thanks in a beautifully humble way.

"Is Noah around?"

"Yeah, but today's family-meeting day. They're in the back. It could be a while."

Charli has been preparing herself to speak to him for most of the train ride, and the idea of coming back later doesn't sit well with her.

"Is it okay if I interrupt?" Charli says. "It's kind of important."

"Yeah, okay," Victoria says, "they're just that way."

Charli goes through the hallway that leads to the stairwell to the inn. Farther down, she once noticed a large room that is often used for larger parties. The doors are closed, but she hears a heated conversation taking place. Something about opening hours.

When their voices return to less passionate tones, Charli knocks on the door. Everyone goes silent as she pushes it open.

The heads of twenty of Noah's family swivel in a synchronistic movement that lights Charli's nerves on fire.

"Sorry to barge in," Charli says, then sets her eyes on Noah. "Could I borrow you for a moment?"

Noah doesn't get up right away. His father frowns. Marianne grimaces. Wesley sits back and crosses his arms. The one-hundred-year-old Helen casts a curious yet unsurprised look. How heavy all of this is.

But Charli holds her ground.

As Noah finally nods and starts to stand, Marianne interjects, "Anything you have to say, you can say to us too."

Noah waves her off. "It's okay. I'll be—"

Marianne wouldn't let him speak. "You might be a runt, but you're my brother, and I don't want to see her walk all over you any longer. Let her have her say in front of us all. Right, Mum and Dad?"

Her mom and dad don't exactly encourage the idea, but they don't bail Charli out either. Noah looks at her with a look of indecision.

"Fine," Charli says. "I suppose it has to do with all of you anyway." She'd prepared for rejection but not this . . .

She swallows her nerves, reminding herself that she's exactly where she needs to be right now. Everything that's happened to Charli these last few weeks has led to this moment.

"Go ahead," Noah's father urges.

She looks at him and then at Noah, where she feels the safest.

"My dad once told me that the hardest three things to say are *I'm sorry*, *I was wrong*, and *Worcestershire sauce*." She mangles the last one, and it makes her smile. Her childhood wasn't all bad.

"I still can't say that one," she says. "But I can say the rest. Noah, I'm sorry. For being an emotional yo-yo and sending you mixed messages and not recognizing what we have between us. And I was wrong not to tell you why I was here in the first place."

She casts her eyes over everyone at the table. "You know what, at the risk of you guys thinking I've lost my mind, let me take a step back. Well, a few steps back, to 1881. The fact is . . . someone in my family generations ago is responsible for the murder of your Lillian Turner, but it wasn't Miles Pemberton, who was sentenced to the gallows."

Noah's family doesn't move a muscle, waiting to see what this loon of an American is going to say next.

"Some of you probably don't even know about the murder—or care about it—but it's become important for me to figure it out. It's a long story best saved for another day, but all the way down to the present day, my family has suffered from trauma due to that murder. I can see by your expressions that Noah hasn't told you any of this. That's the kind of person he is. As good as they come . . ."

She feels instant relief for finally coming out and removing all the untruths. A kind look rises on his face.

"What I can't get over is that I found Noah before I even knew about the connection to your family. I found Noah and fell in love with him, not knowing what had happened with our relatives. If that's not serendipitous, I don't know what is."

Noah gives a curious yet skeptical look.

Charli goes to him and puts her hand on his shoulder. "I'd much rather do this in private, but so be it. There's a fourth thing that's also hard to say." She dives into those eyes. "I love you. I love you. I love you."

The skepticism falls from his face as he sets his hand on hers and gives a smile that maybe says *I love you* back.

Either way, his touch gives her even more courage. "I know that I can be very unlovable, and I know that our future is . . ." She shrugs. "Nearly impossible. But that doesn't keep me from loving you."

He doesn't say a word. Is it not enough? Perhaps he's enjoying this, watching her burn in public. Or maybe he's still trying to decide whether she means it.

That's fine—she'll keep going. "I've never wanted a serious relationship. Never wanted to get married. Definitely never wanted kids. I didn't want to bring them into my world, to make them suffer like everyone else in my family. That has changed since I first met you. I don't know if there's anything between us now. I can only imagine how frustrated you are with me. But that's okay. I just want you to know the truth."

Nothing from the rest of the family, barely a blink.

Finally, Noah chooses to speak, and his words hit straight to her core. "I love you too."

Stars shoot across the sky of her heart. "What took you so long? You had to make me work for it, huh?"

A round of laughter circles the table.

He grins, and it's a look that could push away even the darkest clouds. "I had to make sure you were sure."

"Ah, that's fair. Because maybe I just wanted to embarrass myself in front of your family—because that's what I do for fun. Seriously, can we take this outside now? I'm feeling a little bit like I'm in a Nick Hornby novel."

More laughter fills the room as Noah presses up from the table. "Okay, people. I think we've held her to the fire long enough. Yeah, let's escape before it's too late."

Charli lets out a big sigh.

Then it hits her. "Oh, one more thing." She takes the brooch from her purse. "This was Lillian's. I know that because I have a picture with Miles and Lillian, and she's wearing it. You might not believe this, but Lord Steven Pemberton, the heir of Miles's brother, Edward, gave it to me. I met with him in London this morning. His family has passed this brooch down through the generations as a reminder of their dark past and what is expected of them going forward. He told me the story as it has been passed down, all starting with Miles's father, James, and how displeased he was with Miles and Lillian's relationship."

Charli recounts the details as Steven shared them to her, then lowers her voice. "I know this to be true. It might not matter to you, but the truth matters to me a great deal. Because I believe it can remove some of the negative energy that seems to permeate not only my family, but the Pembertons and perhaps yours as well."

Glancing around the room, it's like she's just shown how a Zoom call works to a bunch of Victorians.

Charli holds the brooch up high and skips her eyes around the room. "If it's okay with you, I am going to take this back home with me and give it to the person who deserves it most: my third great-grandfather, Miles Pemberton. I will leave it on his grave." She likes to hear the pride in her voice when she says his name. Among a long list, Miles Pemberton has taught her how to love, and what could be a better lesson than that?

Helen stares back at her with seasoned eyes and gives a nod, and it's all the answer Charli needs. The matriarch has given her approval; she knows it belongs in Boston with Miles.

Charli sticks the brooch into the pocket of her jeans. "Though it's not my crime and it was a long time ago, I am sorry on behalf of my family for what happened to Lillian. I know with all of me that, just as I love Noah, Miles loved Lillian with every fiber of his being."

She looks back at Noah. "And now I am going to excuse myself while you all talk about the American loon that walked in the door. Don't worry, I get it. I'm feeling pretty loony." She needs him now and tugs on his arm and whispers, "Can we go outside now?"

He grins. "I'd say you've earned it." To his family, he says, "I'll be back in a few."

Marianne stops them as Charli and Noah make their escape. "Hey, Charli. I think you're all right. A little kooky, but that's okay. He'd be lucky to have you. As you know, I've always been curious about Lillian's murder. To know the truth does seem to settle something inside of me. Thank you for that."

"You're welcome," Charli says. She glances around the room. "Nice to meet everyone. I'm headed back to London to catch a flight home. Maybe I'll see you again."

Noah's dad rises first, followed by everyone else. He walks up to her and offers her a hug. "You're a good one, Charli," he whispers to her.

His sincerity breaks through any last fear that remains inside her. "That's how I feel about all of you, truly." She finds his eyes. "I hope to see you again."

By then, his wife and Marianne and Helen are in line, waiting for hugs, and Charli feels accepted in a way with which she's quite unfamiliar.

"You're gonna dump all that and take off?" Noah asks, once they're safely out of the pub. They come to a stop in the middle of the cobblestone street.

"Well, I didn't realize I was going to do that in front of the whole family. Now I need a nap."

He pulls her close and rests his chin on the top of her head. "You are a brave one, Charli Thurman."

Her heart soars.

After a long, comforting moment, he pulls back and clasps her face with gentle hands. "Don't go."

"I have to. I have a flight in the morning, and a boss that is losing patience."

He nods and eases in for a kiss. Her knees nearly buckle as a gasp escapes her lips. They kiss again, uncaring of who might be watching. For those moments, they're all alone, floating on a cloud out into the ether.

He slowly lowers his hands, grazing them across her chest and then wrapping them around her waist, pulling her in. They melt into each other. She breathes him in and soaks up his love, feeling every wall she's ever put up come down in a dazzling display of destruction.

When they pull apart, they're both smiling. It's amazing that they found this connection, and it's nearly comical that they live so far apart.

She straightens his collar, feeling incredible comfort in their touch. "Maybe you could come see me in Boston once your season slows down."

He looks at her as if that were already decided. "You're damn right I'll come see you. I can't stand that we live so far apart; it doesn't feel right." He grunts. "Dammit, I'm going to miss you."

"Me too." They both blink back tears. This is the hardest goodbye of her life.

"We'll always have Winchester," he says.

A welcome laugh escapes. "Don't Bogart me."

His smile is a hug to her heart. "I'm not Bogarting you."

They stare into each other's eyes for a long time, and she revisits some of the moments they shared together. Perhaps he's doing the same, and their smiles crescendo. It's true—it doesn't feel right that they can't be together. Maybe one day . . .

. . . or in another life. Miles and Lillian come to mind, how their love echoed through time. Will there be another couple one day sharing these same feelings, carrying over the fire once ignited by a couple in 1881? Or was there someone before them? What a mystery life and love are, but Charli's sure about one thing, she's glad to be a part of them.

"So this is it," Charli says. "This feels like a good time for me to stick out my hand." She does so.

He laughs. "You're gonna shake my hand?"

"Seems like a logical move. I mean, unless you wanna go back to your place."

They break into laughter, the last one they may share for a while. They kiss, and Charli doesn't want to stop, doesn't want to let go. He apparently doesn't either.

Their kisses turn into one last hug. "Not a day will go by that I don't think about you," Noah whispers into her ear.

"Yeah, me too."

This really is it.

They let go, both backing away slowly, as if they're waiting for something to keep them together. She doesn't want to turn away.

"Bye," he says.

"Bye."

Another few steps.

"Bye," she whispers.

He waves, a slow, steady, agonizing gesture. "Bye."

Charli takes in one last look at this man who has changed her life. She takes a snapshot of him and this moment in her mind, capturing the feeling and the look and the absolute essence of love. No matter what the future holds, they will always share this boundless love. Not even the Atlantic Ocean could extinguish it.

She finally turns away and directs her attention toward the train station. It's time to go home.

Chapter 33

Samuel Hall

Winchester, England
September 15, 1881

As his numbness subsided, his family's betrayal registered more. His mother hadn't even come to see him, hadn't sent a letter. His father, who had called Lillian a whore, and his brother, who had shot her dead, chose to let Miles take all the blame.

It was terrifying, the idea of climbing the steps to the gallows, staring at the rope, knowing he would die with no one by his side. If the fall didn't snap his neck, he'd slowly suffocate. His eyes would bulge out of his head as he voided his bladder and bowels.

Still, he would not speak.

What was there to say?

What was there to live for?

Each day, they slid meals under the door of his cell. He barely ate, only to calm the stomach pain. His ribs protruded from his skin.

Only once per day did he see the daylight, when they escorted him out of the cell to join the others in the yard—most of whom were twice his age and had half as many teeth. Miles had stuck to himself, but they'd clapped him on the back, wishing him well, wishing him to find peace. A camaraderie existed even among criminals.

The day before he would die, all he could think of was Lillian. He could see her eyes as he riffled through the memories. He would think of her when they pulled the lever and his body fell.

Then nothing, a prospect that sounded terribly appealing.

The welcomeness of nothing.

The latch of his cell slid open; Miles snapped to a stand. If he didn't stand quickly, they'd hit him again with the billy club. Though his fellow prisoners were sympathetic, the guards would not look him in the eye, would not offer even a shred of humanity.

He marched beside the guard as they led him through the prison, opening and closing steel doors. The metal parts clicked the last beats of Miles's heart.

It became clear he was being taken somewhere other than the yard. A few more turns and doors took him to a part of the prison he'd never seen. Another door opened, and a flash of sunlight poured in. Miles covered his eyes until they could adjust.

Expecting to see a dangling rope and a crowd waiting on him, he was caught off guard by the waiting carriage. The guard quickly ushered him inside to find a man facing him. His sleeves were rolled up, and he had dirty nails. He jabbed a key into the handcuffs and removed them.

"Do not speak," he said.

Miles couldn't imagine what was happening. Were they about to kill him or set him free? The latter idea was nearly impossible to consider. Who would possibly be helping him? And why?

The driver gave a command for the horses to move, and he sat in silence as they rode for a while around bends and up and over hills. Perhaps it was someone in Lillian's family intent on exacting revenge. But they didn't have the power to get someone out of prison.

Eventually, they were in the forest, and the carriage came to a stop.

"Out," the man commanded.

Miles did as he was told. On the side of the path, outside another carriage, his grandmother stood elegantly in a plaid dress that was bound tight around her skinny waist. A fancy hat decorated with a peacock feather rested on her head.

He tried to speak, but nothing came out. It was like attempting to move a leg that was no longer there.

She came to face him and held out her arms.

They embraced, and again he tried to speak. "How . . . ?" It was as if dust poured from his mouth.

His granny brushed his face. "You need a bath."

Miles tried to smile, but those muscles were dead.

"Tell me you didn't do it, and I will believe you."

Miles shook his head and tried again. His jaws felt rusty, but he found the words. "I didn't do it." It was barely a mumble, but he met her eyes so that she knew he was innocent. "It was Edward. And my father gave me the blame." A tear escaped, leaving a trail down his unwashed cheek.

She reached to wipe it. "I thought it might be something of that nature. We have no time to lose, Miles. I've booked you on a ship to America. It leaves first thing in the morning. I have new papers for you. Your name is now Samuel Hall. I have a room for you as well. Harold will escort you tonight and put you up, then take you to the boat. But, Miles, you can never come back. It breaks my heart to say so, but you will be killed if you do. Do not even write. It's the only thing that I can do for you."

She reached into a satchel and drew out a pouch. "This is enough money to get you where you need to go. The ship's passage has already been paid. I've included some United States bills as well. Find yourself a new life, Miles. Find yourself someone new to love."

He frowned at that. She was speaking too fast, though, and all the information fell heavily on him. A ship to America? Was he truly free or was he dreaming?

Granny dug into the pouch and pulled out the photo of Lillian and him. "I know you are broken, but find a reason to live for her. She'd want that."

He squeezed his granny tight as more tears escaped his eyes.

"You must go," she whispered. "Be careful. And find life again."

"Granny," he managed to get out. He had so much to say but she was rushing him, and he wasn't in the right shape for conversation.

"Yes, my dear."

"Thank you."

She pinched his cheek. "I am sorry."

They held eye contact for a long while. She was the strongest woman he'd ever known, and she'd risked her life for his.

When he pulled away, he hurried into the carriage, holding tight to the purse. He raised a hand for one last wave.

In the morning, Miles went to the docks and found the steamship that would take him to his new life. Dark clouds released a gentle rain. Miles's clothes were as damp as the air. The ship's name was the *Dayton Seacutter*, and she had two giant masts ready for sails and two chimneys already spilling out steam. The commotion around him was near madness as he worked his way to the gate. People dressed in their finest clothes bade farewell to their loved ones.

A man in a blue hat glanced at his papers and said, "Welcome aboard."

All Miles could afford was a nod.

Before he disappeared into the bowels of the ship, Miles turned to glance upon his native land one more time. He'd lost everything here. Could he ever find his footing again?

Miles located his room, which had a small window that looked out to the choppy sea. He climbed into the bed and stared up to the ceiling. It was no different from the prison he'd been in for weeks.

Miles Pemberton.

Now Samuel Hall.

Though a name had been changed, a new existence offered, he had nothing left, barely any will to keep living.

He took out the envelope his grandmother had given him and then drew out the photo of Lillian and him. For a moment he fell back to that day when their lives had been so full of promise. He could still smell her hair and feel her smile.

The loss of her washed over him, and he recalled how it felt to hold her body as her heart stopped beating. He slipped the photograph back into the envelope and let it fall to the floor.

Life was surely not worth living without her.

Two weeks later, they reached New York. Miles had still not said a word. He looked upon this new land from the bridge of the ship and wondered how much longer he could stand breathing.

Where so many that crossed onto land were smiling, he descended the walkway the same way he might walk to the gallows. A man already dead.

Chapter 34

THE MARGARET YEARS

Boston, Massachusetts
1900–1925

New York had been too much for Miles, so he'd caught a train to Boston and never looked back. He'd taken a variety of jobs, anything to keep food on the table. He found no joy, but he could not bring himself to take his own life.

Suicide would have removed his guilt, and the guilt was his self-imposed sentence. He wanted to live out his days thinking of her, punishing himself for ever pulling her into his family.

Nearly two decades after his arrival to the United States, a woman named Margaret Taylor came into his life. Margaret shopped in the grocery store where he worked and would often stop to talk to him. He wouldn't have called her pretty, but she had a warm regard that always seemed to give a lift to his day. She showed a keen interest in him early on, and he thought her mad. He was no company to keep at all.

But she was relentless and kept talking to him, prying stories out of him, including the one he came to tell everyone, that he'd lost his parents to typhoid in London. In turn, he learned about her life as well. Her family had emigrated from Leeds, England, a century earlier.

She lived with her parents and worked at a textile mill that turned raw cotton into cloth. What struck Miles was the way she could illuminate a room by simply being in it. And she had a lively and often inappropriate sense of humor that was a spark of light to Miles's dead soul.

Little by little, Margaret took the darkness from him. Little by little, he started to smile again. One day he took her to dinner. Only a few months later, he asked for her hand.

They married and moved to Cambridge, where Miles took care of horses for Harvard. Soon she was pregnant. A few years later, they were parents of a girl and a boy. Miles tried his best to be there for them, to raise them in a household so different from the one he knew as a child. One with love and support.

Though he'd lost his chance to become an actor, he taught his two children to act, and often they would perform together in the living room, acting out scenes from plays by the likes of Shakespeare and Victor Hugo and Oscar Wilde.

He tried to be the husband that Margaret deserved. It was only sometimes that he faked his happiness. Because he would often think of Lillian. He would take out the photograph that he'd carried with him on the ship and fall back through the years, wondering if there could have been another way.

As he grew older, he began to consider returning to England. He was almost sixty. This would not be a trip of vengeance against his brother. He was in no shape to kill a man, nor was he the murdering type.

No, he wanted to find Lillian's brother, Arthur, and tell him the truth. To apologize for his hand in the murder. Arthur had been good to him, and it wasn't fair that he had been kept in the dark. Miles thought letting out the truth could finally make his heart stop hurting. And he wanted to find Lillian's grave and say goodbye.

In the fall of 1921, he told Margaret that he was going to search for his family and took a boat to England. By now, Samuel Hall was his name, and it took him some time to get used to the name Miles

Pemberton again. He took the train to Winchester and could not believe the change. He hurt more and more as he drew near the city, and when he first set eyes on the Smythun Inn & Pub, he nearly collapsed.

Someone behind the bar told him Arthur was not working but that he could find him at home at #7 Winslow. Miles recalled the location from when he'd first met Arthur and Sadie. He could still see Lillian speaking to the unborn baby with such tremendous joy, and Miles remembered how he was so sure that they would one day have a baby of their own.

How wrong he'd been.

Miles found Arthur in the garden. After a brief altercation, Miles told him everything that had occurred. The men soon hugged, and Arthur took him to Lillian's grave, where he left her flowers and they wept together.

Later, they went to the pub to drink and reminisce of simpler, happier times. In the morning, Miles returned to Southampton and boarded a ship bound for Boston. As he watched his homeland fall away on the horizon, he promised himself he would finally let go of the past and spend the rest of his days being the husband, father, and grandfather that his family in America deserved.

Chapter 35

THE FIGHTER INSIDE HER

Boston, Massachusetts
Present Day

Tiny is great on a leash, and he walks like he's the president's dog as he and Charli approach Miles Pemberton's grave back in Boston. Finding him turned out to be easy. A quick search during the plane ride led her to Findagrave.com, where she entered the name Samuel Hall. He's in section one of the Morris Maron Cemetery in the North End.

She hasn't even changed her clothes since getting home at two p.m. After catching a cab from Logan Airport, she had dashed inside, smothered Tiny in hugs and kisses, and then led him right out the door to finish what she started when she first left Costa Rica.

These older gravestones don't look too much younger here in the New World. Half of them tilt to the side, with lettering that is hard to make out and moss inching up the stone. It's far colder here than in Winchester, though, and the grass has not yet come to life. The only flowers are the ones left by loved ones.

The site of Miles's gravestone takes Charli's breath away. He's buried next to his wife, Margaret. Their gravestones stand three feet apart.

Charli hesitates for a moment, wondering if she's doing the right thing, bringing Lillian back to Miles with Margaret's body right there.

Knowing in her heart that she is, Charli steps closer. The etched wording reads: HERE LIES SAMUEL PHILIP HALL 1863–1925. MAY GOD REST HIS SOUL.

It takes her a while to gather herself as she gets lost in the idea that what is left of his body rests in a coffin beneath her feet. If Frances is right, a little piece of a person's soul remains in their final resting place—no matter whether they are buried or cremated, and that piece is a window into the rest of him, wherever that may be.

Charli leans down and touches the stone, running her fingers along the wording just as she'd done with the carving in the tree. She closes her eyes and feels Miles's presence once again. She senses the pain he must have felt in losing Lillian, in being betrayed. But she also senses gratitude. Maybe she's imagining things, but she believes Miles is grateful for what Charli's done. There is closure now and, therefore, peace.

Tiny pushes his nose into her fingers, and she smiles. He can feel it too.

Lowering to a cross-legged seat, she asks Tiny to lie beside her. He does so happily and rests his head on his paws.

"I don't know how much explaining I need to do, but I came to tell you that I know that you loved Lillian with all of you and would never have hurt her. I know that it was your brother and your father who were responsible. And I hope that if any piece of you is still entangled in this web, and I think it may be, know that all is right now. You are a good man. I know it, and I will make sure the generations to come know it too."

She pulls the brooch from her purse. "I can't imagine this needs explanation. All I can tell you, Miles, is that the love between you and Lillian will never die. If I could talk to you in person, I'd tell you that I would still be stuck in life had I not been awakened by your unrest. By giving you this, I hope you can sense that Lillian still loves you and always will."

With her fingers, Charli digs a small hole in the grass and pushes the hair brooch into it. As she covers it up, she whispers, "May this be the end of our struggles."

Not a second after the words leave her lips, a sense of calm and contentedness wash over her. The joy in her body shoots up out of her, and her heart beams.

She sits there for a while, petting a trembling Tiny, and experiencing a wave of gratitude. It didn't turn out exactly as she hoped, but she'll never be the same. No more pretending. No more self-sabotaging. No more letting Mom win. And no more allowing red or even yellow lights to slow her down.

~

Her father is next. As she drives his way, the sun sets over Boston, its rays spraying like hope over the city. When he answers the door, he cracks a big grin toward her, and it quells the worry that had still been burning inside her. He's still here, still fighting.

She pulls him in tight. "You look good."

He hugs her just as hard. "Honey, you've only been gone a little while. Don't pretend you missed me that much."

"I did."

When they let go, he says, "I thought you'd like to know I turned down a pretty great offer for the boat yesterday."

"What?"

"Hey, we agreed to fight it out. I'm doing my part."

"I'm speechless." There's a sense of unfamiliar optimism that she welcomes, and she wonders where his change of heart is coming from, the constellation or their phone call. Whatever it is, her father is back on track.

As they walk into the kitchen, she asks, "You gonna have room for me in the regatta this year? I'd love to join."

"You can be my first mate any day, Charli. But I do think I might sail the world before too long. I've put the pieces in motion."

"Hold on. What? Really? You should."

He nods with a glimmer of excitement usually reserved for children who are racing out the door to play with their friends.

Her heart fills with joy, so much so that her mouth stretches wide. "You realize you're the best dad on earth, right?"

He kicks out a laugh. "I don't know about that. Just the luckiest dad out there, that's for sure."

She's not sure if *how they got here* matters nearly as much as the fact that they are *here*, in this place where everything seems possible.

"So, what now?" he asks, reaching for the bottle of wine on the counter.

She shares with him all the things that have registered, and she talks about saying goodbye to Noah, how difficult it had been. "Maybe one day we'll be in a place to work it out. I don't know. But in the meantime, I'm going to open my bookstore."

He lights up. "I'd love to see you do that."

"Yeah, me too. A lot to figure out, but there's time."

"What will you call it? Same thing as before?"

"No, I've got something better."

⌒

She's back to work in the morning. And though she's still not in love with this job, it feels like a means to an end now, which makes it far more palatable.

"Ah, Charli, so glad you made it to work today. We're all honored."

Charli is in her cubicle, tapping away at a new report.

Marvin pokes her on the back. "Let's see you in my office, huh?"

"I'm busy right now trying to . . ."

"Nope, we're not gonna have that. Let's go, right now."

She walks down the carpeted hallway and follows him into his office. If he fires her, she'll find something else. Something better.

"Have a seat," he commands.

She sits in one of the two visitors' chairs facing his desk. A bottle of Vaseline hand lotion sits next to a grimy calculator. An Excel sheet stretches across the screen that swings from the wall.

He clicks the door shut. "So . . . how is your mother?"

She turns back to him, uncomfortable that he's behind her. "She's fine."

"Good," he says.

I should come clean, she thinks. *I don't want to lie anymore. If I'm not meant to be here, so be it.*

"And are you glad to be back?"

"No, not really."

"You don't like your job, do you?"

"Well, it's fine, I suppose. I mean, it's better than digging graves. No. I'd rather dig graves, but I don't like dead bodies. It's better than . . ." She has to think hard. He lets her. "It's better than not having a job." How about that for honesty?

He takes the chair next to her—not his on the other side of the desk, but the one right next to her. "I do like your humor. We have fun, don't we? You and I, chatting back and forth."

Cringing at his onion breath, she shakes her head. "No. I don't have fun. I'm just trying to do my job."

He smiles, almost like he thinks she's flirting with him. She sits up straight and moves to the edge of the chair, away from him. He turns to her, puts a hand on her armrest. She's a second away from standing and rushing out the door. Only the fact that she wants the job keeps her still.

"I don't intimidate you, do I?" he asks.

"Not in the least," she says, drawing her hands toward her lap as fast as a tape measure pulls in tape when the button is smashed. She makes eye contact with him. "Is there something you'd like?"

He gives a chuckle that makes her cringe. "Oh boy, is there."

She tightens. He's making a pass at her.

"I don't feel comfortable," she says. If he's not careful, Charli will put up a fight that he never could have seen coming. She's taken her fair share of self-defense classes, and she's not afraid to use what she's learned.

He removes his hand from her armrest. "You know, I give you a hard time, but I think I'm a good boss. I didn't even say anything when you came back with a tan when you took time off to help your mother. Last I checked, no one was getting tans in March on the Cape."

She almost mentions her mother's tanning bed, but that's not who she is anymore. That's not who she's becoming. Instead, she comes clean. "Look, Marvin, you're right. My mother was never having surgery. I was in Costa Rica; that's where I got my tan. Most recently, I was in England doing some genealogical research. I'm sorry I lied about that. And I completely understand if you have to fire me. But I'm back now and willing to put in some hard work."

He smiles at her, as if he's either not surprised or doesn't care. Either way, she's creeped out.

"It's okay," he whispers. "We all tell little fibs, don't we? I think I'm willing to let that go. I've been thinking about ways to promote you, to get that raise that you're always begging for."

His insinuation is obvious and lights the match of her female fury. She's enraged not only at him but at every man who's ever tried to play such a game and for every woman who's been a victim of it. This feels worse than anything her mother ever said to her.

His hand goes up and toward her as he says, "Let's do a little back-scratching. I can help—" The moment he pats her arm, she recoils and backs away so quickly that the chair slams into the floor with a thud. She's on her feet and moving to the door.

"Where are you going?" he asks sweetly. "I'm not doing a thing, just trying to help you."

"I bet you are," she says, twisting the knob, noticing the door is locked. She quickly unlocks it and rushes out as she hears him calling after her. She can't believe this kind of thing still happens.

She rushes to her cubicle and grabs her purse. Her neighbor asks whether she's okay.

"I'm leaving," Charli says. "And you should too."

The woman juts out her bottom lip.

Charli isn't done. Men like this need to be exposed. She places a hand on the cubicle wall and raises her voice. "Everyone, can I get your attention?" It doesn't take a second for the large room to go quiet. Heads turn.

"Marvin just touched me and made it clear that he would give me a raise in exchange for sexual favors. And I quit. I hope you will too. I wish you all the best."

Charli rushes down the stairs and jogs across the parking lot. Never again will she let someone speak down to her or treat her as less than. No, she's done. Because she is the one who determines her worth, and dammit, she is worth something. She's a good person who wants to do the right thing and shine her own light into the world. Even if she never opens a bookstore, *even* if she never finds love, she still matters.

~

After shooting an email exposing Marvin's behavior to every higher-up she's met in the company, she drives out to the Cape. How many times has Charli come out here with hopes that she and her mother will have a nice time, only to return under a dark cloud of sadness? Every. Single. Time.

This visit will be different.

She does not have any expectations.

When her mother opens the door, she says, "Where the hell have you been?" Her robe flaps in the sea breeze. Her lipstick is heavy, the alcohol on her breath flammable.

"Hi, Mom."

"I've been calling you and . . ."

"Yeah, I got the messages."

"No apology, nothing. How easily you forget I dedicated half of my life to you."

Charli recognizes a flash of anger rise up, but she acknowledges it and lets herself feel it as opposed to swallowing it down. She takes her time too.

When she's ready, she says, "I can see how frustrating that must have been. Could we sit and talk? I have some things on my mind."

Georgina notices Tiny for the first time. "If he's coming inside, you need to wipe his paws."

Charli raises a towel. "Way ahead of you."

"Okay, come in. Let me get a drink."

"Could you wait until after, please?"

Georgina groans.

The women sit in the sunroom in two chairs that face the sea. Tiny curls up next to Charli. The water is calm this afternoon, barely a ripple.

"I want you to know, Mom, that I love you. Because of that, I want to tell you a little bit about my life, what I am going to do to change."

Charli doesn't tell her about the constellation or her trip to Winchester. What she says is, "I want the best for you, but I can't be here for you any longer. I need to look out for *me*. I came out here to assure you that I can still love you from a distance, and that's what I'm going to do. Our past is too harsh on me, though, and I'm asking that you respect that. That you respect that I need some space."

For once, Georgina has nothing to say. She licks her lips and stares out to the sea.

Charli adds, "I believe that you have the power to change, Mom. I believe that it's never too late for self-discovery, and I hope that you can find a way to ease your pain."

Georgina slaps the armrests of the chair. "Well, shit, Charli. I don't know what to say. I guess it's good you're finally growing up." A tear rolls down her mother's cheek, and she starts shaking her head back and forth. She looks like she's fighting something back, and then she lets it out, a sob that sprouts in her eyes and comes over her whole body.

"I'm sorry, Charli. I could have done better."

Georgina has never once said she's sorry. Surprising even herself, Charli slides off her chair and wraps her arms around her.

"Thank you for saying that."

"Don't leave me, Charli." She's a wet mess.

Charli lets go and stands. "I'll always be pulling for you. But I gotta go."

"Yeah," her mom says pitifully. "Yeah . . . yeah. Go, please, go." Georgina motions for her to leave. "Please go."

As Charli and Tiny take their leave, a sense of empowerment comes over her, so much so that she feels like she can walk out this door and go and do anything. Because she's done it. She's broken free from those invisible chains that had been holding her back, and the rest of her life will be her reclaiming her lost years and becoming the woman she knows she can be.

Chapter 36

Getting Back into the Groove

Charli wastes no time seeking a new job. After long talks with her accountant and several visits to the bank, she knows what is required to realize her dream of opening the bookstore. She'll take the highest-paying job with the caveat that it's in a healthy work environment, and she'll squirrel away every penny she can to prepare for the onslaught of charges, such as renting the space and buying shelves and furniture, and purchasing inventory. Meanwhile, she'll follow in the steps of her favorite bookstores in their early years and host pop-ups and drum up media interest and run a Kickstarter campaign. It won't be easy, but it can be done. And if it can't, she'll die trying.

A week after returning from England, Charli is catching up with Viv on the phone, which is weird, because Viv hates talking on the phone, when another call comes through. "Hey, I gotta run. This might be a job thing."

"Okay, keep me posted," Viv says.

Charli clicks over. "Hello, Charli Thurman here."

"Hi, Charli, this is Erica with Welsh and Wright."

Charli's insides tingle as she tries to play it cool. W&W are a young firm led by women who manage social media for start-ups. They are within walking distance of her house and are looking for someone to edit and proof social media posts, blogs, and newsletters for their clients.

"Hi, Erica. So nice to hear from you."

"We enjoyed chatting with you and are ready to make an offer. We think you're perfect for our team. And we get it that we might only be lucky enough to have you for a couple of years, considering your bookstore concept, but that's okay. We'll take what we can get."

She briskly paces the apartment as she and Erica work out the details.

"When can you start?" Erica asks. "I know we left that open ended."

"I can start in five minutes if you want me to."

Erica laughs. "That's exactly the attitude that made us all like you so much. Why don't you come in tomorrow morning, and we can hash out the details. Say ten?"

"I'm so grateful. I'll be there."

Charli hangs up and does a dance, then finds Tiny sprawled out on the couch and runs to him. "Guess what. Your mom just got a job. A good job. And I'm so flippin' happy, Tiny." She presses her face to his and closes her eyes. This. *This* is what it feels like to be living.

In that moment, her door buzzer rings. She hops up and pushes the intercom button. "Yes?"

"Looking for Charli Thurman," a muffled voice says. "I've got a DHL package here for you that needs a signature."

She hasn't placed any orders, especially one that would be coming through DHL. "Um, I don't . . . okay. I'll be right there."

Feeling on top of the world, she skips down the stairs and pulls back the wooden door. And then . . . the world stands still.

Noah has a shadow of a beard, which works like magic on him. She has a thing for guys in pink, and he's wearing a baby-pink button-down tucked into dark jeans. A bag hangs from his shoulder.

"You're not the DHL man," she says, her face contorting in surprise.

He doesn't reply, just stands there with that gorgeous smile of his, one side curled up more than the other. The joy of seeing him starts like a tremor and works itself to a rumble inside.

"Is this a dream?" she asks. "Are you real?" She reaches out and playfully pinches his cheek, which only causes him to brighten more.

"You had to be expecting me?"

"Expecting you? You live three thousand miles away. A call would have been nice. What if I'd been shacking up with another Englishman?"

"I would have come in and pummeled him."

They share a laugh.

"And what was with that American accent?"

"It wasn't that bad, was it?"

"It might need a little work. And next time, maybe use UPS or FedEx. Nobody gets DHL packages around here."

"Noted," he says. "For the next time I travel across the world to surprise the woman I can't seem to shake from my heart."

His words are a bubble bath with a good book. Some kind of survival mechanism in her is telling her to play it cool, but she can't. "Yeah, I tried to forget about you, too, but . . . I don't know . . . you're kind of sticky in that way." She's still trying to wrap her head around what has happened, how he's suddenly standing in front of her. "What if I wasn't here? And how did you find me?"

A look of pride rises over him. "I kind of knew you would be."

"How's that?"

"Your friend Viv and I have been chatting."

She shoots her hands out in front of her. "What?"

"I found her on Instagram and told her I was coming to surprise you. She liked the idea and shared your address. And that's why she called you a few minutes ago. Just making sure you were home."

Charli furrows her brow. "You and my best friend are colluding?"

"She's a doll, by the way."

"Yes, she is. I can't wait for you to meet her."

"I can't either. Sounds like we're all going over to your father's marina for dinner."

They're talking as if they were having coffee only this morning. She's truthfully gobsmacked by his presence. "Wait, what? He knows you're here?"

"I think so. Viv says she and her dad are heading over there in a few minutes."

Charli doesn't even know where to start. He's popped over from London as if they'd never strayed from each other. They've texted some, but he gave no indication that he was coming to see her.

"What are you doing here, Noah?"

His face straightens as he stands aside to let two men carrying a sofa pass by. She soaks him in, making sure he's standing here before her.

By the look of his face, he's pleased that he surprised her.

"Could I come inside?" he asks.

She can't get past the pink, how he *knows* that she loves men in pink—she surely mentioned it to him—and how he intentionally wore this particular shirt today.

"Yeah, yes, of course. Let's go upstairs."

Upstairs, Tiny comes charging for him and takes the spotlight for a long three minutes while Charli waits patiently to hear what is going on here, why this man is suddenly in her apartment.

When Tiny finally settles down, Noah stands and looks around. "I love your place." He gestures toward all the books. "Books much?"

"Yeah, the leftovers from the store." She can't take it any longer and is ready to get to it. "What are you doing here?" she whispers, but she knows.

He wanders toward her, dangerously close.

She's missed him so much, and the longing comes back in spades. Her lips go to his like magnets, and it's as if the two of them never parted ways. He pulls her into him, and if she doesn't stop this soon, the whole block is going to be listening in on a romance being written.

Pulling her lips away, she places a hand on his chest. Sure, they left things open, but what is he really here for? Another fling or something more? "Stop. Stop. Good God, stop." She wipes lipstick off the corner of his lips. "You can't just fly over here a week later and jump me."

He allows a concerned look to take over. "Why not?"

"Because."

He touches her waist and steals another kiss. "Because why?"

"Because, because. Because." She adjusts her blouse. "Because."

"You really are a wordsmith, aren't you? You should open a bookstore."

"Don't pick on me."

He lets go of the playful facade. "Look, Charli, I miss you, okay? That's why I came. I miss you, and I want to figure out a path forward— if you have any interest in doing so. I don't know what that is, but I've thought about you every single day since you left. Every hour. Hell, every minute. I booked the trip four days ago. I'm here to find a way to make this work. If you're still interested—"

"I am."

He kisses her.

"I can't hear you," he whispers.

"I am interested," she confesses, and he takes her in for a comforting hug. A few minutes ago she was starting to get used to not having him, and now he's here, and she can't imagine ever losing him.

"But how would we ever make it work?" she asks.

"I left the pub."

"You can't leave the pub. It's your pub."

"I still own my piece, but Victoria is going to run the front-of-house duties now."

"Stop it."

"She got a raise and is moving into a new place a block away. She wanted it for so long anyway."

Charli feels all kinds of giddy inside. "Good for Victoria. I can't think of anyone who deserves it more."

"Yeah, that's the truth."

They stare at each other, starting and stopping and inhaling and exhaling, their eyes searching, making sure what they had translates to a new land.

"I want to be with you, Charli. I will go back when I can to visit. Maybe you'll come with me on occasion. But you are the nonnegotiable in my life. I've got a decent résumé. Surely there's a tech firm or two in this city that will take a chance on me."

"I got offered a job, by the way."

"What?" The delight in his eyes sends her to the stratosphere. "For who?"

She tells him everything, including her plans for the bookstore.

Eventually, he lowers his eyes to his leather satchel, slides his hand in. "I have something to show you. No, not that. Well . . ." He pulls out a copy of the book she'd recommended to him, Chris Whitaker's *We Begin at the End*. "This isn't what I was going to show you . . . but wow. What a book. I'm almost done, so don't spoil it, but I'll tell you this . . . you may have just gotten me back into reading. I like Duchess a lot."

Her body tingles with joy. "Right?"

"We'll talk more when I'm finished." He shoves the book back in, then pulls out an old notebook made of leather, the binding well worn, the edges frayed and discolored. A leather string wraps around it. "My granny and I were cleaning out her attic the other day. Seems you stirred up her own curiosities of the past. We came across this journal. She's never seen it before. Turns out it belonged to her great-grandfather, Arthur, who was Lillian's brother."

"What?"

Noah finally hands it to her. "I spent some time reading it, curious about the murder and my family. And I found something that's damned near hard to believe."

"Tell me already . . . you're killing me, Noah."

"Read it."

"Right now?"

"Yes, right now. Go to the page I marked."

With a curious craving, Charli unties the leather string and pulls open the book. A musty smell rises from its pages. She sits on the couch. Noah sits next to her and watches her.

October 5th, 1921

Miles came to see me. Our son was out of the house by then, and Sadie was visiting her sister in London. I was in the garden when he came. It took me a moment to realize it was him. He was weak and skinny. But when I did, all my anger came rushing back. Of course, I wasn't in my best health either, and he managed to push me to the ground as I tried to swing at him.

Before I could start again, he said, "I came here to tell you the truth."

"The truth?" I said back to him. "You murdered my sister, you bastard. I don't need to know the details."

Miles took me by the coat collar and shook me hard. He said, "How on earth could you think that I killed her? You know how much I loved her."

I don't know if I'm good at reading people, but I knew that he was telling the truth.

"Allow me to tell you what happened."

I nodded. "Very well."

And so he told me of that night, and of his escape and move to the US and his marriage to a woman named Margaret. And of what had led him back here now. He was absolutely riddled with guilt, feeling responsible for her death. He wished he'd not pulled her into his world. Returning to speak to me was his way of attempting to move on with his life.

I know not what to do with the information. Revenge lingers sweet on my tongue. I suppose the days will tell. For now, I am simply putting it here as a way to set straight the truth. This is the best of what I can remember . . .

⁓

Charli reads for ten minutes, doing her best to work out some of Arthur's poor handwriting. She eventually turns to a blank page. "That's all?"

"That's everything we found," Noah said.

She flips back a page. "Your grandmother had no idea it was there?"

"No, but she was excited for you to read it."

She glances to the top and reads the first few paragraphs again. Frances had been right. It was guilt that he'd left reverberating in their family. Though Miles hadn't pulled the trigger, he'd felt responsible, nonetheless. She wonders if he ever found any sort of happiness after losing Lillian. Perhaps not. And that's partially why it's her job to overcome it. For him and for her.

She's about to close the book when she takes another look at the entry date. *October 5th, 1921.* "Hold on," she says. "Wasn't he killed in October?"

Noah cocks an eyebrow. "Maybe?"

"I think so. I have to look." She retrieves her laptop and navigates to the article she saved about the day Arthur shot Lord Edward Pemberton.

"October 10 was the day he died. A few days after he wrote this entry, which gave him time to plan. So this is why he went after Edward all those years later. He'd just found out the truth."

"My God," Noah whispers. "Well done, Charli."

Charli's shaking her head, seeing how it all happened. "I wonder if Miles ever found that out. I wonder if he knew the trouble he'd caused." She runs a hand through her hair. "It never ends," she says.

"What's that?"

"At some point, you have to move on. Or you're bound to keep living the same way." She exhales a breath. "I just . . . I knew the truth, but to read it here makes a difference. Makes me feel like I've found even more closure. Maybe your family has too. Thank you for coming, for bringing this . . . and"—she sets a hand on his thigh, feeling the desire that's been cooped up for too long—"for bringing you."

He leans forward, and she grips the back of his neck and pulls him in. After they kiss, she says, "We shouldn't . . . we're going to be late . . ."

"Yeah, yes, we are," he mumbles back.

"Maybe we should wait—"

It's too late.

Overcome by their cravings, they go at each other, tugging off and slinging clothes across the room, running their hands and lips up and down each other's bodies, pressing against one another in a wildly fierce surrendering, becoming one with each other, writing poetry with their touch and the pounding of their no-longer-lonely hearts.

～

They race to get dressed a little while later. Charli is still buzzing—from his surprise arrival and the lustful fire they lit between them just now—but she's finally coming back to reality and pondering the future.

"I wonder what it would be like to eventually open up a second location in Winchester. Do you think there's room for another bookstore?"

He's buttoning his shirt. "I don't think there's such a thing as too many bookstores."

"Yeah, you're right. Well, it's something to think about."

"I'm into that. You already miss it, don't you?"

"Winchester?" She slips into her shoes. "Yeah, I do. You know, it's my family's town too. You can't hog it."

"I wouldn't dare. I'm already seeing the sign in my mind. The Iambic Inkpot, Chapter Two. Right down the street from the pub."

Charli's seeing it too. Not just another store either. She sees all of Chapter Two, and this guy beside her is on every page.

"Remind me of something," he says, as he laces up his boots. "How do you say 'Worcestershire sauce' again?"

She looks down at him. "Are you going to start picking on me?"

"Oh, c'mon. Do you know how many times I've thought back to that day and heard you absolutely butcher the word in front of my entire family? It's the most adorable thing I've ever heard. Say it for me, one more time."

Charli feels safe enough to give it a try. "Worche . . . Worches . . . no, I can't do it."

A joyous expression fills his face as he reaches for her hand and pulls her down to the couch. "Try it one more time."

"We're going to be late," she says, straddling him.

"Say it . . ."

She rolls her eyes. "Worcestershire sauce."

"Ah, that's it."

Charli leans forward and presses her lips to his ear. "And I love you."

"Right back at you, my lady."

And then running a little late doesn't seem to matter anymore.

Epilogue

THE BOOKSTORE THAT IS

Three Years Later

Life's been wildly busy since Charli returned from Winchester, and there are no signs of slowing down. But that's exactly the way Charli likes it right now. She'll get to a point where she can relax, when she can step away from the store for a few days at a time. But for now, they are in the growth phase, and sometimes that requires digging your heels in and giving it all you have.

Her eyes are focused on the balance sheet that she's been wrestling with all morning. They've been open two months, and she's barely slept, but there's nothing she'd rather be doing.

She loves the distributors visiting with new releases and authors coming by to sign books and read. She finds great satisfaction managing her awesome staff, who all love books as much as she does. And she loves diving into the financial side of things, studying profits and losses, making minute changes accordingly. At this rate she'll have no problems paying back the monthly loan payments to the local bank that was willing to take a chance on her.

Their hard work is paying off. People are supporting them. There's barely ever a free seat in the café. They are ahead of their projections.

The *Globe* gave them a great write-up, calling the Iambic Inkpot "a bookstore that does it right." They like how her "ample seating and delightful coffee" encourage people to stay all day if they'd like.

It's not lost on her that this location, a few blocks from Northeastern University, is far better than the location of the Bookstore That Never Was. The parking is plentiful, and there's a lot of foot traffic. It doesn't hurt that they can walk there in about twenty minutes. Sometimes things don't work out the way in which you design them, but they work out just right, all the same.

Exhausted as she may be, she's never been more proud of herself, and it feels absolutely wonderful to know that she's done it. She's become an entrepreneur. And there's no other person on earth she'd rather share it with than Noah, who has supported her every step of the way—even as he followed his own path and landed a great job with Spotify.

At two, Charli leaves the office and goes out into the store. She's glad to see two long lines at the cash registers. Good for a Thursday afternoon. Through an archway, she sees another line at the café, where they serve freshly roasted coffee, locally brewed kombucha, and some of the best pastries in New England. What she's proudest of is the diverse mix of people spread out on couches and chairs and beanbags, soaking up words. What better calling than to bring literature to the world and create a place where imaginations can run wild.

Charli walks around the store, talking to the employees, making sure they have things under control. She's been preparing them for a week now. It's the first time she's taken time off in three years.

And then Noah comes through the door. Her face lifts into a smile that nearly takes her out of her shoes. He goes straight to her and plants a kiss on her lips. "You ready? I figured I might have to drag you out of here."

"No, I'm pretty sure I can leave of my own accord. And I think everyone in here wants me out anyway. They need a break from the boss."

Noah gestures toward the door. "Uber's here; bags are in the trunk. Shall we do this?" He looks guilty, as if he might have been concocting something bigger than a family reunion. Is there a ring in his bag? She doesn't want to get her hopes up, but she thinks he might propose within the next week, while they're back in Winchester. It's pretty convenient, considering her dad has successfully navigated the Atlantic Ocean with Vivian's father, and they've docked in Southampton. They'll all be connecting in Winchester tomorrow for a few days of getting to know each other at the Smythun. Vivian hasn't answered her calls in two days, and Charli suspects she might be working her way to England too.

Once they're in the back of a Kia Sorento en route to Logan Airport, Noah says, "I talked to the estate agent. He'll meet us tomorrow afternoon to show us the place."

"Aren't we getting a little ahead of ourselves?" Charli asks. "I've barely gotten the first store off the ground."

"It doesn't hurt to look, does it?"

"I guess not." He's really taken by this idea of opening up a store in his hometown and wants to help fund it. Though it's ambitious, she's on board too. Because why not? As she's proven anything is possible.

Charli looks out the window, imagining that she'll be looking out a train window soon as they make their way from London to Winchester. "Going back has gotten me thinking about my first trip."

"Oh yeah? When you came upon Prince Charming?"

"Actually, yes. I can't get over that of all the pubs I walked into, it was yours. And do you know why? Because the avocados at the poke bowl place down the street were brown. That's how I found the Smythun."

"We owe our whole existence to the poor quality of their avocados," Noah says. "We'll have to tell them that tomorrow. 'Excuse me, sir, your subpar produce led to a cosmic love story. Keep it up.'"

Charli chuckles but doesn't want to let go of her point. "There were other weird occurrences too. That guy, Monty, at the LMA. How he happened to know what a Winchester tie looked like. Now that I look back on it, I wonder if he was even real. How I happened to come upon the exact place where Miles and Lillian's photograph was taken. Then nearly running smack into the Palace of Westminster with Big Ben chiming. That stuff never used to happen to me, and now it's almost frequent. I wish I had a better explanation."

"Do you really need one? We've talked about this before. I think there's no doubt that when you're doing the right things, the world seems to open up for you."

"Yeah, I know." She shakes her head as a sense of awe casts her into a spell. "My life was so boring before I met you."

"As was mine, my lady."

A need to capture the moment comes over her, and she digs into her purse for her phone. She holds it out, and they squeeze together for a shot. It is not lost on her that here she is posing with Noah just as Miles had posed with Lillian in Winchester all those years ago.

As she posts the cute picture on Instagram, she thinks back to that night in the pub when she was mentally giving her friends Alice and Melissa a hard time for posting glimpses of their picture-perfect lives on social media. Charli was treating life like a competition, and it's not. What was it that Viv had told her, that love and happiness are universal rights? Everyone has a right to create their own picture-perfect life, and posting it online isn't about bragging—because it's *not* a competition. Like many in the world, Charli simply thrives in connecting and wants to share the joy she's feeling in this moment as it all comes together.

When the car reaches Huntington Avenue, the straight run, Charli gets yet another sign that she's doing something right. She hits Noah on the arm and points, her head dizzy with possibility. It couldn't be true, but it is. She's bearing witness.

Lined up ahead, every single traffic light glows green.

Acknowledgments

Perhaps this is the time to write my acknowledgments . . . at six in the morning on September 12, 2023, as I pore over the developmental edits while tucked away at my writer's cottage on an island in Maine. My eyes are watery as it becomes clearer by the minute how much my editors get me. I don't know what I have done to deserve such fortune, but I have a team of three women who know exactly how to make my story better. And they're so good that I don't have to question their advice. They somehow see into my soul and know exactly what I'm getting at with my stories. They find elements on the page that I didn't even know were there. As I sit here, nineteen days away from my first deadline (thank God no one can see the mess I am right now), I know they're all available and supporting me any way they can. It's more than I could have ever dreamed.

Danielle Marshall, you have understood me and believed in me from day one, and I'm honored to be one of your authors. I trust you and your vision completely, and I can't wait to see where we go together. To the whole Lake Union crew, please know how grateful I am to work with you. It's not lost on me what you've done for my career.

Andrea Hurst, I am so full of gratitude to know you and have you as an agent and editor. As I say in the dedication, you and I vibrate at the same frequency, and it's so nice to be traveling this journey together.

Tiffany Yates Martin, my God, woman, you have the gift. Thank you for giving everything you have to make me a better writer and to make my stories reach their full potential. Your critiques always come with the right solutions, making my life so much easier.

Katie Reed, it was lovely to work with you for the first time. You get story in such a beautiful way, and I can't wait to see where you go with your career. I'm expecting huge things. And I hope you won't forget about me along the way.

To my guru in Spain, Ruth Chiles. You mean more to me than you could ever know. Not only have you helped me drive closer to my potential, but you're the one who gave me this story idea. What a lovely one it is . . . maybe my favorite. Thank you.

To the amazingly talented Jenan McClain, who is a gifted painter and poet and a wonderful friend, thank you for letting me share your poem "Lost Opportunity" in the opening of the story. The moment I first heard you read it, I felt Charli's heart in your words. As you said so perfectly, the poem is Charli speaking to generations of damaged family members; she's finally breaking free. Chill bumps for days! Love you, my friend.

To my Tiki Bar writers' group: James Blatch, Lucy Score, Cecelia Mecca, and Nathan Van Coops. Thank you for being there for me when I'm ready to jump out the window, even if the fall is only one story down. There's nothing like being able to laugh with you every day as we all hack away at this writing life. Nathan, I don't give you enough credit. I'm not sure there's been a book in the last five years that you didn't help me deconstruct. I'm so appreciative of our friendship. And James, thank you for my tour of London. That was one of the best days of my year.

The unsung heroes of my novels are my beta readers, who give so much to me. I have a blast creating with you, and there's no doubt that you are essential to getting my books where they need to be. Among a slew of ways you help, I could never get close to writing female characters without y'all coaching me along. A million thank-yous doesn't seem adequate. Especially Kristie Cooley, who outdid herself with this one; you are a saint. And Lauren Cormier, my secret weapon; I absolutely adore your sense of humor and appreciate your unending support.

Vero and Susana Velasco, I remember the day this novel was hatched. We were on Vero and Sean's balcony in Valencia with your amazing *fideuà* cooking, and I was talking about this seed of an idea, and Vero said, "You need to talk to my sister!" Susana, thank you for sharing your experience. Our phone call is what breathed life into this story.

Lynn Scornavacca, thanks for always cheering me on, helping me promote my work, and creating the superb book club questions. More than that, thanks for being an awesome human. People like you make the world go round.

I'm grateful to Scott Steward and Lara Ford for steering me in the right direction apropos genealogy. I had no idea what I was getting into till we chatted.

To my friends Hunter and Nyree Mack, thank you for helping me get Boston right. I love you so much. Our meeting in Spain was definitely meant to be.

To the folks in Winchester who helped me: my tour guides Erica Wheeler, Kate Mills, and Sandra Showell, and also the Winchester College archivist Suzanne Foster; thank you for helping me bring some verisimilitude to this story. I hope I got enough right that you don't want to wring my neck. No doubt I took some liberties. What a lovely city you represent. I can't wait to get back.

For some reason, my wife, Mikella, and son, Riggs, keep putting up with me. Thank you for letting me disappear into my cave as I satisfy this craving to put words on a page. It's all pointless without you in my life. Seriously, guys, I am lost without you.

To all my friends and family, thank you for your love and encouragement, especially those of you who read my books. I know that can be a little weird when you know the person who holds the pen. Even more, thank you for letting me steal little bits about your lives, as some of my best ideas come from those around me. Being in a writer's life should come with a warning!

And to all the book buyers, librarians, and readers out there . . . y'all make this all possible. It's word of mouth that makes the difference in my line of work, and I'm so lucky to have you out there telling your family, friends, clients, patrons, and book clubs. You can bet your bottom dollar I'll keep giving everything I have.

Book Club Questions

1. At the end of the first chapter—after Patrick breaks up with Charli—what friendly advice would you offer?
2. Do you think that Charli is self-sabotaging because of a lack of self-esteem? Is it a common trait for women? She considers it a foregone conclusion that she will fail at everything. Do you know anyone like that?
3. Have you ever had a day that has gone so poorly you say to yourself, "I must have been a real jerk in a former life, and I'm paying for it now"? Is this karma? Can acknowledging former wrongs change the future?
4. Have you ever had a dream that felt so real that you thought someone out there was communicating with you?
5. Have you looked up constellation therapy? Would you try it? Why? Why not?
6. Are you open to alternative practices in pursuit of your own personal healing?
7. Have you ever had an experience with a manager like Marvin? How did you handle it?
8. Charli's relationship with her mother is a tough one. What do you think she should do?
9. How do you feel about what Charli learned in her constellation therapy session? Could you do this and bare

your soul to strangers?

10. How did you like the time period changes? Did they keep you hooked?

11. Do you believe in the concept of soulmates?

12. Have you ever visited England? How about a true English pub?

13. Discuss your favorite and least favorite characters.

14. Does anyone enjoy genealogy? Do you find the same journey as Charli exciting? It's like being your own personal detective: you never know what you will find.

15. Who could you identify with in this story?

16. Are you satisfied with the way the arc of this story resolved?

17. How did you feel about how Miles's story ended up after losing Lillian?

About the Author

Photo © 2018 Brandi Morris

Boo Walker is the bestselling author of *The Stars Don't Lie*, *A Spanish Sunrise*, *The Singing Trees*, and *An Unfinished Story*, among other novels. He initially tapped his muse as a songwriter and banjoist in Nashville, but a career-ending hand problem sent him scrambling to find another creative outlet. After a stint as a day trader in Charleston, he headed west to Washington State, where he bought a gentleman's farm on Red Mountain, a small wine-growing region in the desert.

It was there, among the grapevines and wine barrels, that he found his voice telling high-impact stories that now resonate with book clubs worldwide. His novels, rich with colorful characters and boundless soul, will leave you with an open heart and lifted spirit.

Always a wanderer, Boo has lived in South Carolina, Tennessee, Florida, Washington State, New York, and Valencia, Spain. He now resides in Cape Elizabeth, Maine, with his wife, son, and two troublemaking dogs. He also writes thrillers under the pen name Benjamin Blackmore. You can find him at www.boowalker.com and www.benjaminblackmore.com.